THE GIRL BELOW

THE GIRL BELOW

Bianca Zander

WILLIAM MORROW
An Imprint of HarperCollins*Publishers*

This book is a work of fiction. The characters, incidents, and dialogue are drawn from the author's imagination and are not to be construed as real. Any resemblance to actual events or persons, living or dead, is entirely coincidental.

FIRST EDITION

Designed by Diahann Sturge

Library of Congress Cataloging-in-Publication Data

Zander, Bianca.

The girl below : a novel / by Bianca Zander.—1st ed.

p. cm.

ISBN 978-0-06-210816-6

1. Young women—England—London—Fiction. 2. Family secrets—Fiction. I. Title.

PR9639.4.Z36G57 2012

823'.92—dc23

2012012394

---

12 13 14 15 16 OV/RRD 10 9 8 7 6 5 4 3 2 1

For Matthew and Hector

THE GIRL BELOW

CHAPTER ONE

London, 2003

IT WAS ONLY MAY, but the streets flared golden like they do in high summer, and all around me the neighborhood sighed with so much privilege that I felt shut out—a stranger on the block where my childhood took place. In the twenty years since we had moved away, Notting Hill had changed beyond recognition, become a kind of joke suburb—part tourist bauble, part film set—and a ludicrous place to say you were from. Of course I'd changed too in that time, but not so much that I was ready to accept the slight. Instead, for the last ten minutes, I had been glued to the doorstep of our old building, staring at a familiar name on the buzzer, too shy to press it but feeling aggrieved that I couldn't get in.

On the other side of a spiked black railing, the basement flat was oblivious to my injury, and bore no trace of our having lived there. Fresh paint slicked the iron bars that guarded the front windows, and behind them our homely green and orange curtains had been replaced with stiff white venetian blinds. Shorn long ago of my mother's pink and red potted geraniums, the patio was bald, and had been industrially water-blasted to remove any residue of dirt or character. Fleetingly, the lemony scent of geranium leaves spiked my nostrils and I saw my mother, hovering over her plants, trimming rogue stems and plucking off blooms that had died.

I had been right, in one way at least, about coming back to London: everything here reminded me of her. She had left behind a trail of crumbs, a dusting of sugar to guide me through the woods.

That day was only my second in London, but already the optimism I had been fizzing with was beginning to seem false. On the long flight over from New Zealand, I had imagined a triumphant homecoming: streamers and banners above a red carpet the length of Kensington Park Road, or at least an easy transition back to my old life. I had been out of the country for ten years, living in Auckland for most of that time, but I had thought that the old life would be waiting for me, that if you were born in a place and had grown up there, you were one of its citizens and it would always take you back.

Other places maybe, but not London. At the Heathrow arrivals gate, no one had been there to meet me. On the way into London on the tube, I had tried smiling at people, projecting a sunny attitude, but I had been met with frowns, and some had turned away. Getting off the tube at Willesden Green, I had gone into a newsagent's to buy a packet of wine gums, had excitedly told the cashier that you couldn't buy them in New Zealand, and he had silently—no, scornfully—handed me my change. Still feeling upbeat, I had walked from the tube station to my friend Belinda's flat only to discover no one was there. Belinda had left a note, and a key, and I had let myself in and sat down on my suitcase—stuffed to the zipper with all I owned—and that's when deflation began. I had come back to London without any plan besides entitlement, and staring at the two-seater couch in front of me that was about to become my bed, I realized what a fool I had been.

The name that had caught my attention on the buzzer of our old building was Peggy Wright: our former upstairs neighbor, a force of nature, someone to be reckoned with, older than my parents but ageless. I remembered her well—her high, cackling laugh, her lipstick-stained teeth—but wasn't sure if she'd remember me, at least not in my present incarnation. At the time we left the neighborhood, I was a scrawny eight-year-old waif in glasses so thick that no one—including me—knew what I looked like behind them. Since then, I had grown tall and robust and switched to contact lenses, but along with those things had come caution, and that's what hindered me now.

From the front stairs, I surveyed the altered street. The most obvious thing missing was Katy's, the junk shop that had doubled as a grocery store, and the first shop I had been allowed to visit on my own—pound note clutched in sticky hand—to buy bread and milk and liquorice allsorts. There was no signage over the door, just a blank awning, but everyone knew the old lady who owned it and referred to the shop by her name. Katy would have been well into her eighties or even nineties back then, and walked with the aid of a Zimmer frame, but she had the smile of a schoolgirl and ran her shop like she was one. Sliced bread and newspapers were her staples, but she sold these alongside a gargantuan pile of moth-eaten trash: lace doilies, books, curios, plates, petticoats, brooches, hats. How any of it got there, nobody knew, but if you spotted something in the junk pile you wanted to buy, Katy would examine it in her shaking hands as though she had no idea how it got there either. She would mutter that she just had to check with her daughter to see how much it was worth. And that would be the last you saw of it. Katy's daughter ran a stall in the Portobello Market arcade, and once alerted to the desirability of certain objects in her mother's junk shop, she whisked them away, polished them up, and rebirthed them as exorbitantly priced antiques. Now in place of Katy's there was a boutique for "*hommes*" with a solitary, art-directed sneaker displayed in its long, gleaming window—nothing else—and I wondered if it was progress or absurdity that Katy's path of excessive bric-a-brac had culminated, decades later, in a store for one-footed Frenchmen.

In front of me, the buzzer beckoned. What did I have to lose? Even if Peggy didn't recognize me, surely she'd remember my parents and that would at least get me a cup of tea and a biscuit. We could talk about Peggy's children, Harold and Pippa, who would be grown, with kids of their own by now. When I was a child, they were teenagers, old enough for Pippa to trip downstairs in her New Romantic get-up and impersonate a babysitter. Her brother, Harold, had been more of a rumor, a floppy-fringed sulker who'd gone away first to boarding school and then to Cambridge University, from where he'd come back arrogant and spoiled (or so my father was fond of saying). Harold did nothing to quash the impression of aloofness, hovering at the edge of Peggy's soirees, shunning endless games of charades, and never lowering his gaze to the level of grasshoppers such as myself.

Pippa, on the other hand, had been my idol, and being looked after by her had been an event. She always arrived in a cloud of hair spray and kohl, armed with secrets from the teenage frontline, and I'd looked forward to the nights my parents went to parties as much as if I too was going out. She would demonstrate the latest dance moves—mostly jerky, New Wave stuff—and if I hounded her, she tossed me a few scraps of advice about snogging and other unbelievable acts. "Don't put on too much lippy or it'll rub off on his face," and, "Never tell a guy you love him straight after you've bonked." She had magnificent boobs, quite the biggest I'd ever seen, and together we'd raided my mother's wardrobe and tried on all her clothes. Unlike her brother, she had not been sent to boarding school, but had made do with the local comprehensive and a hairdressing course at a third-rate polytechnic. My mother, who had gone without haircuts (and many other things) to send me to private school, thought Peggy had done her daughter a great disservice, but anyone who had ever met Harold could tell you that was not necessarily the case.

Spurred on by such memories, I pressed Peggy's buzzer and felt the click of a small electric shock. A brisk voice hissed over the intercom, "Peggy Wright's residence. Can I help you?" She sounded formal, like a receptionist.

"I've come to see Peggy. I'm an old friend."

The woman didn't reply but let me in, and I heaved open the front door, which slammed behind me on a spring. Since we'd lived there, the lobby had undergone a makeover. Instead of letters stacked on the radiator and piled haphazardly on the doormat, each apartment now had its own brass-numbered pigeonhole. The smell was different too, no longer boiled cabbage and mildew, but fresh paint and carpet shampoo. And Harold's bicycle, which had leaned permanently against the bottom staircase, someone had finally moved that too.

I bounded up the first five flights of stairs, eager to see Peggy, but with three still to go I was gasping for breath and had to stop for a rest. Each landing was more or less identical, so it was hard to be absolutely sure, but I thought this floor had belonged to Jimmy, the bogeyman of the building. I had not even known his last name, only feared him, and I'd never stopped on his landing in case he jumped out and threw a sack over my head. When I tried to recall his appearance now, all I could remember was a shadowy, retreating figure, his face a caved-in slab.

Peggy's front door was already open, sweet disinfectant vapors leaking out into the hall. I crossed the threshold, prepared for renovations, but none had been made: the black-lacquered walls, chessboard floor tiles, and accents of orange were, shockingly, identical to how I'd remembered them. So too was the ornamental birdcage, its perches wired with a colony of faded stuffed canaries. Not so much furniture as props, stage dressing for a farce set in 1970s Bohemia. So unchanged was the interior that when I looked in the hall mirror, I was surprised to see an adult face staring back at me.

The brisk woman appeared from the kitchen in white slacks and a white smock, an efficient spring in her white-plimsolled step. "She's just had her afternoon dose," she said. "So I expect she'll be rather groggy."

Too late, I noticed the dim lighting, the hushed, churchlike atmosphere, and regretted my impulsive visit. To arrive unannounced was so terribly un-English. After ten years in the colonies, I had forgotten my manners. Not only that, but something was clearly wrong with Peggy, wrong enough that she required the services of a live-in nurse.

"I'll come back another time," I said. "I'd hate to disturb her."

"It's probably best to see her while you still can," said the nurse, directing me across the hallway. "She's quite weak today but it always cheers her up to have visitors."

Peggy had been moved into Pippa's old bedroom, close to the kitchen, closer to the front door if she needed to check out. The room was dark and cool, with blinds at half-mast and thick net curtains obscuring the warm summer sun. It took a few seconds to locate Peggy, and much longer to recognize her. She was on a trolley bed, wrapped in a cocoon of crisp hospital sheets, the pillows tilted to cradle her piplike head. From her left arm, a drip trailed, and her skin spread like tracing paper over a map of her bones. Most of her hair had fallen out; what remained was aubergine fluff. But she still had her stenciled eyebrows, arched in permanent surprise, and I realized with an odd sting of pity that they must be tattooed on.

Trying not to wake her, I shuffled toward the bed, but a floorboard creaked under my shifting weight and her eyelids flickered open. She had trouble focusing, and looked blurrily up at the ceiling.

"Hello, Peggy," I said, softly. "It's Suki. Suki Piper."

At the sound of my voice she started, and I picked up her dry, weightless hand and squeezed it to reassure her. "We used to live downstairs in the basement flat. I'm Hillary's daughter."

My words did not register.

"We moved away a long time ago and I haven't seen you since—at least, I don't think I have. For some of that time, I've been living in New Zealand. My father, Ludo, went to live there when my parents separated. I think you saw Hillary a few times after that but she . . ." The end of the sentence got stuck in my throat.

Peggy blinked. "Hillary," she croaked, her lips sticking together at the corners. "Darling Hillary."

I tried to give her a drink of water, but most of it rolled down her chin, and I gave up, resting the glass on a side table next to a half-empty bottle of scotch. Alongside it sat a plastic measuring cup with a sticky brown residue on the rim.

When I picked up Peggy's hand again, she pulled on mine, and her eyes danced a little, like they used to. "Lovely Hillary," she said. "How wonderful to see you!"

"I'm not Hillary. I'm her daughter, Suki."

"And how *is* Suki?" With great effort, Peggy lifted her hands to her face and made ring shapes around her eyes. "Pink glasses!" she exclaimed. "Always dancing. Wet the bed when she came to stay with us."

After this, she collapsed, closed her eyes, and began to snore.

Mistaking me for Hillary meant Peggy didn't know, or had forgotten, that my mother was no longer alive. When people forgot I often couldn't bring myself to correct them. Sometimes they started reminiscing about Hillary's beauty, the way she'd lit up a room with her grace, or her legendary abilities to sew and cook, and by the time they asked the appalling but inevitable question, "How is she, your dear mother, Hillary?" the weight of their admiration bore down on me so hard I told them what they wanted to hear. "She moved to Scotland to look after Grandma," I'd explained to one old acquaintance, telling another that she'd gone to India in the midnineties to find herself and was still there on an ashram. Lousy fibs but much kinder on us all. Everyone had loved my mother—no one more so than I—and if I never said out loud that she'd died, then I sometimes believed that she hadn't.

While Peggy dozed, I stroked her hand and took an inventory of her daughter's old room. The dresser where Pippa had teased her hair and kohled her eyes for hours was in the same place, and so was the antique Victorian dollhouse, over in the corner by the window. Pippa had outgrown the dollhouse years before I came on the scene, but she'd remained proprietary of it, and had only begrudgingly tolerated my sticky fingers on its tiny antiques. Though the dollhouse was now dusty and faded, I had never encountered its equal, and I finally understood why she hadn't wanted to part with it. Really, it belonged in a museum—or here in this flat that was so much like one.

I let go of Peggy's hand and walked to the window, curious

to see if our old terrace was visible from up here. Our basement flat had gone through from front to back, with a set of French doors opening out onto a patio. At first, I didn't recognize the chalk paths and lavender pots—it had been remodeled in ersatz French Provincial—and then one or two features stood out as familiar: the way the patio was on two levels, the white gate that led out to the communal garden. But what I couldn't locate—what I was, abruptly, desperate to see—was the pitted iron plate that marked the entrance to the air-raid shelter. This shelter was a relic from the Blitz, a deep concrete bunker where families had gone to sit out the bombings during World War II. My family had gone down there too—only once—but the experience had been so awful, so chilling, that the bunker had quickly come to represent the most terrifying thing in my world. Even now, I shivered to recall the narrow stone stairs that descended into the chamber, how frigid the air had been so far under the earth, how we had not been able to get out.

Once more I scanned the terrace, looking for the trapdoor. Had I lost my bearings or was the air-raid shelter no longer there? Searching again, I found no trace of it, and surmised that it had been filled in or concreted over to prevent anyone's falling in. Good job, I thought with immense relief, for a death trap such as that had no business being in a garden.

Peggy had stopped snoring, and her breathing was weak but regular. When I picked up her hand, she didn't stir. The room had become stuffy, claustrophobic, and I decided I had been there long enough.

Out in the hallway, trying to remember my way to the bathroom, I felt drugged, disoriented, as though Peggy's medication had leaked out through her skin. On the wall next to the phone was a list of emergency numbers, one of which was Pippa's, and I wrote it down on a dog-eared receipt from my pocket. Many of the rooms between Peggy's and the bathroom had been closed up, sealed off, but the door to one of the bedrooms was open, and I saw a mess of books and boxes spilling out. That must have been Harold's old room. How careless and wasteful, I thought, to have so many disused rooms in such a nice flat, when all I needed was one.

It was passing back through the drawing room that I saw her, and froze immediately with the rigid fear of a five-year-old. How could I have missed her on the way to the bathroom? The statue of a young girl kneeling where she'd always knelt, on a dais between two faded velvet chaise longues that had once been cherry red. The dais was varnished mahogany, but the girl's skin was the color of dirty cement. She was rough-hewn, abstract: her smooth granite eyes had no irises. Her tiny hands were folded in her lap, and her hair was in a bowl cut. She wore an old-fashioned smocked dress with a round pansy collar. Peggy had called her Madeline—referring to her by name, affectionately and often, as though she were her daughter or a little friend. She had been real to me too, though not in such a benign way.

As a child, I had refused to be left alone with her, and even in a room full of adults, Madeline could freak me out. It was partly the blankness of her stare, a gaze that nevertheless followed me wherever I went in the room. And partly, it was that she was the same age as me but was stuck being that age and would never grow up. It made me think that inside her was a thwarted adult, who had grown evil over time because she was trapped in a noose of perpetual childhood.

Once, at one of Peggy's especially raucous parties, there'd been dozens of adults in the drawing room, dancing, drinking, laughing, and I was there too, up past my bedtime, and giddily lost in the forest of their legs. For a brief moment, those limbs had cleared, and there was Madeline, motionless but hunting me through the trees. My screams had been so hysterical that I had been taken home immediately—the party over for me and my parents.

On the sofa opposite Madeline's dais, I sat down to observe her from a safe distance. I was curious to know if she'd still have any power over me at twenty-eight years old.

To begin with I was fine, in control, but then outside, clouds passed overhead, casting Madeline's features into shadow. She had not moved, but my first thought was that it was Madeline who had taken all the light out of the room, and before I could reason against it, a sensation of quickening vertigo came over me. When I stood up to move away from her, I felt dizzy and also that I was physically shrinking. Around me, the room seemed to waver, but in a way that was too subtle to grasp. I looked down at my scuffed and ill-fitting trainers, bought in a size too big because I'd meant to use them for jogging but never had. The shoes appeared familiar, but I was sure that the feet inside them weren't mine—that these feet were tiny impostors. I held my hands out in front of my face, spread the fingers and wiggled them, but even these looked counterfeit, rogue hands on the ends of absurdly slender limbs. My perspective had shifted lower down, and for a few seconds, I was a child again—a child who was pensive and scared.

I bit down hard on my tongue, and one by one, the walls of Peggy's drawing room regained their density, and the weight of my adult feet sank into my shoes. Once more, I stood on solid ground, in a London apartment I had not been in for almost twenty years. An apartment so like a museum that briefly, I rationalized, it had pulled me back with it into the past.

That I'd imagined the whole thing was plausible but that didn't change how unsettled I felt—especially when I turned to leave the drawing room and had the uncanny sensation that I was being watched.

Too late, I realized I had turned my back on Madeline, and when I swiveled round to face her, I fancied she was gloating. This amounted to nothing more than a dead-eyed stare—but then again, it never had. The year after next I'd turn thirty, but Madeline still had it over me. Her power was intact, had perhaps even grown. In the old, cowering way, I turned and walked out backward, hoping to catch the very last rays of that untimely summer evening.

CHAPTER TWO

London, 1981

MADELINE WAS NOT the only little friend to dwell behind the stucco facade of Ladbroke Gardens. Downstairs in the basement flat, the boiler cupboard outside our bathroom was home to a hand.

This hand was just a hand—no body attached—and it liked to come out of the cupboard and untie the bows on the backs of my dresses. That was the only thing it liked to do: untie bows. If I was wearing dungarees, or a dress without a bow on the back, the hand did not come out. It did not come out for pajamas, or when anybody else was with me, and it especially did not come out when I wanted it to—though many were the times I climbed into the cupboard and looked for it. Where the hand went when it wasn't in the cupboard, I never knew, but I do know that if it had been attached to a body, it wouldn't have fit in there—the boiler took up too much room.

I was not afraid of this hand without a body. Never had it occurred to me to be afraid of it. The hand untied my dresses; that was the game it played and the sole reason it existed. Perhaps it helped that the hand reminded me of my mother's: soft and feminine but also strong.

I knew what it felt like because I'd once made the mistake of grabbing it. I had been trying to show the hand to my mother, and one day when it appeared, I took hold of it and called out to her. Mum took her time getting to the boiler cupboard, and while she was on her way, the hand and I engaged in a tug-of-war. Strangely, even though I had been the one to grab the hand, once I had grabbed it, the hand started pulling back. Before long, we had traded places, with the hand trying to drag me into the cupboard, and me attempting to shake it off. I don't remember who let go first, but by the time my mother got to the cupboard, I was sitting alone on the floor, rubbing at a red mark on my wrist.

Around the same time—my sixth or seventh year—my parents threw the only party they ever had, a bash so wild and debauched that it's the party I've subsequently measured the success of all others by. They had reason to celebrate. We had literally moved up in the world, bought the flat above us and knocked through a staircase to create a maisonette—so much more posh sounding than a basement. For a while, and at the time of the party, we had two kitchens, two front doors, two bathrooms, and two boiler cupboards—though the hand never ventured to the one upstairs.

The party was in midsummer, a humid weekend in July, and my parents invited the neighbors, including Peggy and Pippa, plus a score of other friends I didn't know they had. There was a costume-party theme, but no one told me what it was and I couldn't work it out from the dozens of pilots, policemen, chambermaids, and slave girls who turned up. In a departure from her usual mild look, Mum donned a corkscrew blond wig and dressed up as Mae West. Eagerly, I helped her to get ready, pulling tight the laces on a corset she had rented for the occasion. She had bought new lipstick too, crimson red, and in the mirror I watched her apply it, then pull back to admire the transformation.

"You look really beautiful," I told her. "Like a lady in a magazine."

"I feel silly," she said, wiping off a little of the lipstick. "And this looks completely wrong." She removed from around her neck the simple oval locket she always wore, and I pounced on it immediately, fingering the silver and fiddling with its latch. She'd bought it in a flea market in Paris and loved it for its plainness—she told me the way it had slowly tarnished over the years made it feel like an extension of her skin.

"Can I wear it?" I said.

Mum hesitated. "Not tonight. I won't be able to keep an eye on you." She put the locket in her jewelry box, and selected another necklace made from dozens of diamantes that I had never seen her wear. "There," she said, putting it on. "Now I look more like a tart."

She pulled herself to standing and hobbled awkwardly out of the bedroom in five-inch stiletto heels, the only pair she had ever owned. When my father saw her, he wolf-whistled. "I might not go away so much if you dressed like that more often." My mother blinked her heavy eyelashes at him but didn't smile.

"Do you like my clown suit, Dad?" I said, sticking out my chest. I was hugely proud of the costume Mum had whipped up on her sewing machine in the week leading up to the party. Together we'd made pom-poms of yellow wool, cutting out cardboard circles and winding the yarn around them to make fat, woolly doughnuts. We'd folded another circle of card to make a pointed hat, topped with a pom-pom and tied under my chin with string. When my so-called friend Esther arrived in a Snow White costume from Hamleys, I was gutted. Suddenly, my clown suit looked homemade, all crooked pom-poms and collapsing hat. Esther's parents were getting a divorce and my mother insisted that I invite her over out of pity. But broken home or not, Esther was mean; she called me four eyes when no one was around.

The most thrilling guests at the party were Jean Luc and Henri, who had come all the way from Paris by ferry and train. They were younger than my parents, perhaps in their early twenties, with long, raffish hair—though my dad had that too—and they smoked a ton of Gauloises. They told each other jokes in French that I knew were dirty from the way my mother made furious hand signals when they told them in front of me.

I thought of the Frenchmen always as a pair, but around Jean Luc in particular, I felt strange. I wanted his attention, but when he gave it to me, I just needed to pee. I think Mum felt something of the same thing because around him she smiled too much and fiddled with the curls on her wig. When Jean Luc came out of the bathroom in a pirate waistcoat—bare chested and exposing a trail of tiny hairs that disappeared under the waistband of his leather pants—she spilled red wine on her dress and rushed off to make sure the chicken vol-au-vents hadn't caught fire in the oven.

Henri was dressed as a crash victim, with a bandage wrapped round his head that oozed tomato ketchup. He didn't make Mum blush, but I think she liked him better, especially after he spent the afternoon polishing our mismatched wineglasses and poking skewers of cheese and pineapple into an orange. The evening before, Mum and I had stayed up late making crudités and a vat of pink taramasalata. But overnight in the fridge the taramasalata had formed an orange crust. When Mum tried to fix it with lemon juice, it curdled, and she had burst into tears before throwing the whole lot out. She was worried there wouldn't be enough to eat almost as much as Dad was worried there wouldn't be enough to drink. Five minutes before the party began, he dashed to the off-license for more supplies and was still out when the first guests arrived.

Pippa brought Lulu, her friend from the polytechnic, who would babysit sometimes if Pippa was busy. Lulu was a stunner. Dad was dressed as a pilot and the minute she arrived he made an embarrassing fuss over her and frisked her French maid outfit, which ended at her bottom in an outbreak of frills. Pippa came dressed as the singer from Blondie, her spiky black hair covered by a platinum wig, and the change made her act in a way that was sassier than usual. When Dad patted *her* on the rump, she cuffed him round the ear and he smiled a little too warmly.

Esther and I had been told we were allowed to stay up until ten o'clock, but when it got that late no one told us to go to bed, so we sneaked around the kitchen taking sips out of abandoned paper cups. Out of revenge for upstaging my costume, I handed Esther a cup of red wine with a cigarette butt in it, but when she didn't see the butt and drank from it, I worried she might die, and told her it was there.

Trying to get all the wine out of her mouth, she had just about choked. "No wonder you don't have any friends at school," she said, adding, "four eyes," to drive home her point.

Tears pricked my eyes. "Four eyes are better than two," I said, even though the retort made no sense. I wasn't clever at being friends with people and always said dumb things and got teased. Mum said I had a thin skin because I was an only child, but I didn't see how having brothers and sisters could stop other children from being mean.

After the cigarette-butt incident we gave up on sneaking drinks and hung out in the disco room. It was dark in there—the floor lamp glowed from under what looked like Mum's dressing gown—and the music was so loud it hurt my stomach. We crept in near the back and hid behind the sofa, where we had a good view but were largely invisible. On the improvised dance floor, adults collided with each other in time to the music, while others bunched together on couches as though trying to keep warm. Surrounded by attentive men, Pippa and Lulu formed a nucleus at the center of it all. The whole night, Dad had been pitching drinks into their hands, with Jean Luc and Henri rushing in to fill the gap when he wasn't around. Now the Frenchmen leaned in with their hips and whispered secrets into the girls' hair.

"What the devil are you doing behind there?"

It was Dad, his pilot hat on back to front. He picked us up, one under each arm, and carried us, kicking, from the room. When he put her down, Esther looked stunned—even more so when he shooed us out the back door and closed it behind us. "My father would never treat me like that," she said, her whisper outraged.

"At least my parents are still together."

In the garden, Mum had put up the Wendy tent, and laid out cushions and sleeping bags. I gave the one with the broken zipper to Esther, and snuggled into the other but didn't feel sleepy. It was dark in the tent, and we were soon telling spooky stories and squealing, which led after an hour or two to a thrumming noise inside my head and then a pinching headache.

"You're taking up too much room," I said, kicking Esther for the umpteenth time.

She fought her way out of the musky sleeping bag. "I need to pee."

"You can't go by yourself, you'll fall into the bunker." I stood up too quickly, and hit my head on a tent pole.

Esther laughed. "Spastic." She was still dressed as Snow White.

I couldn't tell her that I was the one who didn't want to be left outside by myself because of the bunker, so I followed her across the dark patio in my clown suit. We had no torch, and stumbled on a stack of clay pots, which clattered over and broke. At first I thought the French doors at the back were locked, but after an extra-hard pull they came open. Inside, it looked like an elephant was asleep on the bed, and I was startled before remembering it was only the coats. We took turns going to the toilet, then heard giggling from the adjacent bathroom. I told Esther to keep quiet and squinted into the keyhole to get a better look. Behind me, Esther tugged at my clown suit, and tried to peer over my shoulder.

"Don't stand so close. You're making it all wobbly." I shoved her away. Through the keyhole, all I could see was the mist on my glasses—steam from the bathroom had made them fog up. I wiped the lenses and looked again. One corner of avocado bathtub was visible and a gold tap, or half of it. If I closed one eye, I could see a bit more of the wall and a bit more of the taps. Disappointed, I pulled back to let Esther have a look.

"I can't see anything," she said after a spell at the keyhole.

"Maybe they're taking a bath?"

Esther frowned. "In the middle of a party?"

We skulked away from the door, but hadn't gotten far when a groan sounded from the bathroom—followed by a tidal wave of water hitting tiles. We rushed for the keyhole at the same time but I got there first, grabbed the door handle, and elbowed Esther out of the way.

"It's *my* bathroom," I spat. "You're just a guest—remember?"

She shrank back and I looked through the keyhole but

couldn't see the tap—a tangle of buttocks and legs was in the way. Briefly, a gap opened up and I glimpsed what looked like a golf ball in a sock, then the whole lot slammed together as though powered by pistons. I was mesmerized, and wanted to look through the keyhole forever, but a dark shape fell across it, as if someone had pulled down a blind.

"What is it? What can you see? Let me look!" Behind me, Esther grew frantic. She yanked the yellow pom-pom on top of my clown hat until I fell backward, clutching at my neck where the chin strap dug in like a garrotte. Esther leaned forward and spied through the keyhole then recoiled in shock, screamed, and sprang from the door. She gave me a fright, and I screamed even louder than she had. A lumbering, splashing sound came from the bathroom and we hurtled from the door, tripping over each other to be the first to get away.

We made it as far as the bed, and hid behind the coat elephant. In the scramble, my glasses came off, but I couldn't see well enough to find them. I clutched at Esther. "Can you see where my glasses went?"

"Shhhhh," she said. "Someone just came in."

Whoever it was knocked on the bathroom door, then when he or she wasn't let in, they left.

"Let's go back to the Wendy house," said Esther.

I stuck my head above the coats just as a lock turned in the bathroom door. "Wait," I said. "They're coming out."

A vast hulk walked out of the bathroom then split in two—one half tall and thin, the other short and curvy.

"Who is it?" said Esther.

"I don't know," I said. "I don't have my glasses on!"

The two halves rejoined and made a sucking sound.

"They're kissing," said Esther. "It's disgusting."

I tried to shut her up with a sharp look that was more of a cross-eyed squint and stuck my head over the ramparts. I willed the two figures to come into focus, or better still, to turn on the light. The short figure was a girl in a miniskirt. She held what looked like a cat—which she put on her head.

"Is that Pippa?"

"I think so," whispered Esther.

The cat was a wig. I had glanced away at Esther for only a second but in that time the two figures had become three—Pippa and two men. I grabbed Esther's hand in surprise. I wasn't sure if the other man had come out of the bathroom or if it was the same one who'd knocked on the door. They huddled together and laughed, and I thought I saw the outline of a pilot's hat. Trying to make out if that's what it was, I strained my eyes to the point of popping—but to no avail. By daylight the world was a blur without glasses, and by night I was legally blind.

"Did you see who it was?" I asked Esther when they'd gone.

She didn't answer.

"Who was it?"

"Not telling," she said, her smile smug. She was getting back at me for the cigarette butt, and I hated her more than ever.

Ten minutes later of fumbling on all fours, I found my glasses but it was too late to identify the people in the bathroom—they were long gone. Before trundling back to the Wendy tent, I stuck my head into the room where the party was still going on. It was a few shades darker than it had been earlier and everyone moved in slow motion. More of them were sitting down than standing up, and the ones on their feet were leaning against each other so as not to fall over. I searched for Pippa and Jean Luc and Henri, but while I was looking, I accidentally caught Mum's eye and she stood up and staggered toward us. Not taking any chances, I grabbed Esther's arm and hauled her to the Wendy tent, where we lay still and squinched our eyes closed, pretending to be asleep. When no one came to tell us off, what I'd been trying so hard to fake became real, and the next thing I knew, it was light outside and my sleeping bag cover was wet with dew.

When we got up and went inside the flat, it was eerily quiet. Bodies lay stacked on couches and the floor—Jean Luc was slumped against Henri—but there was no sign of Lulu or Pippa. We ate Coco Pops and waited for the adults to stir, and when they didn't we sat down in a gap and watched cartoons on TV. But even that didn't wake them up.

"I'm bored," said Esther. "Don't you have a VCR?"

I didn't even know what that was. "We could try on my mum's jewelry?"

Esther waited reluctantly on my bed while I crept into Mum and Dad's room, past their sleeping bodies, and lifted Mum's jewelry box. Back in my room, I meted out the various trinkets, allowing Esther to try on all but the locket. That one I saved for myself.

"It's very plain," said Esther. "What's inside it?"

"It's a secret." I wasn't lying. Mum had refused to open the locket—she said it was bad luck—and I'd never been able to work the catch. I assumed it had pictures of her and Dad inside it, but the one time I'd asked her to confirm it, she'd smiled and said, "What makes you think I love him the most?" Of course she loved him the most, he was her husband.

I put on the locket and admired my reflection in a scratched mirror that was stuck to the back of a wardrobe door. When Esther's hand appeared in the glass, I thought she was going to swipe it, but instead she closed her fingers around the skin of my neck and pinched it so hard I felt sick. For a few seconds, we simply stared at each other in the mirror, then I lunged for her ponytail and tried to yank it from her head. She flailed for a moment, striking air, then twisted around far enough to claw at me. Naturally, I clawed right back. I don't know who burst into tears first, but before long I was lying on the bed, sobbing into my pillow, while Esther stood, rigid, in front of the mirror, howling at her reflection.

Not long after that, Esther phoned her mother to be picked up, but it was the Filipino nanny, in a Volvo, who arrived to collect her. When Esther saw the nanny, she started to cry again.

The second she had gone, I went into the kitchen to find our sharpest knife, the blade of which was as long as my forearm. Back in my bedroom, I pushed the blade between the two halves of the locket and tried to prise it open, but it wouldn't budge. In a fit of frustration, I put the locket down on a side table and began to hack at the catch mechanism until eventually I sliced it off. This was precisely what I had been trying to do, yet it was only when I saw the snag of broken silver that I realized how awful and irreversible was the thing I had done. I picked up the locket, at least hoping I'd be able to see inside it, but by breaking the blasted thing, I had also somehow cinched it shut.

My first impulse was to return it, damaged, to the jewelry box, and deny all knowledge of the incident. But I felt too guilty and instead put the locket around my neck and resolved to confess just as soon as Mum woke up.

Only later that morning, after calling me into the bedroom, she straightaway asked me to run to the kitchen to fetch a stainless-steel bowl from under the sink, and I did as I was told and forgot about the locket. Mum put the bowl in front of Dad, who thrust his head inside it as though he was about to lick out the remains of a delicious cake mix. Seeing the top of his head, I remembered what I'd seen outside the bathroom the night before, how one of the shapes had been wearing his hat.

"Dad," I blurted out. "Did you take a bath last night, in the middle of the party?"

He looked up from the bowl. "A bath?" he said, his voice in ruins. "Why in God's name would I do that?"

I looked at Mum, who was looking at Dad as though she didn't want him to eat the cake mix. "I don't know," I said. "But some people were taking a bath and I thought maybe—"

"He didn't take a bath," said my mother, shooing me out with uncharacteristic force. "No one did." When the bedroom door had closed behind me, I heard a surge, and Mum exclaiming, "Oh no, the bowl isn't big enough!"

By lunchtime, most people had gone home, but Jean Luc and Henri were still there, smoking cigarettes and coughing while they slugged down small cups of coffee that they'd made in a funny machine on the stove. In the communal garden, they played a rowdy game of hide-and-seek, running between plane trees and diving into bushes, but their rules were haphazard and they didn't seem to care whether they found each other or not. When they tired of that game, they progressed to wrestling, puppylike, on the lawn, rolling and grabbing at each other's pants and untucked shirts. In the early afternoon, they discovered the hatch to the air-raid shelter and Jean Luc asked if we could open it up and go down.

CHAPTER THREE

London, 2003

I HAD COPIED Pippa's phone number off the wall at Peggy's and had rung her the next day, but nearly two months passed before she got around to inviting me to dinner. I didn't suppose Pippa had even noticed it was that long because life had filled the gap, whereas in my case—drifting and friendless—each day I'd felt a little more snubbed. When the invitation finally came, I almost could not go through with it. She'd been brisk with me on the phone, and afterward I'd realized that my adoration of her had been entirely one way. To her, I was probably just a kid she had looked after for pocket money. On top of that, I had fallen for the irresistible lure of a reunion, so cozy when imagined, so stilted in reality.

Pippa had only moved round the corner from her childhood home, to a few hundred meters past the Westway on Ladbroke Grove. Back in the day, the arches of the Westway had been where junkies went to score drugs, the structure itself serving as an unofficial marker between good real estate and bad. Nowadays, the area beyond it was a precinct where fashion designers had workrooms and hipsters bought their first flats. Pippa's building was one of the shabby ones, its Victorian facade battered from traffic fumes and dust. At the front door I hesitated, and wished I'd never called her, never arranged this meeting.

Then, on the third-floor landing, my reservations evaporated in a riot of Mediterranean aromas. I was starving, and in no position to turn down a free meal, especially when the host was married to a chef. Ahead of me, the front door was wide open and Pippa rushed out to embrace me, her green eyes huge and flashing. I'd forgotten she was an exact physical replica of her mother, and though neither woman was conventionally beautiful, through sheer force of personality they conjured up a much more powerful charisma. There were also the breasts—so bountiful that even a woman's eye was drawn to stare.

"Suki, darling!" she exclaimed. "It's so wonderful to see you!" Her voice was louder than I remembered, and more musical. Through her thin clothes, she jangled and pulsed, as if plugged into an electric socket.

"You too," I said, trying not to tense up. It was the first time in almost a year that anyone had hugged me. "I feel so bad about crashing in on Peggy like that. I had no idea she was so ill."

"Don't be silly, she loves an audience," said Pippa. "It's being alone she can't stand. Besides, she's perked up since then, and if you hadn't popped in to see her, you wouldn't be here now."

A few more of my reservations dissolved. "Peggy's better?"

"Much better. Yesterday she ticked me off, for wearing jeans—she thinks denim is so working class—and I took that as a sign she was on the mend. Later on she even got out of bed. One of the doctors said she'd never walk again, but she made it as far as the booze cabinet before collapsing. I expect she wanted to prove him wrong."

"She didn't hurt herself when she collapsed?"

"No, no, she sort of fell into a nearby armchair, and went to sleep with the bottle in her hand. Business as usual there."

I chose this moment to offer up the bottle of plonk I'd bought from the off-license by the tube station. Pippa peered into the brown paper bag, then shrank from it, visibly disgusted.

"I'm really sorry," I said, mortified. "I couldn't afford anything decent."

"Oh dear God," said Pippa, squeezing my arm to reassure me. "It isn't that. The thing is, we—Ari and I—don't drink. And by that I mean we're teetotalers, practically Mormons. We gave it up when the doctors showed us the state of Mummy's liver. We tried AA but couldn't handle all the praying, so now we just keep a sort of honesty calendar. If one of us falls off the wagon, we get a black mark. Don't we, Ari?" She addressed the last part to the kitchen, where, presumably, Ari was hiding. "Suki's here," she said, more loudly. "She's come all the way from Australia to see us!"

"New Zealand," I corrected.

"New Zealand!" she shouted at the kitchen.

I followed her in, where a huge man trussed in a small white chef's apron stood with his belly jutting out to meet the stove. He was the very opposite of all the snake-hipped rogues Pippa had run around with back in the day, but so was almost any husband you could think of.

"Ari," said Pippa, prodding him to get his attention. "I said, Suki's here."

Ari rested his wooden spoon on a tea towel and wiped his hands on his apron before backing away reluctantly from the stove. "Hope you're not vegetarian," he said, holding toward me a hand the size of a bear's.

"Meat is good," I said, patting my stomach.

He smiled vaguely and went back to his pots. Pippa swung open the fridge, giving me a clear view of the honesty calendar, which looked as though it had only just survived a violent game of noughts and crosses.

"That's all Ari," said Pippa, noticing I'd seen it. "He refuses to cook anything without wine. I have to watch him like a hawk. Don't I, darling?"

At the stove, Ari huffed, and I thought, with a pang, of the seven quid I'd wasted on plonk, and how it had been a toss-up between that and my tube fare home. Was it rude, in the home of quasi-reformed alcoholics, to demand a glass of wine from the bottle you'd brought? I was starting to think I might need one.

In the two months that had passed since I first called Pippa, my circumstances had bypassed bad and worse and arrived straight at desperate. I had no family in London anymore, no backstop, and since my arrival the city had been behaving in a way that was downright hostile. In the first month, I had tried to open a bank account in Kensington High Street—the same branch my parents had used—but had been told that I couldn't open one until I'd lived in England for at least a year. "But I was *born* here and lived here for eighteen years," I protested, to no avail. Ten years abroad had apparently canceled out the first eighteen in Britain. The same thing happened at the surgery of my old family doctor in Westbourne Grove, where I went to retrieve my National Health Service number. The receptionist informed me that after ten years without patient activity, they had destroyed my health records. Inland Revenue had just done the same. I found such efficiency hard to believe in a country renowned for its grinding bureaucracy but was told that if I'd come back earlier there'd still have been a trace of me left in the system. As things stood, I felt like the recently deceased.

Pippa took a carton out of the fridge and poured me a large

glass of orange juice. "Now," she said, guiding me back to the living room, "the last time we saw you was at the funeral. Next thing we heard, you'd gone to live with your father in New Zealand."

"I didn't live with him."

"How silly of me," Pippa said. "You were too old. What were you, eighteen or nineteen?"

"Eighteen, but that wasn't it. He lived in the country and—"

Pippa laughed. "I can't imagine the disco king ever living in the country—how absurd."

She talked about my father in a jocular way and I wondered how well she had known him, how much he'd had to do with what I'd seen that night at the party. But it wasn't something I could ask about. "His new wife," I said, "is fully into horses."

She looked as though a light had come on. "Good lord, that's right. Rowan was horse mad."

"You knew Rowan?"

"Not well, no," said Pippa, adding, "only what Hillary told me about her."

For a moment, I was silent, taken aback. My mother had never mentioned Rowan to me by name, or in any other way, and I'd assumed it was because she didn't know anything about her.

"I wish I'd made more of an effort to help you and your mother after you left Ladbroke Gardens," said Pippa. "You do know that, don't you?"

She'd said as much on the phone but I wondered why she felt the need to repeat herself. "You did what you could," I said, parroting what I told everyone who felt bad about not seeing Mum enough toward the end, as if they might have been able to stop her from dying. "Besides, she didn't tell anyone how sick she was. Not even me."

"You didn't know she was dying?"

"I knew she was ill." An edge of defensiveness crept into my voice. "But I didn't know it was terminal."

"Who knows what any of us would do in that situation?" said Pippa, in such a way that I knew she would have done the opposite. "It's a mother's worst fear—well, second-worst fear—and she probably didn't want to scare you."

"What's a mother's worst fear?" I said, feeling stupid that I didn't know.

"One that she can't even bring herself to say out loud."

"Oh," I said, feeling even thicker than before.

For a while we talked about old times, but what Pippa remembered and what I remembered did not seem to converge. She laughed when I told her about Madeline, how after all this time the statue still gave me the creeps.

"Are you sure it has a name?" she said. "Harold and I used to call it the Midget. I tried to convince Mummy to sell it a few years ago to knock off a few bills and what not but she insisted on keeping the bloody thing. Said she'd rather sell her kidneys. I told her no one would want those, they'd be as pickled as her liver. Of course, she didn't find that at all funny. According to her, I don't have a sense of humor. Only Harold has one of those."

From the kitchen came the hopeful clatter of plates, but when Pippa asked how far away dinner was, Ari only grumbled that it would be ready when it was ready. My stomach grumbled back. For weeks I had eaten only as much as I could afford, which was never enough to fill me up.

When we had exhausted the topic of old times, Pippa asked about my current situation—a subject I'd been dreading. Instead of saying I was unemployed, I came up with some rot about being at a career crossroads, unsure of what to do next, and was relieved when she responded, "That's a generational thing, isn't it?" because it meant I could nod in agreement and say, "Yes, we

Gen-Xers are very restless." When she asked if I had a boyfriend, I tried to feign the same indifference, but no one was fooled.

A question formed on Pippa's lips, but she must have sensed this was a touchy topic and didn't ask it. "Would you like another juice?" she said after a time.

"No thanks," I said. "I'm walking."

It had been a nervous joke, but Pippa took it literally. "Walking to where?"

"Willesden Green. I'm dossing on a friend's couch. I'd love to get a flat around here but it's a little too . . ." I hesitated.

"Pricey?" offered Pippa. "Trust me, if we hadn't bought this place in the eighties, just before the property boom, we'd be living in Willesden Green too." She told me they had the top two floors and had managed to convert the attic and build a small roof terrace. "The attic floor is Caleb's territory—where parents fear to tread. Did you ever meet him?"

"Your son?"

"My darling boy."

"I'm not sure." I remembered something about a huge baby, a difficult birth, and months of surgery, nothing appropriate to mention. "Maybe when he was little?"

"Heavens!" said Pippa. "I can't believe you haven't seen him since then."

She went to the foot of the stairs and called out, "Caleb! Caaaaaay-leb!" There was no reply, only the same dull bass line that had been reverberating from up there all evening. "Wait here," she said, setting off for its source.

I went into the kitchen, unnoticed by Ari, and I watched him pour cooked pasta into a colander then lean back as a cloud of steam clipped his face.

"Would you like me to set the table?" I offered.

"Cutlery's in there," he said, pointing with his tongs.

The drawer opened on a junkyard of knives, forks, and spoons, and I searched for matching sets.

"You won't find two the same," said Ari. "She buys them in jumble sales. Don't ask me why. They're cheaper at Asda."

"But not as charming," I said, smiling at the muddle.

"Charming?" said Ari. "More like mad." He carried the pot to the table and handed me a spiked spaghetti spoon. "Dig in."

"Shouldn't we wait for the others?"

"I'd start if I were you. It could take hours to coax his lordship down here."

He didn't need to ask twice. I spooned a pile of noodles onto my plate and breathed in the salty aroma of anchovies. The pasta was perfectly al dente and the sauce tasted better than anything I'd ever made, or eaten, and I was embarrassed by the appreciative noises that escaped as I ate. "This is amazing. You're a chef, right?"

"We used to own an Italian restaurant," said Ari. "But we sold it a couple of months ago. It's being turned into a Pilates studio." He said the word "Pilates" as though it was solely to blame for the sale.

"I thought you were Greek?"

"Yeah, but Italian food is more popular. Or was. Nobody eats pasta round here anymore, too many carbs. They want sashimi, egg-white omelets, bottled air."

"It's working though," I said. "People who live in Notting Hill are the skinniest in the world. They make the average New Zealander look like a whale."

"Really?" he said, for the first time looking interested in something I'd said. "Too much export-quality lamb?"

"And milk, butter, cheese, bacon, eggs. But they're much more sporty too. Always playing touch rugby and training for triathlons."

"How exhausting," said Ari.

"There isn't a lot else to do."

Pippa appeared in the living room, flustered and short of breath. "He absolutely refuses to come down."

"Tell him he has to," said Ari.

"I did. He called me a stupid cow, and other things I won't repeat."

Ari found this funny, but not Pippa. She spooned spaghetti onto a plate, picked up a knife and fork, and carried it to the foot of the stairs, at which point Ari laid down his own cutlery in disgust. "No wonder he won't come down if he gets bloody room service."

"He can't skip meals. He's still growing!" Pippa shot back.

"If he starves, that's his problem," countered Ari.

"And yours," said Pippa. "Although you'd probably expect me to deal with that too." She marched upstairs with the plate.

Next to me, Ari sighed. "Bet you wish you hadn't come to dinner."

"Are you kidding?" I said, trying to be bright. "This food is delicious."

Ari had finished eating and went into the kitchen, where he took his frustrations out on various pots and pans. Then he too disappeared upstairs, leaving me on my own.

I was on my third helping by the time Pippa reappeared, puffy-eyed, Caleb's plate of food demolished. "Sorry about that," she said. "Caleb's not himself at the moment. We think something's going on at school—we're not sure what exactly—but we're going to see out the term there and rethink over the summer hols."

"How old is he?"

"Sixteen."

"That's a difficult age," I said.

"Do you think?"

"It was difficult for me," I said, trying hard to think of an age that wasn't. "And not just because my mother got sick."

Pippa held up her hands. "That reminds me!" she exclaimed. "The other day I found something you'll absolutely love." She went over to the TV and rifled through a stack of VHS tapes that looked like they had been accumulating for years. She put one of the tapes into an antique VCR machine, and gray dots swarmed on-screen, followed by occasional flashes of big hair and talking shoulder pads. "Is that *Dynasty*?" I said, recognizing Alexis.

"Wrong tape," said Pippa, taking it out and tossing it into the dead zone behind the TV. "How frustrating, I had it yesterday." She began to sort and stack dozens of unlabeled and scribbled-on cassettes. "Sorry, this might take a while."

I excused myself to go to the bathroom, but really it was a pretext to be by myself and explore the house. On the landing, I looked into one of the bedrooms and saw an unmade bed—probably Pippa and Ari's. No one seemed to be around, but noises were filtering down from upstairs, not just the loud bass line but something with guitars. At the foot of the stairs I tilted my head toward the muffled noise and saw another landing, and a stepladder leading to what must be the roof. Through an open trapdoor, I could just make out a patch of starless London sky, and, if I listened hard enough, the faint warble of a country and western singer joining the guitars. Was Ari listening to music on the roof?

In the bathroom, I flicked on the lights, and came face-to-face with a giant baby boy, smiling widely under thick black curls, enough for a clown wig. The edges of the photograph were blurred, but in the center his eyes were sharp green constellations. The eyes of Pippa and her mother. Another photo next to it showed the same boy as a toddler, staggering toward the camera on plump bowlegs. Above it, and below it, hung more photos of the same boy, Caleb, I guessed, some black-and-whites, some color, and the pictures continued in a ring around the room. Closer to the loo, the boy was older, and above the bidet, he was thirteen or fourteen, a snapshot taken at a soccer match amid a scrum of other lads. In one, Pippa had her arms in a noose around Caleb's neck, and he looked like he was trying to pull away. The most recent pictures hung on the opposite wall, past the bath, near the door. In these he was a teenager, but utterly androgynous, his translucent skin a canvas for delicate, girlish features. He stared into the camera, sulky and contemptuous. When I sat down on the toilet to pee, his scorn almost put me off.

Just as I emerged from the bathroom, Pippa called from downstairs, "I've found it! Come and see this!"

She was crouched in front of the VCR, stabbing at the volume button. The images on-screen were high contrast and grainy, taken with a prototype video camera, and zoomed giddily around a party. The venue was magnificent, a ballroom of some sort with chandeliers and ornate molded ceilings. I recognized Pippa's brother, Harold, crammed into a white shirt and bow tie, a red cummerbund looped around his alarmingly high-waisted pants.

"Harold's twenty-first," said Pippa. "Mummy hired a ballroom on Exhibition Road to impress his Cambridge chums."

Jiving toward the camera, Harold twirled around, the birthday boy showing off. So he did like to participate, I thought, but only if he was the center of attention. In the next shot, he inhaled helium from a balloon and passed it round to his friends, who took turns speaking goblin. In the middle of a friend's spot-on Monty Python impersonation, Harold snatched the balloon and pushed himself in front of the camera. "My turn, my turn!" he shouted, while his friends looked away politely.

The tape cut to dancing after that, and Pippa sashayed into the frame, cutting a rug with Peggy, queen of the party in peacock-feathered headdress and emerald kimono. The two of them jittered back and forth like birds, moving toward the camera when it appeared to be moving away from them. My mother appeared in a shot, unaware that she was being filmed. The bloom of a teenager was still on her cheeks and she wore no makeup, or none that I could see. Around her neck was the locket, a perfect match for her simple navy shift. She leaned toward Peggy and they shared a joke that was drowned out by loud music. When she saw the video camera she jerked away from it, putting a hand in front of her face. But the more she retreated, the more whoever was filming seemed determined to follow her.

"I'd forgotten she was so shy," said Pippa. "The rest of us were so desperate for attention, but she always got it without even trying."

My father came into the shot and put his arm around her, creating a barrier for my mother to hide behind. She rested her head against his neck and his hand floated up and casually brushed through her hair. Seeing them together, the way they touched each other so naturally, so lovingly, shifted a tectonic plate deep inside me. My jaw contracted painfully, the precursor to tears, and in a lame bid for privacy, I turned away from Pippa and tried to shield my face with my hand.

Pippa, however, had a mother's keen sense of impending distress and drew closer to me, attempted to shush and pat me on the shoulder. At her touch, I reflexively shrank away, and we both saw me doing it but pretended we hadn't. For a second, she hovered with her hand outstretched to try again before withdrawing it for good. The TV erupted in static, startling us both, and Pippa leaned forward to eject the tape.

"Forgive me," she said. "I should never have put it on. Seeing your mother again must have been quite a shock."

She said more, but I was so flooded with emotion that I heard none of it, and a few minutes later, when I found myself outside on the dusty street, I couldn't remember how I'd gotten down the stairs—or even if I'd said good-bye.

CHAPTER FOUR

London, 1981

FOR AS LONG as we'd lived in Ladbroke Gardens, I'd been as scared as I was drawn to the trapdoor that marked the entrance to the air-raid shelter. Even though Dad had explained to me that, forty years ago, it had been the only place safe from trawling Luftwaffe, I couldn't imagine why anyone had willingly gone down there. On the few occasions I had run—nervously, experimentally—across the trapdoor's pitted metal surface, my footsteps had echoed with a hideous boom, and I sometimes worried that at any moment, the entire garden might collapse into the hole. One night, very late, a tapping sound had awakened me and I had looked out into the garden and seen Jimmy over by the air-raid shelter. He had trespassed onto our patio, and was poking at the hatch with a long metal stick, trying to open it. On his head was a miner's lamp, and when he switched it off, he disappeared along with the light. From then on, I thought of the bunker as his domain, that he was its guardian or gatekeeper.

"We can't go down there," I said after Jean Luc had asked, but no one listened.

Dad fetched a crowbar, along with the metal tools he used for basic plumbing and fixing the car. He oiled and coaxed the ancient bolts of the air-raid-shelter hatch, which had rusted shut after years of being trampled and rained on. It took all of Dad's strength plus the wiry disco muscles of Jean Luc and Henri to lift the iron lid, and even then it scraped across the patio paving stones like a car without tires. Once the hatch was out of the way, they stepped back from the cavity and peered inside.

"We need a torch," said Dad, flicking Mum an expectant glance.

"Do we have one?"

"In the laundry," he said, looking down into the hole.

She went inside to fetch it.

Gripping Dad's hand, I sidled closer to the hole. I wanted to peer over the edge, to see inside the bunker, but the thought of going down there made my stomach pitch. I was imagining how dark and cold it was when the path went out from under me and I was jerked upward and swung out over the hole. I felt myself falling and screamed, and fell some more, and screamed again before my father returned me to solid ground, and I stood next to Jean Luc, who was laughing.

"Boo!" he said, his French accent cartoonish. "The little one is afraid, *n'est-ce pas*?"

Henri slapped him on the back. "*Ben oui!*" Of course.

I glared at my father and let go of his hand. His foot hovered above the hole. Was he going to jump in? "Dad! No!"

"Don't worry, there's a staircase. Stone steps leading down."

"Wait for the torch," I pleaded. "Mum won't be long."

A bank of clouds unfurled, turning the garden gray. Mum appeared from the back door carrying a small cardboard box, and held it up to show us. "Candles," she said. "I couldn't find the torch."

Dad opened his mouth to speak but frowned instead. Henri handed him a lighter and Mum opened the box of candles and gave one to each of the men, who passed around the flame and cupped it with their hands.

Mum passed me a candle, but I didn't take it. "Are you really going down there?"

"It'll be fun," she said, as though trying to convince herself. Then her expression changed. "Maybe you should wait up here?"

Being left on my own was the only thing worse than going down there, and I took the candle from Mum's hand.

"It's the last one," she said. "We'll have to share."

Dad went down first, with Jean Luc and Henri behind him. I insisted that Mum follow behind me with the candle, which meant that I was next in line. The staircase was narrow and steep, and we edged down it in single file, my knees wobbling more with each step. By candlelight, it was hard to see much, but the walls on either side were wet and slime grew in the gaps between stones. As we got farther down, the air became dank and wintry and my feet splashed in shallow puddles. I was wearing my school shoes, round toed, with a buckled strap, and the water quickly breached their leather sides and seeped between my toes.

In front of me, Henri turned around and pulled a face, but even with some daylight filtering down from behind me, his features were murky, indistinct. Only he must have seen how scared I was because he didn't try to tickle me or make any more wisecracks—he just turned around and kept going forward. It was very quiet on the stairs, quiet enough to hear the flickering of candle flames and my own breath. I'd counted nine steps when Dad's voice called up from below.

"Bottom!" he said.

made no sound. I was mute, trapped in silence behind thick glass at the far end of a long, dark room. My head grew heavy, then leaden, and rolled to one side and sank in a halo of cold water. The pain fanned out from my head, my chest, pinning down my limbs, but at the center of it, I was shrinking, becoming a wisp. Then the wisp wasn't there at all, only a chill.

When I came to, a candle quivered somewhere overhead, and I saw my dad's face, his worried eyes searching through the murk. I was near the bottom of the stairs. I managed a whimper, the noise an injured puppy might make, and he found me and scooped me into his arms.

Up on the surface, daylight blinded and stung my eyes. I put my hand to my face and touched my glasses. I did not understand how they'd found their way back to me. My father, I supposed, must have picked them up. A while later I realized that the pain had gone. I wasn't even crying, though I was sure I had been right before I passed out.

Dad carried me inside over his shoulder, and with his other not-quite-free hand, tried to comfort my mother, who was shaking uncontrollably. When he put me down on the bed, she started weeping. "I thought it was the end," she said through tears. "I thought I'd finally made it happen, that I'd killed her."

My father laid a steadying hand on her arm. "It was an accident," he said, wearily. "She fell off the step, that's all."

"Nobody pushed me," I said, hoping to clear things up. "I just slipped."

"I know, dear," said Mum. "I know." She attempted a smile. "We've all had a terrible fright, but the main thing is, you're okay."

Dad left me alone with Mum, and she helped me out of my wet clothes. *Was* I okay? I certainly didn't feel it. Everything around me looked familiar but I wasn't sure if I was seeing any of it through my own eyes. My bare skin too felt like borrowed clothes and under my ribs was a growing, hollow patch of hunger for something that wasn't food.

"What is it, weenie?" said Mum, using the nickname she'd given me as an infant, when I'd been small and weak and often sick. "Do you feel unwell? I hope you haven't caught a chill."

I wanted so much to tell her what had happened down in the bunker but when I opened my mouth to speak, I burst into tears, and anything I might have said was swallowed up by long, unruly shudders. Mum pulled me to her chest, and rubbed my back and made hushing noises. "I should never have let you go down there," she said. "This is all my fault."

After a time I stopped crying, but I felt no better, nor was I ready to speak. A hundred horrible images crowded my head but they were too muddled to put into words. "I'm thirsty," was all I could manage.

Mum led me to the kitchen, where she took a box of pineapple juice out of the fridge, left over from last night's punch. "By the way," she said, pouring me a glass, "have you seen my locket? It isn't in my jewelry box, and I know that's where I left it."

She had taken me by surprise—wasn't I still being comforted?—and I guiltily put my hand to my neck, but the locket wasn't there. The last time I remembered wearing it was down in the bunker. What if someone made me go down there again to look for it? "No," I said, quickly. "I haven't seen it."

Mum stopped what she was doing. "Are you sure?"

"I haven't seen it since last night."

She fished around in the pocket of her jeans and held something out in the palm of her hand. "That's odd," she said, "because this morning I found this." She showed me a tiny nugget of silver, the broken catch.

"Oh," I said, feigning surprise. "It's broken."

"Yes, it is." Mum paused. "I found it in your room, Suki. Next to the carving knife."

Blood surged through my head, deafening me. Then, over the noise, squeaked a voice that didn't sound like mine, "It was Esther."

"I beg your pardon?" said Mum.

"Esther did it. We played with your jewelry box when you were asleep."

Mum eyeballed me for a long time, and I stood in front of her, dumbstruck by my audacity.

"And you don't know where the rest of it is?"

I shook my head.

"I knew I shouldn't have taken it off," she said, sounding disappointed. "Even with the other necklace on, I looked nothing like Mae West."

We went to join the others on the lawn of the big garden, and I was given a sandwich but couldn't do more than nibble at it. The adults around me were unusually animated, running over the highlights of last night's party and laughing loudly. Two men who lived across the garden had joined us and it was they who confessed to closing the air-raid-shelter hatch while we were down there. The men had been at the party too, and shutting it had been a hangover prank. It was only once the hatch was shut, they explained through tears of laughter, that they realized what a devil of a time they'd have getting it open. Jean Luc, Henri, and my father hooted at the prank, but my mother, in a private glance, made sure to let my father know just how unfunny she thought it was.

While the adults talked, I sat rigid on the blanket with a tumbler of juice in my hand. I couldn't drink it, nor eat any of the black forest gateau—my favorite—that was handed round at routine intervals, the slices getting smaller and the cream curdling as the afternoon wore on. Every so often, Mum would lean over and stroke the hair out of my eyes or ask if I was okay, and I would nod or smile to mask what was really going on.

Not very far away, in the middle of the patio, the bunker hatch was open, and the magnetic pull of that square black hole made me think I was going to throw up.

I would have run into the flat, but I didn't want to leave my parents' side, even though the later it got, the less often they looked at me, and my mother stopped asking how I was. When night fell, Dad dragged the stereo speakers out through the French doors and someone arrived with fish and chips wrapped in newspaper. They had not long been eaten when a neighbor leaned out of his window and told us off for making a ruckus, and the adults staggered inside with the picnic rug and laid it out on the floor of the living room. I tried to tell Mum and Dad they had left the hatch open and that my Wendy tent was still out on the lawn, but they said to stop fussing and that it was high time I went to bed.

I was sent to my room, where I put on my pajamas. By the window, the clothes I had changed out of earlier were soaking in a bucket, and I peered in at the stained pattern of my strawberry dress. Something was bobbing on the surface of the water, what looked to me like treasure, two pretty white pearls, and I fished them out and in the palm of my hand examined them. Only on closer inspection they turned out to be not pearls, but teeth—a small pair, perfectly formed, very clean. Staring at them, I tasted iron, and a stab of pain echoed in my jaw—the same sensation I'd felt in the bunker, after the fall. I reached for my mouth, frightened to think what I might find, but my teeth, all of them, were still in place.

I began to shake anyway, and the teeth fell out of my hand. One landed in the bucket, where it floated lazily on a fold of the strawberry dress, but the other tooth flew off in a wild direction and disappeared. I half-heartedly looked for it on the floor and under the bed but soon gave up because it wasn't something I really wanted to find.

For what seemed like hours, I lay awake in bed, distressed by the day's events and unable to make sense of them. A lonely feeling had settled over me and I wished that I had told someone what had happened. I worried now that I had left it too late, that I wouldn't remember all the details. But that wasn't all. I had never lied to or kept secrets from my mother before, and doing so made me feel separate from her in a way I didn't like.

When she came in later to check on me, I pretended to be asleep. Watching her cross the room to look in the bucket, my heart thumped so loudly I was surprised it didn't give me away. I ruffled the bedclothes a little, willing her to notice me, to come to me, but she didn't, she just picked up the bucket and left with it.

The night was very still, the air so close it was hard to breathe, and later, when someone went out into the garden to try to close the hatch, the sound of it scraping on the path was jarring, like a skill saw starting up. The noise stopped and, for a short while, all was quiet. I was about to go to the window when I heard male voices, chattering and laughing, before, with a satisfying *thunk*, the hatch found the groove it had been in for decades, maybe even since the last air raid, and finally, it was shut. I waited to feel relieved, but instead all that gripped me was the strange hunger I had felt earlier, as if there was less of me than there had been that morning. And then, under the spell of approaching sleep, I thought of the locket and how, if I had left it in the bunker, it was going to be down there for a very long time.

CHAPTER FIVE

London, 2003

A HAIR DRYER, vacuum cleaner loud, sucked me from sleep, and I realized the flatmates were up before me, eating breakfast in the kitchen and getting ready for work. After leaving Pippa's around eleven the night before, I had walked the three miles back to Willesden Green, stayed up to write in my journal, then collapsed into a deep sleep. Now I realized I'd slept through my alarm clock as well as all the others in the flat. I didn't have my own room but was sleeping in the living room, and had been for almost three months. For the last two, I had perfected the art of invisibility, waking early and going out before everyone else got up; sneaking in late after they'd all gone to bed. Only this morning I'd fucked all that up, and was stretched out in the open like the hobo that I was.

A pair of high heels clacked their way toward me and paused near my suitcase. I'd been too tired to stow it the night before, and was pretty sure I'd left my journal out on top. I winced at the thought of it being exposed, but rather than risk a confrontation

I rolled over and pretended to be asleep. From the shoes, I had a pretty good idea of which flatmate it was, and if she wanted to snoop, let her snoop. Only she didn't. Instead she kicked the suitcase hard, a really fierce kick that I supposed she would have liked to aim at my head—a kick that must have hurt her more than it hurt my suitcase.

Half an hour later, the last of them had left for work, and I got up and surveyed the scene. My journal was out in plain sight, which was careless, but it didn't look like anyone had read it. Watching the video of my mother the night before had unleashed a frenzy of long-forgotten memories, and I had tried to scribble down as much as I could remember about the old days when my parents were still together. I had been doing that a lot lately, writing down events from my past. The present was so empty, so dull, that I didn't have much to say about it.

Ahead of me, my workless day unfurled, a replica of yesterday and the day before it, lethally empty until I filled it up. The easiest way was to shorten the day with sleep, so I closed my eyes again and slept until eleven, when I got up feeling terminally exhausted. In the poky flat kitchen, I stole three teaspoons of instant Gold Blend and pretended the resulting sour mulch was espresso. It tasted so disgusting that it woke me up enough to check my e-mail on Belinda's laptop, my second hit of shame for the day.

Belinda and I had worked on the same community newspaper in Auckland. The office had been short on kindred spirits and we had clung to each other more to keep others away than out of genuine affinity. Soon after moving into her London flat, I'd realized that without common enemies, we had little in common, but by then I needed the friendship more than she did and had tried like hell to keep it going. Lately, I had been feeling more like a parasite. At first she'd encouraged me to use her laptop when she was at work, but after a while she started putting it away in the top drawer of her dresser, forcing me to take it out in secret and erase my tracks after using it. I felt crummy the whole time I was doing it, but was careful never to look at her files, and reasoned that I was doing it for her own good. Without e-mail, I couldn't apply for jobs, and until I had a job, I couldn't move out of her flat.

Progress was inert. So far, I'd e-mailed out hundreds of résumés to HR departments and recruitment agencies without getting a single response. In the beginning, fresh off the plane and brimming with faux Kiwi enthusiasm, I'd actually rung people up, but they'd been so insulted by the interruption of a live voice that I'd given up doing it and now stuck to impersonal e-mails. The London job market was a fortress, and the harder I tried to get in, the more impenetrable it became. All I wanted was a humble temping assignment—office flunky, receptionist, wallpaper—but as August neared, and London shut down for the summer, even that was beginning to seem wildly beyond my reach.

For the third or fourth time that week, I took out my passport folder and considered my last traveler's check, a crisp sheet of paper worth fifty quid if I cashed it. But I was worried that cashing it would signal the beginning of the end, that the second after it became real currency it would be taken from me. Just a few days earlier, I'd left the flat with a twenty-pound note in my jeans pocket, feeling flush, only to reach the tube station and find it had vanished into thin air. I had searched the pavements for an hour, mistaking leaves and lolly wrappers and even a condom packet for the lost note, to no avail, and had had the keenest sense that I had been fucked with, that someone had pinched my money and was hiding nearby, watching me and laughing.

With all the flatmates at work, there was no one to tell me to hurry up and save hot water, so I drained the boiler with a long, scalding shower, and sampled the comprehensive range of salon shampoos and conditioners lined up along the bath. Somewhere in the apartment, a phone trilled, but I'd just squeezed out the last blob of organic seaweed and jojoba frizz-control elixir, and left it unanswered.

I was used to the phone ringing and it not being for me, so I was surprised when I listened to the message and it was from Pippa, something garbled about Caleb bunking off school that had been cut off midway by an electronic pip. I considered calling her back, but doing nothing all morning had resulted in a strong inclination to do more of the same, and instead I sat down on the couch and idly flicked on the TV. Daytime soaps and infomercials were in full swing but the screen was so sun bleached that it was more like listening to the radio. For longer than was healthy, I watched dust particles drift across the living room, staring through them into space until I felt drowsy, too lethargic even to move. A familiar emotion welled inside me, not fulsome like sadness, but a dragging sensation, like the tide going out. In its wake, I felt canceled out. Almost patiently, I waited for the compulsions to begin, and when they did, I was relieved to find them weak, easy to tune out. Even so, I reminded myself to be vigilant, that I could not afford to slip any further off the grid.

The phone rang again, snapping me back to reality, and this time I answered.

"Thank God you're there," said the voice on the other end. "I know you're busy and you've got better things to do, but I've run out of ideas and something you said last night made me think you might be able to help."

"Pippa?" I said. "Is that you?"

Her voice was more anxious than in the earlier message. "Caleb's really in a bad way. I'm worried he's going to do something stupid—harm himself in some way. I desperately want to help him, but he won't talk to me about what's going on. I thought . . . well, I thought he might talk to someone closer to his own age."

"I'm not that much closer," I said, wondering how to convey the fact that I was the last person he ought to talk to, that I needed a little help myself. "If I say the wrong thing, it might be dangerous."

"Please," she said. "I've tried everything else. I know you've been through a lot, and I thought that maybe if you just talked to him about how you'd gotten through it then he'd be able to get through it too. That's all I want—for him to make it out the other side."

"But I'm not out the other side," is what I should have said, but instead I capitulated to her air of desperation. That and the offer of a free lunch, in return for attempted counseling, were I to meet Caleb the next day in the Holland Park Café.

After she hung up, my cell phone beeped—a noise I hadn't heard in weeks—and I discovered a text from my old school friend Alana, inviting me for after-work drinks in three hours' time. I had been trying to see her since I first arrived in London, but she had been away on holiday, then busy at work, and it was only now just happening. In a matter of moments, my week had gone from fatally empty to socially overwhelming.

I set out almost immediately in sneakers and jeans with the idea that I'd walk to Old Street tube station, where Alana and I were to meet, no matter how far away it was. But after an arduous hour of motorway avoidance and sprinting across arterial routes, I limped onto Camden High Street, cashed the last traveler's check, and splurged on an off-peak bus pass. If only I'd bought one at the outset . . .

By the time I got to Old Street to meet Alana, I was a disheveled wreck but bang on time. In the station foyer, I eagerly scanned the thousands of surging commuters for a wistful schoolgirl in gray skirt, blazer, and pumps, her long hair swept artfully to one side. I was still scanning when a sharp-suited woman with a blunt, practical bob approached me and said, "Suki, is that you?"

I couldn't believe this woman was Alana. She looked old, her worn face making it seem like more than a decade since we had last seen each other. "Wow," I said. "You look so grown up."

"And you still look like a student." She looked me up and down. "I'm so jealous."

She couldn't be. Looking scruffy at almost thirty was nothing to be envious of.

An awkward hug ensued, during which Alana's briefcase swung round and thumped me on the back. "Well, I can tell *you* haven't been living in London for long," she said, stepping back to examine me. "You still have a tan, and you seem sort of athletic, like someone who goes to the gym."

"I can't think why," I said, keeping mum about the tramps across London to save tube fares and that I'd subsisted for weeks on a diet of chickpeas and rice. "Do I really still have a tan?"

"Maybe more of a healthy glow," she said. "There's a girl at work from New Zealand who has the same thing. Australians have it too."

"Oh that," I said. "That's from having no ozone layer. You get so fried in the summer that your skin basically never recovers."

On the way to a bar in Hoxton, Alana filled me in on her post-school life, and I listened, enchanted by her private school accent, still as high and fluty as mine must once have been. After A levels, she'd studied economics at Bristol, and gone back to do a postgrad diploma in number crunching when a research job didn't come her way. Since then she'd worked for a multinational accounting firm, but not as an accountant, and although she explained it well, and I tried hard to understand, I failed to grasp exactly what it was she did. She was single, she added, but had her eye on some bloke from work. When she asked if I had a boyfriend, I told her I was happily unattached. We were making excellent small talk, I thought, until halfway down a cobbled side street she exclaimed, "What happened to you after you left? You just sort of disappeared off the face of the earth."

"I went to live in New Zealand. And I ended up staying."

"I know where you went, but apart from a few postcards I never heard from you again." Her tone was reproachful. "I didn't even know if you were still alive."

"I wanted to keep in touch," I said, fumbling for an excuse. "But after a while, everyone seemed so far away. The longer I left it, the harder it was to write. And then it seemed like too much time had passed and I didn't know where to start."

"I thought that's what must have happened," she said. "But it seemed so unlike you to be silent."

There was a note almost of contempt in her voice that I didn't understand. "I know. I'm useless, and by the time e-mail came along I didn't have anyone's address." I'd been lucky to even find Alana again. Her parents still lived in the same house they'd lived in when we were at school and their number was listed. But other friends had been untraceable. "I'm sorry," I said. "After my mother died, it was a weird time."

"I'm sure it was," she said, a flicker of sympathy in her eyes. "Anyway, it's all ancient history now." She grinned. "But you're buying the first round."

And just like that, I was down to my last forty quid.

The bar was hidden down an alley and decorated with mismatched velvet furniture and draped antique shawls, enough touches to suggest a 1920s speakeasy but not so many that it could ever be accused of being themed. At this hour, it was crammed with suits and noisy with the furor of after-work relief.

"I hope you don't mind, but we're meeting some friends of mine here, colleagues, actually," said Alana as we elbowed our way to the bar. Then she yelled out, "Chris! Over here!" and disappeared behind a ridge of corporate shoulders.

Alana's friends—Chris, Mike, and Steve—materialized in identical navy blue suits and one second after they were introduced to me, I forgot which of them was which. The one who made Alana blush I guessed was the bloke from work she fancied, but that didn't tell me his name, and soon I was left to entertain the other two when she and her beau drifted away. Of the two left behind, one was taller and heavier, with a wider chin, but both had cropped brown hair, clear skin, and pale eyes—clean, good-looking blokes, the kind you took home to mother, if you had one.

Next to them I felt like a backpacker who'd been dragged off the street and charitably given a beer, but they seemed to find me fascinating, and raised their eyebrows in amused surprise at everything I said, no matter how inane. It took me a while to realize they were partly laughing at my accent, an odd combination of deep Kiwi and West London posh that flummoxed almost everyone. Partly laughing at me, but not wholly. The taller one soon announced that he'd been to New Zealand and had "totally fallen in love with the place"—a line I'd heard before from a dozen English kids on their gap year. Because I didn't know them, and it was easier, I played along with the version of New Zealand they had in their minds and found myself banging on like a tour guide about black-water rafting, tandem skydiving, nude bungee jumping, and a host of other extreme activities I had never participated in. I didn't tell them I preferred bars to beaches, that I had never been to the South Island, except for a night in Christchurch, or that my experience of the beautiful, unspoiled landscape was that in a nanosecond it could switch to empty and oppressive—a Gothic cathedral without a congregation. At other times, the cities seemed so new they were barely there.

On one of my last mornings in Auckland, I had gotten up early and gone for a drive before the sun came up. It was a Sunday, and the streets near where I lived were still asleep, bathed in weak gray light, everything hazy, undefined. As I drove it looked to me as though all the buildings and cars were slowly fading out, and I remember thinking the time had come to depart from this place, that if I didn't leave, I'd fade out too.

Someone bumped me from behind and spilled beer down my top, and I realized Alana's colleagues were smiling at me in a keen way, undeterred by my sudden silence and oblivious to the gap between what I had been saying earlier and what I had been thinking.

"You should come with us," one of them was saying. "Steve's got a massive tent—big enough to sleep twelve people—and last year we got a wicked campsite near the main stage."

"Yeah, mate, I'm still deaf," said the other one, laughing. He pointed to my empty glass. "Fancy a refill?"

"Sure," I said, and he went to the bar, leaving me alone with his friend, who was the shorter of the two. An awkward silence followed while I tried to think what to say.

"Reckon you'll stay in London once the summer's over?" he said.

"That was the plan," I said. "I don't have a return ticket."

"Brilliant," he said. "So you'll be able to come to Glastonbury with us then?"

I hesitated, not wanting to tell him that I couldn't afford to go, even if I wanted to.

"Go on," he said. "It'll be such a laugh."

"I'll think about it," I said.

I hadn't seen Alana for what was beginning to seem like hours, and I looked around the bar for her, at the same time checking out who else was there. Fewer suits; more art school types; and one or two who looked like they were in bands, or wanted to be. My eye caught on a guy who looked Icelandic—pointed elfin features, blond hair—and just as I thought he was about to turn and look in my direction, someone passed in front of him and he vanished.

"If you like, I can get you a ticket when I get mine. It's cheaper if you get in early." His smile was too expectant, like he wanted me to do more than just go to Glastonbury with him, and when I registered his eagerness and what he was trying to communicate, something changed in me, a switch flipped, and I took an involuntary step away from him, as though repelled. "Thanks, but I'm not sure if I can go."

"Where's Chris got to with our beers?" he said, his face falling briefly before becoming jovial once more. "He must be getting them from a pub down the road."

I laughed, but it didn't quite come off sincerely. So the other one was Chris, and he must be Steve or Mike. He was still smiling at me, a big warm-hearted smile, and the longer he grinned, the more I started to feel like a cat with its hackles up, getting ready to swipe or bolt. "Excuse me," I said, trying to hide the fact that he was the cause of my violent reaction. "But I need to go to the bathroom."

I found Alana in the queue to the ladies', her cheeks and lips restored to their schoolgirl rose by a few pints of beer.

"There you are!" she said. "I've been looking for you everywhere."

"I was by the bar, with your friends from work—right where you left me."

If she noticed my sardonic tone, she ignored it. "I'm so glad you're hitting it off with Chris and Mike," she said. "They're such top blokes." She winked at me. "And single too."

"I'm not looking for anyone," I said. "I told you I was happy on my own."

"Bollocks," she said. "You were always so obsessed with boys. You haven't changed that much—surely?"

"They're not my type," I said, wishing she'd change the subject.

"Oh, that's right," she said, a little archly. "I forgot about you and your types." We had reached the front of the queue, and Alana ducked into a vacant stall. She locked the door and shouted through it, "What about Steve? You have to admit he's a bit of all right!"

I didn't think he was, but she wanted to hear otherwise. "Steve's hot," I said, shouting back. "And he obviously thinks the same thing about you."

Over a flushing toilet, I heard her giggle—had she forgiven me?—then I went into a stall and when I came out she was gone. Fighting my way back, the bar swarmed in front of me, an impenetrable scrum. I considered going home, but didn't want to leave things on a sour note with Alana or the others. Pushing my way through the crowd, I collided head-on with some guy before we sprang apart, both clutching our heads in pain. "I'm very sorry," he said, in a strange, jerky accent, and I looked up and saw it was that Icelandic guy. Up close, he was even more striking, with eyes that could cut through glass. He brazenly looked me up and down before asking, "Which way were you trying to go?"

"Over there," I said, pointing toward where I thought the others were.

"Well," he said, slowly. "This is really a shame."

I returned to the others and tried to act relaxed, like I had when we'd first arrived, but I couldn't think of what to say to Mike that would put things right between us without also leading him on. Perhaps there was nothing, and I ought to just leave. When one of the blokes suggested going for a curry, I saw my out and quickly declined, saying I was tired. Alana seemed less disappointed than Mike, who tried to persuade me to go with them by offering to pay, then, when I wouldn't, insisted on collecting my phone number on the pretext of making sure I got home safely. When we said our farewells, he gave me a crushing bear hug that tried very hard in its pressure to communicate more than just good-bye. I told Alana I would call her the next day, and whispered in her ear, to make amends, that I thought she and Steve would make a cute couple. "Thanks," she said, squeezing my hand as they tumbled from the bar, the boys arm in arm and already belting out "Wonderwall," the hooligan version.

The instant they left, I realized how drunk I was, how far from home. Just thinking about the number of tube changes made me weary. I drifted toward a bald patch in the crowd next to the cigarette machine, and decided to at least sober up before I set off. I was standing there, a few minutes later, feeling self-conscious, when I noticed the Icelandic guy throwing glances in my direction—too many, and too lingering for them to be accidental. He did not look at me expectantly like Mike had. His look was direct, almost a challenge; he was daring me to resist looking back.

Before he even walked over to the cigarette machine and casually dropped in a few coins, I could tell he was a player, but there was something about those men that put me at ease. You always knew where you stood with them, what you were letting yourself in for: nothing.

"What happened to your pals?" he said, pressing the button above Lucky Strike.

"They went to get a curry, but I didn't feel like going."

He opened the cigarette packet before answering. "You made a good decision. These Englishmen, they meet a pretty girl, they have fun together . . . but they always ruin it by taking her for a curry on the way home. They don't know what is sexy. Myself, I don't know either, but I know it's not curry."

Putting down the opposition, false modesty: smooth, but I let him get away with it. He introduced himself. He was Dutch, not Icelandic, and his name was Wouter—the kind of name that only a confident man would admit to outside his homeland. He said he was a multimedia artist and I pretended to believe him, just as I pretended not to mind when he didn't ask what I did or even what my name was. Nor did he offer to buy me a drink, perhaps realizing that he didn't have to.

"How about we go outside?" he said when a surge of new people arrived in the bar. "This place is too crowded—don't you think?"

I had to agree. In the tiny paved courtyard at the back of the bar, he took a small tin out of his jacket pocket and lit a giant spliff. When he handed it to me, I inhaled as lightly as I could and passed it to him, but my throat was still burning from the first toke when he handed it back to me. The joint tasted strange, like chlorine or Jif, but I put that down to London pollution, which often got up your nose just before you were about to eat and made everything taste like the end of an exhaust pipe.

Soon, the thing was only a roach, and I remembered why I didn't normally smoke: marijuana made me want to hurl, especially if I had been drinking. That was probably my last coherent thought.

Wouter put his arm around me, and without any warning, tongue-dived my ear. I leaned away, or thought I had, but all that happened was that the pint glasses on the table in front of us began to list, and the courtyard dipped and folded like swell on a rough sea.

I was way, way too old for this. "Last tube," I slurred, into Wouter's hair—he had dandruff, I noticed as I pushed him away and stood up, knocking something off the table that shattered into a million lethal pieces. Using him as a springboard, I launched myself across the courtyard, but he had attached himself to me seemingly with Velcro and was still trying to snog me when I reached the other side. He was still trying when I got to the tube station, and pushed me up against a wall, sliding a leg in between mine. He managed to undo a few of my shirt buttons, but he was so wasted it was like being mauled by a puppy, and when a tube rumbled toward the platform, I whipped through the barrier to catch it, and left him on the other side, looking hopelessly around for me.

Somehow, I emerged unscathed half an hour later at the Willesden Green tube station, five hundred meters from home, but in my condition, a distance of seven times that. Just before reaching my door, I fell sideways into a shrub that I swear hadn't been there before I left that night. I hadn't fallen over since I was a kid, and the shock of it was deeply insulting, like a punch in the face from a stranger, though I can't say I felt any pain.

In the poky kitchen, I guzzled three pints of water and plundered the fridge for leftovers, finding a pink, three-day-old sausage—was it raw?—and something that had looked like pizza but turned out, when I bit into it, to be only its empty cardboard carton. I stumbled down the hallway, where one of the flatmates jack-in-the-boxed out of a bedroom and told me, in the voice of a mother superior, that the stock market had crashed and it had all gone white.

"What's gone white?"

"Are you all white?" she repeated.

Something flew in the shadows behind her, a bat with a human face, and I ran away.

I should have known that I wasn't going to be able to sleep, but I tripped over the sofa with hope in my heart. Normally when I was drunk or high, I could turn my head to the left on the pillow and the room stopped spinning, but this time I was so far gone it spiraled whichever way I faced. Soon, the wallpaper was rippling too, and I lurched off the couch and zigzagged down the hall to find the bathroom. But someone had moved it, and the next thing I knew, I had taken a tumble and was groping at hulks of ceramic and trying to swim the breaststroke across a deep, black puddle of water.

The bathroom was flooded, not just sprayed with water as if someone had taken a shower and forgotten to use a bathmat but drenched in an unpleasantly cold and glutinous liquid that was black but reminded me of thin, overcooked porridge. It took half a minute for me to recall what the stuff reminded me of: the water in the bottom of the bunker on the day we were trapped down there. In the next instant, as though I had bitten my lip, I tasted blood, but when I ran my tongue over my teeth and gums, there was only saliva.

The bathroom was windowless, and no lights were on in the hallway, but I made my way toward the pale hull of the toilet bowl, rising out of the water. It didn't look far away, but when I tried to crawl toward it, my arms and legs were switched off, and wouldn't do as my brain told them. My neck was weak too, and my head drooped into the cold, thick water. Soil and salt filled my mouth, and I tried to spit it out but couldn't. Just as my neck collapsed, I managed to turn my head to one side and my mouth came to rest only millimeters clear of the foul liquid.

I had taken drugs before, in reckless combinations, but this was different. I wasn't out of it, I was hyperpresent, and fighting for my life. Somehow I found the strength to turn over onto my back. I concentrated on breathing, listened hard to the rhythm of my lungs. Slowly the water receded, started to melt away as if it had never been there, and the tiles were soon only damp. I got to my knees and spewed into the toilet, emptied my stomach of whatever rank poison had been there.

Vomiting broke the spell completely, and I was surprised by how quickly strength returned to my body. I was still a little shaken, but I got up, turned on the light, and looked around the bathroom. It was orderly, solid, even homely, and I picked up my toothbrush and luxuriated in the ordinariness of cleaning my teeth.

I was so relieved that my powers of observation deserted me. Then, treading softly down the hall, I heard a squelching sound and looked down at my clothes. They were soaked through and covered in a kind of mulch. In the living room, I peeled them off, and some of the mulch got on my hands and gave off the odor of mold. I thought back to the shrubbery I'd fallen into, and decided it must have been muddy underneath, though I did not remember it being so. But after everything that had happened that evening, it was a feasible enough explanation, and I tried hard not to think of an alternative.

CHAPTER SIX

London, 1981

IN THE MONTHS that followed my parents' wild party, I waited, tense with anticipation, for my mother to confront me again over the whereabouts of her locket. I thought it was only a matter of time before she spoke to Esther's mother and exposed the fib I had told about Esther breaking it, and each day I rehearsed my confession.

But autumn fell, and still nothing had been said. Mum simply acted as though there had been no locket. She never mentioned it, let alone my part in its disappearance. At first I was relieved, but as time went on, I was utterly bewildered and then finally just plain curious. Why did my mother seem not to miss the locket that had once been so precious to her? When enough time had passed that I was sure I would not be blamed for its disappearance, I found an opportunity to ask her about it. She was sitting at her dressing table, French-plaiting her hair, and I was going through the remains of her jewelry box when I found the silver catch that I had sliced off the locket. I held it up and contorted my face into what I hoped was a look of innocent puzzlement. "What do you think happened to the rest of it?" I said.

Mum abandoned the plait, midfold, and took the piece of silver from my hand. "Someone stole it," she said. "After the party."

"Who?" I said, my chest thumping. "Who stole it?"

"I don't know. It was very dark."

"You saw them take it?"

Mum put the catch back in the jewelry box and snapped the lid shut. "No," she said, seemingly irritated by my question, "I couldn't see well enough. It was late at night."

Though I asked her again, once or twice, her answer was always the same, and soon enough, I forgot about the locket and became preoccupied with other momentous things, such as Christmas. That was the year I ruined it for myself, by myself. At nearly seven, I was far too old to still believe in Santa Claus, but believe in him I did, with a fervor that bordered on religious fundamentalism. Every year on Christmas morning, I woke at three or four A.M.—sometimes as early as midnight—and pounced on the pillowcase bulging with toys at the end of my bed. It wasn't the toys I was after, but their supernatural smell: a sugary aroma of nutmeg, fresh snow, and reindeer fur that to me was the essence of magic. To try and preserve the perfume, I held off playing with my presents for as long as possible, and the same went for not eating the walnuts and satsumas that had been tossed into the sack alongside them. Those I would stow under my bed for safekeeping, where they remained until wizened and black with rot.

At home, no brothers or sisters were there to challenge my zeal, but at school I was forced to defend Santa by using all the skills at my disposal. I didn't mind if other children voiced their doubts, but one day a boy named Charles Pycraft took things too far. He stood on a chair in the middle of the classroom and told us he'd seen his dad sneaking into his room at night with a sack full of presents, and what's more, he'd taken a Polaroid. When he held it up for us all to see I launched myself at him—rather than look. At first Charles laughed, and so did the rest of the class, until he felt my teeth sink into the fat, juicy lobe of his ear. While I ripped his Polaroid into a thousand tiny shreds, he howled his lungs out. As punishment, I was sent to a small library off the assembly hall called the Quiet Room, and was told to stay there and read the illustrated King James Bible until I was sufficiently sorry and in the mood to apologize. At three o'clock, when that mood still had not arrived, I was frog-marched to the cloakroom where my mother stood waiting to fetch me.

"Suki, love," she said, "you mustn't take everything to heart or they'll tease you even more."

Mum often spoke of teasing—as in "Don't cry, he's only teasing"—but I didn't understand why it was my fault for reacting, not theirs for being mean. That was one of the disadvantages of being an only child: you lived in your own head, played yourself at Connect Four, and developed a skin so thin it might as well not have been there.

At school, Charles became a hero because he'd needed stitches ("How many?" the other kids had squealed, ferreting in his hair) and I was called a ninny or a baby for believing in made-up things. After that, I saved my zeal for home, where it blossomed into an obsession. Midyear, I started sending letters to Santa, and by November I was writing daily to butter him up. According to a book I'd read, letters to Lapland didn't need stamps, which is how I bypassed my mother, who always tried to sneak a look at what I was writing.

"Do you know what you want for Christmas this year?" she'd say.

"You don't need to know what I want," I'd tell her. "Only Santa needs to know."

But I needed my mother for something, and devised a plan in which she'd finally give me the ammunition I needed. Mum could be relied on for the truth; she didn't believe in God and said so. She was the one who could verify Santa.

It was a rainy Sunday when I asked her, and she was tackling the weekly mountain of Dad's business shirts, carefully steering the iron round an obstacle course of collars and cuffs. I started out warily by asking if Lapland was a real place, and if it might be possible to go there on holiday, for instance, next Christmas for two or three weeks.

"It's a real place, all right," she said. "In the Arctic Circle, near the North Pole. But I don't know about going there on holiday. That would cost an arm and a leg."

The mere thought of Santa's reindeer skidding about in all that snow made my heart thud, and I took a deep breath to ask my next question, the big one. "So if Lapland is a real place in the Arctic Circle, then Santa must be a real person too—right?"

"You know the answer to that," said Mum, ironing on.

"I know he's real, but the kids at school think he isn't, and I want to prove them wrong."

Mum looked up from the ironing board. "He's real if you think he's real, dear."

"I know, I know, but is he?"

She studied me for a moment, searching for the right words. "If you believe in him, he is."

That sounded like a trick, and I stamped my foot in indignation. "You always say that and I don't know what it means. All you have to tell me is that he's real!"

"I can't do that," she said. "I don't want to lie to you."

"I'm not asking you to lie to me. Just say it."

"Are you sure?"

"Yes!" My excitement grew. Finally, I was going to have proof that Santa was real, and I could go to school and tell all the other kids they were dimwits.

"Well, I suppose you're old enough to know." She sounded sad, wistful. "We did start to wonder why you hadn't found out."

"Found out what?" My stomach flipped a pancake. "What do you mean *found out*?"

"You caught him once, barging into your room with the pillowcase—he tripped on something and woke you up—and the next day you were convinced you'd seen Santa. We couldn't believe it."

"But I did see Santa."

Mum laughed. "I thought I saw a ghost once, but that doesn't mean it was real."

"Santa is a ghost?"

"No, weenie, Dad is Santa."

I was inconsolable, but she hugged me as I wept, and promised to take me to the natural history museum, and to the movies, and wherever else I wanted to go to cheer me up. I told her I didn't want to go anywhere, and probably never would. But there was worse to come. That Christmas, I woke at six out of habit and crawled to the end of my bed to marvel at the bulging pillowcase. For a moment I forgot and was filled with the old exhilaration. I sniffed the air and waited for the intoxicating fragrance to fill my lungs. But there was none. Instead I smelled wrapping paper, sticky tape, walnuts, and orange peel, stuff you could buy at Woollies or any other store. And even though I noticed that the sack was a little more bulging than usual, it was hours before I had recovered enough from the blow to open it.

Christmas vanished that year, and so too did my father, who went on a business trip and never came back.

The first sign of real absence was a box of clothes and shoes that Mum dropped off at the Westbourne Park branch of Oxfam. We often went there to look for unusual fabrics and outdated castoffs, which my mother miraculously recycled into fashionable outfits, but we never donated anything unless it was falling apart, practically in rags. So I was immediately suspicious when she placed a box on the counter and in it were a new pair of brogues, along with a selection of immaculate business shirts and ties.

"Won't Dad be needing those when he gets back from Frankfurt?" I said.

"He isn't in Frankfurt," said Mum, pushing the box across the counter.

The way she said Frankfurt—like it was a type of poisonous snake—made me too scared to ask where he was. Besides, I was used to Dad being away for weeks or months at a time, working as some kind of businessman, and he always came back eventually, his arms bulging with last-minute presents still in their airport plastic bags: colored pencils and pens from Switzerland, chocolate blocks the size of my leg. I looked forward to his return for all the wrong reasons, and this time was no exception.

But the box of clothes didn't add up. Standing by the Oxfam counter, a wobbly sensation spread through my stomach. I'd felt it before, when I left my favorite teddy bear at the newsagent's and he was gone when we went back to get him. Whatever I was feeling must have been written on my face because Mum asked me if I wanted to get an ice cream. I didn't really feel like one but didn't want to miss out on a treat either, so when we went to the newsagent's, I burrowed in the freezer for a Mini Milk. Out on the street, I pulled the ice cream from its sleeve, and straightaway, the long, thin tube fell off its stick and nose-dived to the pavement, but when Mum came out of the shop, I pretended to her that I'd already eaten it.

"That was quick," she said as I covered the milky mess with my foot.

We walked home in silence, and the maisonette seemed bigger and emptier when we got there, as if Mum and I were rattling around in our old life, without a husband, without a dad, not enough of us to fill up the space. *Dr. Who* was on TV, and I watched the opening credits from behind the couch, frightened by the mind-bending music and swirling spiral of doom. When the Daleks bleeped, "Exterminate, exterminate!" I switched off the set and wondered if I'd ever be able to watch shows like that again without Dad's knee to sit on. He'd let me stay up to watch *Jaws* with him once, and every time the shark attacked—or there was even a hint of jaggedy music—I had burrowed into the safety of his chest.

A week after Oxfam, Mum still hadn't told me where Dad was, but by then it seemed too late to ask, so I made do with clues. Mum spent a lot of time on the phone after I'd gone to bed, and I struggled to piece together the missing side of the conversations I heard. There was one, late at night, that was so loud it woke me up. I was wondering if I should get out of bed to see what was wrong, when Mum went very quiet, and then I heard mewling, like a locked-out cat. That got me up, and I hovered in the hallway outside the kitchen without her seeing me.

When she spoke again, she said, "But, Mum, they've already left the country."

She'd said "they." Which meant Dad wasn't alone. I guessed Mum was talking to Granny and she sounded exasperated with her. "He's wanted to leave England for years. We argued about it all the time because I didn't want to go." For a while, she didn't say anything and I thought she'd hung up. Then she hissed, "Because *she's* from there."

I held my breath and waited for her to say more. I waited a long time, imagined Mum winding the cord around her fingers like she did when the person on the other end was waffling. In a feeble voice, she said, "What are you suggesting? That I go all the way to New Zealand just to beg? I don't even know his address."

The names of all the capital cities of the world swirled in my head—we'd been learning them at school—but none matched with New Zealand. I was pretty sure we'd skipped it because the country was too small, just an island, like Corsica or the Isle of Wight.

"That's not going to happen," was the last thing I heard her say before the kitchen door flew open and she came out holding a ball of colored party napkins to her face. "Suki! Why aren't you in bed?"

Too late, I leaped to my feet and scrabbled for the door to the bathroom, waiting to be told off. But Mum didn't say anything, she just stood in the hallway staring at me.

"Sorry, Mum," I said.

"It's not your fault." She sounded waterlogged, upset. "Go to bed."

I hesitated. The right course of action was to do as I was told but instead I threw myself at her. When I squeezed her round the waist, she seemed to give way, as though her bones had only been made of sand. I squeezed tighter, but that made it worse and I fancied she was disintegrating. I choked back a sob and then she was comforting me, picking me up and putting me to bed, stroking the hair behind my ear until I fell asleep.

That night I dreamed the house was on fire and Mum was trapped inside. From the air-raid shelter in the garden, I could see her standing in the hallway, paralyzed. She kept shrinking to the size of a doll, small enough for me to pick up, but I couldn't get out of the air-raid shelter to rescue her. The house became a furnace and she vanished, or burned, or both.

Dad wasn't the only thing to disappear around that time. A few weeks after he left, I went into the living room one Saturday morning to watch cartoons but the television wasn't there. On the shelf where it usually sat there was a clean space in the shape of a television set, and around it, an oblong of dust. I ran my finger through it and yelled out, "Mum! What have you done with the TV?"

There was no answer, so I padded downstairs to the kitchen, where Mum was at the table, studying a plate of toast. When I asked her where she had moved the TV, she looked confused. "I didn't move it."

"Well, someone has. Did Dad take it?"

Mum looked at me, puzzled, and we went upstairs to the living room. There was still no TV on the shelf, only the dust with a finger mark through it. Mum ran round the maisonette, checking all the rooms and opening windows to look outside. She opened the front door, but the TV wasn't sitting in the communal hallway like I guessed she hoped it might be. Watching her anxiety escalate made me queasy. When she arrived at the guest cloakroom on the ground floor, a new addition to the maisonette that didn't yet have bars on the windows, her shoes crunched on shards of broken glass and she held her hand out behind her to prevent me from rushing in. I stared at the broken window, the pieces of glass on the floor. The window was just big enough for a television to fit through, along with a small person, a midget or a child.

I didn't go into the garden much after the burglary, just in case the midget was still around. I thought perhaps he or she lived in the air-raid shelter and was down there watching cartoons on our TV.

In the spring, we got a state-of-the-art alarm system installed. You had to punch in a long sequence of numbers when you switched it on and another long sequence when you switched it off. Mum wrote the numbers on the back of a five-pound note she kept in her wallet, reasoning that if her wallet was stolen, no one would think to examine the note for an alarm code or suspect that's what the numbers related to. Just in case, she added a couple of extra digits to the sequence. She also stapled the five-pound note to the inside of her wallet to stop herself from accidentally spending it.

Each time we opened the front door, Mum grappled with the entire contents of her bag, trying to locate her wallet and the long sequence of numbers before the thirty-second grace period ended and the siren went off. Plenty of times she couldn't decipher her own handwriting and punched in the wrong code, so I learned the sequence of digits by heart and would recite it to her as she attacked the number pad. I don't know what she did when I wasn't there. But then, I was never not there.

At night, we slept with the alarm on. Once inside my room, I had to stay there because otherwise one of the flashing green sensors would spot me creeping around the house. Mum had a red panic button installed by the bed, which alerted an army of security guards and policemen if anything terrible happened. As far as I knew, she used it only once, when a black-and-white tomcat broke into our house and pissed all over the kitchen bench. The cat set off the alarm and Mum pressed the panic button. I always thought it was the sudden, piercing shrill of the alarm that'd made the cat wet itself, but Mum said cats didn't pee when they were frightened, only humans did that, me especially. When she discovered the cat in the kitchen, Mum tried to call the security guards to tell them not to come round, but she couldn't reach anyone on the phone. Once you pressed a panic button, it turned out you couldn't unpress it.

While we waited for the guards to arrive, Mum changed out of her nightdress and into jeans and a sweatshirt. She seemed embarrassed when she opened the door and explained to them what had happened. One of the men patted Mum on the shoulder and asked her if she was going to be okay. He offered to stay the night on the couch, but Mum pulled away from underneath his hand and soon after the guards left.

When they had gone, I climbed into Mum's bed and snuggled next to her. Since Dad left, I had often slept there, but this was different. Usually, I drifted off within minutes, drawn quickly into oblivion by the reassuring presence of my mother, but this time I was seized by the notion that I was the one soothing her toward sleep. I even considered stroking her head but was worried she might think it weird. Once or twice I thought she had finally nodded off, only for her body to jerk violently, as it sometimes does on the cusp of sleep, with that peculiar sensation of falling off a cliff.

To pass the time, I stared at the ceiling, and watched in awe as the dimensions of the room began to distort. One moment the ceiling was a few inches above my head, bearing down on me like the lid of a tomb; a few seconds later it was mile-high open sky. To make it stop, I turned and focused on Mum, but she was shifting too—one moment her head colossal, the next a fragile sparrow's egg attached by a spindle to her body. I closed my eyes, but that just made me dizzy, so I opened them again and watched the show. Was I causing the peculiarities, being tricked by my eyes, I wondered, or were the room and my mother really changing shape? I considered the question for quite some time before realizing, abruptly, that the distinction was meaningless. Whatever I could see in front of me was the reality I was stuck with, regardless of whether it was real or not.

CHAPTER SEVEN

London, 2003

THE MORNING AFTER THE RAT-POISON SPLIFF, I woke to shameful recollections of Dutch elves and flash floods and my own appalling behavior. My limbs had been stretched all night on a medieval rack, and my head throbbed like it had been thrown through a plate-glass window. It was almost midday and I had just enough time to shower and dress and catch a bus to Holland Park (extravagant in the extreme since my last forty quid had mysteriously become twenty overnight).

The park seemed unnecessarily crowded, its paths clogged with tourists and baby strollers, the sandpit crammed with juicy, dribbling toddlers—God, I was thirsty—and I sprinted over them and round them as if they were an assault course I had to get through. Pippa and Caleb were already at the café, seated by the window, and even from a distance, I could see that Pippa had been trying to cajole Caleb, with little success. He clearly didn't want to be there any more than I did—perhaps even less—and as I approached the table, he pushed back his chair and attempted to do a runner.

Pippa caught him by the sleeve. "There you are, Suki," she said, brightly. "Caleb's been so looking forward to meeting you."

"That's total crap," Caleb said, and flicked me a look of such unbridled hostility that I actually flinched.

"Caleb," chastened Pippa. "Remember our deal?"

Whatever the deal was, it held some power, for Caleb groaned but sat down obediently and looked out the window. In the flesh, his expression was more devilishly sullen than it had been in any of the photos, but confusingly, it was grafted to the features of a seraph.

"Well, it's lovely to meet you too," I said.

Pippa fished out her purse and stood up. "Like I said on the phone, Caleb's been in a lot of trouble lately, and I've explained to him that he might find it helpful if you shared your experiences."

At this fresh insult, Caleb stood up again. "I said I'd come here, but you can get stuffed if you think I'm going to hang around listening to this patronizing shit." His voice careened so wildly from low and gruff to choirboy that I couldn't help grinning.

"Fuck off," he said to my smiling face, and to Pippa: "Seriously, Mum, this is totally fucked."

Pippa handed me a twenty-pound note. "Well, I'll leave you two to get acquainted. Have what you like. The food here is delicious."

I sat down for as long as it took Pippa to walk out of the café, then I got up. "Do you want anything? Coffee, tea, a good smack?"

That got his attention. "Shut up," he said. "I'm not allowed coffee."

"Do you want one or not?"

"Okay."

"Cappuccino or latte?"

"Latte."

"I thought so."

"What's that supposed to mean?"

"Nothing. But if you're a good boy, you can have a
as well."

He was so cross he actually snarled—his mood a good ma
for my hangover.

Since my last visit many years ago, the Holland Park Café had been refurbished, and as I waited in line at the counter I wanted to bulldoze its clean Scandinavian makeover. Back in the old days, an Italian family had run the place, treating their customers as though they ought to be grateful to be getting served at all. But their spaghetti Bolognese alone had been worth the abuse—rich, salty, and piping hot. Just remembering the taste of that sauce made me salivate, and I scanned the new menu of organic, gluten-free follies with growing dismay. No grease—nothing that'd come close to soaking up a hangover. In the end I plumped for what was most filling: a carnivorous ploughman's with organic grass-fed beef.

When I arrived back at the table with two coffees, a chocolate brownie, and a nobby-looking stick with a number on it, Caleb scrutinized me as though I were an enemy warship that had just appeared on his radar screen. "So how do you know Mum and Dad?" he said.

"Your grandma lived upstairs from us when I was a kid. So did your mum. She used to babysit me sometimes."

"But you're old," he said.

"And your mum is even older. When she was the same age as you, I was four."

away, staring at a faraway tree. I remembered feeling like that at his age, so absorbed by my own mood that other humans were invisible.

My ploughman's was taking forever, and I considered dabbing up the brownie crumbs from Caleb's plate before realizing how gross that was. "When did you turn sixteen?" I said.

"A few weeks ago."

"Did you have a party?"

"No." He rolled his eyes. "Parties are for dicks."

"And what do cool people do instead?"

"They definitely don't say 'cool.'"

I'd encountered surly teenagers before, but he was taking things to a whole new level. "Look, I know your mum thinks I'm going to give you all this great advice, but I don't have any, so we may as well just skip the lecture and have something nice to eat."

Caleb had been picking at the Formica table with his thumbnail, and where he'd been working, there was now a hole. "Suits me," he said, with a shrug.

I rummaged in my bag for a book. A few days earlier, on the bookshelf in Willesden Green, next to a hopeless selection of microwave cookbooks and empty CD cases, I'd found a dog-eared copy of *Lolita*. I'd read it before, but years ago, and had forgotten how funny it was. Even better, I couldn't remember what happened at the end.

After blurring through half a dozen pages—reading hung-over was like driving through heavy rain—I became dimly aware that Caleb had been twisting his head to see the book's cover, but every time I looked up, he turned away and pretended to be draining the dregs of his already empty cup. I held up the book so he could take a proper look. "Have you read it?"

"I've heard of it. Isn't it about a perv?"

"You mean a pedophile?"

"I don't know. He's like a creep or something."

"Would you like to borrow it? Then you can find out."

"No." His answer was too quick, too emphatic.

"Well, you can't anyway," I said, determined to make the situation as difficult for him as he was making it for me. "It doesn't belong to me."

I resumed reading. When my ploughman's arrived, it was predictably weedy and didn't go far in soaking up either stomach acid or my revolting mood. I put down the novel while I ate and sensed Caleb's continuing interest in it, as well as the pride or stubbornness that prevented him from admitting it. He eyed my food too, but when I asked him if he wanted any, he said he wasn't hungry. I didn't see how that was possible—seeing as his hips were so thin they barely held up his pants.

We sat like that, in unhappy companionship, for another half hour or so, long enough for me to pseudo-read ten pages, and spend Pippa's change on a gluten-free rubber ball masquerading as a muffin, washed down with a second coffee. Caleb ate nothing, did nothing except destroy the tabletop, and mostly, I ignored him. But toward the end of the hour I remembered Pippa's anxious tone on the phone, and felt guilty for spending her money and not at least trying to help her son. "So what do you do when you bunk off school?"

Caleb looked surprised that I'd spoken. "Nothing much."

"In my day, the cool kids used to hang out on some church steps near the school, smoking. They always went to the same place, and always came back to school chewing gum to hide the smell. About once a week, they got caught."

"What's that got to do with me?"

"Well, nothing, because you're obviously not that stupid."

His mouth rippled with a smile before he remembered to scowl.

"On the other side of it, if you were mostly a geek and did all your homework on time, you could get away with bunking because the teachers didn't have time to come down hard on everyone—only the ones who were failing."

"I'm not a geek," said Caleb.

"I know, but you might get away with more if you at least did your homework."

He thought this over for a moment. "That sounds naff."

"It worked for me," I said, and shrugged.

I glanced away and saw Pippa bustling across the café toward us. She looked happy—perhaps surprised to see that Caleb was still there. "I see you two have been getting along famously," she said, eyeing the two empty cups on the table. "Caleb, you didn't have a coffee, did you?"

"She had two," Caleb said, with haste. "And an enormous ploughman's lunch and a muffin."

"Well, good for you," said Pippa, smiling broadly at me. "Told you the food here was delicious."

Caleb stood up. "Can we go now? All the new games will be gone."

"What kind of games?" I asked, curious.

Caleb looked at his mother—clearly warning her not to say anything.

"There's this one with a cute purple dragon," said Pippa. "It flies around a castle, rescuing princesses and collecting treasure. What's it called again, darling?" She glanced at Caleb, who was giving her a dark look.

"I haven't played that for about five years," he said.

"Well," she continued, "whatever it is, we have to restrict his use or he'll play it twenty-four hours a day—no toilet breaks or even dinner." She patted Caleb's slim torso and laughed. "If he ate any less, he'd disappear."

"Mum! Can we please just go?" His petulance made him seem younger, still a child. He didn't even have chin fluff yet, I noticed.

"Wait for me outside," said Pippa, and once he'd gone, added, "I'm sorry he was such a little shit."

"Don't worry," I said. "We've all been there."

"Well, I'm really very grateful to you, and I wanted to ask if you're still sleeping on your friend's couch?"

"It's getting to be a bit of a problem," I said, tired of pretending.

"Splendid," said Pippa. "Because I have a proposition for you."

Before she even told me what it was, I started to feel uneasy.

"We got our dates muddled up and Peggy's nurse, Amanda, has booked to go on leave right before our holiday. It took us so long to find someone Peggy likes that I can't bear the thought of trying to find a temp. I visit every day, of course, but she needs someone there the rest of the time to make sure she doesn't get into any bother. She's still very frail, and can't do everything for herself."

I saw where this was going and was filled with dread—mainly because of Madeline, and what had happened on my last visit to Peggy's apartment. But Pippa misread my thoughts, and added, hastily, "We wouldn't expect you to do any of the messy stuff—changing sheets and all that. It's more that she needs companionship. She gets lonely, especially at night."

"You want me to stay over with her? In her flat?" Just saying the words sent a chill through me.

"Well, yes. You'd have your own room. Either her old one or Harold's, seeing as she's moved into mine."

It didn't matter which room I was in—I was never going to spend the night there. "Can I think it over?" I said.

"Sure." Pippa seemed surprised that I hadn't accepted. "It's only for a week. We're all going to Greece after that. Peggy too."

I glanced over at the café door and saw Caleb scowling in at us. "I'll call you," I said. "I think I have a temping assignment next week."

"Of course," said Pippa, clearly disappointed. "You've got my number."

After they left, I went for a walk through the Holland Park woods, where I'd often played as a child. My prep school had been nearby, behind a church, and we had walked to the park in crocodile formation, two by two, holding hands, in every sort of weather. The park had been the scene of some of my greatest humiliations, and, when I thought about it, absolutely none of my triumphs. The worst had been my attempt, in front of the entire class, to scale the six-foot-high metal fence that ran down the middle of the park, separating the sports fields from the cycle lane. At the top of the fence, I'd balanced for a moment between two metal spikes, then jumped, only to be snagged by the hem of my gray gabardine skirt. I had hung upside down from the fence, flailing and screaming, for just long enough to wet my pants before the fabric ripped from arse to hem and I fell.

Peeing my pants had been my standard response to any great fear or surprise, and the last and only time I had ever stayed at Peggy's, at age seven, I'd wet the bed. I had woken in the night, desperate for the loo, but had not been able to leave the room for fear of crossing Madeline's path. Peggy had been really nice about it, had even said I could stay over again one night, but I wouldn't even consider it. Even now, I found it abhorrent.

When I got back to Willesden Green, the place was empty, the flatmates all still at work. That morning I'd been in such a rush to get to the park that I'd left my cell phone behind, and it was beeping incessantly, telling me I had two new messages and three missed calls. They were all from the same number, the texts banal: "It's Mike. Let me know if you get this text," and because I hadn't let him know: "It's Mike. Is this your number? Let me know." Finally, a voice message inviting me to dinner then changing his mind and downgrading to drinks.

Reasoning that any other action would be false encouragement, I deleted the lot.

I went into the kitchen to make a cup of tea before the flatmates got home from work, which was generally when I made myself scarce. Lately, I'd been running out of things to do at night, but a few libraries were open late, and I'd found a local park where you could watch people play floodlit tennis. As I heated water and rummaged for a tea bag I considered where I could go tonight—not too far, in my hungover state. And then I found The Note.

It was in Belinda's handwriting, but someone else had added to it, and I imagined the flatmates writing it together, perhaps over breakfast. They'd left it propped up behind the kitchen taps, where I'd be sure to see it if I got a drink of water or filled the kettle—except that I hadn't gone into the kitchen before leaving that morning, there hadn't been time. I was familiar with these kinds of notes; they were how people in flats communicated with each other when things had become really septic, usually over unwashed dishes or unpaid rent. In block capitals, this one said: "Suki, too fucking much"—an arrow pointed to the sink, where someone had left her dirty clothes to soak—"You have to leave. Today." The word "today" had been written in such a rage that in places the ballpoint went right through the piece of paper.

With horror, I realized what was in the kitchen sink: the jeans and top I had been wearing the night before. I must have put them in there to soak, although I didn't remember doing it. The water around them was rust colored, and what looked like a few twigs had risen to the surface. Above it floated the now familiar stench of mold.

Under the circumstances, the note was diplomatic.

By half past four I had packed my suitcases, thrown out the jeans and top, and removed all traces of myself from the flat. Before leaving, I returned the note to its shelf behind the tap, and placed my front-door key on the kitchen table. Then I called my friend Alana, who answered on the third ring.

"I need a place to stay," I said after we had exchanged greetings.

"I'm at work," she said, flatly.

"I meant after work."

"What? Tonight?"

"I've got nowhere else to go."

"Are you sure?" Her resistance troubled me, but I could not afford to analyze it.

Sitting on my suitcases at the Barbican station a couple of hours later, I looked so forlorn, so raggedy, that a businessman threw fifty pence at me with an admonishment not to spend it on grog. Not for the first time, I thought of the check my father had offered me, and how different my situation might be if I'd accepted it. Then again, it was entirely possible that I would have frittered it all away on clothes by now, and I'd be no better off.

Alana arrived an hour later than we had arranged, and didn't apologize, though she did help drag one of the suitcases along three blocks of crooked pavement to her flat. "I haven't had a roommate since I moved here," she said. "Living by myself is the best."

I was surprised to find that Alana lived in one of those sixties council towers that you see on TV being detonated before they collapse one day on top of their inhabitants. At least she lived on the ground floor, far below the suicidal balconies crammed with washing lines and dustbins.

"I was on the waiting list for years before I got this place," she said, letting me in. "It's nicer on the inside than it is from the street." She was right, it was nicer, cozy even, and I envied the amount of space she had for herself, space she evidently wasn't too keen on sharing.

I handed her a plastic bag of groceries I'd salvaged, not stolen, from Willesden Green, and she inspected the contents warily and stuffed them into a low cupboard. The bottle of wine I'd bought got a better reception, and I opened it while she put a frozen pizza in the oven. I told her about Mike and his flurry of texts, though I'd meant not to. Alana picked up where she'd left off outside the toilet stall, demanding to know how I was so sure I didn't like him when I didn't even know him. "Because there hadn't been a spark," I told her, but she wouldn't let it go, and I sensed she was annoyed with me in a more general way that had nothing at all to do with Mike.

After a few glasses of wine, she seemed to relax, and we sank back into the old routine of recalling the most recent dramas of our lives in amusing and elaborate detail. She finally got it out of me that I had given up on men only because the latest in a long line of destructive breakups had been such a train wreck that in the aftermath, it had hurt too much to have hope.

"You went out with a bunch of assholes," she said a little dismissively when I had finished explaining. "It was a bad run, that's all."

She didn't understand, and I knew I could never explain, how a bad run left its mark—that at the end of it, you were not the same person you had been at the start. Every time you went through a breakup, it took something from you, leaving less of you to give to the next one, and the longer the bad run went on, the harder it was to offer up what little was left.

When I was done with talking about men, I moved on to my family (which took us through another bottle of wine) and to being broke and unemployed—out came a bottle of foul coffee liqueur her great-aunt had given her for Christmas—and for good measure, I doubled back and added in those final messed-up months in Auckland—hard to leave out—at which point it was half past eleven and Alana announced that she was spent. She went to tip her glass of coffee liqueur down the sink, and I told her not to waste it, that if she didn't want it, I'd drink it—but she must not have heard me.

"The couch folds out," she said, fetching sheets and a blanket from an airing cupboard. "It's a bit lumpy, but I shouldn't think that'll bother you much."

While I was trying to work out if that was an odd thing to say, I was swamped by a wave of nostalgia for the after-school phone marathons and sweet delusions of our girlhood friendship—a wave I needed to share. "There's something so great about old friends who really know you, who understand you," I began, with a lump in my throat. "Living in New Zealand, I really missed that. I always had to make new friends, and we didn't share any history. Not like I do with you."

"Yes," she said, matter-of-factly. "We used to have a lot of fun."

She was tired, she said, shutting the door to her bedroom, and so was I. So tired that my second hangover came early, while I lay on the lumpy sofa bed, staring at the ceiling and worrying about how many flats, how many lives, were stacked on top of that thin piece of particle board.

Scanning over the evening's conversation, it struck me that I couldn't remember a single thing Alana had told me about her life. Not because drunkenness had wiped out my memory, but because she hadn't told me anything. Then, with a mix of horror and shame, I realized that was because I hadn't let her get a word in, that I'd done all the talking—*all* of it. I had been rabid, had frothed at the mouth. But it was too late now to go back and put a stopper in the bottle. I could only apologize, and try not to do it again. Over breakfast, I would make amends.

But by the time I woke up, Alana had gone. She hadn't left a note, but I wrote one to her saying thanks for the bed, and then I called Pippa.

"I'm so pleased you'll do it," she said, the relief clear in her voice. "I think Peggy took a shine to you, and we had so much trouble finding a nurse she liked. Most of them weren't posh enough and she complained about their 'dreary accents' when they were reading to her."

"I have to *read* to her?" I hadn't meant to sound rude, but reading aloud was the pits.

"Only if you feel like it. But it's either that or listening to her stories, which can get a little . . . repetitive. You know what old people are like."

"Not really," I said. "My grandmother was more interested in telling people what to do than in boring them to tears."

"I met her once, I think," said Pippa. "Is she still alive?"

"I don't know," I said, truthfully. "So, can I start straight-away?"

"If you want."

Pippa made arrangements for me to pick up a key from her place, and I was about to hang up when she said, "By the way, what on earth did you say to Caleb?"

Oh dear. Had he told her about my bunking advice? "Nothing much," I said, tentatively. "We hardly spoke."

"Are you sure?"

"I asked him a few questions, but he wasn't exactly chatty."

"Really?" she said, sounding surprised. "Because on the way home, instead of renting a game, he insisted on going to the library and getting out a stack of books. When we got home he went straight to his room and we haven't seen him since—well, hardly, except for dinner, which he wolfed down in five seconds." She paused. "He's never wanted to read books before. I'm a little freaked out."

It did seem like strange behavior, though I could guess what book he'd gotten out—along with a few decoys. "Did you see what he was reading?"

"He wouldn't show me."

Making my way to Notting Hill that night with my suitcase and a key, I felt like a gypsy. My sense that London owed me something had vanished. Maybe if I'd been born in another part of the world I could have returned there and felt like a native, but London wasn't like that. It was too full to take back a stray who had carelessly given up her place.

And yet, for now, I had a key to our old building. It was shiny, freshly cut, and turned easily in the well-used lock. The heavy front door had a rubber skirt and shushed across the carpet in a satisfying, moneyed way. When I stepped into the lobby, a bright chandelier lit up overhead, and the brass central heating grille gleamed like a new Rolls-Royce.

I climbed the wide staircase one flight at a time, and just before I reached each new level the landing would be illuminated, the lights triggered by an invisible sensor. At first I was grateful for the ease—my hands were full with heavy suitcases—but as I climbed higher up the building, my pace slowed, and the lights began to time out before I reached the next floor and the next sensor. For half of every flight—then gradually more—I was plunged into a darkness that my eyes found hard to adjust to and was forced to walk blind up the stairs. I looked for a switch but found none. To keep abreast with the lights, I tried to pick up my pace, but the more I tried to rush with my heavy bags, the more out of sync I seemed to get. Finally, when I arrived at what I thought was Peggy's floor, the lights didn't come on at all.

In the dark, I put down my suitcases and groped in my bag for the key. It fit easily enough into the lock, was only a little sticky, but when I tried to turn it, the thing wouldn't budge. For almost a minute, still in darkness, I persisted, twisting the key back and forth and trying to shift the door slightly in its frame to see if that would help. I looked up and down the shadowy staircase and out the window at a stand of muscular oak trees, their wide trunks dappled in the moonlight, and that was when I realized something was wrong. From Peggy's floor you looked above oak canopies at the sky. Once more, I studied the door. It had no number, just a tiny metal eyehole in the center.

It wasn't Peggy's door. This was Jimmy's floor. A spasm of fear radiated from my stomach and I tried to pull out the key, but I must have already turned it too far in one direction, and the jaws of the lock had clamped around it. Jimmy's name hadn't been on the list next to the buzzer and I had taken it for granted that he had moved out—but what if he hadn't? My fingers plucked uselessly at the key as voices issued from the belly of the flat behind it, quiet at first, then shouting. Loud music started up, as rowdy as a fairground ride, and I jumped back, letting go of the key. It sat in the lock, reproaching me. I was being a scaredy cat, but knowing that didn't help.

The music then changed abruptly to classical—the sound track to an ad I recognized. It was only the TV, rocking through a commercial break. Of course Jimmy didn't live there anymore. The realization calmed me enough to have another go at the key, to tweak it with more patience until it released.

Halfway up the next set of stairs, the blessed lights came on, and stayed on until I reached the landing outside Peggy's flat. My hands on the key chain were shaking, but I found the right key and turned it in the lock.

CHAPTER EIGHT

London, 2003

ONCE I HAD GAINED ENTRY to Peggy's apartment, what came over me first was relief. The lights worked, and the tatty interior was comforting, lived in. A hearty soup or stew had been warming in the kitchen, and the aroma of it was still in the hallway, canceling out the usual unpleasant smells. Pippa's instructions had been to call out to Peggy as soon as I arrived, in case the old woman thought someone was trying to break in. Peggy was expecting me, but she had a leaky memory for comings and goings, and Pippa said it defaulted to paranoia if she was taken by surprise.

I put down my suitcases and called out her name once or twice, first in a quiet voice, then a little more loudly. When there was no answer, I assumed Peggy had gone to sleep. The door to her bedroom was closed, and I carried on down the hallway in search of a room that was empty—Pippa had told me to sleep in whichever one I could physically get into. Some rooms, she'd warned me, were entirely full of boxes. First, I came to what I thought had once been Peggy's bedroom, and pushed open the door, or tried to, but something was blocking it, a small trunk or a piece of furniture. The door gave a little, but I didn't want to force it open. I made my way down the hall and crossed the drawing room to get to Harold's room, switching on as many lights as possible along the way. I meant not to look at Madeline, nor to think of her, to focus only on where I was heading, but before I could stop myself, I had looked in her direction—and looked again, because she wasn't there. In the place she normally sat there was only a dark square on the floorboards where her dais had prevented the wood from fading.

Instead of relief that she wasn't in her usual spot, however, I was transfixed by the idea that she had learned how to move and was following stealthily behind me, gliding even, just outside my line of vision. But when I looked behind me, the apartment was deserted.

I told myself to buck up, and carried on to Harold's room. It was, as Pippa had predicted, almost impossible to fight my way through the abundant boxes, but I found too that most of them were stacked by the door, as if someone had gone a little way into the room, hurriedly dumped the cartons, and left. Once you got past them, the room was quite sparsely furnished, with a dresser and a double bed, sagging in the middle but heavenly compared to the couch I'd been sleeping on for months. At first I meant only to test the mattress before getting up to clean my teeth and undress, but once I was lying down I didn't want to move, and despite the strangeness of the situation, and all that was lurking outside, I pulled the eiderdown up around my shoulders and fell into a deep, untroubled sleep.

It was only the next morning that I saw the dust, lying thick on every surface of the room, including, I noticed with dismay, on the adjacent pillow. Some of it had gotten into my throat in the night, and the first thing I did when I sat up was cough. It was very early, only a gray film lit the morning, and I crept through the flat to get a glass of water. Peggy's door was still closed and everything else appeared undisturbed since the night before.

In the kitchen, after pouring myself a drink from the tap, I poked around in the cupboards for a vacuum cleaner. I found one of those old-fashioned ones that resembled a set of bagpipes, and wheeled it down the long hallway to Harold's room—far enough away that I didn't think Peggy would hear it. Plugged in, the volume was impressive, but it had no suction, and its metal head was so huge that it was beyond maneuvering, especially through the death valley of Harold's books and junk. Still, I gave it my best shot, and only came to a halt when the vacuum cleaner fell into a pothole. On closer inspection the hole turned out to be more extensive than I'd thought—in fact, a whole section of parquet floorboards was missing. Under the desk by the window, and along one wall, perhaps two dozen blocks of it had been pulled up and stacked to one side, leaving exposed an adventure playground for mice. When I went around the room a little farther, I saw that other patches of floor had been pulled up and replaced, but badly, so that pieces of parquet jutted out here and there at hazardous angles.

That was when I gave up on vacuuming, or any other sort of housework. Instead of cleaning Peggy's flat I tried to clean myself in the decrepit bathroom. In place of a proper shower there was one of those hose devices that was meant to fit snugly over the bath taps, but instead sprayed water all over the bathroom. England was the only place I'd been where such devices were still in use—not only in use but overused and repaired, with duct tape and lengths of string. At least I wasn't using it in winter when showering under it would lead to hypothermia.

By the time I had dressed, it was almost eight, and I made Peggy a cup of tea and knocked on her door. When there was no reply, I called out to her, "Peggy? It's Suki. Are you awake?"

I thought I heard shuffling, and tentatively pushed open the door, but when I went in, her hospital bed was empty and she wasn't in the room.

Back out in the hallway, I noticed a rattling sound from behind the door that had been wedged shut the night before, as though someone was trying to force it open from the other side, and by the time I got there Peggy had squeezed herself halfway out.

"Good morning," she said. "I appear to be stuck."

"Let me help you." With a little undignified shoving and pulling, I got her through. Once she was out, I tried to open the door all the way, but it was still stuck. "Is there a wedge under the door?"

"A wedge?" she said, quite bewildered. "Whatever do you mean?" Her hair was wrapped in a turban, and a pink satin bathrobe fishtailed behind her—the 1930s movie star, waiting for her lover to drop round for cocktails and barbiturates. She saw the cup of tea I was carrying and brightened. "Is that for me? How lovely."

I took her by the arm, and sat her down in a nearby chair, where she gulped her tea and asked for another, "With a spoon or two of sugar." At the end of that cup, she said, "One more. I don't quite feel strong enough to get up just yet."

I was amazed that she could get up at all. Only a few months earlier she'd been on her deathbed, written off by her own nurse. Since then she'd filled out, and no longer resembled a living skeleton. But it was only after her third cup of tea that she finally revived enough to really notice me. Then she said, "Oh, you're not Amanda."

"No, I'm Suki. I came to visit you a few months ago. I used to live downstairs with my parents—Hillary and Ludo."

"Why are you here?" she said, as though she hadn't heard me.

"I'm going to help you for a bit while Amanda's away. She's coming in later to say good-bye."

"Forty years on my own, I think I can go to the lavatory by myself. What did you say your name was?"

"Suki. Suki Piper."

"Aha," she exclaimed. "I knew your sister. She wore little pink glasses and was always dancing. Do you know she came to stay with us once and wet the bed?"

"I think you're talking about me," I said. "I don't have a sister."

Her face fell. "Oh dear. I'm so sorry. I just remembered what happened to her." She took my hand. "Forgive me."

"Forgive you for what?"

"I forgot your sister died of cancer."

"She didn't. But my mother did. Hillary."

"Hillary had cancer?" She looked confused. "But I saw her a few months ago and she was fine."

"That was me too, not Hillary."

Peggy stared for a moment at the stuffed birds in their cage. One was hanging upside down from the perch, its feet bound by twine. "I think I might need an extra cup of tea this morning," she said.

I was relieved to discover that I had only to escort Peggy to the door of the lavatory, but she insisted on going in alone. To conserve energy, she spent most of her time in a wheelchair, but could walk short distances when it suited her. At half past ten I found her in the kitchen, answering the siren call of her midmorning whiskey. The liquor brought a splash of color to her cheeks, and contrary to what I'd expected, she was much more lucid afterward. "This is our little secret, you hear?" she said, stashing the bottle in an old-fashioned flour bin. "It's almost all gone, but I shall send you out later to replenish our stores."

I did not appear to have a say in the matter. Soon after, Pippa arrived amid a bustle of plastic shopping bags, and put away groceries on low shelves where Peggy could reach them—cans of soup, mainly, plus a few packets of mouse-colored biscuits. Mother and daughter air-kissed on both cheeks, their skin not actually touching. Pippa had dyed her hair, I noticed, as did Peggy, who grabbed a swatch of it. "It looks a little brassy," she said. "Did you do it yourself?"

"Mmm-hmm," said Pippa, noncommittal.

"It's the wrong shade for your complexion. Brings out the red in your face." Peggy puffed out her cheeks to demonstrate. "You must always go to a salon. I have told you this before."

"Thank you," said Pippa, straining to be courteous. "Remind me to consult you next time." She noticed that her mother's cardigan was fastened incorrectly, and rebuttoned it while Peggy huffed discontentedly. In a schoolteacher voice Pippa added, "Why doesn't Suki wheel you into the drawing room while I make us all morning tea? You can show her your photographs."

At the mention of photographs, Peggy perked up. "Don't push too fast, or it makes me feel giddy," she said as I steered her out into the hallway. The wheelchair slid easily along the tiled floor, and it was an effort to slow the pace to one that suited Peggy. "I've always imagined having a wallah to do this," she announced as we reached the end of the hall. "Like the maharajahs did in India. I don't think they minded at all, the wallahs. In fact, I think they rather enjoyed it. So much better to be civilized than living in the jungle eating bananas, don't you agree?"

She was too old to be dissuaded from her colonial fantasies, so I opted to play along. "Where to now, memsahib?"

She pointed to the far wall. "Over there."

I had been in the drawing room dozens of times but had never scrutinized the wall of photographs directly opposite Madeline, probably because Madeline herself had always distracted me from doing so. "Did you get rid of the statue?" I asked, hopefully.

"Get rid of Madeline?" said Peggy, outraged that I had even asked. "Of course not. She's like a daughter to me." She had stopped in front of a photograph of herself in a feathered headdress looking young and haughty, a small, impish boy trying to climb up her leg. "You remember dearest Harold, don't you?" she said. "Such a sweet little boy. Liked to hang around backstage, waiting for Mummy to finish." She pulled me closer to the photo so I could get a better look, then pointed to another picture of Harold in a suit and graduation gown. "So terribly bright. Do you know he graduated from Cambridge with a first class honors? Isn't he handsome?"

I nodded, though I didn't agree. Harold had shadowy, deep-set eyes, and his mouth was soured by a sneering expression. "I didn't know you were an actress," I said.

"Oh yes," she said, sweeping her arm over the entire wall. "As you can see, I worked with all the greats. It was a marvelous time. Of course, they're all dead now. And I'm almost there."

Most of the photographs were black-and-white studio poses, with autographs scrawled across them, and there was only one other shot of Peggy, standing next to a short, dapper man.

"Is that Harold and Pippa's dad?" I asked, recalling that their father had been an actor.

"Heavens, no! Their father was a scoundrel. You won't find any photos of him here. I burned every single one." Peggy stroked her finger across the photograph glass. "That's Laurie," she said, swooning at his name. "He *should* have been their father but he died."

The man in the photo was intriguingly effeminate, with kind, amused eyes, and he and Peggy looked to be sharing a joke. I asked if he had died in the war, but Peggy ignored my question.

"You can stop gawking now." She pushed off from the wall, obliging me to follow the wheelchair as it careened in the opposite direction. "I should like to sit by the window."

On our way past the chaise longues, I examined the dark patch of wood where Madeline's dais had stood. Long scratch marks on one side showed the direction she'd been dragged in but the marks stopped abruptly, as though she had been lifted up off the floor.

As we neared the windows, Peggy's reptilian hand gripped my arm. "Ahh, Hillary, I do so love the sun! What a gorgeous day." She nodded her head around the room, surveying her kingdom. "Tell Pippa to brew the tea for longer. She always makes it too weak."

Pippa appeared in the doorway with tea and biscuits, a formal arrangement on a tray. "Last time you said it was too strong."

"Well, it was," said Peggy, surveying the tray. "Is that shortbread?"

"Yes."

"You know I don't eat biscuits."

"So don't eat any." Pippa poured a splash of milk into each of three teacups.

"I prefer not to have things like that in the house."

"You don't normally have *any* food in the house, Mummy. Only grog."

"Not anymore," said Peggy. "You won't let me."

Pippa sighed. "And I'm sure you've found ways to get around that."

Peggy shot her an indignant look. "Just what are you implying?"

"Nothing, Mummy, nothing at all."

For half a minute, everyone sipped tea as starchily as ladies in an Edwardian costume drama. The sun obliged our charade and added its summery warmth, but it was too bright for Peggy and she held her hand up to her face.

"Hillary, do be a darling and fetch my sunglasses," she said to me, an order, not a request. "They're in my room, on the dresser, I should think."

I stood up to obey. "The room you got stuck in this morning?"

"I believe I said, 'in *my* room,' didn't I?"

"You did."

"Stop it, Mummy," said Pippa. "She isn't your servant."

They continued to bicker as I left the drawing room. In the hallway, I came to the door of Peggy's room—her original bedroom—and tried to push it open but met with the same resistance I had the night before. I was bigger than Peggy and wasn't sure if I'd be able to squeeze through the gap, so I pushed a little harder to see if the door would give way. Inch by inch, whatever was behind the door slowly moved, until the gap was wide enough for me to fit through.

The room was dark, unnaturally so for such a bright day, and I stood still, just inside the door, while my eyes adjusted. I didn't think I'd ever been into Peggy's real bedroom before, and it was both larger and messier than I expected. Clothes and shoes sprouted from every piece of furniture and lolled about on the floor—not really clothes at all, I saw on closer inspection, but costumes: piles of slippery silk and feathers and winking diamantes. No wonder I had never been allowed in here as a child—it was little-girl heaven, a giant dress-up box filled with vintage treasures. I would have broken things, accidentally on purpose, just like I had ruined my mother's treasured locket.

So overwhelmed was I by all the finery that I forgot to look behind the door to see what had been blocking it, and when I finally did look, I wished that I hadn't. There was Madeline, parked next to the bed, kneeling beside it, in fact, close enough to be petted by whoever was sleeping there. Her granite head was being used as a hat stand, and a satin undergarment was draped from her shoulder, but the indignity made her no less menacing. I should have guessed it would be her behind the door, but instead I felt ambushed, as though Madeline had won the first round in a blindfolded parlor game.

In different circumstances, I would have taken hours to find the sunglasses, handling as many gowns as possible along the way. But with Madeline watching, my hands were paddles, swiping blindly at things and sending piles of necklaces and garter belts flying in all directions. I was so flustered that after a time I wasn't even sure what I was looking for, and had displaced so many of Peggy's things that it looked like the dresser had been savaged by a dog. Finally, I saw a pair of ridiculous sunglasses—huge and round, like dinner plates—poking out from the top drawer, and I grabbed them in my shaking hands and fled.

Out in the hallway afterward, my reaction at seeing Madeline seemed about as credible as being strangled by a psychotic feather boa, and I recovered almost as soon as the door was shut. I'd had a panic attack; that was all.

"You took your time," said Peggy when I returned. "But I suppose a little snooping won't hurt anyone."

Pippa laughed. "She wasn't snooping—have you seen the state of your room? I'm surprised she found anything in there. I'm surprised you can even find the bed."

Their sniping sounded gentler than it had when I'd left, and I guessed a truce between them had been reached. Either that or they'd worn each other out. I handed Peggy her sunglasses, which obscured most of her face and made an indentation on her papery cheeks. She looked glamorous though too, a skeletal version of Jackie O in her Greek phase.

"You look ready for our bon voyage now," said Pippa.

"I don't know why you're so excited," said Peggy, looking out over the top of her sunglasses. "It's one of the lesser Greek islands."

"Which means it's unspoiled." Pippa wiped a dribble of tea from her mother's chin. "You'll absolutely love it. Ari's family can't wait to make a fuss over you."

"What makes you think they won't put me to work in the taverna like the rest of you?"

"We'll only be working some of the time," said Pippa. "The rest is a holiday."

"And what if I get sick again?" Peggy's mouth turned down at the corners. "I don't suppose they have proper medical facilities."

"Don't be so morbid. It's the middle of summer." Pippa wiped a finger of dust off the windowsill. "It'll do you good to get away from your museum."

"Harold will look after me. I'll ring him tonight in Australia."

"Canada, Mother. He lives in Toronto, remember?"

"Well, they're both part of the Commonwealth," said Peggy. "And there's no need to shout." She tried to take a sip from her cup, but it slid out of her hand and smashed on the floor in a pool of milky tea. At the calamity, Peggy started, and Pippa put out a hand to steady her.

"Have you heard from him lately?" she said, more gently.

Peggy didn't answer, but I saw, as Pippa knelt and carefully gathered up the pieces of broken china, that her jaw was clenched.

"Well, neither have I," said Pippa, when she'd finished picking up the crockery. "Suki, would you mind getting a tea towel from the kitchen?"

I was still rifling in the cupboards looking for one when Pippa came in to throw out the broken cup.

"Is she well enough to go to Greece?" I said.

"It was her idea," said Pippa. "She campaigned with her doctor to be allowed to go. But she enjoys being difficult. If we changed our minds and said she had to stay here, she'd want to go with us." She pulled out a tea towel from perilously close to the moonshine flour bin and handed it to me. "Did you enjoy Mummy's fantasy wall?"

At first, I didn't catch on. "You mean the photographs? She told me she was an actress."

"She was an understudy in a couple of plays," said Pippa. "Eventually she became a theater publicist—a very good one too. That's why she has got so many autographed photos, and why she isn't in any of them."

"Except for the one in the headdress," I said.

"Costume party," said Pippa. "She had plenty of those."

"That's what I remember most about her—the amazing clothes," I said, feeling a rush of sadness and sympathy for Peggy's failed ambitions. Perhaps it didn't matter that she'd only acted the part of an actress. Flouncing around in Kabuki gowns had been a kind of performance. Who cared if it hadn't been on a stage?

Pippa settled on a stool by the window, and didn't look like she was in a hurry to go back to the drawing room. "I wish she'd let go of all that," she said. "She hangs on to all those bloody gowns and some of them are worth a fortune. Soon they'll be so ruined they won't be worth a thing."

Money troubles, it seemed, were all around me. "Couldn't she sell this place? Move somewhere smaller?"

"She doesn't own it," said Pippa, as if this was something I should have known.

"But the rent must be astronomical!"

"It would be if she hadn't been here since the sixties. She pays peppercorn rent, and no one can kick her out. She's got absolutely no savings, and most of the time we have to help her out with bills. This place costs a fortune to heat." Pippa sighed. "I shouldn't be so hard on her. She made so many sacrifices when we were growing up. Harold's education didn't come cheap, nor did the trimmings that went with it."

"You didn't want to go to university?"

"Me? At university?" She sounded surprised that I'd even asked. "I was far too interested in makeup and boys—as I'm sure you remember."

"You taught me everything I know about makeup. And I should have listened more to what you said about boys."

Pippa laughed. "It was such a shame when you and your mother moved out of the flat downstairs. But I suppose I can understand why she wanted to get rid of it."

"She didn't want to—we moved because Dad wanted to sell the flat. That was the one time he got in touch."

"What?" said Pippa. She looked like she had been slapped. "You mean he cut you off?"

I had never heard anyone describe it so harshly, but she was right, we had been severed. "Mum didn't like to talk about it."

"I'm not surprised," said Pippa. "How awful."

That night, Peggy asked me to read to her from one of the romances on the nightstand by her bed. I was about to start from the beginning of the slim volume when she snatched it from my hand and opened it near the end. "Start with the climax," she said, getting comfortable against a bank of old feather pillows. "I can't stay awake long, so you have to cut to the chase."

I made the mistake of glancing at Madeline before I complied, and Peggy followed my gaze. "Isn't she lovely?" she said. "She was a gift from my darling Laurie."

"She's very . . . lifelike," I said, choosing my words carefully.

"I think so, but the others can't see it. She'll be out on the curb the minute I'm gone."

"Wherever I go in the room," I said, "I feel like she's looking at me."

"I know," said Peggy, reaching out to stroke Madeline's face. "I never feel lonely when she's here." She smiled. "Of course, it's even better to have human company. Especially someone who isn't in a uniform."

From her corner, Madeline glared.

"Did you move her in here yourself?" I asked.

"Heavens, no. She weighs three times as much as I do. But Amanda came up with the ingenious idea of popping her in the wheelchair and trundling her down the hall." Peggy pointed to the large dresser on the door side of her bed. "Only we couldn't get the wheelchair past the dresser, so she's sort of stuck behind the door."

After I'd read a single page, Peggy was sound asleep, and I tucked the quilt into the small of her back. Standing away from the bed and looking at her sleeping body, I suddenly felt very alone, and realized that I'd enjoyed having company as much as she had. Being useful, feeling needed, had been nice, and I went back to the living room, acutely aware that I was neither.

There was no TV in the flat, only books and whiskey—at least I knew where that was hiding—and with Madeline tucked away in Peggy's room, I felt relaxed enough to take a nightcap on the chaise longue with a 1978 issue of *Vogue* that I had found in a stack under the coffee table. But after only a couple of sips, and a dozen or so pages, my eyes began to droop.

I went to my room tired but sober. It was a silvery night, pretty, and after getting changed into summer pajamas, I opened the curtains and climbed into bed. The moon was out, a pale disk filmed over with smoke. No stars, but I'd stopped looking for them in London's light-polluted skies. Harold's room looked out over the communal gardens, and the rustle of oak trees was surprisingly loud considering the constant low hum of people and televisions and traffic underneath it. For an hour or more, I lay there with my eyes closed, waiting for sleep, but every time I came close to drifting off, some thought pulled me back to consciousness. Round and round these thoughts went, until my body drummed with restlessness. I was thirsty too, perhaps because of the whiskey, so I got up and walked through the quiet flat to get a glass of water, turning on lights as I went. The kitchen was empty, and smelled of the sweet tomato soup I'd heated up for our dinner. I drank a glass of water, and filled it again to take back to bed, then turned off the fluorescent bar in the kitchen, and returned to the hallway, where I did something uncharacteristic—I turned off that light too. It was very dark but in time my eyes adjusted, and I made my way through the shadows to Harold's room. I had braced myself to feel constant fear in Peggy's flat, where she and her little friend lived, but walking alone along the checkered hallway, I felt nothing except nostalgia, and the old familiar gnaw of unwanted solitude.

Back in Harold's room, I put down the glass of water next to the bed and climbed in. Glasses off, I shut my eyes to sleep. I was calm, hydrated, warm, tired; I should have drifted off immediately, but could not. This time it was a noise that kept me awake, a scraping sound coming from the garden, as if someone was dragging a heavy iron spade along one of the concrete paths. The noise stopped, but then I was bothered by a deep absence of sound, as though I had descended to the bottom of the ocean. No oak leaves rustled, no traffic hummed; all the TVs and their owners had been switched off. So dense, so complete was the silence that I put on my glasses and went to the window to see what it looked like.

Everything below was incredibly familiar, like the scene in a postcard that's been stuck to the fridge for too many years. There was the paved patio and white gate; the neat begonia beds with their border of pebbles; the barbecue area my father had built out of salvaged red bricks. On the tiny patch of lawn, someone had been ten-pin bowling and left the game out for the night—only they weren't bowling pins, they were wine bottles. My gaze lingered on the flattened carcass of a Wendy tent—primary red and yellow with five or six tent poles sticking out like broken ribs.

When the truth about what I was looking at sank in, I sprang from the windowpane, and steadied myself against an adjacent wall. Nothing in the room had changed—the bed was messed up where I had been lying in it, and the glass of water on the bedside table was as full as it had been when I set it down. The thing that was wrong was outside, in the garden. Not just the tent, but in the seconds before I looked away I was sure I'd seen a rectangle of black beyond it, slightly larger than a cot mattress.

But how was that possible? I steeled myself to look again. Leaning carefully toward the glass, I gripped the sash window frame so hard that a splinter of chipped paint jabbed into the soft skin under my fingernail, but the pain of it was canceled by what I saw out in the garden in plain sight. There, at the end of the begonia beds, was the hatch to the air-raid shelter, peeled open like the lid of a sardine can.

Two or three times more, I experimented with moving away from the window for a moment, then looking back out to make sure that what I'd seen was actually there. It was, every time. There was no mistaking the layout of the garden, exactly as it had been when I was a child, no mistaking the rectangle of black or the debris that had been left out on the lawn the night after the party.

The windowpane was damp where I'd pressed against it, and I stood back and wiped away the condensation. Real moisture from my breathing, something you could run your finger through, unlike the mirage on the other side of the glass. I rubbed my eyes, but that made no difference. The old garden was still there, as alluring as it was filled with menace.

I decided to open the window. It had been so long since anyone had done so that it took some effort to force aside the half-moon catch between the two sides of the sash. The windowpane itself moved easily enough, but I soon discovered the sash cord was broken, and the weight of the glass in its frame bore down on my hands with tremendous urgency and pressure. Still, I got the thing open, and propped up the sash with a hardback Dickens omnibus from Harold's schoolboy collection. With much trepidation, I leaned a little way out. The night air was still, but also sultry, humid. With one eye on Dickens—his long-windedness holding fast—I leaned out a bit farther and dared to look down.

One of the French doors—*our* old French doors—was open, and light spilled out onto the patio. A shadow fell across it and a male figure walked out, followed by another and another—three men in all—their laughter like gunshots on the still night air.

For a second or two, I watched with awed curiosity before I reacted physically to the ghastly spectacle—one of the men was my father—and reeled backward and upward, dislodging the book and sending the window frame downward with the force of a guillotine. The sound of it slamming was enough to wake the dead, and I dropped to my hands and knees and crawled, at great speed, toward the bed.

Once in it, I pulled the musty feather quilt over my head, but it wasn't quite thick enough to block out the dreadful scraping noises of the hatch being closed, or the giddy, drunken voices, including my father's, that accompanied the endeavor. The only mercy—and I was absurdly grateful for it—was that from four stories up, I could not make out a word they were saying. After a time the scraping, talking, and laughing all stopped and I guessed that the men had gone back inside, wherever that was, this world or another. The garden, the building, the room, fell quiet once more, not the thick silence of ten minutes earlier but the ordinary hum of late-night London. I could have climbed out of bed and gone to the window to see if sight matched sound, but by then I had run out of gumption, for that or any other task.

CHAPTER NINE

London, 1991

OVARIAN CANCER: one of the most deadly, one of the most invisible. I didn't see it coming. Not just because there was nothing to see, or because Mum hadn't wanted me to find out, but because for most of the two years she was having aggressive treatment, I was trawling the lipstick counters and movie foyers of Notting Hill, lost in a haze of bus-stop crushes and top-forty pop hits. I was sixteen. The first few times she went to hospital and my grandmother came to look after me, I thought it was serious, but after Mum had been admitted half a dozen times and was, on each occasion, returned to me in one piece, her absence became routine. I was free to fixate on what all teenage girls fixate on—boys. In my case, I wanted to know why I had grown up to be one of those girls with whom they did not fall wildly in love. Cancer had nothing on that, and try as I might, I cannot go back to redress the oversight.

By that age, I had worked out that my rotten luck with boys had little to do with looks or even personality—plenty of plain, irritating girls in my class were met at the school gates by a different boy each week—and more to do with a hidden magnet you were either born with, or, tragically, born without. If the magnet wasn't there, you couldn't get one, or even pretend you had one; you just had to learn to live without it, to watch from the sidelines while girls with magnets made off with all the loot.

That year, Alana and I were hung up on noses. Every single boy we saw in the street, on the bus, in the park had to have his nose rated and classified according to a complicated set of criteria. At the bottom of the sliding scale was the worst kind of nose: large and bumpy and Roman, the sort a French lothario would sport (off the scale altogether was anything potato shaped or bulbous). At the top—the very pinnacle of proboscis perfection—was an RP: a pointed, girlish ski jump of a nose, as sported by the pointed, girlish actor River Phoenix, or "Riv," as he was to us. To see an RP in the flesh was to fall instantly, swooningly in love, and warranted an immediate four-hour phone call to discuss the details of the nose and its owner. This would be followed by weeks of frustrated stalking in an attempt at further sightings.

On the art department photocopier at school, we made River Phoenix wallpaper and used it to cover the walls of the common room. A competing group tried to do the same with Keanu Reeves, but they got as far as wallpapering the Coke machine before the art department started charging for photocopies and their commitment faltered.

I talked to Mum about boys, but only enough so she thought I was normal, not a lesbo like the PE teachers at school. Any more than that and I risked getting "the lecture," the one that began with "boys only want one thing." But as my seventeenth birthday approached, the lecture began to grate in a new way, for it only served to remind me of what I wanted too but wasn't getting. I'd had enough of talking on the phone about hypothetical movie star boyfriends and their noses; the stuff of my mother's direst warnings was what I most craved.

For that, I turned to my only other friend, Jo. As eleven-year-olds, we had shared a passionate interest in dressing up as pop stars and had videotaped each other miming with tennis racket guitars to Madonna and A-ha, but Jo had moved on since then. Not only was she on the pill, but her boyfriend Adam practically lived with her in the attic of her parents' Notting Hill mansion.

It was Jo who introduced me, that summer, to Adam's best friend, Leon. I had seen him before from a distance, a solid brick wall of a boy, definitely no RP, but my friends thought he was good looking, and their opinions mattered to me as much as my own. One afternoon after school, still in uniform, Jo and I caught the bus to Kensington Park Road, and she let us in through the gate of the communal garden across the road from her house, near where I had once lived. After Dad left, Mum and I had moved to a rented flat in Shepherd's Bush, a small two-bedroom place with a bathroom but no proper living room, only a carpeted extension of the kitchen (stunning view, also, of a slice of railway and the Shepherd's Bush roundabout).

Once inside the garden gate, Jo and I made straight for a thicket of mulberry bushes in the center and Jo parted the leaves with both hands. "Have you ever gotten high?" she said, smiling her dreamy smile.

A fleet of nerves spread through me. Keen as I was for experience, I had read that taking drugs even once was enough to set you on the path toward becoming a junkie—one of those walking skeletons I had seen huddled under the Westway as a kid. "Will I be all right for school in the morning?"

"Of course, silly, it's only hash," said Jo. "Me and Adam do it all the time, practically every day. You'll just feel relaxed, that's all."

Jo was so relaxed that she often spent the entire day in the common room with a hot water bottle on her lap to ease menstrual cramps. She was in the bottom class for French and math, her brain muddled by all that sex and whatever this hash thing was. "Okay," I said.

We found Adam and Leon reclined on their school bags in a circle of grass, fiddling with scraps of paper and something brown and crumbly in a shoe polish tin.

"I love this place," said Jo. "It reminds me of a fairy circle."

When Jo said things like that, it was best not to reply. She went over to Adam and nibbled his lip. "Sweetheart, I missed you so much today."

Adam ruffled her hair and continued with his paper work while I sat on the grass and watched Leon. His fingers were short and stubby, like raw chipolatas, and from the way he smiled at me but said nothing, I gathered he knew this was a setup.

On the first puff nothing happened except that I coughed after trying to smoke it like a cigarette. Jo let the smoke curl out of her mouth in wisps and reclined on the grass, opening her eyes to gaze at the sky. The next time it was my turn, I copied her. Was the sky a more intense shade of blue than it had been five minutes ago? Or was it just that I was looking at it from directly below, and the shift in perspective had made me dizzy?

I tried to concentrate, to note every nuance of the experience so I could write it down later and cross it off my list of things to do that were grown up and deviant, but my senses were unusually dulled. If anything had changed it was that I felt boxed in, paralyzed by a second-by-second sense of déjà vu. Lying there on the grass, I got the strangest idea in my head that I had moved without actually moving. Leon was suddenly in a patch of grass to my right and when he asked me a question, my reply was so muffled I couldn't be sure if he'd heard me.

He tried again, speaking slowly, as though I didn't understand English. "I said, 'How are you feeling?'"

I blinked at him and tried to form a sentence, a simple one that expressed my displeasure that he was lying so close, but my tongue had expanded until it was a tennis ball, jammed into my mouth and glued there with peanut butter. My contact lenses had also dried up and were coming unstuck from my eyeballs, which made me think they were about to pop out. I shut my eyelids against their escape. "Go away," I mouthed, but heard nothing.

Leon's hand landed softly on my thigh, the chipolatas searching for the hem of my gray wool skirt. I tried to roll away from him but must have rolled in the wrong direction because soon, his lips were on mine, his tongue forging ahead, slimy with saliva, past teeth and gums, toward the tennis ball and the peanut butter. Someone was kissing him back, and for a second I felt sorry for her, until I realized it was me.

I tried to clamp my mouth shut.

"I've liked you for ages," Leon said, clawing at my striped school shirt, only to be foiled by a white Cure T-shirt underneath.

"Hmuh," I said, as discouragingly as I could, but not really doing anything to stop him. The part of me that wasn't repulsed was curious to see what he'd do next.

Leon climbed on top of me. He didn't seem to mind that I wasn't kissing back, and several times kissed the side of my face as passionately as if it were my mouth. With one hand under my Cure T-shirt and another on the grass for balance, he floundered away on top of my skirt, pushing his hips backward and forward in a rhythmical motion as if I were a pencil mark he was trying to rub out.

After a long sigh, he fell on me. For a minute or two I stared at the greasy hair near his part and then he abruptly stood up and walked off into the bushes. He had his back to me, but I watched him grab a handful of hydrangea leaves and unzip his pants. When he turned around to see if I was watching, I pretended to be asleep.

The next day at school, Jo rushed up after assembly and congratulated me for giving Leon the best hand job he'd ever had.

"The best what?"

She needled me in the ribs. "You're a dark horse, aren't you?"

Whatever a hand job was, Leon must have wanted another one, because the next night he rang me after getting my phone number from Jo. He made me do all the talking, as though he'd already done the hard work by dialing my number. For the next two weeks, he rang me every night at the same time, until one night I accidentally invited him over.

We smoked hash on the tiny balcony off the kitchen, leaning back against the wall and burying the roach in one of Mum's plants. In my bedroom, I played Leon the new Cure record, even though he said he had already heard it on the radio. We listened to the first side lying on the carpet between the two speakers, the volume turned up so loud it made the windows rattle.

When Leon tried to kiss me, I rolled away. "Wait until we get to side two. It's more romantic."

"Yeah, side two blows my mind," he said.

But when side two came on and Leon tried again, I found I preferred listening to the music without his tongue in my mouth. He started tugging at the hem of my shirt and I was petrified he would expect another hand job that I didn't know how to provide. "I'm starving," I said, pulling the needle off the record halfway through a song. "Would you like a ham sandwich?"

Having a boyfriend felt more like homework, a thing to get through and endure rather than the state of nirvana I had imagined. Most of the time Leon was there, I daydreamed about being by myself. I wondered if other girls felt the same way, or if I had just picked a dud.

I wanted to ask my mother if it was normal to be asked out only by boys you didn't like, but before I did that, I'd have to admit to her that I had gone out with one. It was a conversation that felt long overdue, and I made up my mind to tell her on my next visit to hospital. She had been in for ages this time, but had reassured me this was a good thing, that she was finally getting the right sort of treatment. On that next visit, I was peering at Mum through the door to the oncology ward, thinking of the best way to tell her, when I was blindsided by the odor of rotting fish. Mum was sitting up in bed, waiting for me, and when she saw the look on my face she reached for a can of room freshener that was on the cabinet next to her. "I'm sorry about the smell," she said, spraying her cubicle so much that particles of the stuff settled briefly, like a sleet shower, on our heads. "It ought to be gone in a day or two."

I thought the smell was her leftover dinner, that she'd had something unappetizing to eat, but a few minutes later a nurse walked in with a tray and removed a plastic dome from over a plate of steaming roast meat and vegetables. While Mum was eating it, the fish smell came back, and put me off telling her about Leon. I felt disgusted by her, then ashamed of those feelings, then angry and frustrated at her for not being a normal, healthy mum. Round and round the feelings went, driving me from her bedside.

On subsequent visits, I tried to be more sensitive, but I was hopeless at gauging how ill she really was. I was so used to her puffy, sallow complexion, her bloated thinness, that I couldn't tell if she looked better or worse than the day before—if she was deteriorating or on the mend. What had she even looked like before she got sick? Would she ever not have cancer? Once or twice my mind roamed forward to another possibility, to a future without Mum in it, but the concept was so alien that I couldn't even hold the thought. So long as my mother was in front of me and breathing—however labored or wheezy that breathing was—she had vitality enough to anchor my world.

I turned seventeen then eighteen, stumbled through A levels, finished school. Mum got better then worse then better again. A pile of university prospectuses, still in their envelopes, crowded the side table in the living room. I had decided to take a gap year, but as the summer ended, nothing came along to fill it. I thought about getting a part-time job but didn't know where to start looking.

Autumn arrived, and the pavement outside the cinema filled up with dry, brown leaves. I still spent an unhealthy amount of time there, soaking up the atmosphere, living for Thursday when the new releases came out. One Friday night, Mum and I went to the Shepherd's Bush Odeon to see *Sneakers,* starring River Phoenix, my choice. By then, my crush on him had waned, but like a lapsed member of some brainwashing cult, I still went to see all his movies. Halfway through the film, Mum said she had to leave and would meet me afterward in the lobby. I thought it was because she didn't like the movie, and wished, after she had slipped out, that I'd let her choose something better.

But I was wrong. The film wasn't it. She didn't feel well; she had chills. She'd had that symptom before, but I should have known something more was up from the way she behaved, later that night, as if she was packing to leave the country. She made lists of bills that needed paying—the electricity was on its final red warning—and signed a couple of blank checks. She inventoried the fridge, threw out everything that had gone off, or was about to, and started to tidy the kitchen cupboard. Midway, she gave up, leaving packets of rice and noodles in disarray on the table. Lazy and distracted by a breakout of pimples, of all things, I remember that I watched all this but didn't help. We went to bed early. Mum said she was tired.

She must have called the ambulance sometime in the night, but because she had called it herself, I was lulled into thinking it wasn't an emergency, just an easier way to check in routinely to the hospital. I climbed into the vehicle next to her, half asleep, while Mum surrendered to the gurney as if she was sinking into her seat on the last flight out of town. The ambulance pulled out onto the Shepherd's Bush roundabout. There was no traffic, but the siren switched on, loud and urgent, and that's when I was gripped, finally, by a funguslike dread.

For most of the next day, which we spent in the ICU, Mum was delirious one minute and lucid the next. The last unequivocal conversation we had was about some dry cleaning she wanted me to pick up, then later on, breathing rapidly, her forehead slick with sweat, she stopped making total sense. My father got a mention—"he left you with nothing, the prick"—but so did her childhood cat, who had been run over by the milk truck. "It happened all the time. They smelled the milk." She would form sentences then reject them, as though trying out a new foreign language—the language of the dying. When she did get her words out, she left gaps that I had to sew up. "You'll see," she began at one point, before a long pause, "me again."

"See you where?"

"In the garden."

I assumed she meant heaven, that we'd be reunited there, until I remembered she was an atheist. "But, Mum, you don't believe in God."

"I don't." She laughed—phlegmy, jarring—and batted the skin near her neck. "After the party," she said. "You were wearing the locket."

I wondered if she was out of it, free-associating, or if this was my last chance to confess—or try to. "The morning after the party," I began, "I was fiddling with it when it accidentally broke. I was wearing it when we went down in the bunker but afterward it wasn't around my neck. I think I left it down there—it must have come off."

"No, no, no," said my mother, adamant. "You kept it."

"I didn't," I said. "I really don't know where it is."

Mum hadn't been sad up till then, but quite unexpectedly, her eyes filled with tears, and she turned her head away from me to speak. "But I know you have it. I saw you wearing it."

I was devastated. For more than a decade, Mum hadn't said a word about the locket, but it turned out that all along she'd known I took it—and worse, thought I'd been hiding it from her. "I swear I don't have it," I said, hoping she'd believe me.

Mum didn't say anything more or even look at me again, and a woman in a white coat fiddled with the tube that was taped to her arm. When she was done, Mum sighed, and her hand I'd been holding went limp. Her chest heaved and her eyes were still open, but her gaze was glassy, remote.

"We're doing all we can," said the woman in the white coat. "You should get some rest." She signaled to an armchair in the corner of the room but offered no clues as to how I might sit in it without letting go of my mother's hand. It didn't occur to me to move the chair.

Parts of that night, I missed. Important parts, like the moment Mum died. I remembered things leading up to it: hushed voices, interludes of calamity followed by long periods of staring at the lino floor, so highly polished I could see up my own skirt. But however many times I sidled up to it from different angles, the part where she took her last breath remained stubbornly blank. To me it was a moment of failure, a lapse in concentration that cost me the game. I feel ashamed of the lapse, almost fraudulent, as though I have only been pretending I was there.

Other moments, other sights, couldn't be gotten rid of, left behind pockmarks: Mum's face set in a yellow, waxwork mask. The strange-smelling treacle that spread out on the sheet from beneath her until it was noticed and then covered by a nurse.

They let me sit with her for a long time. I was given a cup of tea and a biscuit, neither of which I touched.

Sepsis, the doctors said. After years of illness, her immune system was spent. They pumped her full of antibiotics, tried frantically to find something that would help her fight the infection, but even as they were pumping, I think the doctors knew that what they were doing was futile. It was all for show—a show for me, I supposed.

When it was over, a friend of my mother's picked me up from the hospital. I didn't know what day it was or how long we had been there, cut off from time in the bright, windowless rooms of the ICU. The friend drove me home but wouldn't let me stay there on my own. By the door, we had a standoff. I didn't want her to come in; she insisted. I gave in, but stubbornly ignored her, went straight to Mum's room, shut the door, and climbed into her bed. The sheets felt clammy, earthbound, but the surrounding walls were sheened in silver, and I thought it was Mum, that she had manifested in the wallpaper as a kind of seraphim. I didn't want to close my eyes on her, to abandon her, but I'd been up for days and was quickly mown down by an unstoppable freight train of sleep.

In the morning, the wallpaper seraphim had gone, and a little after nine Granny arrived to take care of the rest. I stayed in Mum's room, wearing her clothes, while she attacked the flat, her grief masquerading as a cleaning hurricane. I found a hatbox that I thought had been full of Mum's hats, but it was brimming with medication in brown plastic bottles, enough analgesics to relieve the whole street of pain. In the same hatbox were mementoes from my childhood: a lock of fine hair, tied with a ribbon; the plastic identity bracelet from around my newborn wrist; and wrapped in a tissue, a clutch of milk teeth. At the sight of the teeth, I felt a muted surge of adrenaline and tipped them out on the bed. There were a couple of tiny pointed fangs, and some flat, straight ones in varying sizes. I wondered if any of them were the ones I had brought up from the bunker in the folds of my dress, but I did not have the heart, that morning, to examine them, and I never saw them again.

I refused to let Granny hug me, but she was only the first to invade. Starting that morning and continuing for days, hordes of people arrived with casseroles and cards and flowers. So many bouquets arrived by courier van that they had to be flung in the bath. Who were all these people and where had they been for the last two years? I didn't think, in that whole time, we'd had anyone over or received a single invitation to dinner. At first I tolerated the smothering, the condolences from strangers, but as the days wore on, I grew belligerent and locked myself in Mum's room. That's when I found her building society book, and a note that said: "For Suki: my password, just in case." So she had known. She had made preparations. She had known I would come in here looking for a way out.

By the day of the funeral, I'd shut down completely. Why had everyone come to inspect my grief? And why did they keep trying to feed me? Didn't they know I wasn't hungry, that I might never eat again? When some relatives of my mother's asked if I'd like to go and live with them in Edinburgh, I was openly rude. "Scotland," I said. "Are you kidding?"

I had already bought my plane ticket with the money from Mum's savings account. The flat we lived in was rented; I thought Granny could sort through the chattels.

Not long after Mum was cremated, I caught the Piccadilly line to Heathrow Airport with a single suitcase, no ashes. Briefly, as the plane wheels lifted off the tarmac, a shadow of regret passed over me, but I blamed it at the time on shifting air pressure, a moment of queasiness as my body adjusted to the change in altitude.

CHAPTER TEN

London, 2003

FOR FIVE OR SIX HOURS after I had seen the old garden from Harold's bedroom window, I remained under the covers in a tight ball, coming down off the fear and confusion that had gripped me like a fever. Explanations came and went in that time, but none that made sense, and as light started creeping into the room I decided that the garden had been an apparition, an elaborate hoax on the part of my imagination. I had seen the air-raid shelter because I wanted to see it, not because it was there.

Still, getting out of bed that morning, I approached the window in a cautious mood. What if the apparition hadn't gone away? I needn't have worried—there was nothing out of the ordinary to see. The garden was back to the way it had been the day before, terra-cotta pots in two parallel lines reaching out from the back door, surrounded by paths made from chalk. The only thing there that I hadn't noticed before was an ornamental orange tree, clipped into submission, in keeping with the garden's unbending design. A few months ago I'd looked upon that symmetry and loathed it, but that morning I found it a reassuring sign that the world was, after all, a sane and rational place.

Just to be certain, though, I decided to go down and see the garden for myself. But first I put my head through Peggy's door, and listened for reassuring sounds. Yes, she was out for the count, her breathing punctuated by something that was either a trembling snore or flatulence.

Pippa had left a note to say the keys to the garden were on a small rack in the kitchen, and I took them and went down the communal staircase, meaning to let myself out through the back door. Only, where I had remembered there being a back door, there was none. The communal stairs stopped at ground level, and the end of the hallway was blocked off with a wall. To get out into the garden, I'd have to use the main gate on Kensington Park Road. It was inconvenient to have to walk along the street and around the corner just to get into the garden, and I realized why I'd hardly ever seen Peggy or Pippa out there.

The morning was crisp, not at all summery, and as I crossed the lawn to find a patch of sun, I recalled the strange humidity in the night—so different from the current dry atmosphere. At that early hour, the garden was empty save for a man smoking a cigarette while his dog squatted at the base of a tree. He wore pajamas under his jacket and looked both surprised and displeased to see me. When the dog stood up, he stubbed out his cigarette on the tree trunk and quickly moved on.

I hadn't visited the communal garden since childhood and was surprised by how small it was. Running wild and unsupervised around it with the other children who lived on our street, it had seemed enormous, a continent of jungle and grassland with areas we'd mapped out, prosaically, as Big Wood, Small Wood, and the Dark Forest, where none of us dared to go. I'd played uneasily with the other children, their savage games shocked me—and I was equally fearful of being left out. One of the boys always had matches to set fire to anything that wasn't sopping wet, and both boys and girls had taken turns to squat under the drooping willows of Big Wood to see who could do the biggest shit. I'd not told my mother about those games in case she forbade me to play in the garden, but I once came home with a scorch mark on my dress and she had wheedled it out of me, while I cried, that we had been lighting fires.

I stood on the communal lawn and viewed our old flat from the garden side. The patio gate was invitingly open, but I walked past it a few times before working up the nerve to go in. In the few days I'd been staying at Peggy's, I'd seen no one coming or going from the basement, and that morning all the windows and doors at the rear were heavily curtained and shut. It was impossible to tell if the people who lived there were away or just sleeping, but I told myself I wasn't really trespassing because it had once been my home. I decided to make my visit a quick one though, just in case, and slipped through the gate and walked hastily over to where the entrance to the air-raid shelter had once been. I ran my foot through what was now a chalk path. Some of the gravel displaced, and I saw that it was only ornamental, a thin layer of white stuff spread over concrete. Unconvinced that I had been searching in the right area, I rubbed away the chalk in a few more patches, but found no metal plate underneath, just a continuation of what appeared to be newly laid concrete. Satisfied the hatch was no longer there, but also slightly disappointed, I smoothed over the chalk as best I could and made my way over to the French doors, still in place, but freshly painted in chic gunmetal gray.

"Excuse me," said a sharp voice from above. "But can I help you?"

I looked up to where a woman leaned out of the first-floor window—what had been my parents' bedroom after the flat was turned into a maisonette. Her hair was wrapped in a fluffy white towel, and she wore a matching robe.

"I'm sorry," I called up. "I'm staying upstairs with Peggy."

She frowned. "We don't know anyone upstairs."

"I used to live in the basement flat. There was an air-raid shelter in the garden. Do you know if it's still here?"

"An air-raid shelter?" she repeated. "I don't think so."

"Do you know if it was filled in?"

"I'm not sure I know what you mean."

"Never mind." I made my way toward the gate, and tried to end the encounter on a friendly note. "I like what you've done with the garden. It looks really smart."

"We haven't touched it," she said. "We're renting."

I promptly left the garden and decided to walk down to the delicatessen on Chepstow Road to grab a takeaway coffee. The place thronged with people in suits grabbing breakfast on their way to work, their sense of urgency palpable. Next to them I felt tranquilized, and realized I hadn't left Peggy's flat for more than two days, nor seen or spoken to anyone other than the old woman or her daughter. My world had reduced to the size of a dot, and the shrinkage felt permanent, irreversible.

When I returned to Ladbroke Gardens, I found Peggy in her room, down on her hands and knees and wielding a large pair of dressmaking scissors. In the other hand, she held a necklace, a long string of pearls with a diamante pendant. She appeared to be trying to unpick the curtains, but had so far succeeded only in cutting a large hole. The scissors she was using were serrated, and the curtain, where she'd hacked at it, had a manic, toothy grin. She hadn't heard me calling out her name after I let myself into the flat, or even coming into her room, and when she finally saw me standing next to her, she dropped the scissors in fright.

"Hillary!" she exclaimed. "I forgot you were here."

"I wasn't," I said, not bothering to correct her. "I went out to get a coffee. Do you need a hand? Those scissors look rather sharp."

"No, dear, I'm quite all right," she said, stuffing the necklace into the pocket of her dressing gown and casually moving the scissors out of sight. "But I would so love a cup of tea, if you wouldn't mind?"

"Sure." I lingered, hoping she would explain what she was up to, but it was clear she was waiting for me to leave.

No wonder I was losing it, spending all my time with an old bat who had taken to secretly chopping up her own curtains. Then and there, I resolved to try harder to reestablish myself in London, to rebuild a normal life, but before I could take even the first step toward doing so, Pippa came round that afternoon with another offer she was adamant I should accept. She wanted me to stay in their flat for the month of August while the family was in Greece. I thought it odd that she had left it so late to arrange a house sitter, but, delighted to be able to put off paying rent or asking for favors from long-forgotten friends, accepted right away. Then Caleb, who had come along reluctantly to visit his grandmother, piped up, "Don't we normally just put the alarm on?"

"We don't normally go away for such a long time," said Pippa, resolutely. She went to give Peggy her bath, leaving Caleb and me alone in the kitchen. He had a black eye, quite a shiner, the kind that you really only got in a fight.

"I'd hate to see the other chap," I said.

"What's that supposed to mean?"

"Only that I bet you roughed him up for doing that."

"Fuck you," he said, so aggressively that I guessed the opposite was true. Pippa hadn't been specific about the trouble Caleb was in at school, but I wondered if he was being bullied.

"You must be looking forward to getting away," I said. "Having a break from school." And so ended our conversation.

"Going away with the family isn't a break," he said. "It's a fucking nightmare."

I was surprised and relieved when the rest of my stay at Peggy's passed without incident. Amanda returned to resume her duties, ruby red after a week in Marbella, and Pippa came to fetch me and my suitcases in her green Citroen 2CV, a car whose nearest mechanical relative was the tin can. When we arrived at their place, Ari hardly looked up from the TV and Caleb was nowhere in sight. Without fanfare, Pippa showed me to my room on the top floor, on the same landing on which, on my first visit, I had been tantalized by a glimpse of the ladder to the roof. That day the ladder was stowed, which intrigued me even more.

My room was small but cozy, with bare floorboards and a window that looked out over the garden. It was furnished with a single bed, a chair, and a desk with drawers, but I liked the austerity. Compared to Peggy's, the room verged on hospital clean and I looked forward to settling in, to sleeping well in the chaste narrow bed.

"There's a wardrobe," said Pippa, opening it. "But I'm afraid it isn't completely empty. Some of my old junk is in there—a few boxes and clothes I can't bear to get rid of." The boxes were old tea chests like the ones my parents had stored stuff in, the same logo stenciled on the side. Pippa took out an armful of garments to make room for mine and I realized she was as much of a hoarder as Peggy. After taking out the clothes, she couldn't shut the closet door; it didn't seem to fit properly in its frame. "One more thing," she said, pointing to a small door I hadn't noticed when we came into the room. "The attic bathroom, used by his lordship, who is not the tidiest or most considerate person in the world."

She opened the door and we looked into the tiny bathroom at a cramped shower stall, toilet, and miniature sink, then through an open door to the space beyond, where Caleb was sprawled on his bed, punishing an air guitar in front of a blaring stereo. He was really getting into it, contorting his face with heavy-metal menace.

When Caleb saw us staring at him, he hurled himself off the bed. "Fucking retards!" he yelled, slamming his body into the door to shut it. "Fuck off! Fuck you!"

Pippa flinched at the abuse, but she couldn't help smiling, and even though I could tell Caleb was mortified, I laughed too. "You'll have to work out some kind of system," she said. "Or use the bathroom downstairs."

"There's no lock?"

"Caleb shut himself in there one day about a year ago and refused to go to school, so we had it taken out." She lowered her voice, conspiratorially. "He's not exactly thrilled about sharing his floor with anyone, but he'll get over it. He's really such a sweetheart once you get to know him."

I wondered how that was ever going to happen.

Later on, after supper, I unpacked my suitcases, lined up the few books I had along the narrow windowsill, and tried to hang my clothes in what remained of the closet. Caleb came through to tell me we should keep our respective bathroom doors closed at all times, and that I should always knock before I went into the bathroom, even if I thought no one was in there.

"Suits me," I said, and waited for him to skulk back to his bedroom, but instead he hovered in the doorway. "You can come in," I said, eventually. "I won't bite."

"I don't want to," he said. "But this used to be my room."

"So?"

"I had to give it up so you could stay."

"Well, thanks," I said, and turned away, expecting him to leave. But he didn't, he just stood in the doorway, openly taking an inventory of my belongings.

"Do you keep a diary?" he said, pointing to the pile of notebooks in my suitcase.

His impudence was annoying me, so I decided to annoy him back. "What music were you listening to?"

He reddened. "Why do you want to know?"

"I don't," I said. "I just didn't pick you as the hair-metal type."

He went back to his room and I heard no more from him. Before going to sleep, I wrote for a while in my journal, breaking in a new notebook because the old one was full. The house was quiet when I finished; I had stayed up later than I thought. The room was stuffy and I opened a window and leaned out. Down below, the back gardens of Ladbroke Grove stretched out in neat compartments, separated by brick walls and the occasional tree. In the neighboring garden, there was even a vegetable patch, and I marveled that anyone would want to eat whatever produce managed to grow there. I looked around the bare room, and my gaze kept returning to the closet. What if those tea chests really had belonged to my parents? What if they'd accidentally left something in there? The next thing I knew, I had flung open the wardrobe and was opening one of the boxes, convinced of the possibility.

The first yielded paint-splattered clothes and a jumble sale of unmatched cutlery, saucers, and cups. Pippa's stuff. The second tea chest was heavier, and difficult to drag out of the cupboard. While I was shoving, one of its metal strips scraped loudly against the doorway, giving me quite a fright. I stopped to see if the noise had woken up anyone, and sure enough, a thumping noise came from Caleb's room.

He went into the bathroom, and I leaped up to turn off the light in case he noticed I was still awake. The walls were thin, and I could hear a long stream of urine splashing into the bowl. He didn't flush the toilet, but went back into his room and dragged what sounded like a heavy object in front of his door. His room fell quiet, and I turned my attention back to the tea chest. I was being nosy, but my urge to explore the tea chest and find something that belonged to my parents was stronger than my willpower to resist it. Before long, I'd prised open the lid.

Art materials took up the top half of the chest, a raggedy canvas, rolled up, and a box of crusted oil pastels. Underneath those was a spindly wooden mannequin with movable arms and legs, the kind we used to practice life drawing with. I'd been given one for my birthday once, when I was going through an art phase, and had experimented with it enthusiastically, bending it into different poses, only to discover that its flat wooden chest and mechanical joints were nothing like the human body.

When I reached into the box again, my hand jumped back from what it touched: a strange, hard object with a firm center and protruding stems, like a starfish or a giant tarantula made of wood. I stared into the chest, hardly breathing, but it was too dark by the wardrobe to see anything, so I brought over the bedside lamp and shone it into the box. There, in a black velvet glove, was a hand with long, thin fingers, about the same size as mine. I reached into the box and picked it up, noticing how little it weighed. The glove peeled off easily, and inside was a jointed wooden hand, also used for life drawing. We'd had one of those in the art room at school.

I put the hand back in its glove and held it as though we were shaking on a deal. The gesture was enough to bring back a sharp recollection of the past, and briefly the wooden hand turned into my hand in the cupboard, the one that had untied the bows on my dresses. I experienced then a strange jolt, not déjà vu but its opposite, a conviction that the way I had always remembered the hand might be wrong. What if I had seen this wooden hand at Pippa's and had transferred it, in my imagination, to the boiler cupboard? The theory seemed plausible, but it didn't resonate except in a cold, scientific way—and the hand in the cupboard had been neither of those things. It had been warm, as human and alive as I was. But how could that be?

One by one, I returned the objects to the tea chest and found that I was shaking. Discovering the mannequin hand had unnerved me to the core. Not just because it was creepy, but because it had rattled my sense of certainty that how I remembered the past was how it actually was. Now when I thought of the hand, my memories of it were unmoored.

I climbed into bed but saw that I hadn't put away the tea chest. It was out in the middle of the room, and behind it, I had left the wardrobe doors wide open.

I had to put the tea chest away before morning, or risk Pippa seeing it, but there was something about the wardrobe that made me not want to go near it. The black space between the two open doors no longer seemed neutral, but pulsed with a presence that was strangely malevolent. Worse than that, it seemed to be exerting a magnetic pull.

Keeping one eye on the wardrobe, I hurried into the bathroom and closed the door behind me. What was I so afraid of? I tried to breathe it out, to talk myself down, and as I did so, I realized I was exhausted, worn out with anxiety—so much so that the floor between shower stall and sink looked inviting. When I lay down, I noticed how grubby it was, dirt crammed into the grooves between the tiles and tiny coils of hair behind the column that supported the sink. But with one glance I was able to take in the entire room, including both doors, firmly shut, and the thought of that was comfort enough to lull me into sleep.

I woke up when Caleb, in striped pajamas, walked into the bathroom, eyes sleepy, a hand clamped over his crotch. He didn't see me until he had stumbled into my head. "Fuck!"

My embarrassment equaled his, and I rolled out of the way. "Sorry, I fell asleep."

"In the bathroom?"

"I guess I must have been sleepwalking." I had never sleepwalked in my life.

We returned to our rooms to regroup, then avoided each other for several days.

As a guest in Pippa's house, I never quite felt sure where the boundaries were. She'd glibly told me on many occasions to make myself at home, but hadn't meant it literally, as I discovered to my cost. The second or third morning I was there, I came downstairs to find a note pinned to the fridge telling me to help myself to food, except for the leftover lasagna, which was being saved for Caleb's dinner. The note put me on edge, and from then on I was careful not to eat or drink too much, except for coffee, which I allowed myself almost unlimited quantities of. The disturbance in the wardrobe continued to bother me, and I spent two more fitful nights on the bathroom floor, and a third downstairs on the couch with the TV on low so as not to wake anyone. After a week of this, I was so utterly frazzled from accumulated sleep deprivation that I wasn't sure if the disturbance had caused my insomnia or if it was the other way round. I didn't mention anything to Pippa because I didn't want her to think I was a nut job; if that happened, I'd be out on the street.

One night I got back from a walk in the park—I had been

trying to wear myself out with exercise—to find Pippa wrestling with a basket of washing. She was trying to separate Caleb's socks and underwear from Ari's slightly bigger ones, and when she said, "It's make your own dinner night, the servants are on strike," I thought she meant I hadn't been pulling my weight around the house.

Downstairs in the kitchen, Ari told me to help myself to baked beans, which he'd heated up in a pot on the stove. "Finish them up," he said, handing me a bowl and pointing to a loaf of sliced bread for toasting. I ate in the living room, watching TV with Ari, and just as I was finishing, Alana finally returned one of the dozens of calls I had made to her mobile.

"I'm sorry it's taken me so long," she said. "I've been terrifically busy."

"Me too," I said, though the opposite was true. I tried to arrange another outing, but Alana was booked up, and sounded stressed. "Is everything okay?" I said. "Is it Steve?"

"Steve? No, he's great." She softened. "Actually, he's lovely. He took me to Paris for the weekend."

"Wow, he didn't seem like the romantic type."

"Exactly what type did he seem like," she said, unexpectedly sharply, "to you?"

I had offended her, in a way that wasn't easy to put right. "He seemed nice," I said. "Really nice. A top bloke."

"You never liked nice," she said.

The edge was still in her voice, but as I opened my mouth to defend myself, Alana cut me off.

"I was going to get it over with the other night," she went on. "But you were so drunk I didn't see the point."

"I'm sorry about that," I said, wincing. "I was excited about hanging out with you—I got carried away. There's no one else I can talk to about how weird things have been lately—moving here, being unemployed, not having anywhere to live. I have terrible insomnia—"

She interrupted me. "Please don't start."

"Start what?"

"Telling me everything that's wrong with your life. You're just making it worse for yourself, and you have no idea how draining it is for everyone else."

I was about to defend myself by explaining that my life really *was* messed up right now—that I wasn't exaggerating—but stopped just in time. "We've been friends since we were fourteen," I said. "You know I'm not always like this."

She said nothing—passively disagreeing with me.

"You think I've always been draining?"

"You've always been intense," she said. "Yes."

In a matter of seconds, my closest girlhood friendship revised itself, then collapsed. "Why didn't you tell me?"

She sighed, as though she couldn't believe I didn't already know. "Because I felt sorry for you."

Sorry for me because my mother had cancer and was dying? Or because I was such a loser? I didn't have the stomach to ask. "Well, you had me fooled," I said, struggling to keep the hurt out of my voice.

"I better go," said Alana, sounding relieved. "I'm sorry if I've upset you."

I put the phone down. My jaw was stinging, about to crack. Pippa was heading toward me with a saucepan thrust out in front of her.

"You ate the last of the baked beans," she said. "What's Caleb going to have for dinner?"

I looked into the dirty saucepan. "Ari told me to eat them," I said, backing away from her and trying to leave the room before I cried. Halfway up the first flight of stairs, I started to lose it, and by the time I had slammed the door to my room and flung myself on the bed, I was a puddle of childish sobs and dramatic, shivery wails.

Pippa had followed me up the stairs and started patting the bedclothes, trying to find me, but that only made me curl up in a ball and pull them more closely around myself. "It wasn't my fault!" I cried out. "Leave me alone."

"Listen to me, Suki," said Pippa, whose persistence had finally gotten past the duvet. "I didn't realize Ari told you to eat them."

"Go away," I said, covering my face.

"Come on, Suki, I'm just trying to help."

"I don't need your help," I said, staying covered. I knew I was being ridiculous and immature, but it wasn't enough to snap me out of it.

"You have to let someone in," said Pippa.

Under the duvet, I froze, listening, cringing.

"I know you've had a hard life," she continued. "But at some point you've just got to let it go and move on."

I didn't go downstairs again that night, and woke up the next morning on the floor of the attic bathroom with my legs stretched into the shower stall. A damp towel was wedged under my head and my shoulders were covered by a threadbare satin quilt, though I did not remember fetching either of them. When I pushed open Caleb's door, his room was empty, his faded superhero bedspread in a heap on the floor. I looked in the mirror and hardly recognized the person there. Excessive crying had rinsed the color from my cheeks and left red rings around my eyes. Reluctantly I went downstairs, where Pippa was bustling in the kitchen, listening to a radio drama and cooking scrambled eggs. She said nothing about the night before and quickly turned down the radio when she saw me. "Sorry about the racket," she said. "*The Archers Omnibus* is my only addiction. There's coffee in the pot if you want some."

"Thanks, it smells great."

When I sat down at the table, she put a plate of scrambled eggs in front of me and told me to eat up. Dressed in his soccer kit, Caleb stomped in from somewhere and devoured his own plateful of eggs in about three mouthfuls. When Pippa went into the kitchen to fetch the coffeepot, he briefly looked over at me. "You were sleeping in the bathroom again," he said.

"Did you put the quilt over me?"

"Don't be stupid." I thought he looked a little flustered when Pippa came back, but I didn't challenge him. I was too tired, too shamed. Caleb got up, left his dirty plate on the table, and tied a sweatshirt round his hips, preparing to leave.

"Are you playing on Wormwood Scrubs again?" said Pippa.

Caleb ignored her.

"Please don't go near the prison," she said, as if he had responded. "And don't hang about afterward smoking—even if that's what the other chaps do." Caleb rolled his eyes, but Pippa continued, still undaunted, "And if it starts to rain, shelter in a bus stop until it passes."

"For God's sake, Mum, it's the middle of summer." Caleb was already in the doorway, but he paused there and smiled sweetly. "Can I have a fiver for lunch after the game? A bunch of the guys are getting burgers." He picked up Pippa's purse from the hall table and handed it to her.

"I wish you'd get something healthy," said Pippa, passing him a tenner, and gratefully receiving her reward, a peck on her cheek. When he'd gone, she said, "He's a little sod, but I can't bring myself to say no to him. One day, when you're a mother, you'll understand."

She seemed sad, resigned, and I felt ashamed at having behaved so childishly the evening before. "I'm sorry about last night," I said. "My best friend dumped me."

While Pippa listened, I recounted my conversation with Alana, and began to understand a little of what Alana had been trying to tell me. The epiphany was an uncomfortable one; a glaring blind spot had been shown to me, and my first thought was that I wanted to see Alana and behave in a different way. Only it was too late for that. Even if she agreed to meet up, it would be futile to try to get her to change her mind about me. I could be different in the next friendship, but that one was history.

Pippa thought so too. "Not all friendships last. Do you remember Lulu? Impossibly long legs, and a gorgeous face to go with them . . ."

"Of course," I said. "She came to a party at our flat. I think my dad had a crush on her."

Pippa laughed. "Everyone had a crush on her—she was exquisite, and a total nightmare to be best friends with. If you ever fancied a bloke, you couldn't let her within a hundred miles of him."

And yet it had been Pippa who'd scored at my parents' party. "That was a wild night," I said. "Or at least it seemed that way to me."

Pippa drummed her fingers excitedly on the table. "Oh yes! *That* party. Lulu was a little minx that night." She blushed. "And so was I."

"I suppose she's married now too, with kids?"

"I don't know," said Pippa. "I haven't seen her for about ten years."

I was surprised, and then sad. "How did that happen?"

"Lulu always had men hanging off her—miniskirts and stilettos were invented for girls like her—but she could never make anything last. I don't even think she liked men all that much. When we were young, it didn't matter, it was all just fun. But we got older, and everyone settled down except her. She kept on partying, not just at the weekends but all the time. I think she started doing lots of coke, and fell in with a crowd in King's Cross who were into hard drugs. Whenever I bumped into her, she asked me for money, and if I didn't give her any, she'd take off. The last time I saw her she was sitting outside a tube station—I went up to talk to her—and she was so out of it she didn't even recognize me."

"And that was the last time you saw her?"

Pippa was rueful for a moment, lost in reminiscence. "I think she might have overdosed, but I'd rather not know."

We began to reminisce about the babysitting days, and Pippa's description of me was one I hardly recognized. "You were very high spirited," she said. "Always dressing up and entertaining everyone with your imaginary worlds."

I wondered what had happened to her, this other, more charming me, whether she was gone for good or if it was possible to revive her—if she was in fact waiting patiently to be brought back to life.

Not two days later, Caleb decided to exert his will on a larger scale. The first sign of trouble was his persistent uncooperativeness in packing, even though the family was leaving in three days and would be gone for a month. At first Pippa thought he couldn't be bothered, but when she started doing it for him, he sabotaged her efforts and hid all the clothes she had packed. Then, when his passport went missing, Caleb said he knew nothing about it, but after turning his room upside down, Ari found the missing passport tucked into an old comic. When they confronted him about what he was up to, Caleb announced he wasn't going to Greece. Ari was furious and took a swing at Caleb before Pippa got in the way and tried to calm things down. Then Ari exploded at both of them.

I heard nothing more about it until Pippa knocked on my door, late, two nights later. She said she hadn't discussed it yet with Ari but she had been thinking that it might not be so bad if Caleb stayed in London with me. I thought it was a terrible idea, but I just said, "Does Caleb know about your plan?"

"It was his idea," she said. "At first I thought it was too much responsibility to put on you. But then I came round to the idea. You might be a good influence on him—he might open up once we're not around."

"And Ari?" There was no use trying to talk Pippa out of it—I could tell she had already relented—and I was grabbing at the only straw I could think of.

"He'll get over it. The second he sits down to an ouzo with his brother."

Two days later, with Ari in a funk, they left without Caleb. I took them to the airport, and drove the car back on my own. I had never driven before in London and it took me twice as long to get back as it had to get out there; I followed the wrong lane out of a roundabout, and wound up south of the river in a suburb that might have been Putney or Barnes. By the time I got back to the flat, it was dark, and Caleb was hunched in front of the TV in the living room with the lights off, frantically pushing buttons on a gaming console. On the screen, a lone high school jock was fighting off an army of bloated, pale green Samurai warriors. I picked up the box next to the console. "Samurai Zombies?"

"Promise you won't tell Mum. She thinks it's too violent."

"I expect I'll tell her right away—the instant she calls."

"What?" he said, losing concentration long enough to meet a grisly end. "Fuck!" he said. "I was nearly on the next level."

"I'm not going to promise anything."

"What?" He looked at me again—shocked that I had disagreed with him—but I had decided, on the way back from the airport, that the only way I could survive the next month was to show him who was boss.

"You heard me," I said, and went upstairs.

Ari had told me I could use the car while they were away, but in Central London there was no point in driving, so I went into their bedroom to leave the keys there. Their room looked like a rogue tornado had passed through, and I wondered if I ought to tidy up, just a little. I hadn't really been in their bedroom before and couldn't resist looking round and trying out the bed, which was an enormous king-size futon, of the kind I hadn't seen since the late nineties. The futon hadn't been made, and the bedding smelled a little funky, but after all the sleepless nights I'd had, it was devilishly inviting, and I lay down on it, meaning to rest only for a moment. But once I was lying down, all the exhaustion of the last few weeks arrived at once, and I succumbed to a kind of half coma. Must get up, I told myself as I relived the day as a sequence of increasingly wonky moments—getting squashed by Peggy's antique trunk in the back of the car, catching a plane with no wings, driving off the side of Putney Bridge . . . and then, as I got really woozy, I imagined someone was lying next to me on the futon, a man who smelled of Christmas morning—that delicious aroma I remembered from when I was a kid. I didn't know who the man was, but he smelled so good that when he rolled over and started to kiss me, I put my hand on the small of his back and pressed my mouth into his. All at once the man's back narrowed, and the bones shrank under his skin, and I realized he was a boy, that it was Caleb I was kissing–Caleb who tasted so good.

It was such a vivid, startling dream that it propelled me out of sleep and off the bed in the same instant. My pulse raced as

I looked around the room, but it was empty, static. No one else had been in the bed except me. The door was still closed, and beyond it I could hear the steady click, click, beep of a gaming console downstairs. It was nothing more than a dream, I told myself, just a man morphing into a boy who happened to be Caleb.

I was tired, and losing it—nothing that couldn't be fixed by a good night's sleep. I went downstairs to make a cup of milky cocoa to help me nod off, and walked past Caleb, who was sitting in front of the TV, engrossed in his game. He didn't look up, but I thought he was going to, that somehow he knew about the dirty dream but was pretending he didn't.

Standing by the kettle, waiting for it to boil, I tried not to look at him, but he seemed always to be at the edge of my field of vision. Without Ari and Pippa there to act as a buffer, the flat seemed smaller, too intimate, and I wasn't sure that Caleb and I should be in it alone.

The kettle pinged, and I jumped as though I had been caught in a compromising act. I had been meaning to offer Caleb a cup of cocoa but changed my mind in case he read more into the gesture than was meant. Instead I fled upstairs with my drink in hand, spilling a little on the carpet, and not even wishing him good night.

CHAPTER ELEVEN

London, 1993

THE FLIGHT TO NEW ZEALAND was long but not long enough to account for the shock of how different it was from England. I hadn't prepared myself for arrival in a strange country—had thought of nothing but fleeing—and the only thing the same was the language. Auckland was a wall of moisture, bright and hot, and I sleepwalked through customs, where men in short shorts and long socks inspected my bags for insects. I wheeled my trolley out from behind a screen and emerged in the arrivals hall, where a crowd of eager faces intently scrutinized my features before passing me over, for the next new arrival.

The ugliness of Auckland shocked me: suburb after suburb of sand-colored bungalows, their newness punctuated by short, spiky plants and an occasional outburst of trees. It was drizzling and sunny at the same time, and on the backseat of the minibus, I broke into a sweat without lifting a finger: I couldn't, it was stuck to the seat.

In downtown Auckland I checked into a backpacker hostel

on a street with massage parlors and strip joints at one end, banks and law firms at the other. I asked for a single room and was shown to a shoe box on the sixth floor with a window overlooking a ventilation shaft, down which people had thrown Coke cans and cigarette butts that were impossible to retrieve. Outside my window, an air-conditioning unit sounded like it was trying to take off, and the air was thick with insects.

Time slipped through the cracks. I woke and thought I'd wet the bed, but it was only sweat. I took a shower but had no soap, I couldn't get clean, couldn't wake up. I lay in bed trying not to think about either Mum or food, but ended up alternating between the two until I had a headache. Laughter burst from the corridor, British and Swedish accents, the sound track to international sex. I drank a whole liter of water and went back to bed.

When I woke, my eyes were gummed together. Cramps squeezed my stomach, and I felt light-headed. Dressing in whatever was close at hand, I went outside. The pavement was melting tarmac, and when I looked into the distance, objects shimmered as if they were underwater. The sun was so bright it obliterated the edges of things, and my eyes squinted shut in protest. I found a small supermarket and bought cheese, chocolate milk, and a loaf of bread, and when I paid with a hundred-dollar note from the airport exchange, the man at the counter commented in a language I didn't understand. Back in my room, I stuffed the bread and cheese into my mouth in pieces, washed down with milk from the carton.

For another two days, I stayed in my room: dozing, thinking, sweating, eating, until I started to feel as if I had fused with the bed. On the third day, I got up in the late afternoon, took a hot shower, dressed in decent clothes, and went downstairs to find a phone book. Dozens of Pipers were listed in the Auckland directory, but none with the first name Ludwig. My father, whose grandparents were German, had been named after the famous composer, but only official documents used the elongated version.

The discovery that his name wasn't listed was more crushing than it ought to have been, and I realized that looking him up in the phone book had been the extent of my plan to find him. I had no idea what to do next, so I went into a bar and ordered a Mexican beer. The barman wouldn't give me one; he insisted I drink New Zealand beer instead. "It's the best in the world," he said.

Unwilling to make a scene, I handed over a ten-dollar bill and went to sit by the window, as far away from him as I could get. The brown beer was foul, with a heavy, bitter aftertaste, but it was cold and I drank it thirstily. A tall man with angular shoulders and dark hair was in the bar, and as soon as I saw him I knew he would come over. He had heard me talking to the barman and asked what part of London I was from.

"West," I said. "I went to school in Hammersmith." Even then, I knew better than to mention Notting Hill.

"That explains your posh accent."

"I'm not posh."

"'I'm not posh,'" he said, mocking me.

I stood up to leave. I was way too tired to have a sense of humor.

"I'm sorry," he said. "It's just that I love the way you speak. It's so quaint." He placed a hand on my upper arm. "Please. Let me buy you a drink."

Unused to day drinking, after two gin and tonics, I was tipsy, and he'd told me his name was Hamish. He claimed to be an actor, but I didn't believe him. He didn't have the right sort of face. But I told him I was looking for my father, and he suggested I try the library, where they had national phone directories, fewer than twenty for the whole country. "New Zealand is a series of villages," he said. "Sewn down the middle by a two-lane highway."

"You make it sound like a sock."

Hamish laughed. There was something about him I liked, and when he offered to take me on a scenic drive of Auckland, I said yes. The gin had made me reckless, but I sobered up once we were in his car and the doors were shut and locked. He drove us along the waterfront, past thousands of yachts, their white masts jousting against the horizon. He told me one in eight people in Auckland owned a boat.

"Is that an official statistic?"

"Every year, they count."

"They do not."

"They did once, in the eighties."

The marina ended in an industrial port, containers stacked like Lego bricks, their sides painted in wacky Russian fonts. Behind them, a cone-shaped island rose out of the bay, and Hamish told me it was a volcano with a Maori name, Rangitoto.

"I hope you're kidding," I said.

"Don't worry, it's extinct," he said. "Dormant for thousands of years."

We drove through undulating streets, past houses that were prettier and more colonial than the ones I'd seen on the way in from the airport. The car climbed a steep road toward the summit of a hill, and Hamish said it was another extinct volcano. At the top, we got out of the car and peered into a crater cup filled with grass and sheep. A strong wind blew me into Hamish, and he put his arm around me. I asked if we could go.

We drove in silence to the hostel, and when we arrived Hamish wanted to come in.

"No," I said.

"I just want to keep talking," he said.

When I opened the door, he followed me in. The shoe box, with two people in it, was crowded, the single bed the only place to sit. We had nothing to say, and I suddenly felt like I had been shot with a tranquilizer gun.

"You should leave," I said. "I need to sleep."

I got into bed with my clothes on, and Hamish sat on the floor with his knees pulled up in a triangle. "I'm quite comfortable here," he said.

My head sank into the soft pillow and the rest of my body followed. Lying down was wonderful, the bed a sort of heaven.

"You're very beautiful," said Hamish, from a distant place, perhaps another room.

Only the pillow heard me say, "Bullshit."

All had gone quiet, except for the air-conditioning unit, droning on. I was sinking, slowly, heavily, downward, with no will to climb back up. At the bottom, there was a volcano, upside down, sheep swimming in a coffee cup. Train noises, but no train, and my name whispered down the tracks.

"Suki. Oh, Suki. So *posh*." The last word grunted.

I paddled upward, felt my eyes pinch as I surfaced. I'd fallen asleep with my contacts in again. Heavy breathing—not mine—and at the edge of my vision, blue jeans concertinaed around a pair of hairy white knees. Higher up: hairy buttocks, tensed flanks, and an elbow, still in its shirtsleeve, pumping.

"Oh, for fuck's sake," I said.

Hamish said absolutely nothing, just pulled up his pants and left.

I took a cold shower and tried to wash away what I'd seen. And came smack up against what I wanted. Not sex with Hamish, but sex all the same.

Since ending my nonrelationship with Leon soon after it began, I had gone back to pining for boys I didn't know or who weren't interested in me. Between that and my mother's continued disapproval, I had somehow forgotten to lose my virginity. I was pretty sure I was the only one in my peer group who hadn't, so I fell into the habit of pretending, cagily, that I had, whenever the subject came up. This had gone on for so long I worried that if I did finally try to have sex, everyone would find out I'd been lying and the humiliation would be double. But now that I was in New Zealand, what did any of that matter?

In a downtown bar, I met a surfer with salt-bleached hair. With a bottle of tequila on the backseat, he drove us out to a west coast surf beach in his yellow Holden Kingswood station wagon. I would not normally have noticed what type of car it was, but he was so proud of it and repeated the details so many times on the way out there that long after I had forgotten the sex, I remembered the make and model of the car. I would never again see one without thinking of that night, without remembering how I had sat on the sand dunes afterward while a vial of lemon-and-barley syrup trickled down my thigh. I wished I'd thought to bring a towel, and perhaps a paperback, something to read while I waited for him to sober up enough to drive us home.

The next morning, I felt ready to meet my father, and found his address in the library, just like Hamish had said I would. The very same afternoon, I went to the bus station to buy a ticket for Hamilton, where the directory said he lived.

The cashier said, "Are you sure that's where you want to go?"

I checked the address. "Yes, why?"

"It isn't a tourist destination, that's all."

"I'm not a tourist," I said.

Past the city limits, the countryside was so green it could have been AstroTurf. I hadn't telephoned ahead, I'd been too nervous, too unsure of what to say. The coach followed a swollen river for many miles before approaching a town that was far uglier even than Auckland. Wide streets with barnlike stores sold fertilizer and tractors. The coach pulled into a bus terminal, an open-air glue-sniffing bar, and I hesitated before climbing off.

At a nearby tearoom, I showed Ludo's address to the woman behind the counter. She told me no buses went out to where he lived, and that I'd be lucky to find the place, even in a car, even with a map. Thinking like a Londoner, I set off on foot, but after an hour, I hadn't even reached the city limits, and I sat down on the side of the road, defeated. For forty-five minutes, I watched cars stream past, too scared to put out my thumb, until finally a white van just stopped. The woman driving it had brown skin—not Maori but something else—and the backseats were jammed with handicapped kids.

"Are you lost?" she said, too friendly.

"I'm trying to find Koro . . . Koro-ma . . ."—I showed her the map—"this place."

"Hop in," she said. "I can take you as far as Temple View."

I climbed into the front seat—watched vigilantly by her passengers—and read the sticker on her dashboard. JOY, it said, and underneath: JESUS FIRST, OTHERS SECOND, YOURSELF LAST.

At Temple View, she let me out. The name of the town wasn't a joke. Rows and rows of identical white-brick bungalows collected around a temple the size of a mountain, every single window in the place net-curtained against sin. In the shade of a cypress pine, I waited, until it felt like the eyes of the town were on me—even though I couldn't see a soul. I set off down the road and had walked a few kilometers, thumb out, sweating under my rucksack, when a large four-wheel drive swooshed to a stop on the verge in front of me.

The passenger window slid down and a mane of blond hair leaned out. "You shouldn't be hitching," she said. "It isn't safe."

She seemed cross that she'd had to stop to tell me this, and I apologized. "There isn't a bus that goes where I want to go."

"Where's that?" she said.

I reached for the map but realized I'd left it in the white van. "Kora-something?" I said, pointing down the road.

"Koromatua?"

"Yes, that's it."

The woman drummed on the steering wheel for a moment before getting out to open the boot, where she put my backpack next to a pair of muddy boots and a bag of poultry wheat. She was absurdly tanned, and moved in an urgent, choppy way. Straw clung to her jacket, and the inside of the car smelled of horses. She pulled out on the main road as though she was driving a rally car. "Your accent," she said. "Are you English?"

I nodded.

"My husband's English. We met over there."

Her erratic driving put me on edge and I wondered if we were going in the right direction. "Do you have a map?" I asked. "So I can show you where to go."

"I know this area. Just tell me the address."

"Flint Road."

"Flint?"

"Yes, do you know it?"

"We live on it," she said, and looked at me strangely. "What did you say your name was?"

"I didn't. It's Suki."

The car swerved off the road into a ditch and the woman turned in the driver's seat to glare at me. "Suki *Piper*?"

I felt sick and a little creeped out at the same time. "How do you know my surname?"

But she was ten seconds ahead of me. What Hamish had

said about the smallness of this country was even truer than I could have imagined. In a sharp voice that I would come to fear, she asked, "Why do you want to see him?"

Her name was Rowan and she had been married to my father for ten years. They had two children, Lily and Simon. She smiled when she said their names. After she told me all this, we pulled out onto the highway again and drove for a while in heavy silence before turning off the road and cruising down a long gravel lane, across cattle bars, and passed through a remote-controlled gate. The parklike grounds were dotted with cows and sheep, a few horses. A ranch appeared, sprawling, with porticos and stables, a garage the size of an aircraft hangar. The car came to a stop in front of a barn, where a handful of brown chickens scratched in the sand.

"Wait here," said Rowan. "Your father isn't home."

She disappeared inside. I got out of the car and went over to a tabby cat lounging in the sun. A tag around its neck read FLEA. "Aren't you a lovely boy?" I said, stroking the soft white down of his tummy.

"Flea's a girl, and she's not allowed inside," said a child's voice from behind me. "She sleeps in the stable with Felicity—my bestest pony."

I turned, then tried to hide my shock. It was like looking in a mirror at myself at age five or six. She even wore bottle-top glasses. The little me scratched her head. "Are you a friend of Mummy's?"

"Not exactly. But I think we're related."

"I thought so," she said. "You look like my cousin."

"And you must be Lily?"

"Mum called me after a flower because she thought I was going to be pretty."

"You *are* pretty," I said, although I'd felt the same way at her age.

"I'm not. I wear glasses. Which means I can't be a ballerina. Not a proper one." She attempted a pirouette and crashed into my shoulder. "See?"

"You just need to practice," I said. "Besides, I used to wear glasses like yours and now I don't."

She looked quizzically into my eyes. "Did you get new eyes?"

"No, but I have tiny glasses *inside* my eyes."

"Ouch," she said. "That might be too painful for me."

I stood up and noticed that Rowan had been watching us from the front porch. Lily ran to her and was pulled into a hug.

"It's my cousin," she said, kissing her mother. "My new cousin!"

Rowan kept her arm around Lily, blocking the door. "Ludo's on his way home," she said. "He shouldn't be too long." An older boy appeared in the doorway behind them. He looked me over then went back inside.

"You better come in," said Rowan.

Their house was messy and smelled of wet dogs. Rowan told me to wait in the kitchen, where a round, dark-skinned woman was gathering her things together. Rowan handed her an envelope and they chatted for a few minutes about the children's day before the woman, who must have been a nanny, left. Seconds later, Rowan and the boy—who must have been Simon—were swallowed up by the huge house and I was left alone in the kitchen. Lily had parked herself in front of the TV in the next room, occasionally glancing over her shoulder at me to see if I was still there.

I'd made a mistake coming here, I realized. I was unwelcome. But I was also filled with the same overwhelming longing that I'd felt as an eight-year-old, waiting for my father to come home after a business trip, his arms laden with big, guilty presents. Often, that longing had been the best part, better than actually seeing him.

After almost an hour in the kitchen, tires crunched on gravel and a car door slammed. He was home.

The man who walked into the kitchen was smaller than I'd expected, and very nearly bald. But I recognized his eyes, never smiling in unison with his mouth.

After all this time, what should I call him? "Hi, Dad."

"Suki," he said, pronouncing my name as if he hadn't said it, or perhaps even thought it, for many years. He came forward and shook my hand, then briefly and clumsily touched my shoulder. "What brings you to our neck of the woods?"

He was starchy, as if he had just been introduced to a stranger. "I'm on vacation," I said, and looked at Rowan, who had arrived and stood in the doorway.

"Well, it's certainly a surprise," said my father. "When Ro called me up I could hardly believe it."

She moved to his side. "*I* believed it," she said. "As soon as I saw you, I knew who you were." She paused. "And why you were here."

Her tone was oddly suspicious, as though I had come to steal the family silver, but any awkwardness was softened by Lily, who launched herself at Ludo and covered him with kisses. "Daddy, Daddy, Daddy!" she squealed. "You're home early! Is it because you wanted to see our cousin?"

Ludo looked puzzled. "Your cousin?"

"She's our sister, you dummy," said Simon, who had sidled in and was hovering near his mother.

"I don't have a sister," said Lily. "Only a stinky brother."

Rowan looked sharply at Simon. "Don't. She doesn't understand."

I had been trying to ignore their exchange, but it was hard when I was standing right there. Lily fell quiet and leaned into our father's neck as if she had done something wrong. "You're confusing her," said Simon, and sulkily left the room. He was about ten or eleven, as old as my father's new marriage, old enough to have been conceived before they left England. As soon as I figured that out, I wished I hadn't done the math.

"You will stay for dinner, won't you?" said Ludo, impersonating a country squire.

"Is there anywhere else around here to eat?"

Ludo snorted then turned to Rowan. "Well, darling, it looks like word about your awful cooking has finally reached London."

"It was a joke," I said, wishing I hadn't made it. "I was trying to say how remote this place was—this place is so remote that I'd be lucky to find anywhere else to eat."

Ludo was laughing, but not Rowan. "Let me see what I can rustle up," she said, trying not to show her hurt.

My father had been right about her cooking, but it was a good match for the conversation that was potholed with topics we were all anxious to avoid. Rowan and Dad talked cheerfully about their marriage as if it was Ludo's first, as though he had come to Rowan with a clean slate, and when he talked about his family, his children, it was clear that in his mind he had two of them, not three. But I was no better. When Dad asked me to fill them in on the last ten years of my life, what I came up with was drier than a school prospectus. I couldn't find a casual way to tell them the bleeding obvious—that my mother had died a few weeks earlier—but no sooner had I made the omission than I realized I had missed the most natural window in which to say it. Now if I brought it up, it would be a bombshell, a conversation stopper, everyone looking at me and wondering why I hadn't brought it up earlier. I would look like a fool.

"I suppose you'll be traveling around after this," said Dad. "Isn't there a sort of circuit that you young people take on your gap years?"

"I don't plan to go bungee jumping, if that's what you mean. It isn't really my thing."

"Oh, but you must," said Rowan. "You haven't been to New Zealand unless you've gone bungee jumping. And white-water rafting too."

"Mum," said Simon. "You told me those things were too dangerous and I could never do them."

"I only meant that you were too young," she said. "But Suki is old enough."

"Sure," said Simon. "Whatever." He left the table in a huff.

By dinner's end, I was tipsy, and so choked up on my terrible omission that I worried it might burst out of me in a stream of projectile vomit.

"Is the food really that terrible?" asked my father, noticing my untouched plate and no doubt greenish face.

"I'm a little tired, that's all," I said. "The bus really took it out of me." I tried to smile at Rowan. We had not seen eye to eye on a single topic all evening, and I was unsure if it was a simple personality clash or if she had been disagreeing with me on purpose. If I told them about Hillary now, I could not count on her sympathy, and decided that it would be better to tell my father when we were alone.

That night I stayed on a daybed in Rowan's sewing room. Long into the small hours, I was kept awake by the rise and fall of an argument, traveling down the corridor from Ludo and Rowan's bedroom. They were still going at it when I fell asleep, though less ferociously than earlier.

At dawn, I went into the living room, where Lily was perched in front of the TV, eating Cheerios out of a cardboard box. When

I sat down next to her, she pushed the carton under my nose. "Would you like some breakfast?" she whispered.

"Thanks, but it's a little too early for me," I said.

"Shhhhh," she said. "You can't make any noise until the little hand gets to the rabbit." She pointed to a clock above the TV, where someone had put a rabbit-shaped sticker over the number 7.

"Only another hour to go," I whispered.

Lily giggled. "I'm not allowed to pick my nose either but sometimes I do."

"Me too," I said. "It's fine so long as you don't eat it."

She moved closer to my ear, and the *whoosh* of her breathing tickled my eardrum. "I do that sometimes too," she said, and pulled away to see my reaction.

When I smiled, she put her finger into her nostril then licked it. "Yum!" she squealed, forgetting to be quiet, then remembering and covering her mouth. She snuggled into me and sighed, and for a few delicious moments I experienced what it would be like to have a kid sister, someone who trusted me implicitly, someone I could hug whenever I wanted. Then she wriggled away, shook the cereal packet in my face, and squawked, "Cheerios! Cheerios! Yum, yum, yum!"

Later that morning, Rowan left for work—her farewell businesslike, shot through with relief—and the nanny arrived to take the children swimming. After they'd left, Ludo came in and sat down at the table where I was eating toast, then got up and paced to the sink.

"Has anyone shown you round the stables?" he said.

"There wasn't a tour," I said, "when I arrived."

In the long stable block, Ludo introduced me, by their names and breeds, to a series of twitchy mares and stallions that all stared back with disdain. In one of the stalls, a man in gumboots shoveled manure and nodded when he saw Ludo. The horses looked expensive, high maintenance, like certain kinds of women, and for the first time since I'd been on their property, it dawned on me that my father must be rich.

"Rowan represented New Zealand at dressage," he said, stroking a shiny flank rather timidly, then backing off when the animal bristled. "But she missed out on going to the Olympics. She was sabotaged. By one of her teammates."

"'Sabotaged'?" The word was so Agatha Christie. "How?"

"She came down with food poisoning the night before the trials. She was the only one who got sick."

"It wasn't just bad luck?"

"She was the best rider by a mile. The rest of the team was jealous. Poor thing. It was a real blow. She gave up riding for a while. Went to England. Married me. Now she just rides for fun."

"Went to England. Married you," I repeated. "Just like that."

"In a roundabout way, yes." My father cleared his throat. "How's your mother? I noticed that you didn't mention her last night."

We had come to the end of a row of stables, and the cat, Flea, was reclining on a bale of hay in the sun. My hand shook on her fur, and sensing tension, she sprang up and ran away. For a moment my fingers hovered above where the cat had been and I felt my throat constrict. I hadn't answered Ludo's question yet, and didn't know if I could. I walked to the window, and watched a handful of chickens pecking at something that had been thrown on the ground. Still with my back to him, I said, "She had cancer."

He didn't say anything, and after a while, I turned round and glanced briefly at his face. He was processing what I'd said, noting my odd choice of words. His look was confused but still cheerful. I looked out the window again. The chickens had gone from the yard, leaving behind a square of mud. Why wasn't my father saying anything? I opened my mouth to say one more sentence, one string of words that I had to get out, but gearing up to speak, a gulp of air caught in my windpipe. "She died," I said, swallowing the words, so I had to repeat them. "She died and the funeral was a week ago."

I heard what sounded like a sharp intake of breath and the word, "Christ." When I turned around, Ludo was gazing in the direction of one of the horses but was transfixed by another scene, one that was playing inside his mind. His throat muscles were going crazy, gulping down an invisible drink. His eyes had filled with water, and he blinked to cover it. But he didn't look at me, or move my way.

I left the stables and walked quickly into the house. I would have kept walking all the way to Auckland if I had known in what direction to go, but instead I went into the kitchen and packed up my things and waited for a lift.

Ten minutes later, Ludo drove me into Hamilton, back in control behind the wheel of his executive sedan. "I'm sorry about losing it earlier," he said. "It was a terrible shock. I was once very much in love with your mother. She was so attractive."

I wasn't prepared for the anger that hit me like whiplash. "Is that why you loved her?" I spat out. "Because she was *attractive*?"

Behind the steering wheel, my father stiffened. "That was one reason," he said. "But of course there were others."

"Such as?"

"She was a great cook."

"What?"

"And a great mum to you."

"Was she?" I said. "She didn't even tell me she was dying." I didn't know what I was saying—a lunatic ventriloquist was moving my mouth up and down.

"Perhaps she didn't want to frighten you." He surprised me

then by laughing—as though he had just remembered something funny from long ago. "And to think she was always so worried that something would happen to you."

Why did he think nothing had? And just like that, my anger turned to self-pity and free-flowing tears. I scratched at the threads in my jeans then stared out the window, trying to stop them. We had left the country behind, and were driving past car yards and lurid fast-food joints that were big enough to drive a truck through. I missed London, the compact scale of its streets and corner shops, all of it so much less vulgar.

Ludo was still smiling to himself, and when he noticed I was watching him, he looked guilty.

"What is it?"

He reddened. "I was just wondering if your mother, you know . . . if there was anyone else after me."

I was appalled. "Are you asking if Mum had a boyfriend before she died?"

"It's none of my business, I know."

"You've got that straight."

We were back at the bus station, where the winos were enjoying a breakfast of meth and glue. Ludo circled the car park and found a spot as far away from them as possible. He stood with me at the bus stop. My backpack looked funny next to his business suit. "I'm sorry about all that stuff with Rowan," he said. "She doesn't like to be reminded of the past."

"Is that what I am?"

My father looked ever so slightly troubled. "It's more that we came to New Zealand to start a new life. That's why everyone comes here."

"A new life," I repeated. "Without the old one."

Ludo plunged his hands into his pockets and looked at the

ground. "It was your mother's idea not to keep in touch. She thought it would be easier for everyone, and I went along with it."

It was easier for him, I could see, to say that it had been her idea. And I would never know whether that was true or not.

My coach arrived, and Ludo carried my pack over to the luggage compartment. He pulled out a white envelope from his pocket and handed it to me. "Don't open it until you're on the bus," he said. "I really am sorry about Hillary."

I took the envelope and hoped for a moment that it held instructions for what I should do next, but it was too light, too thin, for that.

"It isn't much," he said. "But I hope it helps."

The bus was almost empty, and I found a window seat and stowed my bag on the overhead rack. Ludo's sedan was still in the car park, but as the bus pulled away, I couldn't see him anywhere. I tore open the envelope as soon as I sat down. In it was a check for eight hundred dollars, made out to cash: an extravagant amount, a respectable charity donation. I folded the envelope carefully and pushed it to the bottom of my backpack, out of sight, but not entirely out of mind. I wondered what I'd buy with the money, or if I was the one being bought.

CHAPTER TWELVE

London, 2003

WHEN ALONE IN OTHER PEOPLE'S HOUSES, I figured everyone snooped, even if just a little bit, glancing at a private letter, opening a drawer that was already ajar. I hadn't meant to do so much of it at Pippa and Ari's house while they were away, but I seemed to be so often bored, and the only one there. I was in their bedroom one afternoon when the phone rang and I jumped, feeling caught red-handed. I was shaking when I picked up the receiver and heard Pippa's voice on the other end.

"It's only me," she said. "We've arrived on Skyros—though I'd hardly say in one piece." The journey had been arduous. On the way, Peggy had fallen ill with a mysterious travel-related ailment—Pippa's tone implying that it was all in the old lady's head. In Athens, they'd taken Peggy to a doctor, but she'd pronounced his surgery unclean and had refused to be treated by him, forcing Ari to sneak back and beg him to write out a prescription for penicillin, codeine, tranquilizers—anything to stop her complaining. Since arriving in Skyros she'd made a miraculous recovery and was now spending her waking moments directing Ari's mother and aunts in the shifting of furniture and beds. "I'm already exhausted," said Pippa, coming to the end of her tale. "I think we shall just send Mummy back in a cardboard box." She paused. "I don't mean that, of course."

She sounded disappointed when I told her Caleb was out, and said she'd call back in a day or two to speak him. "I'd get you to call us, but Elena doesn't have a phone."

Earlier in the day, Caleb and I had had a quarrel of sorts after he'd come into the kitchen, accidentally knocked a bottle of sweet chili sauce out of the fridge, then left the resulting red gunk and broken glass to seep across the floor. I had been walking around it for an hour when he reappeared downstairs with his jacket on.

"I'm going out," he'd said.

"And the sauce?"

He'd looked at it, then at me. "What about it?" he said.

"Well, aren't you going to clean it up?"

He had zipped up his jacket and was already heading for the door, but just before he got there, the little shit had turned around and said, "You should get out more."

He was right about my getting out more, but instead I had mopped up the sauce then gone upstairs and wandered into Pippa and Ari's room. It was promisingly messy but no intrigue was forthcoming. They did not seem to hold on to letters or even newspapers, and most of the paperbacks on the nightstand were dusty but unread. Under the bed, I'd found a decrepit rowing machine left over from some nineties fitness fad and a few odd socks, but nothing uncommon. Especially no diaries or journals. Married folk suffered angst, I was sure, but I supposed they couldn't very well write it down in a notebook for their spouse to discover and read.

On the opposite side of the room from the bathroom, there was a walk-in closet, knee deep with piles of ground-down sneakers and stilettos, and more clothes on the floor than on hangers. I had been peering into it when the phone rang.

After Pippa had hung up, an even more extreme boredom took hold than the one that had driven me into her room in the first place, and for the second time that week, I climbed onto the vast futon and fell asleep. When I woke up, some hours later, the sky was a murky gray that left me unsure as to whether it was twilight or just an overcast English afternoon. The house had no pulse, nothing stirred, but sitting on the bedside table in my sight line were Ari's keys, which I'd deposited there after dropping Pippa and Ari off at the airport. Besides the car key, the chain held half a dozen keys, and as I lay there staring at them, I had an idea.

The ladder to the roof screeched as I pulled it down, and when I lost my grip and it crashed to the floor, I jumped out of my skin. On the way upstairs I'd turned on as many lights as I could, but up near the padlock it was dark, and I fumbled with the keys and dropped them. Inwardly, I was ashamed of myself for being so nosy, but not so much that I was prepared to turn back. On my third attempt the padlock yielded, and I was faced with a stiff bolt that gave way only after I'd figured out how to pull it from exactly the right angle. But once it gave, the hatch swung open easily and landed on a soft asphalt cushion.

Up on the roof, the night was clear, with a weak moon hanging on the horizon. I wondered how another entire day had slipped away without my participating in it. Drawn to the shaft of light coming from the hatch, insects ricocheted off my head as I looked around at the neglected roof terrace. What must once have been a thriving garden was now a cemetery of dead stalks and broken clay pots.

In one corner of the roof stood a wooden structure no bigger than a sentry box. It had one tiny window and a peeling black door that rattled but didn't open when I tried the handle. None of the keys on Ari's chain fit the lock, and I searched unsuccessfully under pots and on the door ledge for something to open it with. But when I tried the window, it creaked open and I was able to reach in and unbolt the door. This counted as breaking in, I supposed, but there was no question of giving up now, not after overcoming so many obstacles to get here.

Inside, Ari's lair was tidier than I expected. The compact space was furnished with a coffee table and an easy chair, with the rest given over to the worship of music. An entire wall held built-in shelves, and these were crammed with vinyl records, their spines creating a library of sorts. On a low table sat an old-fashioned turntable and amplifier, and a pair of ungainly headphones. The brown plastic case of the turntable was so lovingly maintained that it showed my reflection, and its chrome dials were polished to a high shine. On the coffee table, a chipped Bakelite ashtray sat empty but caked in soot, recently used.

The easy chair was accommodating, and I sank into its soft cushions and flicked through the nearest row of records, all preserved inside plastic covers. Once or twice a rogue *Playboy* or *Penthouse* tumbled out, but they were the same vintage as the records, more coy and amusing than pornographic. Ari's filing system had an order, but it took me a while to gauge its logic. Albums were grouped together by artist, but not alphabetically. Rather, they seemed to be filed by decade, with the 1950s and '60s closest to arm's reach. Ari was in his early forties; the records were too old to belong to his youth, but they were clearly his favorites, as he had collected multiple copies of the same album. There was a lot of Chuck Berry and Little Richard, hardly any Beatles, but what looked like more than one set of the complete works of the Rolling Stones. I counted eleven copies of the same album, a strange-looking thing with what appeared to be a hamburger or a wedding cake on the cover. I took one of the records out of its sleeve. The vinyl felt heavy, satisfying, and I remembered how when I was a child Dad had told me off once or twice for messing with his records. I thought I'd played with them in secret, but my hand had been too small to span from the edge to the hole in the middle without leaving telltale finger marks.

Once the record was in place on the turntable, I lowered the needle gently and it skated over the dusty surface, looking for a song. I plugged in the giant headphones and a tinny guitar riff leaked out into them. The first song was familiar, off a movie sound track, but I didn't recognize the mournful one that came after it. Before long, I was leaning back in the chair with my eyes closed, oblivious to everything except the sounds that flowed through my ears and acted on my bloodstream like a narcotic. By the end of side one, I felt tipsy, as if I'd arrived at the sweet spot of a really wild party. My foot had been tapping of its own accord for some time, and no doubt other body parts too, when I became aware that I wasn't alone in the shed. Someone was standing behind me.

I pulled off the headphones and spun round to see Caleb standing in the doorway, arms folded, all smirk.

"Don't stop your funky moves," he said, mocking me.

"How long have you been standing there?"

"A while." He paused just long enough for me to blush. "I've never been in here before—only looked through the window. It's kind of cool."

I felt I ought not to tell him I had broken in. "The door was open."

"I bet it wasn't," he said, grinning. "Dad's really psycho about this place. He won't let anyone in because he thinks we'll scratch one of his precious records. For ages, I thought he was up here surfing porn but when I told Mum, she laughed and said he didn't even know how to switch on a computer. But I still thought that's what he was doing—lots of my friends' dads do it and they're techno retards. Anyway, Mum was right, but Dad still won't let me in the door."

Caleb had never been so talkative, or so friendly, and the sudden change in him put me on edge. "We should go downstairs," I said, lifting the needle off the record.

"What were you listening to?"

"The Rolling Stones."

"Dad's always trying to get me to listen to them. He says they're the best band on the planet, but when you see them on TV, they're like a bunch of granddads in try-hard clothes." He reached past me and grabbed the record cover, sending out a wave of such strong heat that I moved away from him. He didn't notice, had already thrown the Stones to one side and was pulling records off the shelf three at a time, oblivious to his dad's filing system.

"What about this?" he said, holding up an album with two topless women in see-through knickers on the front.

"Don't you think we should go?"

He chucked the record on the turntable and unplugged the headphones, filling the shed with a raucous late seventies disco riff.

"All right!" he hollered. "These chicks are awesome."

"I don't think that's the band on the cover," I said. "I think they're just models."

Caleb hadn't heard me. He was hunting through cupboards and looking behind things, but some miracle had prevented him from rooting out the seventies bush porn. "I'm sure Dad's got a fridge in here, somewhere," he said. "He's not allowed to drink, but I've seen him sneaking up here with dodgy brown paper bags." He swung back one of the shelves to reveal a tiny, ingenious fridge stocked with beer, from which he took out two cold bottles of ale, then pulled a key ring with an attached bottle opener from his pocket.

"Do your parents know you drink?" I said when he handed me a bottle.

"Doubt it. Mum's too busy having fits about what Dad drinks, and he's too busy hiding from her that he's an old soak. Mostly I stick to spirits—vodka and stuff—but beer's okay if you haven't had much to eat."

"You drink vodka?"

He nodded. I didn't know why I was surprised. I had too at his age. We'd bought cans of Coke and tipped them half out then filled the rest up with vodka so we could drink on the tube without getting caught. One time I had polished off the remains of the vodka bottle straight and had spewed all the way home on the night bus. "Do you still have to get girls to buy your booze?"

"Girls?" he said, as if they were an alien species. "Why would you do that?"

"Because girls look older."

"Nah, the guys I hang out with are older than me, so they buy all our shit."

"And they give it to you for free?"

"No, they make us pay." Caleb was on to his second beer,

having guzzled the first in little more than a gulp, and his face had begun to bloom. "That chili sauce went everywhere this morning," he said, miming an explosion.

"I'm glad you think it was funny."

"It was, rather." He flicked open another beer and handed it to me. "Sorry about buggering off. I couldn't be arsed cleaning up, but I was going to later on."

"Sure you were." I took a sip of the beer and wondered how we were going to replace all the missing bottles. Caleb had turned up the volume on the stereo and suddenly took hold of my wrist.

"Let's pretend we're at a party," he said, pulling me to my feet. "And we're not the only ones dancing."

He spun me around in a clumsy twirl and I tried to follow his lead but my knees tensed up.

"Don't be such a square," he barked. "I saw you dancing before, so I know you like it." But something about his youthful swagger, his proximity, made me lose my nerve even more, and Caleb gave up and dropped my hand. For a moment or two, I did an old-person's shuffle, while he bounced around in a wild pogo, ricocheting off the record shelves and walls until he stumbled and landed heavily on the turntable case. The lid made a hideous cracking sound and the needle scorched across the record before skidding clean off.

Into the sudden, deafening silence, he said, "Fuck me!"

I stared at the turntable, where a fault line wended its way from one side of the case to the other. We could replace the beer, but this was different. I felt the giddy spirit of the evening desert me. "We really should call it a night," I said, starting to tidy up, but Caleb was selecting another record from the shelf.

"Bob fucking Dylan," he said. "Awesome!" He was beginning to slur his words, and I wondered if he'd already had a few drinks before he came up here. It would explain why he'd been so friendly.

"Come on, let's go," I said. "Before we destroy anything else." I had it in mind to come back up the next day to assess the damage—without Caleb.

"Wait, wait, wait," he said, before, with exaggerated, inebriated care, he launched the needle across the record. But nothing happened. The turntable wouldn't revolve. He tried to push it round with his hand, and a sick, whining sound escaped from the speakers.

"Holy shit, it's really broken," he said, cracking up. "Dad's going to fucking kill you!"

"Kill *me*?" I said. "You're the one who broke it."

"Yes, but I'm not the one who busted in here—am I?" He shot me a challenging look and held it for a moment or two, letting me sweat. Then he cracked up laughing. "Relax, I'll take one for the team," he said. "I'm already in deep shit with Dad, so a bit more won't make any difference."

We stood sipping our beers for a moment, but it was deadly quiet, airless and hot, the space too cramped to be alone in with Caleb.

"We really should go downstairs," I said, and as much as was possible began to put things back the way I'd found them. Caleb gulped the rest of his beer and took another out of the fridge, stowing it in his back pocket. The weight of it made his trousers droop below the hem of his T-shirt, and escaping from the top of his waistband was a curly sort of down. "One for the road?" he said, offering me the last beer.

"No thanks."

With the lights off, the crack in the turntable case wasn't so noticeable, but on the way down the ladder the incident worried me for reasons other than who would take the blame. Granted,

I had broken into Ari's shed on my own, and the music had loosened me up, but in the short space of time Caleb had been there I had basically lost my head.

On the landing outside my bedroom, Caleb turned to me. "Maybe you should sleep in Mum and Dad's room."

"Do you think they'd mind?"

"They won't even know." He glanced in my room. "What did you see in there that freaked you out so much?"

"I didn't really *see* anything. It was more of a presence."

He laughed. "You've been sleeping on the bathroom floor because of a *presence*?"

Said like that, it sounded ridiculous. "I guess so."

"If it's only a presence, then it's all in your head. So tell it to go away."

"It's not that simple," I said.

"Yes it is." He gave me a friendly punch on the shoulder. "Don't be such a wimp."

Caleb was right; it was beyond silly to be frightened of a cupboard. That first night in Pippa and Ari's room, I slept dreamless and undisturbed, putting it down to my newfound determination to be more courageous.

When I woke the next morning, Caleb had gone out, leaving a note on the dining table to say he was at a friend's house. Midmorning, a temping agency called to get me in for a typing test the following week—the first appointment in my diary for almost a month. For the rest of the day, I did washing and housework, interspersed with long periods of staring out the window or into space. The only time I left the house was to walk to the supermarket at half past five, when it was jammed with after-work shoppers filling their baskets with pre-prepared meals and wine. Using Pippa's money, I splurged on indulgent groceries, the kind I hadn't bought for months, but by the time

I'd carried it all home and put the food away, I couldn't be bothered making anything more gourmet than a ham and mustard sandwich. While I was eating it, Caleb sent a text saying "Hi how R Stones," so I sent one back that said, "Are you home for dinner?" but got no reply. Later, when I tried to call his mobile, it went straight to voice mail. He had told me he never checked messages, so I didn't leave one.

At midnight, I woke on the couch with a stiff neck, an infomercial for body bronzer blaring at me from the TV. No messages from Caleb, but outside, Friday-night revelry had taken over the street. The bass from a nightclub almost a hundred meters away, under the flyover, was making the windows vibrate. There had been a time when staying home on a Friday night would have made me anxious and depressed, but now it was the idea of going out and jostling in a bar with strangers that seemed perverse. I thought of the night with Wouter and the spliff and how out of practice I'd been, how my body had no longer been able to tolerate what I'd once put it through all the time.

Before going to bed, I checked Caleb's room for signs of his whereabouts, but found no appointment diaries or wall calendars, or evidence of any advance planning. At sixteen, as long as you knew what parties were happening on the weekend just ahead—and as long as you were invited to them—life was as organized as it needed to be. The same went for washing. In the corner of Caleb's room was a pile of his clothing, and I started to sort it, until I came across a stash of crumpled, matted tissues. With a jolt, I realized what was gluing the tissues together and dropped them, along with the washing, vowing never again to set foot in his room.

I tried Caleb's cell phone one more time before calling it a night and going upstairs to sleep in Pippa and Ari's room. I slept okay at first—it was after one, and I was tired—but as the night wore on, I woke at regular intervals, imagining that the front door had opened and I'd heard Caleb staggering in. But always, straight after the initial noise woke me, the house was silent, and I realized I'd been tricked.

So preoccupied was I with the routines of insomnia that I failed, at first, to notice that the closet door was open about a foot. I was positive I had closed it before going to bed. I didn't like leaving any cupboard doors open—not this one or the one in my room. Once the lights were off, that dark space always seemed to take on a life of its own.

I was about to succumb to the usual fit of anxiety when I remembered Caleb's admonishment not to be such a wimp.

Feeling emboldened, I grabbed my glasses and got out of bed and strode to the closet to show the damn thing who was boss. I put my hand on the wardrobe door, near a simple wooden handle, and pushed, using a regular amount of force, not too violent, not too gentle. But the door stayed where it was. I pushed again, a little harder this time, and the door recoiled by a fraction, then settled back on its hinges. There was an odd springiness to the movement, unlike if the door had been jammed open by an object.

When I tried the other door, it swung open without obstacle, which only made its twin seem more perverse, more unchained from the laws of physics. If the door hadn't been open in the first place, I wouldn't have gotten out of bed, so I reasoned—if that was the correct term—that the closet had been trying to get my attention. That it wanted me to go in.

In the event that it should change its mind, I propped a chair against the wide-open wardrobe door, and walked two steps into the closet, far enough that I was really inside it, and not standing half in the bedroom. On either side of me, clothes hung on parallel steel rails, which pointed to the back of the closet.

When I'd been in a few days earlier, I was sure a third rail had been there, positioned low against the back wall for suits and shirts, but I found this time that I couldn't see that far, that the back of the closet was obscured by a heavy gray curtain.

Thinking that's what it was, I put my hand straight out in front of me to determine what fabric it was made of, expecting it to feel like a kind of heavy velvet. And at first it did feel velvety, or perhaps a little softer, like the fur of a rabbit's pelt, only the surface of it had no resistance. It allowed me to put my hand in it, then through it, until my arm was invisible below the wrist. I felt a pressure on the tips of my fingers, as though they'd been fitted with tiny suction cups. This tension was gentle but irresistible, slightly ticklish, and I let it pull my hand forward, reassured by the downy warmth of the substance it was passing through. At a certain point, when my arm had disappeared up to the elbow, the pulling sensation stopped, and I found I was able to move my hand around in an open space on the other side of the curtain. This hand then came into contact with something, a knot of fabric, and I toyed with it for a moment before a wave of recognition hit me. The knot of fabric was a bow, and whatever it was attached to was moving and very much alive.

As though bitten by something with very sharp teeth, my hand withdrew with such force that it sent me reeling backward into the wardrobe, where I lost my footing in a wreckage of sneakers and tennis rackets.

I fell sideways, grabbing a handful of dresses on the way down, and the sheer gracelessness of the movement snapped me out of whatever spell I'd been under just moments before. Flooding with adrenaline, I scrambled from the floor of the closet and didn't stop running until I reached the kitchen, where I turned on every light and the wireless, to hear if the rest of the world was still there. First to escape from the tuner were atmospheric farm noises, a pastoral program about raising pigs. The broadcaster had gotten right inside the pen and held the microphone almost up the pig's snout as it snuffled and rooted in a pile of rotting vegetables. He described the scene in great detail, but the more I listened to the program, the less like real life any of it sounded. I switched off the radio and tried the television, but that too was stuck on late-night filler, infomercials and Bible clowns talking about the end of the world, nothing that was reassuring. The loudness of it blocked my senses, and I worried that if anything crept up behind me, I wouldn't hear it approaching. I thought of what was upstairs, and a quiver ran down my neck.

CHAPTER THIRTEEN

Auckland, 1997

BY THE LATE NINETIES, I had lost my way so thoroughly that I was beginning to think I would never find it again. I was still in New Zealand, which I had neither planned on nor could account for, and the longer I stayed there, the more remote and unreachable London seemed. Partly it was the plane fare, too princely a sum for my meager restaurant wages, and partly it was a state of mind. After that first nonreunion with my father, I had simply hung about in Auckland, found a flat and drifted through university, then become too useless to save up enough to leave the country. I understood what everyone meant about being stranded in paradise, that if you couldn't get out, it turned into a prison.

At twenty-two, I was working in a faux-French restaurant on Christmas Eve when Scott, my first love and nemesis, walked back into my life and asked me to marry him.

The evening had not begun well. When I arrived at six for my shift, the place was packed with red-faced office workers who'd been drinking buckets of chardonnay and eating nothing since lunchtime. Anton, the maitre d', was already in a state of high agitation—too much speed, too early on, I supposed—and the second I appeared in the kitchen, he threw an apron at me and told me to get straight out on the floor.

"But I'm early," I protested. "Can I at least have breakfast?"

"Babe," he said, tossing the remains of a steak béarnaise into the scraps bin, "it isn't my fault you fucking just got out of bed."

Lately, I had been keeping vampire hours, going to bed sometime around dawn and getting up a few hours before work started at five or six. That afternoon, I'd slept in and had had just enough time to shower, dress in my waiter's uniform, and race down to a department store on the main street to pick up Lily's Christmas present. Rowan had already paid for the present and had given me detailed instructions on where to pick it up. The next day, she was expecting me to arrive in Hamilton with the gift in time for Christmas lunch. It was the first time in years that I'd been invited—the year before they had flown to Rarotonga without telling me—and I was trying not to believe it was only because they'd needed a courier.

For dinner I had two short black coffees and a sneaky cigarette on the kitchen fire escape, where I hoped Anton wouldn't find me. I was still out there, sneaking a second, when I glanced into the restaurant and saw a familiar figure heading for the men's toilet: Scott. The scoop of his neck, the quiff at the front of his hair, the slope of his nose—his features were as familiar to me as my own, maybe more so. And that brief sighting was all it took for my mood and confidence to plummet.

The last time I'd seen Scott was a few weeks after we broke up, at least a month before. He had summoned me to his flat on a Sunday morning with no explanation other than that he had something to tell me. I had gone eagerly—I still wasn't over him—and had stood on the porch with a swelling of hope in my heart. With barely a greeting, he had guided me to the living room, and told me to sit down on a wooden dining chair that had been placed in front of the stereo.

"What's going on?" I said.

Scott kneeled on the floor next to my chair and pressed play. "Listen carefully to the lyrics," he said, then put his head in my lap.

I recognized the opening bars immediately. It was Elvis, his favorite, my least, and a track that was slow and saccharine.

The first line, "Maybe I didn't treat you . . . quite as good as I should have," had been a doozie. But as the song went on, I became confused. When Elvis pleaded, "Tell me that your sweet love hasn't died," I wondered, did Scott want me back? Or did he just want *me* to want him back? I wasn't even sure, now that it seemed to be on the table, if that's what I wanted. Which had been the problem all along. When I wasn't with Scott, I pined for him, like a lost limb, but when he was in the same room, as he was now, I felt nothing—not just for him but full stop. My emotions went blank, along with my mind. The longing was gone but his being there erased me, turned me into a cipher, and I didn't know which of those two things was worse.

At the end of the song, Scott had stood up and I saw that he had been crying. "Now you know exactly how I feel," he'd said, apparently proud of having expressed himself so clearly. But I was baffled. I had been about to ask him what he wanted to do about these feelings he had, when he announced that he had to go into the office, but he could give me a lift somewhere seeing as it was raining. That was it, and that was Scott: chivalrous and cold in equal measure.

Since then we had not even bumped into each other, even though I lived less than two blocks from his apartment.

I stayed out on the fire escape a little longer, defying Anton, delaying the moment when I'd have to go back out to the restaurant and face Scott.

As if on cue, Becky sailed into the kitchen carrying an armada of dirty plates. "Fuck, it's busy," she said, putting down the plates and rubbing a red indentation on her arm. She looked at my face. "Shit, doll, are you all right?"

I swept her into an alcove and whispered, "Scott's here."

Becky's eyes widened. "Are you sure?" But she could see from my face that he was. She reached under her apron and pulled out a tiny piece of folded paper, which she pressed into my hand. "Save some for later," she said, and winked.

I went into a stall in the ladies' toilet and closed the door. Usually, we waited until toward the end of the shift to have a line, but occasionally, in emergencies, we had one early.

The speed was bitter, and hung in a lump at the back of my throat, but soon after taking it, I felt the familiar rush of clarity, and the aftertaste was easily fixed by a slug of vodka behind the bar. When I stood up, Scott was heading toward me, smiling the alligator smile that early in our relationship I'd mistaken for debonair.

"Suki Piper," he said, enunciating every syllable in a proprietary way. He leaned on the bar and looked me up and down for a moment, as if he was appraising goods in the window of a shop. He liked to use silence to his advantage, and was waiting for me to speak, I knew.

"Would you like a drink?" I said.

He nodded. "And I wanted to see you."

We were still standing like that on either side of the bar when Anton came up behind Scott and slapped him on the back. "Scottie, my boy. You're up early. Got any samples for us to try?"

"I'm off duty," said Scott. "But I'm sure we can find something else to do." Scott was a wine rep who preferred to conduct business at night when he could most enjoy his customers' hospitality. He smiled roguishly at Anton and an understanding passed between them, an understanding I recognized all too well.

"Suki," said Anton, "look after table five. They just ordered coffee, but try the dessert menu one more time. I think the fat chick's about to cave." He drummed Scott's arm with a series of friendly punches and led the way to the staff room. I knew where they were going; it was where Scott always went on a Friday night, where he had taken me about a month into our relationship to induct me into his shady world of rolled-up banknotes and powder. He had cleverly waited until I had fallen in love with him before revealing his habit, before taking me to the staff room to lovingly chop up my first line. He was proud of being the one to initiate me, and even more delighted when I turned out to be a fiend.

When Anton returned to the restaurant floor, he reeked of cigar smoke and peppermints, his favorite amphetamine *digestif*. Scott was heading for the door, about to leave, when he turned back and walked to the coffee machine where I was standing. "I'm heading to Dagger," he said. "You should come up for a drink when you finish."

I hated how he did that, made a suggestion but didn't ask outright. I also knew that I would go meet him, that I couldn't help myself.

He leaned over the counter and whispered in my ear: "I miss you, Sukes."

After he left, the restaurant got busier and louder before starting to empty out as people went home to wrap their Christmas presents and stuff them into stockings or hide them under trees. The store had already wrapped Lily's present in garish pink paper; all I had to do was get it, and myself, to the bus stop.

After putting all the chairs up on the tables and polishing the last piece of cutlery, Anton poured us all cheap fizz to celebrate Christmas and the end of the shift, which irked because the week before we'd asked for, and had been denied, a monetary festive bonus. I drank the champagne thirstily and poured another glass. I was nervous about meeting Scott. Becky had offered to come along for moral support, but I told her I preferred to go alone. "Okay," she said. "But I'll be at Kuzo if you need me."

"I'll be fine," I reassured her.

"Just don't sleep with him again, okay?" she said. "He's a scumbag."

I smiled at her. Since breaking up with him, everyone had told me what Scott was really like, but while I was with him, no one had said a thing.

When I got to Dagger, Scott was surrounded by his cronies, but he left them to settle in a corner booth with me. He went to the bar and came back with a bottle of champagne—the French stuff, he refused to ever buy fake—and two plastic flutes, like you'd find in a picnic set or on a boat.

"Kind of ruins the effect, don't you think?" he said, pouring out the bubbles, which smelled of freshly baked bread.

"What are we celebrating?" I asked, my voice flat because the speed had worn off.

Scott leaned in closer and put his hand on my knee. "You look tired," he said. "I'm worried about you."

"Why?" I said, defensively. "I'm fine."

"Suki," he said, gently cupping my chin in his hand and forcing me to look at him. "I know you better than that."

I took a huge gulp of champagne and said nothing. Scott put

his hand around mine on the plastic flute stem, gripping me with warm fingers. With his other hand, he brushed the hair from my face and swept it behind one ear. It was so easy to respond to his touch, to forget the hurt and turmoil of the preceding months, to surrender to my longing for intimacy. Involuntarily my body leaned into his, reacting to the familiar pull of his closeness.

"We should just get married," he said, settling back into the seat and scooping his free arm behind my back.

"What?"

"We should get married." His words hung surreally in the air.

"You're joking—right?"

"Why would I joke about that?" he said.

Scott's proximity and the mellow warmth of the champagne had me intoxicated, but from five fathoms down came the voice of unwavering reason. "We can't get married," I said. "We're not even going out."

"Being married would fix that."

His sureness threw me into turmoil. Some of the happiest times of my life had been with Scott, early in our relationship, when I'd tasted the first sweet sip of reciprocated love, but so had some of the worst, all the mornings I'd woken up to find him missing, only to have him come in a few hours later reeking of booze and lousy excuses. "Being married wouldn't change anything," I said.

Scott shrugged. "It might make me good."

"I'm not marrying you to find out," I said.

Scott laughed. "Then there's nothing more to talk about." He drained his champagne glass and stood up, looking at his watch. "I'm supposed to be meeting Anton in a minute."

Following him out to the pavement, I wondered how he could offer to spend the rest of his life with me and snatch it away moments later. While he had been proposing, I'd felt sure of myself, in control, but now that he was walking away, I was overcome with wild emotions. "Wait," I said. "You just said we should get married. Doesn't that mean anything to you?"

"You said you didn't want to."

"So that's it—either marriage or nothing?"

"That's it," he said, adjusting the lapels of his jacket.

I had begun to sob, quietly at first, but then with real despair. He tried to quiet me down, to prevent a scene, and when that didn't work he started to back away, to disown me. I clutched at his clothing, half blind from the flooding in my eyes. "That isn't what I want," I said, pathetically.

"What *do* you want from me?" he said.

The question was so insulting, so belittling—as though I didn't even have the right to want anything from him—that I finally let go of the jacket and watched him walk away.

Seven minutes later, I pushed past the doorman at Kuzo and stumbled down the long staircase into the basement. They were having a drum 'n' bass night and the place was decked out in camouflage netting strewn with orange emergency tape. Sweat dripped from the ceiling and huge speakers shook from the effort of spitting out bass. I fought my way past heaving shoulders and found Becky, sitting on her friend Justin's lap in the corner by the bar. We didn't speak to each other—we couldn't, it was too loud—but she saw I'd been crying and put her arms around me, enveloping me in a damp hug. She pulled me into the bathroom, where we shoved our way into an empty stall and hunched over a small plastic bag of wet brown crystals. "Lick your finger," she ordered. "This shit is too sticky to snort."

At the bar, we demanded flaming Quaaludes, and washed them down with vodka and tequila shots, toasting, "Fuck you,

Scott," with each one. There was only eighty dollars in my account to last until next week's payday, and I had spent it within twenty minutes. The brown speed was good and strong, but it made me thirstier than I had ever been in my life and I was relieved when we ran into Guy, a regular at the restaurant, and his mate Rupert, who had a face like a potato but was rich and liked to buy everyone drinks. I didn't care who they were or what they looked like, I just wanted them to pay for it all and they did, round after round of shots, vodka, tequila, and schnapps. When I took speed, I could drink as much as I wanted without falling over or suffering the calamity of a hangover, and before long I felt dazzling and witty. Guy and Rupert were my new best friends, and the night opened up in front of us, a Christmas cracker of possibilities. Getting into the festive spirit, we raised our glasses to Jesus Christ and sang him happy birthday. Then I overhead Guy saying something to Rupert about Charlie and I said ugly things and flattered and lied until I got some.

I took Becky with me into the toilet stall, where we laughed and fell into each other as we poured out a tiny cloud of the white powder. "Just a bit more," I said to Becky, shoving her elbow so that a teaspoon of cocaine fell onto the toilet seat.

"Shit!" she said, laughing. "We better leave some for Guy."

We tried to get the powder back into the packet, but our coordination was off and most of it drifted across the seat in white puffs, which we chased and licked with our fingers. "Don't worry, he's loaded," she said, cutting up what was left and inhaling it greedily through a ten-dollar note. "Merry fucking Christmas, Suki!"

We stared at our wide, sparkly eyes in the dimly lit bathroom mirror and I was sure I had never looked so beautiful. "I feel like dancing," I said.

"Me too," said Becky, and we jumped in the air and kissed.

Hours and a lifetime later, a dull glow filtered through the glass bricks of the skylight above the back bar of Kuzo. Outside it was daylight, but I had convinced myself that the bar was still suspended in the night before. I lit a cigarette and looked in the packet: only two left. Apart from the barman, Lewis, the place was deserted. Becky had gone home with Rupert and Guy to their flat in Saint Heliers, but at the last moment I'd changed my mind about going with them. It was a long taxi ride there and I'd had an unlovely vision of how the hours after that would unfold, especially with the kind of deficit Becky and I had racked up. Everyone would sit around on the patio with their sunglasses on, drinking and smoking pot until they came down enough to sleep or at least lie horizontally in a dark room. When that happened, there would be sex, or the expectation of it, and even though I was wasted, that was the part I shrank from the most. It was never a question of being forced to put out, but if you didn't, you had to be prepared for the hostility that followed. Rich young lads didn't take girls home for company—they had guy friends for that—and after the deed was done, they happily left you on the bed with your knickers round your ankles, feeling like you should have gotten paid. Except that we had already been paid, at Kuzo, in large amounts of booze and fags and coke.

Staying in the bar with Lewis seemed like a simpler option. He was the bar manager, and like everyone in the district, knew Scott, and knew about our messy breakup. When he offered me another line, I took it, even though I was already shaking so much that my coffee cup rattled on the saucer when I put it down. The new line of speed wiped away the effects of the alcohol and instantly sharpened my focus, but when I looked around at the objects in the shadowy bar, they formed a surreal jigsaw that held no meaning. The longer I stared at a chair or a table, the less I was able to recognize it as either of those things.

"I'm hungry," I said, even though it wasn't my stomach that was empty.

Lewis had closed up the bar and there was no avoiding the bright glare of the pavement any longer. When we walked out onto Vulcan Lane, the buildings looked to me like cardboard scenery.

At the corner, Lewis hugged me and said good-bye. Through his thin shirt, I felt a ragged heartbeat and was overcome with an urge to cling to him. "Do you want to come up for tea?" I said, trying to sound light, but hearing the desolation in my voice.

He held my hand for a moment. "I can't." He tipped his cap and let it settle back on his head. "Merry Christmas though."

"You too."

When the lift doors opened, the painted scenery of the apartment I shared with Becky and two of the chefs at the restaurant gave way and let me in. There was a ringing in my ears that I hadn't noticed in the bar, where there had been low music playing, or in the street, where there had been traffic. The door to my room was wide open, and a boy was standing by the window. I was startled at first to see him and then I remembered: his name was Liam, he was the brother of one of my flatmates, staying with us until he found his own place. He was much younger than me, fresh out of school, but he had kind eyes and this sage-like quality that made him seem older.

He was embarrassed at getting caught in my room, but I told him not to leave. I didn't want to be on my own. "Are you okay?" he said, and looked at me with such gentle concern that I had to tell the truth.

"I feel like a ghost," I said, through chattering teeth. "Like I'm not really here."

Liam reached out for my hand, the one nearest him, and tried to warm it. "You'll be okay in a couple of hours."

"You think so?"

"I know so."

I wanted to believe him, but the stickiness of his palms was making me think of a schoolboy who hadn't washed his hands all day. When my amphetamine-fueled gaze zeroed in on the skin on his face, it was oily and caked in zits. Sagelike qualities? What was I on? "I think you better go," I said.

I went into the bathroom with my contact lens case and stood in front of the sink to remove them. The first one came out easily enough, but my eyes were dry and I struggled with the second. When I finally got it out I put on my glasses, which had broken across the bridge and were stuck together with masking tape. I was ashamed of them but couldn't afford another pair, and made do by never wearing them in public.

"You look different with your glasses on," said a voice behind me, and I looked around to see Liam standing in the doorway. I didn't know how long he'd been there, but his posture was relaxed, as if it had been a while.

Mortified that he had seen me in my glasses and had apparently been watching me without my knowledge, I shrieked, but he didn't move. So I shoved him out of the bathroom, hard. "Don't look at me, you fucking creep!"

His kind eyes buckled, then his legs. He landed clumsily on one knee and I realized, a little too late, that I'd behaved like a total bitch.

"Please," I said, more gently. "I want to be alone."

I got into bed and pulled the duvet over me, trying to get warm. It was the middle of summer, but my bones were cold. Sticking out from the end of the bed, a swatch of candy pink wrapping paper caught my eye. The pinkness of it didn't make sense; it was way too bright, an insult of color. I stared at it for a whole minute before I remembered what it was. Lily's present. *Fuck*. It was Christmas morning. How could I have forgotten? I looked at the bedside clock. It was not quite ten thirty but my bus to Hamilton had left an hour before. Rowan and Ludo were expecting me for dinner. Or was it lunch? Was dinner at lunchtime on Christmas Day? I had never known the rules. Maybe another bus left later. Or maybe it didn't. I would worry about that after I'd had some sleep. I closed my eyes, but they continued to dart about, and the cogs in my skull whirred ceaselessly, so that every thought I had seemed to double back on itself and play in a loop. The fibers of the mattress absorbed me and tendrils of it grew up and over my body, weaving me into a sleep pod out of which there was no escape.

CHAPTER FOURTEEN

London, 2003

ON THE MORNING AFTER I put my hand through the strange curtain in the closet, the phone rang in the living room, and I answered it through a fog of sleep, taking a moment to recognize Pippa's distressed voice on the other end. I had been dozing on the couch, and didn't remember at first how I'd gotten there. Then I tasted bittersweet tea, saw the half-empty cup I had made in the small hours, and the events of the night before played back in a delirious slide show. By the time I tuned in to what Pippa was saying, she was telling me about a fall in the courtyard, that they would have to take Peggy to the mainland for X-rays. They'd be out of reach for a few days and she wanted to speak to Caleb before they went. That was when I remembered that Caleb was still missing.

"He's not here," I said, fumbling for an excuse. "Soccer practice started early."

"At half past seven?"

"I know. Must be a big match this week."

"Wow," she said. "Your influence is working already." She told me to make sure he cleaned the mud off his soccer boots when he got home instead of leaving them in the sink to fester. I was also to give him a hug from her. I promised I would, and felt terrible for lying. If Caleb really was missing, I'd just made matters worse.

To make amends, I resolved to spend the day looking for him, and got in the shower at once. Under piping-hot water, I planned my search route: first, Wormwood Scrubs, followed by his school, then the local cinema—where I'd go, but, realistically, he wouldn't. I'd call his cell phone at regular intervals throughout the day and also ring home in case he'd returned while I was out.

When I stepped out of the shower, the bathroom was opaque with steam, and I opened the window to a gust of cold air, the first sign of summer's end. I was in the downstairs bathroom, had forgotten to bring a towel, and the only thing at hand, apart from the pajamas I'd had on the night before, was a flimsy satin dressing gown of Pippa's. I'd just put it on when I heard the doorbell ringing, not serenely like it normally did, but a crazed *bing-bong bing-bong bing-bong.* Caleb must have forgotten his key and gone bonkers from waiting on the doorstep for so long.

I ran to the intercom and buzzed him in, saying, "Thank God you're home." Caleb made no reply over the receiver, but I heard the downstairs door click shut behind him. His feet on the stairs were slow, deliberate, as if he had on lead boots and was very tired.

Pippa's satin dressing gown was now wet through, transparent, and I grabbed Ari's gabardine raincoat off a hook and put it on. Then, when I opened the door, I thought I really was going berserk. Caleb stood in front of me—only he had aged overnight and was forty years old.

He stepped into the living room, looked up and down at my wet hair and raincoat, and it was then that I recognized the scowl, the imperious look directed at me. "Harold?" I said. "I thought it was Caleb."

"And you are?"

"Suki. I'm house-sitting."

He repeated my name to himself, as though trying to remember where he'd heard it. "Where is everyone?" he said. "I've just come from Peggy's, but the place was deserted. It struck me that I might be too late."

"Too late?" I pulled the raincoat more tightly around me.

"That the old biddy had already croaked."

"She was alive this morning when Pippa called from Skyros."

"Skyros?"

"She fell over in the courtyard or something. I don't think it's serious."

"Fuck." He sat down heavily and sighed. "You're telling me they're in bloody Skyros?"

"Were you expecting them to be here?"

"Rather. Peggy called me last week to say she thought the end was near and that she'd cut me out of the will if I didn't make it over. Of course, she was being overly dramatic and has nothing whatsoever to pass on, but I got it that she needed to see me."

"And you didn't check in first with Pippa?"

He got up. "I thought Pippa didn't want me to come at all—at least that's what Mummy told me over the phone."

In photos, I hadn't really noticed Caleb's resemblance to Harold—or maybe I hadn't wanted to—but in person, it was uncanny. They even had the same rebellious expression, only on Harold it had set into a sneer.

"You look familiar," he said, scrutinizing me. "Were you one of the au pairs?"

"I used to live in the basement of Ladbroke Gardens, with my parents, the Pipers."

He frowned. "No, I don't remember you."

"I looked different then. I wore pink glasses." I mimed the spectacles, because it always seemed to help. As I did so, the raincoat drifted open and I hastily pulled it closed.

It was open for only a second, but it seemed to make all the difference to Harold's powers of recollection. "Oh yes, now I remember—your mother was an absolute doll!" he exclaimed and shook my hand vigorously. "And your father—wasn't he something of a cad?"

Though it was true, I couldn't possibly agree with him. "My mother passed away," I said, feeling flustered. "She had cancer."

"Christ," said Harold. "What a terrific waste."

"Yes, I suppose it was."

I excused myself and went upstairs to my old attic room to get dressed. On my way down again I saw that Harold had put his suitcase in Pippa's room and strewn his clothes across their bed. I went in to retrieve a book I'd left on the bedside table, and my pajamas, which were screwed up in a heap on the bathroom floor. By the time I got downstairs, Harold had made a pot of coffee, and was connecting the telephone line to his laptop, so that if Caleb tried to call, or the police, they wouldn't get through.

"I'm expecting a call," I said. "Do you mind doing that later?"

"I won't tie up the line for long," he said, powering up his computer. "Where's my nephew? Still asleep?"

"Soccer practice," I said, spreading the lie a little further.

Not long after, I set out to look for Caleb. I had gone as far as his school in Holland Park when I realized what a futile search I was on. He could be anywhere in London, or, by then, anywhere in the world. I exited the park by the gate opposite the Kensington Odeon, and went into the cinema foyer for the sake of nostalgia. Every Thursday on our way home from school, Alana and I had taken a detour past here to see what new films were on. We'd pored over the posters in the lobby, really studied them, got up close and rubbed our fingers on the glass. We had even kissed one once. Only this time when I remembered it, the memory had changed: I saw myself kissing the poster and Alana hanging back a few feet, thinking I was weird. I had never realized before how unstable the past was, how easy to color and revise.

Harold was out when I got home, and I went straight upstairs to my room intending to write in my journal, but got sidetracked by the book I'd been reading, a trashy bestseller I'd found by Pippa's bed. So engrossed was I that when my right arm and leg went dead from the strange position I had been lying in, I ignored the numbness until I was wracked with pins and needles. As the spasms hit, I rolled on the bed, gasping and groaning in pain—which was exactly the moment Harold chose to appear in the doorway.

"Sorry to interrupt," he said, drinking in the scene and also my bungled attempts to cover what I was doing—the book, but also the writhing. "Jilly Cooper," he pronounced with emphasis. "Always a racy read."

"I found it in Pippa's room."

"Oh, you needn't convince me," he said. "We all read that in the eighties. It was compulsory."

I stood up from the bed and tried to laugh. "Yes, I think my parents had a copy."

"My mother had half a dozen. She used to give them away at dinner parties." Harold scratched his chin and looked about the room, apparently stalling. "Look," he said, finally. "The thing is, I'm dying for a pint. And I thought you might like to join me." He looked briefly at his feet and laughed. "It's a terrible habit, but I find getting drunk is the best way to get over jet lag."

I vehemently did not want to go, but no excuse came to mind. "I'm not really dressed for an outing," I said, pulling, rather stupidly, at my rag of a T-shirt.

"I was thinking of the local pub," said Harold. "You'll fit right in with the junkies and hobos who hang out there."

I didn't know what to say, so I didn't say anything, and then, when the awkward silence had gone on for too long, we both tried to speak at once.

"I didn't mean—"

"I don't want to—"

Harold cleared his throat. "Well then," he said. "Another time."

"Yes. Another time."

He went off to the pub on his own and I stayed at home to wait for Caleb. If he hadn't returned by the following morning, I decided, I'd have to call the police, then Pippa, in that order. But at a little after midnight the phone rang.

I thought no one was on the line at first, then a male voice in the background barked: "Is that your parents? Give it here." I thought I heard a tube train shunting into a station, then a voice closer to the receiver said, "Suchi? Zatchoo?"

"Caleb?"

Ten minutes later, I was shown into the guard's office at the Ladbroke Grove tube station, where Caleb was slumped over a desk, his bloodshot eyes at half-mast, his face pale green and bloated. One side of his nose was crusted with blood from a cut.

On the other side of the desk, a hulking man looked up from

his crossword. "I don't usually bring them in here, but he was about to get beaten up. Someone shoved him off the train then got out after him, and he spewed on the other guy's trainers. That's when they started kicking him. They took off but I think they knew him—he was calling out their names."

I was horrified. "I'll get him out of your way," I said.

"And you are his—?"

"Sister."

He looked surprised. "There's a fine to pay, of course."

"What for?"

"Traveling without a ticket and damage to LTA property."

At that moment, Caleb looked up from the desk and winced at the harsh fluorescent lighting. He tried to speak but couldn't manage it, and a torrent of pale yellow liquid poured unobstructed from his mouth, like water from a tap. When it stopped, I hoisted him up from the waist and dragged him to the door. Ribbons of slime decorated his shirt and pants and he weighed so little it was like picking up a chopstick.

"You can't just leave," said the guard, torn hopelessly between running after us and salvaging what he could from the floodplain of his desk.

Out in the station foyer, Caleb puked again. I tried fervently not to record the lurid egg yolk yellow of his vomit, but knew it was likely now embedded in my brain forever. On the hundred-meter stretch between the station and home, he kept himself together, then a dollop escaped on our way up the communal stairs. In the living room, I propped him up on the couch, and fetched a glass of water and a bucket.

"Take small sips," I advised, helping him hold the glass upright and guiding it toward his lips. Chips of gravel were stuck in the gash on his nose, and I wondered how they had gotten there and how to get them out. "Jesus, how much did you drink?"

He did not reply, but before I could stop him he gulped down the glass of water.

"Nother one," he said.

Filling up the glass at the kitchen sink, I heard what sounded like the whoosh of a bath overflowing, but by the time I got back to Caleb, it was too late.

"How could you have missed?" I said, taking the empty bucket from him.

Searching in the kitchen for a mop, I heard Harold's voice, and got back to find him, in a pair of threadbare pin-striped pajamas, surveying the scene with baffled amusement.

"Don't just stand there," I said, trying not to look at his hairy potbelly. "He's your bloody nephew."

I made him hold the bucket while I mopped up and I made him help me carry Caleb upstairs, and it all took much longer than it should have. Harold was fussy about who should go at the front and recoiled from the slime on Caleb's clothes. Halfway up, Caleb revived and looked at Harold and burst out laughing, then turned to me and said, "What's my cock of an uncle doing here?"

In the attic bathroom, I told Harold I'd take it from there, and held Caleb's head over the toilet until I was sure he had finished spewing. Manhandling him into bed, I felt like a boarding school matron doing what needed to be done, but as I peeled off his soiled shirt and trousers, I hesitated, as though I really ought not to be doing it. With only his boxers on, Caleb's limbs were thinner and more childlike than I had expected, and his arms were covered in bruises. Looking more closely, I saw they were only smudges, that he'd been drawing on his arm with a felt-tip pen. Next to a girl's face, her mouth fixed in an enthusiastic O, I could just make out the ruined sketch of a spurting penis.

As best I could, I recovered my matronly outlook and flipped him over onto his side so that if he vomited in the night he wouldn't choke, and I pulled the duvet right up to his chin. After that, I went downstairs and drank a mug of Ari's cooking wine. The bottle had been standing next to the stove for months and it tasted like vinegar, but at least it took the edge off, and washed away the smell of all the puke I had just cleaned up.

That night I was so tired and so relieved to have Caleb home that I went up to my old attic room and slept like the dead. The next morning I felt more refreshed than I had in weeks, and even sang to myself as I made a pot of coffee. Harold had gone out early—he'd asked to borrow Ari's car keys—but had left his laptop and papers strewn across the dining table. I remembered Pippa had told me Harold wrote screenplays, and, deeply curious, I picked up a few pages and gave them a cursory read. The formatting was hard to follow at first, but I was able to pick up the gist of the scene. A masked crusader rushed into a burning building to rescue a woman who wore nothing but stilettos and a transparent wet raincoat . . .

I dropped the papers immediately and tried in vain to unread what I'd read. How much had Harold seen under Ari's raincoat when it had gaped open? And had he asked me to the pub because of it—not as a friend but as a date?

By midday, there was still no murmur from Caleb, and I carried up to his room a tray of sugared black tea and dry toast. My knock on his door went unanswered, and his room, when I went in, smelled strongly of alco-sweat. When the tray landed on the bedside table, he finally stirred. "Ouch," he mumbled, touching his nose. "What happened?"

"I think you got the shit kicked out of you."

"Yeah, I remember that part. But how did I get here?" Struggling to sit up, he noticed he wasn't wearing a shirt. Then he peered under the covers to see what else he had on. "Who undressed me?"

"You were unconscious." I pointed to his crumpled clothes. "And there was vomit on everything except your underpants."

He pulled the duvet up around his shoulders. "I threw up?"

"You really don't remember?"

A startled expression crossed his face. "Did anything else—did someone—?"

"Did someone what?"

"I don't know." He looked grave. "Maybe you should tell me."

I told him about fetching him from the tube station, about all the spewing, and about Harold being there, and he listened intently, as if hearing it all for the first time. When I got to the part about missing the bucket, he chuckled.

"You can't laugh at that," I said. "You didn't have to clean it up."

"You're right. Sorry." His face fell. "Wait, did you say my uncle's here?"

"He arrived yesterday."

"Shit," he said. "Mum's going to kill me when she finds out I got wasted."

"You think Harold will tell her but I won't?"

"You wouldn't tell her," he said, with absolute confidence.

"What makes you think that?"

"Nothing." I was sure there was something but couldn't guess what it was. "You just seem cooler than that," he said.

I had been meaning to tell Caleb off, but his comment so threw me that I left his room without doing anything of the sort. After everything that had happened, how could he possibly think I was cool? And why did I even care? It was the answer to the second question that bothered me the most.

By early afternoon, Harold had returned with two cardboard boxes of books and papers he'd picked up from Peggy's. He'd found the key to her flat on the same chain as the car keys and had gone for a spontaneous visit. I was in the kitchen when he got back, lethargically making myself an instant coffee—I had mainlined the last of the espresso that morning—and he saw what I was doing and said, "That's it. We're going to Holland Park Café. Now."

I was too taken aback to refuse, and seven minutes later found myself scurrying after him up the steep cycle track to Holland Park. "There's absolutely no point whatsoever in strolling," he said, when we reached the café. "If your heart's not racing, it doesn't count as exercise."

We sat in a fenced-off enclosure, on sturdy wooden furniture that was crusted in places with lichen. The day was crisp, with a breeze that flurried nearby leaves and blew my hair into my face. It wasn't bright enough for sunglasses, but the light had a penetrating quality that made the pores on Harold's nose stand out. I wished I had not looked at them so closely, for afterward the lunch felt too intimate. Harold had been talking about the visit to Peggy's flat, how morbid it was, and I was only half listening until he mentioned that someone had ripped up the floorboards in his old room.

I told him I had seen them when I stayed there. "Do you think it was Peggy?" I asked. "I saw her cutting up curtains."

"It could have been. But there were a couple of strange incidents a while back with her neighbor Jimmy."

I was immediately intrigued, but at that moment our lunch arrived and Harold started banging on about his twenty-first birthday. He had found the old videotape at Pippa's and watched it that morning. He told me that Peggy had taken out a huge loan to pay for the extravagance. "That was how she operated," he said. "She handed you the moon and stars then expected you to spend the rest of your life being grateful."

"She took out a loan just to pay for a party?" I said, shocked.

"It was the same with my education. She sent me to all the best schools and reminded me every day of her sacrifice." Over the next thirty-five minutes I got an in-depth account of Harold's Cambridge years—term-time escapades with what he referred to as "the sons and daughters of the ruling elite," and interludes at home with his alcoholic mother. "She always wanted to know who I'd met and what I'd done with them, and when they were going to offer me a job—even when I was only halfway through my degree." He said he would never have gone to Cambridge if Peggy hadn't forced him. His education had been nothing but a burden, creating enormous expectations he couldn't possibly live up to. And so it went on. He seemed to have a chip on his shoulder about almost everything. He didn't fit into the upper echelons he had been educated alongside but had been rejected by everyone else for being overeducated, too posh. He was, he said, virtually unemployable. In his mind, all his misfortune, his sense of alienation, was Peggy's fault and hers alone. At least those had been the bits I could follow.

While I digested what he'd said, it occurred to me that Harold was trapped in a version of his life story that had ended decades ago—or would have, if he'd let it. The thought of ending up like him when I was in my forties, still stewing over what my parents had or hadn't done to me as a child, was dismal, and it struck me that there had to be a cut-off point, where it all stopped being their fault and started to become my own. "It's definitely going to rain," I said, standing up and feeling the first drops on my face.

Harold stood too. "Mind if we check out the old loggia before going back? I haven't been there for years."

I minded, but he was already halfway across the lawn, so I followed him. The rain began its promised assault, first in fat, cold droplets, then in squalling sheets, forcing us to take shelter on a stone bench in a secluded alcove. In different company, the circumstances might have been romantic, but as they were, I felt horribly trapped. Harold's monologue had moved on to his divorce, the long, slow, ordinary breakdown of his marriage—the kids got older; they grew apart; had affairs; tried counseling, didn't work—and as the tale went on, I had one of those terrible epiphanies in which you see an aspect of your own personality that has hitherto been hidden: I suddenly saw myself having swapped places with Harold, carrying on like he was, complaining about my life to Alana and a host of others before her. I didn't have to worry about ending up like Harold in my forties; I had already been like him for years.

"Anyway," said Harold, finally catching his breath. "Enough about me. Now it's your turn."

I was still cringing from the epiphany, vowing never to speak of myself again. "I think I'll pass."

"Tell me why you came back to London. I mean, isn't everyone else trying to emigrate to New Zealand—the clean, green paradise of the Pacific?"

"New Zealand isn't all it's cracked up to be." I stood up, pulling my jacket over my head. "I don't care if we get wet," I said, and dashed across the boggy grass in search of the nearest crowd.

That evening, the three of us sat down to dinner. Harold had nearly burned down the kitchen cooking steak, but the result was surprisingly tasty. I told him so but got no reply. He was still sulking about my running away from him in the park. Sitting next to him, Caleb said very little either; he was still zonked from alcohol poisoning and ate like a trucker, then disappeared upstairs. After a second bottle of wine, Harold started to thaw, and by the time we loaded the dishwasher, he was whistling a medley of show tunes—*Evita* mainly, with a smattering of *Cats*, nothing post-1985.

It was then I remembered that I hadn't found out about the incident with Peggy and the floorboards. "What happened?" I said, filling up the sink with hot, soapy water and preparing to attack the burned pan. "Was Peggy trying to find something?"

For a moment, Harold said nothing, and I thought he was still sulking.

"Maybe," he said, finally. "The business with Jimmy really got to her."

Even now, I was too nervous to say his name. "Was he as bad as everyone said?"

"Worse," said Harold. "Much worse." He told me that Jimmy had been waiting in line to be hanged on the day that capital punishment was abolished. Year later when he was released he came to live in Ladbroke Gardens with the woman who had been his barrister and who, for such treachery, was disbarred. On the whole, Harold said, Jimmy kept to himself, but he could be extremely intimidating when provoked. Harold's abandoned bicycle had caused one such episode, after Jimmy got so sick of it being in the hallway that he began urinating on it. Harold never used the bike and didn't even notice, but after a time, the urine began to leak through the floorboards and seep into the ceiling of our basement flat. When my mother worked out what had been causing the smell, she was livid and charged upstairs. Jimmy, apparently, had been meek. But about a month later, when my father was knocking down walls and clearing out rubble to convert our flat into a maisonette, Jimmy came downstairs with an ax to complain. At this point in his tale, Harold noticed a bottle of wine in the pot cupboard and took it out.

"I wouldn't drink that if I were you," I said, recognizing the bottle as the one I'd brought on my first visit to Pippa's. "It was the cheapest in the off-license."

He ignored my warning and unpeeled the stopper, then poured himself a healthy glass.

"Actually, can I have one too?"

"Sure," said Harold.

"So wait a minute," I said, trying to piece together Harold's story. "Jimmy hacked the floorboards? I thought you said Peggy did it herself."

"She did," he said, grimacing as he swallowed a mouthful of the wine, followed by another. "Years later, after Jimmy died, the person who bought his flat decided to renovate. When their builders ripped out the walls and ceilings, they found hundreds of stolen wallets and credit cards—stashed there by Jimmy over a period of twenty years."

"And that's what Peggy was looking for?"

"Possibly, but she got done over by him in a different way. Just before my birthday one year, she got a phone bill so huge it would have bankrupted her to pay it. She complained to BT, but they didn't believe she hadn't made all those calls—especially when they found out she had teenage children." Harold downed the rest of his glass and poured another. "Peggy read us the riot act, and the phone got cut off for six months while she paid off the bill in installments. But guess what the builders found?"

"That Jimmy had been using her phone?"

"He'd run wires up through the ceiling. The whole thing made Peggy really paranoid—and I guess she only got more so with age."

It hadn't been open for long, but the third bottle of wine was already half empty. "Hopefully I'll sleep better tonight," I said, finishing off my glass.

"Insomnia?" said Harold. "I get that too. Sometimes it's so bad I can't drive the next day."

"Because you're so out of it?" I said, thinking of all the strange things that had been happening.

He nodded. "There is one thing that helps though, I find."

"What's that?"

He gave me a bold look. "Well, sometimes not sleeping can be a sign that the body is trying to rid itself of certain energies—energies that can be destructive if we don't release them." He raised his eyebrows to see if I'd gotten his meaning—which I had, loud and clear.

"I'm not that drunk," I said, quickly. "But thanks for the advice." I drained the sink and turned on the dishwasher, a dinosaur of a thing that got loaded and unloaded and reloaded with the same dirty items until they eventually came out clean. Harold went into the living room, and I heard the late news come on.

Later in my room, I settled down to read, but it was a humid night and I found it hard to concentrate. Before attempting to fall asleep, I decided to take a cool shower. I'd been under the showerhead for several minutes when I thought I heard someone moving about in my bedroom. I had left the bathroom door open a fraction, as per Pippa's instructions—to let the steam out so the bathroom didn't go moldy—but I'd made sure the door from my bedroom out into the hallway had been shut. The noise wasn't exactly loud, but I had sharp hearing, perhaps to compensate for my lousy eyesight. I listened again, but heard nothing, and continued rinsing my hair.

The faucet groaned when I turned it off, and water still

dripped from the showerhead. I reached out from behind the curtain to grab a towel and heard the noise again. Looking through the gap in the door, I registered a glimmer of movement, but by the time I had wrapped the towel around myself and gone into my room, it was vacant. The door out to the hallway was closed, but when I listened carefully I heard someone thumping down the stairs, and not long after, a door slammed.

CHAPTER FIFTEEN

London, 2003

NOTHING SUPERNATURAL ABOUT getting spied on in the shower, but creepier in its own way than all the other stuff that had been going on, and I went to bed that night feeling deeply unsettled. Sleep eluded me, and I leafed through a copy of a trashy New Age novel I'd picked up off a bookshelf downstairs. In the early nineties, this book had been all the rage, and I remembered Alana reading it and raving about it and urging me to do the same. About a third of the way through the book, I had almost been lured in by its notion of meaningful coincidence when I turned the page and came smack up against a printing error. The whole middle section of the book had been printed twice, leaving the ending off altogether. My first thought was that it was some kind of joke—perhaps even a prank edition. What better way to poke fun at a book about synchronicity? But then, spurred on by the lateness of the hour, the gullible part of me took over and I began to see the misprint as part of a larger and more sinister puzzle. Stuff like this had been happening to me for weeks, and if the book was to be believed, I was fucked.

I made the mistake, then, of glancing over at the wardrobe door, the one in my room that had a hard time staying closed. Even now, it was open, but shouldn't have been. Before getting into bed, I had placed a chair in front of it to keep it closed, but since then the chair had moved and the door was ajar. The only remedy would be to replace the chair with something heavier, so I got out of bed and began to slide the desk across the carpet. At first, the thing shifted easily enough, but one of its legs caught on the carpet and it came to a halt, sending a carefully balanced tower of notebooks crashing to the floor. The noise was thunderous in the quiet house, and I held my breath while I waited to see if it had woken anyone up.

When it seemed that it hadn't, I shunted the desk free, and searched the carpet for the object on which it had snagged. My eyes fixed on what looked like an ivory trinket, its surface luminous against the carpet's dull weave. I bent to pick it up and placed it in the palm of my hand, where the trinket transformed into something more organic, a small front tooth, its root tapering off at a strange angle.

I dropped the tooth immediately, but even so my hands felt contaminated and I ran to the bathroom to wash them. With the door shut, I scrubbed and scrubbed with warm water and soap until my hands felt raw, one scrub away from bleeding. In the mirror was a surreal cartoon of someone who'd just had a fright, eyes bulging in a pale moon face. Perhaps it hadn't been a tooth, but a bead or a button. The bedroom had been dark, and I hadn't taken a proper look before dropping it. Except that I had.

Someone was knocking on the bathroom door, I realized, and I opened it to Caleb's sleepy face. "What's going on?" he said. "I heard banging."

"My books fell off the desk," I said, stuttering.

"Are you all right?"

"I found a tooth."

In Caleb's expression, I saw how pathetic that sounded.

"It's probably one of mine," he said. "Can I see it?"

We went back to my bedroom, turned on the light, got down on all fours, and crawled over the carpet looking for the tooth, but like a contact lens that had popped out of my eye, never to be found again, the tooth had fallen from my hand and disappeared. After ten minutes, we still hadn't found it, and I sat down on the edge of the desk, despondent.

"Are you sure it was a tooth?" said Caleb. "Maybe it was just a button or something."

"No, it was definitely a tooth. A small front tooth." I had only wanted it to be a button.

Caleb sat on the edge of the bed and yawned. "It must have been mine," he said. "This used to be my room—remember?"

"You're probably right. I'm still a little freaked out about the, ya know, presence, that's all."

He flopped over and frowned at the ceiling. "Have you heard the noises?"

"What noises?"

"Children's voices. They whisper sometimes."

A bolt of such hysterical fear went through me that I laughed out loud. "What do they say?"

"I haven't heard them for a while, but they were mostly taunts, like at school. They talked about me like I was the stinky fat kid and they were coming to get me. Like they wanted to kill me." His voice fell to a raspy whisper. "Kill him. Kill him. Eat his heart."

We fell silent, listening, but heard only the faint rumble of Harold's snoring, coming from downstairs. He'd been trashed when he went to bed, and I thought, with a shudder, that he must have been the spy. A strange rustling sound came from the bed, where Caleb was lying, and when I looked over, he was scratching his skin and pulling at his hair, eyes rolling back in some kind of fit.

"Caleb, are you all right?" I actually went over to the bed to get a closer look.

His chest heaved with silent spasms, and he was laughing hard enough to choke. "'Eat his heart,'" he repeated. "You should have seen your face—it was priceless."

"You scared the shit out of me." I tried to laugh, but felt like crying, and turned away, only to come face-to-face with the damn wardrobe. Even with the heavy desk slammed up against the door, it had found a way to spring open a fraction.

"Sorry," said Caleb. "I was trying to make a joke of it—so you wouldn't be frightened."

I was sick to death of feeling like such a sissy, and went over to the desk and hauled it away from the wardrobe. I flung open its doors, and pulled out all the boxes and other junk. "Who are you?" I said to the empty space. "And what do you want?"

The wardrobe did not reply.

"I've got an idea," said Caleb. "Why don't we stake it out? Like they do on TV."

I thought he was kidding, but he wasn't.

"It'll be fun," he said. "And anyway, nothing will happen, because I'm here."

Half an hour later, we were propped on our elbows, facing the wardrobe, bedded down on pillows we'd dragged from our beds. The wardrobe doors were wedged open, the desk on one side and a tea chest on the other, and in the middle was an empty space.

"I feel silly," I said.

Caleb zipped up his sleeping bag and handed me the torch. "Then you can take the first shift."

"We're not taking shifts," I said. "We're in this together." But within minutes he was fast asleep, and I was watching light patterns flit across the ceiling.

It was never completely dark in the city, or even very quiet, but the night was peculiarly still, as if the neighborhood had been covered with a tarpaulin. I looked over at Caleb, breathing slowly. His sleeping face was exquisite, like something out of a pre-Raphaelite painting. I wanted to run my finger down the length of his nose and over the bow of his lips. I wondered if his skin felt as smooth as it looked, and tried to imagine what it might taste like. Then I caught the direction my thoughts had been going in and stopped them. Caleb was just a boy. I had no business thinking about him in that way, none whatsoever.

I shone the torch into the wardrobe and directed the beam upward, illuminating a lone spider in its web. Next to my head, the carpet smelled of dead beetles and shoe dust, and something like sour milk, the stain from a spilled coffee perhaps. The torch was rubbery and heavy in my hand, and I felt my grip on it loosen as my body relaxed. Lulled by Caleb's regular breathing and the sound of distant traffic, I let my eyes close, just for a minute or two, and enjoyed the weighty feeling of exhaustion. The torch swooned to the bottom of a coffee pond and I swam through floating beetles toward a pair of dirty socks. How long I was under, I'll never know, but the pull upward was violent and complete, as though being wrenched from a hot bath and held up naked in a blizzard. Gasping, I opened my eyes, or thought I had opened them, but nothing registered except darkness so thick it was like trying to see through oil. I thought the disorientation was because I had been asleep, but rather than abating as I came to, it increased.

The only thing I was sure of was that I was no longer in the attic bedroom. Wherever I was, it was claustrophobic, with a harsh smell of mildew and wet concrete. Overhead, thick earth bore down and my hands, I realized, were lying in a puddle. My clothes had become heavy with water.

The experience was dreamlike, but it was not a dream. Instead, it was like being pulled backward through time to a distant memory, reliving it with perfect sensory recall. In the dark, when I reached out, I was able to touch the dry nylon coverlet of Caleb's sleeping bag, but when I tried to shake him, my hand was too weak to close around the fabric. My voice, when I shouted his name, went backward into my throat.

Shifting my weight to try and stand up, my hand struck a group of small, wet objects that were smooth and hard, like pebbles. Straightaway, from their irregular shapes, I knew they were teeth—not just two but enough for a whole set—and my hand shrank from them, colliding with other debris. The water was crowded with matter that hadn't been here on my first visit, and I groped at textures that were hard, like bone, but also slick. Mixed in with those were fragments of organic material, hair perhaps, and fingernails, an unholy bric-a-brac of human remains. In protest at the strong smell, my nostrils clamped shut. My chest heaved in a sob that I couldn't hear, and in spite of a rising feeling of disgust, my hands kept searching through the swill for something I'd lost. On my hands and knees, I crawled forward, and encountered a familiar child's leather shoe, rounded at the end with a metal buckle and an old-fashioned T-bar strap.

My fingers closed like a vise around the shoe, and in the same instant a tapping began, quiet at first, then louder and more insistent. The rotting odor receded, replaced with the doughy smell of a sleeping body, and I was completely dry, no longer submerged in water. Before I opened my eyes, I noticed that one side of my body was jammed up against an intense source of heat, but the knocking sound distracted me from that. My eyelids flicked open, I was back in the attic bedroom, and there stood Harold, framed by the doorway, his body a dark silhouette.

Three or maybe five seconds later, I clocked that Caleb had shunted over in his sleep until he was crammed hard up against me. I rolled away from him, but too late. From his vantage point by the door, Harold would have seen Caleb and I wedged together, my belated attempt to roll away from him, and worst of all, my stunned expression—a possum caught in headlights. I reached for my glasses, and put them on.

In the early morning gloom, the look on Harold's face was hard to make out, and he was unmoving, silent.

"Hi," I said. "How long—how long have you been there?"

"Long enough to figure out what's been going on in this house," he said.

While I tried to think of something to say, Caleb sighed awake, registered it was morning, and looked over at the wardrobe. "You didn't wake me up for my shift," he said. "What happened?"

Harold cleared his throat and flicked on the light switch, startling Caleb. "I'm sorry to interrupt your slumber party, but Pippa just called from Greece."

Something in his tone made us both sit up and try to look awake.

"It's Peggy," he said. "Her fall was worse than anyone thought, and because it wasn't treated immediately . . ." He trailed off.

"Is she okay?" I said.

"Not really, but she refuses to go to Athens, where they could treat her. She wants to stay put in Skyros, come hell or high water."

"What does that mean?" said Caleb.

"It means we need to get there as soon as possible," said Harold. "And that includes you, Suki."

"Me?"

"Yes," said Harold. "All three of us."

"Great," said Caleb, throwing off his sleeping bag. "That's just fucking wonderful." He got up and stomped to the bathroom, banging the door shut behind him.

"Why am I going too?" I asked Harold.

"I don't know," said Harold. "You tell me." He looked meaningfully around the room at the pillows, torches, and junk piled up on the bed. Surely he could also see that my sleeping bag was zippered to the top, as Caleb's had been.

"You don't think—" I began, but didn't know how to continue.

"You might want to put this room back the way you found it," said Harold, and turned on his heel and left.

Alone in the attic room, I felt a stinging sensation in my hand, and unclenched my fingers from around the phantom shoe. On the palm of my hand, small, but very clear, was a dot of blood where the pin of a shoe buckle had gouged a hole in my skin.

CHAPTER SIXTEEN

London—Paris—Athens, 2003

OUT THE TRAIN CARRIAGE WINDOW, London's backside was on display, and even at six A.M., eyes clogged with sleep, I couldn't look away. Satin sheets and flannelette, cloth nappies, magic knickers, garter belts, socks, tights—even the things people didn't want you to see had to be washed and hung out to dry. Some gardens were profuse with vegetables and roses, scattered with abandoned children's toys and signs of life. Others were barren squares of concrete, windswept or clogged with litter, and I wondered if whoever lived there was as untended, as unloved, as their backyards.

But I was only distracting myself. The discovery of the tooth and what had happened afterward—the grisly remains in the bunker—were still fresh in my mind. I was worried too about what Harold had surmised from what he had seen. I didn't think Pippa would have summoned me to Greece and paid for my ticket solely because she wanted to tell me off, but in the absence of another, it was the only explanation that seemed plausible.

At such short notice, no direct flights from London to Athens had been available, so we were taking the long route to Skyros, catching a train and hovercraft to Calais—the tunnel train was fully booked—and flying out of Paris. We would overnight somewhere near Athens and catch the ferry from a nearby port.

The night before, Harold and I had been sent to Peggy's apartment to pick up items on a list given to us by Pippa. Peggy wanted some of her personal belongings brought to Greece—photograph albums, various mementos, and a heavy white fur coat. Despite the Skyros heat, she would not budge on the fur coat, though her request to bring over Madeline had, thankfully, been refused. While we were over at her apartment, Harold and I had gone into his old room and he had shown me the clipped wires under the floorboards where Jimmy's illegal phone line had been disconnected. Jimmy had stuck the wires to the plaster with pale green putty that looked like chewing gum. I hadn't noticed the wires when I was staying there, or the scratch marks around them, as though a small dog had been digging under the floorboards.

"Maybe she thought he was still down there," said Harold, poking his finger into a crumbling plaster hole in what would have been Jimmy's old ceiling.

"Maybe he is," I said, half joking, half not.

While we were at Peggy's, Harold was civil with me, though I had been on edge, wondering when he would mention the sleepover again. It wasn't until the next morning, when Caleb was with us, that he reverted to being frosty and sarcastic—or perhaps I was reading too much into his mood and he was just tired. Whatever the case, we almost came to blows over Peggy's extra suitcase, a giant, cumbersome thing that required the three of us to cooperate in ways that were beyond us at that or any other time of the morning. Still, we made it onto the train to

Dover, and Caleb immediately fell asleep with his head against the carriage window, oblivious to the greasy smear next to his face that someone else's hair gel had left behind. Harold was reading one of the left-wing newspapers, holding it up in front of his face to shield himself from the rest of us, and I closed my eyes and pretended to snooze but could not. At Dover, we boarded a hovercraft, and watched uneasily as it farted its way to inflation. Hovercrafts had seemed so futuristic once, but now the thing just seemed like a relic, unseaworthy and rank, especially inside the grubby main cabin where the wet carpet ponged of diesel and latrines.

We took our seats and I thought of coffee, teased by the sweet smell of powdered hot chocolate that began to waft through from the onboard cafeteria. We were lined up in a row with Caleb in the window seat, but any views that might have been there were obscured by fog and violent hurls of sea spray.

"Can I get something to eat?" said Caleb, turning to Harold. "I'm famished."

"There won't be anything decent."

"I don't care." He climbed out past Harold and rolled his eyes when he got to me.

"I'll go with you," I said.

A long queue curled around the refreshment kiosk, and everyone in it looked grim, deflated from rising too early. Even Caleb had bags under his eyes, and was yawning enough to make his jaw snap.

"Has Harold said anything to you about the other night?" I asked when we were in the queue.

"Nope," he said. "He just told me to stop pissing around and pack my shit."

Briefly, I caught another whiff of the onboard toilets, and it reminded me of the dreadful smell in the bunker. I wasn't sure how much longer I could keep it all to myself. "That night while you were asleep," I ventured. "Something did happen."

"Why didn't you wake me up?"

"Because I'm not sure if it happened, or if I imagined it." I thought of showing him the scab on my hand, but without the shoe that put it there, it didn't seem proof of anything. "And it wasn't the wardrobe this time."

"Well, whatever it is, I'm sure it won't bother you in Greece." He laughed. "I don't think ghosts can swim the channel."

I wanted him to be right but was afraid that he wasn't. "What if I'm the ghost?" I said. "Or I take it with me wherever I go?"

We'd reached the food cabinet, where I lost Caleb's attention to a hundred plastic sandwiches and pastries in dinky cardboard boxes. "Can I get whatever I like?" he said.

"Go crazy."

Fifteen minutes later, midchannel, the hovercraft buzz was at its most deafening, and Caleb sat beside me looking green. He got up suddenly and lurched toward the aisle, clutching his stomach. I got up to follow him, but Harold reached out to stop me. "He doesn't need you to hold his hand," he said.

It was the first time he'd spoken to me since we'd boarded the hovercraft.

"I wasn't planning on it," I said.

Harold gave me a challenging look. "Are you sure about that?"

"Whatever you think happened the other night," I said, "you're wrong. Caleb was just trying to help me sleep, that's all."

Harold said nothing, but I suddenly remembered his carnal cure for insomnia, and realized I'd only made things worse.

"I'm going to get another coffee," I said, and decided not to mention it again.

We arrived in Calais as disheveled as if we'd been traveling for weeks. Back on dry land, after emptying his guts at sea, Caleb was ravenous again, and tucked into a stale *pain au chocolat*, while Harold stood on the concourse and smoked. Already the journey was starting to feel like punishment.

At Charles de Gaulle Airport, Caleb rode up and down the conveyor belts of the central dome, waving at us and pulling faces until, at the end of one trip, he decided simply to vanish. With less than half an hour to go before we had to board our plane, Harold dispatched me and my schoolgirl French to find him. I wandered the concourse, bewildered by foreign signage and shoving hordes, until I too was lost. The airport was hideously chaotic, overrun with thin, jabbering women and fat, smoking men, and an intimidating array of security guards and military police with guns. I wanted, very much, to lock myself in the toilet.

In the end, it was Caleb who found me and not the other way round. I was buying bottled water at a kiosk when he punched me on the arm and said, "*Salut!*" then tried to blow a smoke ring in my face. He seemed perfectly at home, another *louche garçon* with a Gauloise packet hanging from his shirt pocket.

"Where were you?" I said. "We're going to miss the plane."

"*Je suis un flâneur,*" he said, with a pretentious flourish.

"*Oui,* and *je suis un rock star.*"

We caught the plane, but only just, and Harold was furious about it for as long as it took him to pass out with a deep snore on the seat between us. Within seconds, Caleb was tapping me on the arm, asking me to order an extra glass of wine for Harold so he could drink it. When I refused to, he turned up the volume on his headphones and turned his back on me, the model of a sulking teenager. It was silly to even analyze it, but telling him off, and the casual way he'd rebuffed me, made me feel like I was his mother, and I wished that I hadn't said no.

Hours and hours later, we were in the back of a hot, cramped bus from Athens to the port of Kymi when I first noticed that Harold had been crying. Only then did it dawn on me that his cantankerous mood probably had nothing to do with Caleb or myself. We were on our way to Skyros because his mother was dying, and I of all people should have had a little empathy.

Our hotel was a fleapit in an industrial quarter by the port, half the letters missing from its neon sign. In the dim lobby, Harold went to the reception desk to check in, while Caleb and I sat on our bags in the cracked marble foyer, yawning our heads off.

After what seemed like forever, Harold came toward us looking glum. "They didn't get our reservation," he said. "They've one room vacant, a double, and the best they can do is a trundle bed."

"Fuck that," said Caleb. "I'm not sleeping on a trolley."

"There aren't many hotels here," said Harold, wearily. "But the girl at reception said she'd ring round to see if anything's available."

The thought of more travel was torture. "I'll sleep on the cot," I offered. "It's sort of the only arrangement that works."

Harold nodded. "Caleb and I will have to share."

"No fucking way," said Caleb.

In the small, ovenlike room, we put down our bags and turned on the ceiling fan. It scudded to life and wafted hot, stale air over our faces.

Caleb flopped on the double bed. "I'm hungry."

We all were, in the inexplicable way jet lag stimulates the appetite, and set out along a strip of kebab joints and all-night bars, grateful to abandon the hotel. It was well past midnight by the time we sat on the curb munching souvlaki, but a gang of olive-skinned urchins was still up and playing in the street, terrorizing a scrawny orange cat and her litter of emaciated kittens. The day had been a hot one, and the stench of baked rubbish was intense but not unpleasant, just all part of the new and vivid sensory imprint of Greece.

For the first time in weeks, I felt energized and awake, but I was out of sync with our itinerary. Our ferry left at seven the next morning, and before long, we were back in the oven, trying to sleep. The beds had lumpy horsehair mattresses over squeaking springs and made a cacophony as we took turns to get up and use the bathroom. Caleb wore pajamas and tried to build a protective wall of pillows down the center of the bed he was sharing with Harold, who came out of the bathroom bare chested, wearing a towel fashioned as a skirt. He climbed in next to Caleb, and fumbled under the sheets before dropping the towel to the floor.

Caleb sat bolt upright. "You're not going commando, are you?"

"Y-fronts. I don't like to feel restricted when I sleep."

Caleb wriggled closer to the wall, while overhead the ceiling fan flapped as though it were trying to take off. The tepid breeze that reached my face smelled of unwashed travelers, with a top note of garlic *tzatziki* and lamb. Harold fell asleep almost immediately, his snoring a low, steady rumble, but hemmed in next to him, Caleb pitched and moaned. "I can't sleep," he said. "I feel like a rotisserie chicken."

"It's your pajamas," I said. "They're too restricting."

"Shut up."

Exhaustion had caught up with me, but there wasn't enough oxygen to go round the room, and each time I reached the edge of consciousness, a mosquito screamed in my ear, and I swiped at it pointlessly in the dark. An hour passed before Caleb kicked the wall in total frustration. "I don't see why we all have to go. Granny hates it when we make a fuss over her."

"I don't think we're going for Peggy's sake," I said. "Your mum wants the family to be together."

"Even Harold?"

"Shhhh," I said, pointing to the bed. "Peggy's his mother too."

A loud squeak came from the mattress springs as Caleb catapulted himself out of bed and tugged off his pajama top. Briefly, his bare silhouette appeared in front of the neon hotel sign, his bony shoulders bent over like a spoon.

"What are you doing?"

"Escaping."

Even though he was asleep, I didn't want to be left alone with Harold. "Wait for me."

We headed out in no particular direction but soon found ourselves at the port, drifting alongside a fleet of decrepit fishing boats and freighters, and set off aimlessly along a jetty that pointed out to sea. On one side of the jetty the water was smooth, oily, but on the other it slapped up against the rocks in angry waves. Caleb and I had been walking along the jetty for half an hour or so when it seemed to narrow, and the sea became rough on both sides. The concrete under our feet was wet in places, and once or twice a wave washed clean over it.

I looked over my shoulder to see how far we'd come. Expecting to see the port behind us, I was shocked to discover nothing there at all. Everything, all the freighter hulls and fishing boats, had been washed away, and the only thing left was the sea. On the horizon was a dim orange glow, the faint promise of dawn. I wondered if my eyes were playing tricks on me, and, a little more slowly, I traced the line of the jetty as it arced away from us. But still, nothing was there except ocean.

"Caleb, stop," I said, feeling panicky. "Turn around."

"What is it?"

"Behind us. The port isn't there."

He scanned the horizon in the direction my finger pointed, then turned right around until he was facing out to sea. "It's that way," he said, as if I was a complete moron.

"What do you mean?"

"We turned around about ten minutes ago and started to walk back."

"What?"

For a few minutes I watched him continue to walk in the wrong direction, away from the port, and was too stunned to say anything. When it was obvious he wasn't going to wait for me, I trotted after him. "Caleb, you're going the wrong way. You're heading out to sea."

He looked over his shoulder at me and frowned. "No, I'm not."

He waited this time while I examined the horizon in both directions, looking for some kind of landmark. But there was nothing. I was completely lost.

"You'll just have to trust me," he said.

His stride was confident as we set off in the direction he indicated, but my legs had become jellylike, uncooperative, and I struggled to keep up. For another five minutes we walked in silence, then a chugging noise that had been in the background grew louder behind us and I turned to see a lantern bobbing in the air, some fifty meters offshore.

"What's that?" I said, peering at the ghostly vision.

"Have you totally lost your mind?"

I looked again at the bobbing light, and saw that it was bolted to the top of a pole, that behind it was rigging and a white cabin. It was a fishing boat, heading back to port, and as it pulled alongside, a couple of fishermen who'd been pouring fish guts over the stern waved at us.

"*Kalimera!*" yelled Caleb, and one of the fishermen called back, "*Kalimera!*" and held up a still-flapping fish.

"That means good morning," said Caleb, turning to me. "Come on, race you there!"

I tried to run but could manage only to trot, and as we neared the wharf the sky began to lighten and I saw, with relief, that we were back on the docks where we had started. Circled by screeching cats and gulls, the fishermen had already started unloading their catch, and the salty smell of fresh seafood wafted over to us.

Caleb bounded toward the boat and started negotiating with the fishermen in a flurry of pidgin Greek. While he did so, the first sun of the morning burst over the horizon, dipping everyone, including Caleb, in soft, golden light. Despite having had no sleep, Caleb's hair, cheekbones, eyes, and lips were at their pristine best. In three years' time those features would be testosterone coarsened, ravaged with stubble, but that morning he was caught in the last instant of perfection before boyhood ends, and staring at him gave me a pain in my chest.

I hadn't noticed that one of the fishermen—so tan he looked like a sandal—was nodding in my direction and saying something to Caleb that was making him shake with laughter. He handed Caleb a fish wrapped in newspaper and slapped him on the shoulder. When he trotted back, Caleb was still chuckling. "Guess what he wanted to know?"

I looked at the giant fish. "If you had a refrigerator?"

"No." Caleb grinned. "He asked if we were on honeymoon!"

"Who?"

"You and me, dick."

"And what did you say?"

"That you were my mother!"

His insult hurt, and I was too tired to hide it. "I'm not that old."

"I know you're not," said Caleb, giving me a friendly biff on the arm. "And that's why I told him you were my sister."

Daylight arrived quickly, and with it, heat. There hadn't been time to shower the night before, and I was desperate for one now. As we retraced our steps along the port, the surrounding streets clattered to life. Roller doors flipped up to reveal hidden shops, and awnings unraveled over café tables that had been stored away for the night. Searching the sun-glazed streets for a familiar landmark, I realized for the second time that day that I was utterly lost.

"Do you have any idea how to get back?" I asked Caleb, who had stopped at a kiosk to buy sweets for breakfast.

"I was following you," he said, shoving a square of lurid pink bubble gum in his mouth.

After clumsy negotiations, Caleb got directions to a Hotel Triton, which we thought was the name of our accommodation. We'd found the port easily enough that morning, but the route back was convoluted and seemed to take longer than the way there. We cantered the last few streets, and as we piled into the Triton's lobby streams of sweat ran down the groove of my back. Harold stood at the desk grilling the night concierge—"How could you *not* have seen them leave?"—and barely keeping it together.

"Here we are!" said Caleb, heroically.

Harold whipped around and glared at him. "The ferry leaves in twenty minutes—I'm not even going to ask where you two have been."

"Fishing," said Caleb, and held up his prize.

"Not now," I said, and shooed him toward the stairs.

In a state of panic, we stuffed clothes into suitcases, and hurriedly checked under the bed for stray socks and underpants. Clothes sprouting from his half-zipped backpack, Caleb called out to me, "I don't care if we miss the ferry. This hotel's fucked, and Harold's a cock."

Running for the ferry, we retraced our steps for the third time. Caleb jogged with the fish under one arm and tried to keep abreast of Harold, who was surprisingly nimble, while the best I could manage was a lopsided scuttle, held back by fatigue and wayward suitcase wheels. When I had dropped too far back behind the others, I picked up the suitcase, and the plastic handle burned painfully into my hand.

Up ahead, a grim-looking ferry called the *Achilea* honked its departure horn, and the gangplank swung away from the dock as we drew alongside. Harold waved frantically at the shipping steward, who was methodically fastening a small metal gate, and started shouting at him in a mishmash of English and Greek. For a tantalizing moment, the gangplank shivered while the steward decided our fate.

"Please, please!" begged Harold. "My mother is dying!"

"Your mother?" said the steward, his English perfect.

He lowered the gangplank and showered us with condolences while we filed past, silent with gratitude. The main ferry cabin was stuffed with squeamish tourists and rowdy locals whose grandmothers, children, and breakfasts were spread out on every surface. Already it smelled as though the toilets were overflowing, and we ventured outside to the aft deck and a row of wooden benches. But after so little sleep, I couldn't stand the idea of sitting upright for six or seven hours on a plank of wood, and when I moved to a shady corner of the deck and collapsed against a funnel, Caleb followed. Harold was giving us the silent treatment and remained on the bench, inspecting his ankle where the strap of his orthopedic sandal had rubbed a blister.

The ferry chugged out into the harbor, and I closed my eyes and sank into my suitcase. A few minutes later, a warm weight fell against my shoulder, and a swatch of hair tickled my neck. Caleb had fallen asleep on me, though who knew if he had meant to. With bright sunlight burning an orange pattern on the inside of my eyelids, I tried to imagine how we'd look to strangers, or even to Harold, but I lost consciousness before I could make a decision about what if anything to do about it.

Some time later, I woke with a jolt and Caleb rolled off my shoulder and onto the deck. "Ouch," he said, sitting up and noticing the patch of drool on the shoulder of my T-shirt. "Did I do that?"

I was surprised by how little I minded. "It'll dry out soon enough."

He looked around at the sun-blazed ship. "How long was I out for?"

"An hour maybe? I don't know. I've been asleep too."

The ferry swung round unexpectedly, and the change in direction threw us out of the shade. "There's still ages to go," said Caleb, pulling a sweater out of his knapsack. He scrunched the sweater into a ball, placed it in the crook of his neck, and leaned against my shoulder again. "I'm going back to sleep," he said.

Where his bare arm fell against mine, my skin goose-bumped. He sighed a couple of times and relaxed into sleep. To lean on me once had been careless, but to do it twice was something else, and before I could stop it, my pulse quickened, and a warm feeling spread over me. It was followed by an ugly jolt. What was I doing? Caleb was barely sixteen—a half-formed newt who drank and smoked but didn't yet shave. Nothing could come of this, nothing good.

I needed a bathroom, but not so badly that I was prepared to get up and look for one, and soon fell into a clenched half sleep. The ferry chugged on and on, and periodically I gazed across the railings to the edge of the sparkling sea but saw no land. The hours started to sag and lose all shape, until it seemed we had spent our entire lives at sea on this crusty ship. Next to me,

Caleb's legs were folded girlishly underneath him, and his wrists hung limply in his lap. He looked vulnerable, like a child who had fallen asleep on an adult he trusted, and I felt ashamed of the path my thoughts had taken, the way my body had reacted.

An hour or so later, it was Caleb who walked unsteadily to the railing and stared out across the frothing wake. After hours of inertia, my own legs were stiff and uncooperative, and my contact lenses were like sandpaper against my eyes. I joined him at the railing, feeling queasy and dehydrated and terminally zonked. He pointed toward the starboard side at a cluster of blue-black fins on the horizon.

"That's Skyros," he said. "We're almost there."

CHAPTER SEVENTEEN

Auckland, 2001

I HADN'T SEEN or heard from Ludo in months when he called out of the blue inviting me to lunch. He said he was coming to Auckland on business, and maybe I'd like to meet him at one of those new al fresco places on the Viaduct Basin that were springing up to cater to the Americas Cup. Ever since securing the prestigious event, the city had gone all St. Tropez, or tried to, and in the formerly industrial quarter next to the harbor a miniature gin playground was hastily being built. To cope with the expected influx of seafaring Eurotrash, thousands of Aucklanders had upped their intake of champagne and oysters, while women, single and married, had been enthusiastically taking French lessons to better seduce any incoming Eurosailors.

I had been doing neither. In fact, I could hardly bring myself to go down to the harbor and look, such was my contempt for anything to do with the enterprise.

A hundred yards out from the restaurant I identified Ludo, sitting on the terrace in a beige linen suit. The restaurant he'd chosen was all white, even the floor, and at midday already full of red-faced gents sucking oysters from their shells and trying to chat up their waitresses. I'd come straight from the office, where we spent all day on the phone, and felt scruffy and incongruous in sneakers and an ill-fitting shirt. As I approached my father, the jerks at the next table openly appraised me, and I tossed my hair and scowled at them to let them know how little I appreciated it.

"You look different," said my father, shaking my hand, formal as ever, and pulling back my chair in a show of chivalry. "Have you had your hair cut?"

"I dyed it. Supermarket red. You look younger. Have you had work done?" Hard as I tried to temper it, my sarcasm was always out of control around Ludo.

He ordered a dozen shucked oysters and ate them in front of me, washed down with champagne, pausing at regular intervals to ask if I was sure I didn't want one.

"No thanks. They taste like snot to me."

He didn't like it when I was vulgar, but I enjoyed the look on his face when I was. "Order whatever you like," he said. "It could be a taste of things to come."

"What does that mean?"

He sipped his champagne and winked. "You'll see."

That sounded ominous, and I perused the menu while waiting for the charade to come undone. Unless I'd done something wrong, or they needed collecting from the airport or a last-minute babysitter when they were in town, I never heard from Ludo or Rowan. I'd received no invitations to spend Christmas with them since the time four years earlier when I had failed to turn up with Lily's present and arrived the next day with such a foul hangover that I'd passed out at the dinner table after one too many of my father's aperitifs (apparently, Rowan had held my head over the toilet while I spewed, though I did not remember, or subscribe to, that part). When I came round, Dad and I had a huge row over the past, a continent he refused to revisit, and the argument had ended with me hurling a framed photograph of his children at the wall. The frame had smashed, and I had left the house immediately, hitching all the way into Hamilton at two in the morning. Ludo had gotten in touch with me a few months later to say we ought to meet on neutral territory from then on, which I understood to mean that Rowan had finally banned me from the ranch. So this was how it was: a few times a year he took me to lunch. Once or twice I'd seen my father cruising the streets of Auckland in his late-model four-wheel drive—he came up for business all the time—and though I'd thought about waving to him I never did.

The restaurant menu was convoluted seafood, and I ordered something prawny with pink lobster mousse that said it came in a basket with fish-egg decoupage. Waiting for this impossible creation to arrive, I asked politely after Rowan and the children and my father's business and listened to the latest installment of their mishaps and triumphs. Rowan had fallen from her horse in the last round of dressage at an event in Christchurch—she was competing again—and Simon had taken up rowing and was already trying out for the New Zealand under eighteen team. Lily apparently had developed "weight issues" and did nothing all day except sit in her room and listen to "God-awful head-banging music." Out of all of them, she was the one I could most relate to.

Ludo wanted to know what I'd been up to, and I gave him the abridged version: work was the same, but someone on the community newspaper I worked for was leaving, and I hoped to get a promotion by the end of the year.

"Good for you," he said. "It's great to have a taste of a career before you settle down. That way you can pick it up again later if you get bored."

I had long suspected that my father measured my worth, if he measured it at all, in the proximity of wedding bells and booties, and even though I knew his attitude was deeply sexist, it still hit me where it hurt. His frequent attempts to matchmake for me with blockheads he worked with only made things worse. During dessert, he even hunched his shoulder toward the jerks at the next table and with a wink said, "Gee, there sure are a lot of hunks at this place."

"Dad," I said, as one of them turned and looked in our direction. "Please don't."

But he either hadn't heard me, or was determined to humiliate me, and before I could stop him, he was waving at the men and smiling in my direction. "You see?" he said, when they waved back. "It's the easiest thing in the world to meet a guy."

"I've already met someone," I said, quietly.

"Great," said my father. "What's his name? What does he do?"

"You won't know him," I said. "So there's no point in telling you." I traced a pattern on the tablecloth with my finger. "What did you want to talk to me about?"

Ludo tried to refill my glass from an empty champagne bottle, and even though I protested, he insisted on ordering another one. "We're going to need a toast," he said.

"To what?"

"All in good time."

The champagne arrived and was opened with ceremony. Dad put his briefcase on the table and took out a checkbook. On the top line he wrote my name, then he started on the figures and kept adding zeros. When he was finished, he handed it to me. "Voilà!" he said.

At first I thought it was a joke, that you couldn't write personal checks for that much, but when I looked at Dad his expression was too expectant for it to be fake.

I said, "What did you do—rob a bank?"

He looked bashful, almost as if I'd guessed the truth, and said, "Of course not. It's only what you deserve."

"So *I* robbed a bank and forgot about it?"

He chuckled, as if he was stalling, and carefully folded his napkin. "It's something I've wanted to give you for a long time, but haven't been able to until now. I think I told you business is booming."

I put down the check on the white linen tablecloth and stared at it. Underneath my father's signature was printed PIPER ENTERPRISES LTD. The check had my name on it and was crossed in the top-right-hand corner so no one else could cash it, but I left it on the table while I picked at dessert, a pot of creamy white stuff that smelled sort of fishy.

"You don't seem very excited," said Ludo, pouring more champagne into my already full glass.

"I'm just in shock. That's five times what I earn in a year."

"Really? But you're a journalist."

"Exactly."

Ludo went over to the till to pay and came back and put his briefcase on the table. "There's just one thing—I almost forgot." He laughed. "My accountant needs you to sign this document confirming that you received the money as a gift." He handed me the document, printed on the legal letterhead of a large firm of city solicitors. I tried to read the first paragraph.

"Even I don't understand the details," said Ludo. "But the gist of it is that I'm not trying to tax dodge." He handed me a pen and pointed to the dotted line at the bottom, the place where I should sign.

"I'm too tipsy," I said. "Can I sign it later?"

"Wouldn't you rather bank the check straightaway?"

Scanning the letter for a phrase that made sense, I stumbled upon the words, "In lieu of legacy." I read them again. "What does that mean?" I said, showing the phrase to Ludo.

He looked closely, or pretended to. "Well," he began carefully, "I suppose it means I'm giving you something you're owed."

"But isn't a legacy what you get when someone dies?"

"It can be, but a person can give it to you while they're still alive."

"Why would they do that?" I said, feeling dim, and wishing I hadn't drunk so much champagne.

"Maybe they think it would be more useful to you now."

"I see," I said, but didn't at all, and picked up the check and the document to try and make sense of it. Instead I got a queasy feeling, the same one I had when I discovered a mistake in the galley of an article just after it had gone to print. "I really don't think I should sign anything when I'm drunk."

"Please, Suki," said my father. "I really want to give this to you. And I know you need the money."

I was folding the document to put in my handbag when Ludo took it from me.

"What's there to think about?" he said. "It's a windfall." But the way he made it sound as if I'd just won the lottery without even buying a ticket was what finally stopped me from signing.

"I can't do it," I said. "It's too weird."

On the way back to the office I passed by my favorite clothing store, where the new summer range was on display in the window, and regretted my decision. I was up to my neck in debt, had three credit cards and a student loan. Why hadn't I just signed the damn document and run away to Paris with the check? Was I that much of an idiot?

That night I had a date with the new guy I was seeing, Edward. I hadn't told my father his name because I didn't want to jinx anything. Since breaking up with Scott I had suffered a long drought of unrequited obsessions broken only by the occasional desperado one-night stand. Edward was the first guy in five years who looked at me and saw something more than either an unsexy friend or a late-night opportunity, and for that reason I ignored what I otherwise might have considered a series of early warning signs. I was too delighted, too relieved, that at last someone liked me, and well before the point at which a relationship is deemed to have legs, I had thrown out caution and eagerly gifted him my heart.

I had never been out with a lawyer before, or anyone even remotely professional, and I noticed that my friends took the relationship more seriously after I told them what he did. However, I was more interested in his passion for films. He followed only the work of what he called "true auteur directors," and he delighted in educating me on all that I'd missed (which was nearly everything). One of Edward's favorite things to do was to invite me over for curated movie marathons. These he took very seriously, and once one had begun, there was no question of it finishing early, even if I was tired. One night, it was after midnight when he took the final DVD out of its box and put it into the player. Five minutes into the film, the subtitles blurred into a hairy black line, and my eyelids tanked.

I remember Edward tried to prise them open, but to no avail. When we got into bed, I found that I couldn't pass out like I had on the couch. Edward was lying too close, and my limbs found ways to slide in his direction. He had his back to me, and I caressed his slim, smooth hips.

"I thought you were tired," he said.

"So did I."

"Then what are you doing?" His voice was flat, and my hand

retreated. I had not known what I was doing, but whatever it was, I kept doing it, like a puppy that returns to the owner who beats it. One night he asked me to name my top five albums, and when I had picked the *Dirty Dancing* sound track, which I had liked very much growing up, he'd laughed, unkindly. I should have laughed too, at his pretension, but instead I doubted my taste.

My hope was kept alive by the times he would soften and take me to bed, where he would whisper intimate confessions about his life. As an eleven-year-old he had been sent to boarding school, where an older boy had raped him with the handle of a cricket bat. He had never told a soul, and the secret had almost devoured him. When he was sixteen, he had tried to kill himself. He was only telling me these things, I reasoned, because he trusted me, because he loved me, and on the promise of that, I trailed around after him for another few weeks.

Sometime around then, a letter arrived from Rowan.

Dear Suki, it began, *It's not my thing to write letters, so that should tell you how upset I am by what's happened.*

I knew I should stop reading, tear up the letter and throw it away, but I couldn't help myself.

> *Your father and I have worked bloody hard to provide for our children, and we don't want you to take it away from them. Considering your past behavior toward us, Ludo's offer was extremely generous, and it just shows your selfish attitude that you turned it down. The money is more than you're owed, given what your parents' flat sold for in the eighties. You probably don't realize this, but houses in London weren't worth much then. If it had been up to me, we would have offered you less. Don't think that by holding out for more, the*

> *amount will go up. It won't. Ludo doesn't know about this letter, so there's no use ringing him up to talk to him about it. He said he was going to try giving you the check again, but I don't know why. I know you're too greedy and won't take it.*

There was more, but it was more of the same. I had to read the letter a few times to work out why she was so angry. From what I understood, my father had taken more than his share from the sale of the London flat and there was some kind of deficit that she was worried I was angling to take back from them.

When I showed the letter to Edward to ask for his legal opinion, he agreed. "She's trying to buy you out of Ludo's will."

"But I don't want any of that," I said, thinking of the ugly ranch and muddy paddocks and the stables full of twitching horses. "And besides, he's still alive."

"She must think you're waiting to make your move."

"I have a move?"

"You'd be surprised by how many people do."

That was one of the last sane conversations I ever had with Edward. That same week, he started accusing me of fucking his friends, and the more strenuously I denied it, the more proof he seemed to find of my guilt. I had always thought jealousy might be flattering, but the look in Edward's eyes when he accused me of cheating was sheer lunacy, not affection. A few weeks later he dumped me, though it should have been the other way round.

Breaking up with Edward took me to a level of devastation I had never known before. Not because he had been a great love—we had been together barely two months—but because I believed it was the end of love, that he had been my last chance, my last shot. I was not yet twenty-seven, which I knew was hardly old, but I felt worn out. On the day we broke up, I experienced what felt like a power outage in the region of my heart. It was done with being battered, had decided to shut down for good.

I went to Wellington for a week to get away from it all. The capital was in the grip of an Arctic wind when I arrived, and I stayed in a dreary self-contained studio on the tenth floor of an industrial concrete block. It had a tiny balcony shaped like a çage, and a view of an abandoned building site that had been turned into a car park. When I had "settled in," I picked up the phone and worked my way through a short list of phone numbers. I had hoped to see Becky, but a message told me her cell phone had been deactivated, and when I tried her home number, a flatmate told me she had moved out long ago. When I couldn't reach anyone, I decided to go out on my own.

The city was jammed with after-work drinkers, and I fought my way through them in bar after bar, pretending to look for someone who was never there. I found a pub where hundreds of blokes and their girlfriends were crowded in front of a rugby match on a giant screen, but the boisterousness of the crowd unnerved me, and I left without ordering a drink. It was too early to be out alone, though, when everyone was just getting started, so I went into a liquor store that was next door to an Irish pub. The girl at the counter had pink shiny skin and ginger hair, and chirped at me in a thick Irish accent when I handed over my money. I had not understood a word of what she'd said.

"Excuse me?"

"Can I see year eye dee?" she repeated.

"My eye what?"

"Your eye-dentification," she mouthed, slowly, as though I were retarded. "So I can check you're over twenty?"

I held up my driver's licence, which had a picture of me taken when I was at university. She looked from me to the photograph and scowled. "You need a new picture, love," she said. "That one looks nothing like you."

Maybe it wasn't me. I certainly didn't feel like the girl in the photograph anymore.

I bought cigarettes and hurried back to the gray box of my studio room to smoke them with wine. As I fumbled with the swipe card, I heard the phone ring on the other side of the door. I missed the call, but when I got in, a red light was flashing on the telephone. There were no instructions about what to do, how to retrieve the message or make the flashing stop, so I ignored it and went outside to smoke in the cage of a balcony, sitting cross-legged on a metal grate. Cars and bits of pavement were visible through the gaps and for a split second I imagined what would happen if the cage came unattached from the wall. The wine had been supposed to act as a heater, but my feet and hands were frozen, and I ran inside and, seeing a NO SMOKING sign propped up next to the empty fruit bowl, smoked with my head hanging out of an open window. I'd already downed most of the bottle, but instead of getting me drunk, the wine had combined with the nicotine to cause my nerves and thoughts to race unrelentingly.

I had the strangest sensation then that I had somehow left the real world behind, and had gone to a place that didn't exist. I had taken annual leave, and it would be weeks before anyone realized I was missing. Starting to panic, I tried to call friends in Auckland to tell them where I was, but it was Friday night and none of them was home, not even my best friend Susan, who had a young baby and never went out. I even started calling my father, but remembered Rowan's letter, and stopped in the middle of dialing his number. Desperate to talk to another human, I rang a pizza delivery chain and ordered whatever was on special.

They said it would take forty-five minutes, so I switched on the TV and flicked through random images. Then, in the middle of taking a pee, the phone rang again, and I ran to answer it with my jeans half zipped.

"Hello?" I said, eagerly, hoping Becky had somehow tracked me down.

"It's me." His voice was robotic.

I felt sick. "How did you find me?"

"I was worried about you and I called your work. They said—"

I held the phone away from my ear and stared at the tiny plastic holes where Edward's voice was leaking out. Maybe if I didn't put the phone back to my ear, I could pretend he wasn't there. Maybe he wasn't there. Right from the start, the phone had been playing tricks on me. I followed the cord to the wall and pulled it out at the socket. The flashing red light finally extinguished and the rest of the phone went dead.

Had I really talked to Edward? It seemed unlikely that he would have found me here. But if not him, then to whom had I spoken? I scanned the studio's gray walls for clues, but found none—nothing in here reminded me of anything. Even the clothes in my suitcase did not look like mine. My driver's license showed a picture of a familiar young woman, but the girl in the liquor store had been right not to recognize her. Neither did I.

The pizza arrived. On it was pink and yellow goo that had fused with the gray cardboard box it had come in. I wasn't sure that it was really food. I was out of wine; had three cigarettes left, then two, then one. I emptied the ashtray on top of the fake pizza and the ash stuck to the topping like fine black pepper. I tried not to think of Edward, but he surrounded me. The walls of the room were his skull, and I was sitting inside his head.

I lay down on the bed to go to sleep and that's when it started. Without prelude, my mind became fixated on a list of ways to kill myself. I thought at first that I must be the one writing this list, but soon after, I realized I wasn't in control of it, that the list was writing itself. It had invaded my thoughts like a virus.

Whether I had my eyes open or closed made no difference. The list kept scrolling, demanding that I pay attention to its methods, perhaps ten or twelve in all: strangulation by hanging; an overdose of pills; falling from a tall building or bridge, like the one that spanned Auckland Harbor. Nothing very original or creative, just the basic methods, brutal and efficient. These unfolded step by step like the safety instructions at the start of a flight, only the attendant (who was me) had gone rogue and was demonstrating death instead of self-preservation.

As time went on, I found I was no longer simply a passive bystander watching myself carry out the methods, but was experiencing a set of corresponding physical sensations: the vertiginous urge to jump; the long, slow trapeze of falling.

Fifteen feet away, the open apartment window beckoned. From there it was only a matter of stepping off a metal bar, of surrendering to the open arms of gravity. Why had I left the window open? I wanted to shut it but could not risk getting close enough. Instead, I gripped the mattress with both hands and closed my eyes so I wouldn't be able to see it.

But the list was not so easily thrown off course. Just down the road, it announced, was an open-late supermarket where boxes of aspirin and razors were stacked prettily on the shelves. It reminded me that a speeding bus would also do the trick; or a train if one was at hand.

I tightened my grip on the mattress. I had thought, before this, that when people committed suicide they had done so by choice, that they'd *wanted* to kill themselves. But I saw now that suicide wasn't something you chose. It chose you. It was a compulsion, a command, and the margin for survival was narrower than a pin.

In the end, my own probably came down to luck: I was good at insomnia, at wakefulness, at hanging on to consciousness when I should have been asleep. Nodding off or even just zoning out for a minute, in this case, would have been fatal. That's when the list would have pounced.

Sometimes, when I have gone over the events of that night in the gray box, I have seen another outcome very clearly. I have imagined myself losing awareness for a second or two and walking to the window and climbing up on the cage and jumping off without hesitation. Mid-fall, I come to, and the last thought I have before I hit the pavement is that no one will ever know I didn't want to jump.

CHAPTER EIGHTEEN

Skyros, 2003

"WATCH THIS," SAID CALEB, crossing the ferry to where Harold was napping on a wooden bench, his head resting on his camera bag, his leg tied to his suitcase by a garish silk tie.

"Don't," I said. "He's fast asleep."

But Caleb picked up the suitcase and made to run off with it, so that Harold's leg jerked in the same direction and he rolled off the bench. "Stop!" he called out, landing awkwardly on all fours. "Stop, thief!"

Caleb laughed hysterically, "It's me, you knob. Can you look after our stuff while we get something to eat? Seeing as how your security system rocks."

"You little toad," said Harold, still half asleep, but Caleb dumped his bag there anyway, along with the fish, which had started to reek after basking all day in the Aegean sun.

"Sorry," I said, and was about to take my suitcase with me, but realized how heavy it was and put it down next to Caleb's. "Actually, do you mind?"

"Just get me a fucking coffee," Harold said through clenched teeth.

For breakfast or lunch, or whatever meal it was, we bought cans of thick chocolate milk and a packet of dry, sugary biscuits that tasted, well, foreign. After sucking on diesel fumes for seven hours straight, everyone in the canteen had turned into zombies and stared in our direction without seeing anything.

"I'm still hungry," said Caleb when the biscuits were all gone, and the ship answered him with a booming honk.

Out the salt-smeared window, a jagged coastline dotted with white cubes and brooding fir trees loomed ominously close. "Come on," I said. "We don't want to be late again."

Even though we raced back to Harold, he'd already lined up all our suitcases, ready to disembark, and was pulling at the newspaper around Caleb's fish.

"Don't touch that, it's for Mum," said Caleb.

Harold screwed up his nose and grimaced. "Lucky her."

Passengers surged toward the exits, jamming corridors and doorways with children and bags, and we were swept along in the crush, too tired to resist. For almost a minute I was squashed up against Caleb, my nose in his hair, his buttocks pressed to my groin. Better than the other way round, I thought, and blushed at what I'd been thinking. Another surge set the crowd moving again, and I was shoved into an old man, all thoughts of any kind put out by his sour armpits and garlic breath.

For a moment I lost sight of Caleb and then he reappeared up ahead of me, leaning over the railing, searching for his mother in a sea of bobbing heads. Harold was on the gangway, struggling with his and Peggy's suitcases, and I felt guilty that I hadn't helped him. I spotted Pippa among the crowds on the wharf and made my way toward her. The others got to her first, while I was still on the gangway, which swayed from the combined weight of so many bodies. Caleb turned to look for me and tapped his mother on the shoulder and pointed in my direction. I waved, but Pippa didn't wave back, or even smile, and I dropped my hand, already paranoid.

When I finally reached them, Caleb had just presented Pippa with the fish, which she held aloft, as though it were a trophy, before treating her son to a long bout of hair ruffling and kisses. "That's enough, Mum," he said, pushing her off.

Harold stepped forward to embrace his sister, and she stepped to one side to avoid him. "Hello, Harold," she said, suddenly brittle. "Mummy can't wait to see you." She turned to me. "Suki, you look like death. You'll fit right in with the crowd at the villa." Her voice was strained, and she talked in a rush. "I'm afraid we can't hang about. I've left Peggy alone with Elena and she's probably knocked her out with her bells and smells by now." She laughed fakely at her little joke and touched me briefly on the shoulder. "It's a bit of a hike to the house, but if we're lucky we might be able to hire a donkey."

There was no donkey, just a backbreaking, thigh-burning climb up the steepest hill in Skyros with the midday sun drilling a hole in my skull. Pippa set the pace, trotting up ahead with Caleb and his bantamweight rucksack, while behind them, Harold and I dragged and shoved our suitcases as well as Peggy's up the knotty, cobbled street. By the time we arrived at a low wooden door set into a white plaster wall, I had begun to wonder if perhaps this was all part of an elaborate punishment. The door opened onto a courtyard paved with pebbles, with rooms that looked invitingly dark and cool off it on three sides. On the fourth side a low, whitewashed wall dropped away to a magnificent expanse of azure sea and sky, creating the illusion that it might be possible to dive off the wall and straight into the ocean. A fig tree grew in the corner of the courtyard, and I thought I was seeing things when a sort of troll hobbled out from under it and made a beeline for Caleb. It flung its arms around him and pinched his cheeks and clucked and cooed a string of Greek at him.

"This is Elena—Ari's mother," Pippa said, adding more quietly, "she doesn't understand English, but I wouldn't worry about that because she doesn't seem to understand Greek either." She patted her ears, which I took to mean the old woman was deaf, and excused herself to go and check on Peggy.

Elena put her knobbly hand around my waist and said, "New Zealand. *Kalimera!*"

"Thank you," I said. "Your villa is lovely."

Her face folded into a gummy smile and she quickly released me and whisked Caleb off toward one of the cool, dimly lit rooms. He had his arm around her too, and she fit snugly under his shoulder, the flag of her black head scarf peeping out over the top.

Seconds later Pippa reappeared, and Harold said, "It's good to see you. You look great—so tan and healthy, not like us."

We looked like refugees after three days in the back of a lorry, but I didn't think Pippa looked much better. "I can't think why," she said, brushing off Harold's compliment. "I've hardly been outside since we got here."

"And how is Mother?" he said.

"Not good," said Pippa. "She's asleep at the moment, but we can pop in to see her if you like."

Peggy had been set up in a small, airy room that overlooked the flat roofs of the village slopes. We stood in the doorway so as not to disturb her. She was asleep in a modern hospital bed, the sort that cantilevered in the middle, and Pippa whispered that they'd had to drag the sodding thing up the hill on the back of a donkey cart. The room smelled faintly of rubbing alcohol and disinfectant, and Pippa gestured to a small white tube that trailed out of Peggy's arm and hooked onto a receptacle by the bed. "It's a morphine pump," she said. "Most of the time it knocks her out, but occasionally Lazarus rises from the bed and starts barking instructions."

Harold smiled. "That sounds like my mother."

"She wanted to see you the second you got here," said Pippa. "You should probably give her a kiss."

Rather stiffly, Harold moved to the bed and pecked Peggy's forehead once.

"She's dying," said Pippa. "It isn't contagious."

Harold bristled, but I saw why he'd held himself back, and was shocked by it too. Instead of the tan she'd hoped for, Peggy's skin had lost all pigment, and peeled off her body in chalky layers. Her hair had thinned out too, what was left standing up from her head in downy, newborn tufts. She was really only a collection of bones, except for her abdomen, which was horribly distended.

Pippa saw me staring at the protrusion. "It's fluid," she said. "An edema. It means her organs are failing."

We shuffled back out to the courtyard, more sober than when we had left it, only to be baked alive by the midday sun. Under my clothing, my unwashed skin was starting to itch. "Would anyone mind if I took a shower?" I said.

"Of course not," said Pippa. "I'll show you to your digs. It's a bit of a squash I'm afraid, but we'll all just have to rub along." She still held the parcel of fish, and tentatively started to unwrap it until the smell overpowered her. "Where did he get this?"

"I don't know," said Harold, before I could answer. "Suki and Caleb absconded this morning—we nearly missed the ferry—and that *thing* was their excuse."

Pippa looked at us both blankly and smiled. "Well, Elena will know what to do with it." She disappeared into a room I assumed was the kitchen, and came out carrying two glasses of water. "We boil our drinking water here," she said, handing one to each of us. "I wouldn't advise drinking from the tap—just to be on the safe side." She led us into a long, narrow room next to the kitchen, where shuttered windows cast a weak gray light. The floor was pebbled, like the courtyard, but most of it was covered with faded red and blue woven mats. Around the room were platforms at varying levels, and these were crowded with patterned cushions and textiles, discolored from age or too much sun. At the far end stood a shrine festooned with candles and effigies, the centerpiece of which was a life-size statue of the Virgin Mary holding a midget Jesus nailed to a cross. Both icons were plastic and wore lurid halos made from fairy lights, switched off at that time of day.

"This is where you'll be sleeping," said Pippa, pulling open a striped curtain with a spindly ladder behind it. At the top of the ladder was a platform and a thin, rolled-up mattress. "Elena sleeps over there." She pointed to a mass of pink lace and quilting directly underneath Jesus and Mary. "She's terribly sweet, but snores like a walrus, so I hope you're far enough away. There wasn't anywhere else to put you, I'm afraid."

"Am I sleeping in this room too?" said Harold, looking around at the other platforms.

"No," said Pippa. "This is the girls' dorm, and you're bunking with Caleb."

"Great," said Harold. "I couldn't be more thrilled."

Left alone in the crypt, I lifted my suitcase onto the platform and climbed up after it. The space was about six feet wide, with no railing and a drop of about the same distance. With the curtain shut it was almost private, but also strangely coffinlike, and I was acutely aware of Jesus and Mary just over yonder, watching, praying, leaking their plastic tears. Above my mattress, nailed to the wall, was a wooden bleeding heart, its paint rubbing off in places.

I was considering where on the platform to stow my suitcase when the sounds of an argument, heavily muffled, filtered through the wall. The baritone voice I recognized as Harold's, and after a time I heard Pippa yelling too. Most of what they were saying was indecipherable, but at the peak of the crossfire I heard Caleb's name spat out in the same sentence as my own, by Harold.

Consequently, I arrived at supper that evening in a state of high apprehension. Whatever Pippa and Harold had been arguing about, I was sure would come out. But I was also starving, and allowed myself to be distracted by a feast of stuffed peppers, tomato salad, oven-baked bread, and rich, bubbling moussaka. Elena might have been doubled over with osteoporosis, but she was no slouch in the kitchen. Even Caleb's fish, grilled to a crisp, looked good enough to actually eat. Though once it was on my plate, my stomach disagreed.

"Is something wrong with your meal?" asked Pippa, pointing to it.

"Not at all," I said. "It's amazing."

"It's the fish, Mum, it's rotten," said Caleb, spitting out a mouthful.

"Nonsense, darling, we don't let good food go to waste in this house." Pippa looked at her husband. "Do we, Ari?"

At the sound of his name, Ari looked up, but he had missed Pippa's question. Since arriving in Greece, he had been even less present than he had been in London.

"Tell them we don't waste good food," repeated Pippa.

Ari looked down at the untouched fish on his plate. "It's revolting, Pip, and the last thing we need on top of everything else is food poisoning."

"On top of my mother dying, you mean?" said Pippa.

Ari didn't reply, but Caleb banged his fist on the table. "Mum, I told you it doesn't matter about the stupid fish!"

Pippa turned to her son, blinking furiously. "Darling, it was awfully thoughtful of you to buy it for me. I just don't know if I can eat it." She pushed her chair away from the table and stood up, looking at Ari. "As for you . . ." she said, starting to cry and covering her mouth with a napkin before heading in the direction of her room.

"You know I didn't mean it like that, Pip," Ari said to her retreating figure.

The rest of us were quiet after she left, except for Elena, who continued to chew and slurp as though nothing had happened. When she had mopped her plate clean with a piece of bread, she smacked her chops in delight and squeezed Caleb's hand, saying something in Greek I couldn't understand.

"You're welcome, Grandma," replied Caleb, with an imitation smile. "At least someone enjoyed the fish," he said to us.

Immediately after supper, Caleb took off to his friend Yanni's house, and Ari said we probably wouldn't see him from now on. "They've been best friends since before they could walk; he practically lives over there."

"Why didn't he want to come if his best friend lives here?" I asked.

"He was testing us," said Ari. "Seeing if we would bend to his will."

I told myself that not seeing so much of Caleb would be a good thing, though inwardly I had lurched with dismay. When the meal ended, I excused myself and went to the sarcophagus to try and sleep. I was half strung out with exhaustion, but Elena had been into the room since the afternoon to light a few candles, turn on the halos, and generally fill the place with a toxic cloud of frankincense and myrrh. Out of desperation, I tried covering my head with a pillow, but couldn't breathe at all, and I was still wide awake when Pippa came in later and called out to me. By the time I'd put on a T-shirt and pulled back the curtain, she was already halfway up the ladder.

"Golly," she said. "You wouldn't want to climb up here after a few drinks." She was rueful about the scene at dinner, and ashamed that I'd had to witness the hostility between her and Harold. "I can control myself at first, but the tension builds up so quickly—then, when he comes out with one of his ludicrous allegations, I just go ballistic at him."

"That's family," I said, too afraid to ask what he'd accused anyone of. "They know how to push your buttons."

"Yes, but he's also a stirrer," she said. "He says things just to get a reaction."

She trusted me too much. "Pippa," I began. "I know you think I'm a good influence on Caleb but—"

"Oh you are," she said. "He's already changed. That thing with the fish was so sweet, so considerate. He hasn't done anything like that for years." She climbed onto the sleeping platform and made herself comfortable. "Only it made me feel terrible."

"Because you had to eat it?" My comment barely registered, and I noticed that Pippa was distracted, struggling over the right words. "Have I done something wrong?" I said.

"I wanted to tell you before we left, and it's been on my mind ever since we got here," she said, finally.

"I can explain—" I began, but was cut off.

"I was very young," said Pippa. "And I thought it was all just harmless fun—we all did back then." She looked down at her lap and rubbed at an imaginary mark on her shorts. "We even called it bonking, like sex was just some kind of party game."

She paused to gauge my reaction, while I tried to keep up

with the change of direction the conversation was taking. Was she about to confess to sleeping with my father in the bathroom that night at the party? "It's okay," I said. "I really don't want to know."

"I had that job in the florist's on Portobello Road," she continued, ignoring me. "I worked there all through school and afterward, when I was at the poly. At first he used to come in himself to buy small bouquets, nothing flash, but after a while he started to ring up from Frankfurt or wherever he was working and would ask for the flowers to be delivered."

She was talking about my father; he had bought flowers from the shop she worked in. Why was she talking about that? "He wasn't fussy about blooms, but they had to be specific colors: oranges and reds, really quite garish," she continued. "Over time, the arrangements got bigger, more expensive."

"Mum hated cut flowers," I said. "She must have thrown them out before I even saw them."

Pippa bit down on her lip. "They weren't for her, darling."

An attack of dimwittedness came over me, and I pictured a bouquet left on the wrong doorstep, flowers getting pelted with rain. "Who were they for?"

"I feel so bad about it now," she said. "But at the time—I suppose I was too preoccupied with myself. And your father was so charming. He used to take us all out for drinks—not just me but my friends too. Champagne cocktails at Annabel's, the works. Once or twice she came too. We all knew what was going on, but no one told your mother."

I suddenly understood. Rowan had been in the background all along. In a blink my childhood was reshuffled, all the hidden cards revealed. "How long did this go on for?" I said. "The flowers and all the rest?" I couldn't bring myself to say her name.

"A few years, perhaps."

"A few *years*?"

"None of us ever thought he'd leave your mother," said Pippa.

Then, with utter clarity, I saw the ace of spades that had been in the deck all along. "She was pregnant," I said. "Simon, their son, was born not long after they left."

"Yes," said Pippa. "I wasn't sure if you knew."

"I knew the timing was close, but I didn't know how close." I was quiet for a moment, thinking things over. "I can't believe you knew Rowan, that you had drinks with her." I hadn't meant it accusingly—I was merely astonished—but to Pippa it sounded that way.

"If I could go back and change my part in it, I would," she said.

I wanted somehow to reassure her that it hadn't been her fault. "All you did was make up bouquets, have a few drinks."

"I did more than that," she said. "I helped to deceive your mother while your father went out and had fun. I didn't see it that way until I had a child of my own. Then I deeply regretted all the lies."

"Well," I said, choosing my words carefully, and scarcely able to believe what I was about to say, "telling the truth isn't always possible. You did what you thought was the best thing—at the time. Telling Mum might have made things worse."

"I know," said Pippa, and smiled. "I suppose that's ultimately why I didn't tell her." She rubbed her eyes and leaned toward me. "Anyway, good night," she said, giving me a warm hug. "I'm so relieved to have that off my chest."

"It's nothing, really," I said, hugging her back.

After she left, I lay awake, grappling with the implications of what she'd told me. I had been lying when I'd said it was nothing. For some reason I had always felt that my father had cheated on me and not just on my mother, and now I understood why. By starting a family with someone else, he had cheated on the one he already had. All the feelings of resentment I had tried to deny suddenly bloomed inside me. No wonder Rowan had been paranoid that I was going to take them to the cleaners, for she knew I had every reason to. For a few minutes, I let my blood boil with righteous indignation, but then I just felt worn out and sad. Fleecing Rowan was no use to my mother, and it couldn't deliver me a childhood with my father in it.

I drifted off to sleep, only to wake abruptly some hours later from a feverish dream set in a vast mansion haunted by unspeakable horrors. I sat up in bed, thinking that an overload of fear had woken me, only to realize, a few moments later, that what had actually roused me was a noise: a blunt, metallic scraping sound that was still there—iron dragging on concrete.

I was sleepy, and it didn't click at first that I'd heard the noise before. Then I remembered *where* I'd heard it, and all the air went out of my lungs. It was the same noise I'd heard that night at Peggy's flat, when I'd looked out the window and seen . . . what had I seen that night, exactly? In the weeks since, I'd tried not to analyze it because each time I had, nothing became any clearer.

But there was the sound again: a metallic scrape coming from the courtyard, as clear as if I were dragging the hatch open myself. I reached next to the thin mattress for my glasses. My hand was shaking, and they wouldn't settle properly on my nose. There was no lamp on the sleeping platform, only a candle, but I didn't have any matches, hadn't noticed any in the room. But perhaps I didn't need to turn on the light—after all, what I wanted to see was outside, not in the crypt. I was wearing only knickers and a singlet, and quickly pulled on a pair of jeans. My flip-flops were at the bottom of the ladder, and I climbed down slowly. Shuffling across the pebble floor, my foot caught on one of Elena's knotted rugs, and I briefly pitched forward, taking fright. Over by the shrine, the old woman's pink and white bedding heaved, but it wasn't true about the snoring, she made no sound at all.

I reached the door, which was slightly ajar, and pushed on it with my hand. At my feet, through the door, was a short flagstone path and clipped grass, Notting Hill green. The door swung shut again, and I remained still, with my hand on the wood. Behind me was Elena's room—the faded rugs and Jesus and Mary, their halos glowing faintly, neon lit. But in front of me, on the other side of the door, was what? Not the courtyard, not Elena's villa. Not what ought to be there.

Once again, I pushed the door open, and held it open with my hand. I took a step forward so that one foot landed on soft grass. In front of me was a homemade brick barbecue, a small, square lawn littered with empty wine bottles, and the discarded red slip of a Wendy tent. Everything I'd seen that night at Peggy's, but right here, within arm's reach. I put my hand up in front of me and moved it forward, waited to meet resistance, but felt none, only a different kind of heat; the air through the door was swampier, like just before a downpour.

I lowered my hand and inched my right leg forward, leaving the other behind so that I straddled the doorway. The temperature on either side was subtly different, but both places were warm, summery, strangely inviting. Without thinking, I shifted my weight onto the front foot, and swung the other leg forward so that all of me was outside in the garden—*my* old garden from when I was six years old.

Not trusting what I was seeing, I stepped back through the door, into Elena's room. But the garden was still there on the other side. I crossed the threshold another four or five times and then, satisfied that I wasn't going to be shut out, I stepped resolutely into the garden. At first, being there felt like coming home, but as I walked a little farther my legs began to shake, and after a meter or so I stopped and looked behind me.

The door I'd come out of was an old servants' entrance that I'd forgotten was there. It went nowhere, had been blocked off long before we'd lived in the basement flat. This was the same door, I now realized, that had confused me when I was staying at Peggy's and had imagined a direct exit from the communal lobby to the garden.

Only then did I have the wherewithal to examine my surroundings more closely. The area immediately around where I stood was perfectly solid, tangible even. When I bent to feel the grass, it was springy to the touch, and slightly damp. I walked onto the patio and crouched down. The flagstones were smooth, and the grooves between them were gritty with soil fragments and dust that adhered to the ends of my fingers.

But looking across the communal garden, and beyond that into the distance, I noticed that the trees and masonry had soft edges, that they melted into one another, became indistinct. The waxiness of it unnerved me, and I had the sense that at any moment it might all collapse, taking me along with it if I was still there.

The thing I most wanted to see—but was also afraid to look at—was over to my right, on the other side of the flagstone patio. When I finally had the courage to glance over, I could just make out the edge of it—of the hole—and next to that, the hatch of pitted iron. The bunker was open, the same as it had been that night at Peggy's, only this time I was at ground level, close enough to feel the vertigo that insisted I was going to fall in.

Pulled by that irresistible force, I moved a little closer, near enough to see moss growing around the edge of the iron plate. I moved closer still, until the top step that led down to the chamber of the air-raid shelter came into view. Seeing the step below that one sent a shiver through the hairs on my head, and I thought of the horrors that were down there. Not just the teeth and the T-bar shoe, but the lingering smell of decay, and the soup of hair and bones.

As if replying to my thought, a soft whimper sounded from the pit of the bunker—such a tiny sound that it was almost negligible, and I wondered at first if I had imagined it. To better hear, I dropped to my hands and knees, and lay down next to the hole with my fingers curled around its mossy edge. Cautiously, I put my ear to the cavity and listened. For half a minute, I remained stationary but heard nothing, and then a piece of soft moss crumbled off in my palm. Beneath it the soil churned with earwigs, squirming in all directions and wriggling blindly toward my hand.

Mice and rats I could tolerate, but insects were another case entirely, and I got up and shook the dirt from my hands, danced around on my tiptoes as if I was infested with the things. At that exact same moment a high, desperate wail escaped from the bunker, followed by a heartbreaking moan that sounded like a child in pain crying out for its mother. Halfway through, the moan was cut off, as though the creature making it had been strangled or plunged underwater.

So disturbing was the combined effect of the moan and the earwigs that I found myself mechanically stepping away from the hole, first walking backward in slow, deliberate strides, then turning around and legging it toward the service entrance. In the doorway I paused, and turned round to face the bunker. Someone, a child, was trapped down there, and I had to go back for her. Was that why I kept returning to this place?

I had retraced my steps almost to the service door when a sharp guffaw tore through the air and a man stepped through the French doors of our old flat and out into the garden. Two other men followed, also in raucous hysterics, snorting with abandon. Among the voices, I recognized my father's low chortle, and for a moment or two I simply listened in a kind of trance, before it clicked that my presence in the garden was an unthinkable anomaly. I was trespassing across space and time. What would happen if they saw me? My nerves caught up with me and my heart began to pound. Whatever blip was occurring, I did not wish to cross paths with a giddy, young version of my father. I wasn't ready to have that experience, not now, or ever.

I resolved to return to Elena's room, and as I crossed the threshold of the service entrance and found myself back on her hard, unforgiving pebble floor, relief flooded through me. I was back in Skyros, back in the present. But when I turned around and looked back through the door, the view of our old garden was still there. I could even put my hand through the doorway, touch the humid, pre-storm air. I leaned on the doorjamb and peered into the garden. Some ten or fifteen meters away, the shadowy figures of Jean Luc, Henri, and my father were heading toward the air-raid hatch. They bent down and each took one side of it and tried to heave it a few inches off the ground. Mere seconds later they dropped it again, and the sound of clanging iron reverberated around the garden. The three of them fell about laughing—the gleeful, irrepressible hysteria of wine-addled youths—so intoxicated that they seemed unable to continue with their task. But a few minutes later they had recovered enough to try again. On the third try, they finally succeeded in placing the hatch over the hole. They didn't bother fastening the bolts, just staggered off toward the flat with linked arms—all except Jean Luc, who loitered by my mother's prize geraniums. I realized after a time that he was relieving himself, though the procedure seemed to take him longer than necessary. His elbows stuck out at odd right angles and he was struggling with something, perhaps a zipper. After what seemed like an age, he got it sorted, went inside, and the garden was deserted.

For a short while longer—perhaps only ten seconds—I stared at the apparition in front of me, until I had the sense that my vision was failing, that the scene was rapidly going out of focus. Gradually, like a windscreen demisting, the distortion lessened, but as it did so I realized the scene in front of me had changed. Instead of the old garden, I could make out the dark outlines of a stooped fig tree and a low wall, the solid features of Elena's courtyard. The evening light was a little bluer than it had been a few minutes earlier, but the time of night I judged to be approximately the same—give or take twenty years.

I felt shattered—not just physically exhausted, but mentally done in, as though I'd been trying to figure out complex algebra that was far beyond my ability. I managed to climb the ladder to my sleeping platform, to lie horizontally on the small, firm mattress, and the instant my head connected with the pillow I was out for the count.

CHAPTER NINETEEN

Auckland, 2002

WHEN AFTER SIX MONTHS the suicide list still hadn't gone away, I paid for sessions with Arthur, a Jungian psychoanalyst who had been recommended to me by my doctor. Before that, I had gone to see a psychiatrist who had offered me a choice between two brands of psychotropic drugs. I'd told him I didn't want either, that I thought perhaps drugs were what had gotten me into this mess in the first place, and he had sent me on my way with a condescending look and a flyer for group counseling.

Arthur was fiftyish, with a beard and sad, suffering eyes that made me think of paintings of Jesus with nails through his hands. He worked out of a small room with obscured glass windows at the front of a weatherboard villa, where I sat on an overstuffed couch next to a jumbo box of man-size four-ply tissues. Only once did I reach for the tissues, when I'd come to my session after a particularly grueling day at work, but Arthur reached for them often, whenever a story I told made him cry.

"Don't you feel sad when you tell me that?" he'd ask, dabbing his eyes.

"I don't know," I'd say, and I'd really mean it. Often when I talked about my past, I noticed it was easy to articulate the events, but not so easy to feel the emotions that went with them. A lot of the time I felt nothing at all. I told myself it was the falseness of the situation that was restricting me. Arthur was genuinely kind, but I was paying him handsomely to listen, he wasn't doing it out of the goodness of his heart.

On and on I talked, until I ran out of saliva, and week after week, Arthur said very little. He was fascinated by my dreams, and got me to recall them in detail at every session, but when I asked what they meant, instead of telling me outright, he'd ask cryptic questions until I came up with my own unsatisfactory explanations. It was like hiring a translator who then refused to interpret the foreign language you didn't speak.

In one of our early sessions, Arthur asked about my father, and why I'd stayed in New Zealand instead of going back to London, and I had replied, "Because I like it here."

"Do you?" he said. "You haven't been very happy."

"I prefer this to going back to Grandma and all that."

"All that?"

"Grief, I suppose. London is where Mum died."

"But ten years is a long time away from your homeland. Were you hoping the situation with your father would change?"

"To begin with, maybe, but not anymore."

"When did you last see him?"

"Only once since he offered me the check. He tried to give it to me again."

"Do you regret not taking it?"

"Sometimes."

"And did you tell him about the list? About being suicidal?"

"I haven't really talked to him in a while."

"When did he last call?"

For only the second time in Arthur's office, I reached for a tissue, and he waited patiently while I used it.

"Not having any family to fall back on," he said. "That must be very hard."

His pity rankled, and I sat up straight and blew my nose. His wife and children were playing noisily in the backyard behind the villa—I'd seen them arrive home in their Volvo. What did he know about having no family, about being alone? I had left his office in a snit, but later that night, listening to music in my room, I realized Arthur had only been trying to make me see that I no longer had a valid reason for remaining in New Zealand. I was refusing to accept that I'd never have a prominent place in my father's life, and it was the only thing that was holding me here.

In another session, from out of the blue, I had recalled how the whole family had been trapped down in the air-raid shelter. I told him about the teeth, about the move across the bunker that I couldn't account for, and as I was telling him I had the strangest sensation that perhaps it had all happened to a parallel version of myself who shared my experiences but wasn't me. "Is that normal?" I asked. "To feel like a bystander in your own past?"

"It's perfectly normal to disconnect from traumatic experiences," he said. "Do you have any other memories like that?"

"There's the hand in the cupboard," I said, and told him about the way it had untied my dresses in a sort of game. Even as I was telling him, I knew he'd have a field day with the implications of a mysterious, meddling hand, and duly, he seized upon it as tremendously significant but wouldn't say why.

"Do you think it's a suppressed memory of sexual abuse?" I suggested, half joking.

"Well, do you?" he said, not joking at all.

"The hand was real," I said. "In fact, I'd stake my life on it."

"That's very interesting," said Arthur, nodding his head. "Have you always believed in things other people can't see?"

"Only when it comes to men," I said, surprising myself, and finding it was true. "I see qualities in them that aren't there. Then I fall in love with my own creation."

"What a fascinating observation," said Arthur, making a note with his pencil. He often jotted things down while I talked and told me the reason he finished the hour early was so he could write up his notes before the next patient arrived. Early on, I'd assumed his notes were what I was paying for, that at some future interval, I'd be handed a dossier along with a diagnosis and a cure. When that didn't happen, I began to feel increasingly duped.

"Have you figured out what's wrong with me yet?" I asked after three or four months of weekly visits.

"It doesn't work like that, I'm afraid," said Arthur. "You have to come to your own realization."

Two weeks later, after a period of no realizations at all, and a bill of almost two thousand dollars, I lost patience and rephrased my question in a less polite way: "You must have worked out by now if I'm fucked in the head?"

Arthur laughed. "Do you really believe that about yourself?"

"You're never going to tell me, are you?"

He shook his head. "It isn't for me to say."

As the weeks dragged on, I grew tired of talking about myself, and couldn't shake the feeling that I was locked in a game with no end and no rules. Often at the close of an hour I had a sore throat but no insights, though I did notice that on the days I went to see Arthur the list was quieter, more subdued.

Toward the end of summer, I found enough courage to quit

my job and book a ticket to London, and once bought, I pinned my hopes on going back there. New Zealand was to blame for making me depressed, and leaving would be the cure. It wasn't just about what had happened with my father, or with men; the country had a melancholy side. Flip paradise over and all that wide-open space with too few people in it became an echo chamber for your own thoughts. I wanted to go to a city that was noisy and polluted and crowded with people. I thought it would be safer there, that with so many bodies jostling and colliding, I might be able to leap from my skin into someone else's.

Through the southern-hemisphere autumn I daydreamed of escape, though I failed quite spectacularly to plan any details of the new life I was heading toward. Instead I got carried away with the rightness of it all, the synchronicity of returning to London after exactly a decade.

I didn't tell my plans to Arthur because I feared he would imply, with pointed questions, that I was running away. Then one morning, after a spell of cold, wintry weather, I arrived for my appointment at his office and Arthur said, "It's a glorious day. Why don't we take our session outside?"

"Okay," I said, surprised and a little unnerved.

We walked the leafy streets around his office, past gabled villas with sweeping driveways and canopied trees, and arrived at a small reserve, open on one side to the road. Arthur laid out a checkered picnic rug, the sort men keep in the back of their cars for romantic dates, and he sat down on it with stiff crossed legs. I tried to copy him, but was wearing a skirt, and ended up in an awkward posture with my legs twisted uncomfortably to one side.

"How have you been this week?" asked Arthur, in the same manner he began all our sessions.

"Fine, I guess."

He looked at me expectantly, waiting for more, but I said nothing. A woman with a pram and a young child in tow walked past, and she glanced in our direction for a second longer than she needed to. Did she think Arthur was my boyfriend, or, worse, did she realize he was actually my shrink?

"Don't worry about her," said Arthur. "Pretend we're still in my office."

"Sorry," I said. "I thought she was looking at us."

"Tell me how you've been," said Arthur, fixing me with his kind, sad eyes.

Away from the squishy couch and the box of tissues, his question seemed unnatural, prying, and his voice too loud. I felt exposed.

"Is something wrong?" Arthur's brow creased with concern and he leaned a fraction closer and placed his hand tentatively on my arm. "You don't need to feel uncomfortable," he said. "I'm not going anywhere. You're safe."

But his words sent panic coursing through me, and I shrank from his touch as though he was diseased. What were we doing together on a picnic rug in a secluded park? Was he coming on to me? I was sure a line had been crossed, and every molecule inside me turned against him. "I don't like it here," I said, flatly. "I want to go back to the office."

"Of course," said Arthur, immediately getting to his feet. "Wherever you feel more comfortable." He stood up too quickly, and his papers scattered in a gust of wind. With pathetic flapping movements, he chased them around the small park. I should have helped him but embarrassment paralyzed me, and I turned away, pretended I didn't know him. On the walk back, I hurried ahead, picking up speed whenever Arthur tried to catch up. Back in the office, he tried to continue the session, but I felt no less uncomfortable and couldn't shake off the sensation of disgust. "I need to go," I said.

"I'm sorry," said Arthur. "It was foolish of me to suggest going to the park."

His apology made him seem even feebler, and it was all I could do to stay long enough to get out my checkbook and pay him.

"This one's on the house," he said, flustered that I was leaving. "We've barely had half a session."

"Good-bye," I said, quickly, and walked out of his office for the very last time, the only time I'd done so without feeling robbed.

CHAPTER TWENTY

Skyros, 2003

MY SUSPICIONS THAT PIPPA hadn't summoned me to Skyros wholly to atone for her guilt were confirmed the morning after I arrived when my duties began. She didn't say as much, but it was obvious they needed an extra pair of hands—women's hands. In times of sickness and death, women were still expected to cook, clean, and change soiled bedding, whereas men were permitted to invent reasons to be absent. Or they didn't invent reasons but simply made themselves scarce, as Ari did, a little after nine in the morning, telling Pippa not to worry, that he wouldn't need lunch—as though by eating out he was somehow doing her a huge favor. I didn't know where Harold was, and cared even less, but the news that Caleb had also gone off for the day, to the beach, was a blow. I had wanted to talk to him, to attempt to tell him what had happened the night before. Just having to say out loud that I had gone back in time and visited the communal garden would make it seem like a thing that was impossible, and when Caleb laughed and dismissed it as nonsense, I would laugh too and think he was right.

Soiled sheets, at any rate, were a distraction, and directly after breakfast Pippa set me to work in the laundry at a cranky cast-iron washing machine that refused to spin clothes and shuddered off its support blocks in protest. Wet clothes had to be wrung out in a mangle, which is how they ended up if you didn't feed the garments in at the correct angle and speed. One load took me two hours, and after I'd hung it all out in the sun to dry, my shoulders were almost as bent out of shape as Elena's. I was sweating too, and cursing under my breath, when Pippa appeared at the end of the clothesline with a glass of iced water. After I had gulped it down, she said Peggy had asked to see me.

"Are you sure she asked for me by name? She always calls me Hillary, and I stopped trying to correct her."

"Oh yes," said Pippa, pulling us under the fig tree for shade. "She asked for the young woman who'd read to her so nicely—she remembered your name and also that you had taken a shine to Madeline."

"I haven't taken a shine to Madeline. She gives me the creeps."

Pippa laughed. "It's probably just another one of her stories. The other day she started going on about a fellow in the village square who had asked for her hand in marriage—I expect she was reliving something that happened years ago. She's been babbling a lot about her old lovers, especially the gay one."

"Peggy was a lesbian?"

"God no, but she was in love with a gay man. She probably showed you his photograph on her fantasy wall."

I recalled the short, effeminate man with the big smile. "The one she calls the love of her life?"

"His name was Lawrence," said Pippa. "They worked at the same theater. He was a raving queen, but in those days you got arrested for buggery, so they came to an arrangement."

"You mean she was his beard?"

Pippa nodded. "Something like that. He was fond of her too, maybe not in the same way, but fond enough to get engaged."

"But they never married?"

"No. It was a very sad business. Just before the wedding, he was arrested in the toilets on Hampstead Heath. He couldn't face going to court and he hanged himself."

"That's so terrible," I said, and felt that it really was a double tragedy. Not only had the suicide list won but Peggy had lost someone she loved dearly, knowing all the while that she had not been enough for him.

Peggy was dozing when we went in, but she still had her pinkie looped through the handle of a teacup that rested precariously on the counterpane. "Is that really tea?" I whispered, while Pippa tried to unhook Peggy's finger from the cup without waking her. "She doesn't normally take it black."

Pippa shook her head. "I gave in," she said. "It seemed mean to take away her best chum so near the end. But so as not to offend Elena, I made her pretend it was tea."

Just then Peggy stirred, and her eyelids flicked open as though she'd had a fright. She stared at us both.

"Suki," she said, perfectly lucid. "I thought you'd never get here."

"It took a while, but here I am." I took her hand, the coldest thing on the island, while Pippa turned to fiddle with the morphine pump. "And I brought all the stuff you asked for—even the fur coat. Your hands are freezing—perhaps you need it after all."

At the mention of the coat, Peggy's eyebrows—or at least the tattoos of them—shot up. She put a shaky finger to her lips. "Sshhhhhh. Not now." She glanced at Pippa, whose back was turned, and gave me a stern look. "Not in front of her."

I was too busy the rest of the day to think anything more

about it. Pippa had me doing odd chores in the kitchen and laundry, and by the time the sky was darkening and she suggested that I go for a walk round the village, I confessed I was too tired to do anything but eat and go to bed. Caleb hadn't come home yet, but I convinced myself this was a good thing.

For once I nodded off without any trouble, but I was still jet lagged and had set my bedtime too early. I woke several hours later in the dead of night with the sense that I'd already had my quota of sleep. For a few minutes I lay on the platform, listening for strange sounds, but only the ever-present chorus of cicadas could be heard. We were too high up to hear the sea, though I sometimes caught the tang of salt in the air, and I suddenly longed for a swim. The night was balmy, and I didn't see why I couldn't go then, when no chores had to be done and everyone else was asleep, so I pulled off my bedclothes with the idea of rummaging in my suitcase for a swimsuit. I had packed a bikini too, but thought the one-piece more modest night attire, and put it on under shorts and a T-shirt. For a towel, I took the one I'd used that evening after a shower.

I climbed down the ladder, slid my feet into sandals, and set off across the pebbled floor, wary this time of the obstacles I'd tripped on the night before. The door to the courtyard was ajar, and I slipped through the gap and closed it behind me in an easy, fluid movement, trying, I supposed, to be stealthy.

I was preoccupied with thoughts of my swim, so it was a shock to realize that I was in our old garden, its features set out gloomily in front of me, like the pieces of an abandoned chess game. Despite the warm night, the air of melancholy sent a chill through me, and I wanted to turn back immediately.

But I remembered the child in the bunker—and I hesitated, standing my ground.

Something had changed from the night before. A few moments passed before I figured out what it was, why the scene looked so forsaken. For a start, it was gloomier. No light spilled from the flat, and the moon was completely obscured by cloud. Rain was in the air—or at least the tension of it—and I recalled that the night after the party had signaled the end of my Wendy tent. I had woken the next morning to find it floating in a pool of mud—salvageable, only we hadn't bothered. It had stayed outside for weeks, browning and rotting, and we had simply thrown it away.

With less light, it was harder to make out the air-raid shelter, and I had taken a few steps down the path before I realized the hatch was in fact closed. Next to it, a dozen rusted bolts lay helter-skelter along the path. I went over to them, to the hatch, and tested the metal surface warily with my foot. Bending down, I listened for the child but heard nothing, only my own tight breaths, high up in my chest, anxiety escalating.

The men had been and gone.

They had come out into the garden, put the hatch in place, and stumbled back inside. It was the right night, but I had arrived too late—perhaps by only a few minutes, or longer, by a few hours. I remembered the geranium plants, and went over to see if they were still wet. Sure enough, their leaves had been recently sprayed by a phantom Jean Luc, meaning my tardiness had been a matter of minutes.

Why was I here if the hatch was closed? It didn't make sense. I went back to the air-raid shelter and banged on the plate with my fists. "Wake up!" I yelled to whoever was down there, and lay down on the hatch to listen.

No one answered, but even if they had, the hatch was too heavy for me to lift. The first fat drops of promised rain landed on my bare forearms. I didn't remember London ever having rain like this, so tropical in pelt, so warm on my skin, and within seconds of the deluge beginning the garden started to flood. Water pooled on the lowest flagstones and ran along the patio in furious rivulets, surged into the narrow slit between the concrete path and iron hatch. Before long, my clothes were soaked through, my feet submerged, and I imagined water cascading down the steps of the bunker and flooding the chamber below.

Whoever was down there would drown—if it wasn't already too late.

I felt angry, helpless, sick to the very bottom of my soul, but also glad that the poor wretch down there wasn't me. For although I was soaked through, the instant I chose to I could leave this horrific scene and return to midsummer Greece. Only then did it occur to me that perhaps I couldn't, that perhaps I'd left my return until too late. For if I'd arrived in the garden a few minutes after the men had closed the hatch, then it was all about to dissolve—with me in it.

Until that moment, I did not know what sprinting was—how fast it was possible for my legs to run. I moved like a tornado, but very nearly not fast enough. When I reached the service door, it was already going a little out of focus, and I stepped through it and turned around to see that the garden had blurred beyond recognition. It remained so for another moment before clarity slowly returned, and with it the view of the courtyard.

Shaking with nerves, I walked over to sit on the low white wall, where the view of the ocean began to calm me. I wasn't sure how long I'd been sitting there when I heard footsteps behind me and looked up to see Pippa walking out of Peggy's room. She tiptoed toward me, and the first thing I noticed was how drawn her face looked.

"Is Peggy okay?" I said.

"She's the same," said Pippa. "I've been in with her all night. I couldn't sleep."

"I can't sleep either. Too hot."

She frowned. "Did you go for a swim?"

"Actually, I was about to," I said, before glancing down at my T-shirt and shorts, and seeing they were wet through. "I mean, yes. Yes, I went for a swim. What I meant was that I was just about to take a shower."

I could see that I had confused her, but she just yawned and said, "Good idea to have one now, before the morning rush."

In the tiny bathroom, I peeled off my wet shorts and T-shirt and wondered if perhaps I had gone for a swim and imagined the rest. But when I held my clothes up to my nose, they gave off the fresh scent of rain, not the sharp tang of salt.

It occurred to me that I ought to find out what the time was—something I hadn't bothered with for weeks. I wasn't sure at what exact point I'd stopped paying attention to alarm clocks and watches, but I hadn't even switched on my cell phone since arriving in Greece. I found my phone in the bottom of my backpack, and it had enough charge left to switch on and display London time. From memory, Greece was two hours behind GMT, so I calculated it was about half past three in the morning. Working backward, I figured out I must have woken at around three fifteen that night, and gone out into the garden a few minutes after the hatch had been closed. Which meant that the night before . . .

I caught what I'd been trying to do—calculate the time I'd need to wake up to be in the garden before the hatch closed—then realized how bonkers it was to assume that the time twenty years ago would be concurrent with now. I could no more predict when and where the garden would appear than I could control what Caleb would do next.

Then, exactly as I had the night before, I felt wiped out, my brain aching from the effort of trying to understand something wholly irrational. I was already in bed, had climbed up the ladder to find my phone, and minutes later passed out cold.

The sleep was a short one, and I managed to get up and dress and make it to the kitchen for breakfast before the men took off for the day. Elena was the only one absent, and while the rest of us tried to drink coffee and eat toast in a civilized manner, Caleb horsed around in the kitchen and wasn't satisfied until he had knocked a basket of onions off the bench. I was trying to avoid eye contact with him, but had been aware of his every move, and laughed involuntarily when the onions spilled.

"That's it," shrieked Pippa, reaching her wit's end at the early hour of eight in the morning. "After you've picked up the onions, you can bugger off to the beach—anywhere except hanging around here being a bloody great pain in the neck."

"You should come with me, Suki," said Caleb, juggling the onions instead of picking them up like he'd been told. "The beach is terrific, really top notch."

"I can't," I said. "I promised to stay here and help with Peggy."

"Oh no you don't," said Pippa. "You've been here two days and haven't left the villa yet. We can't send you back without a tan."

"You need my help, and I really don't mind," I said, trying to be emphatic.

Pippa cleared away my plate from in front of me. "We'll manage fine without you, and on top of that, I absolutely insist."

I caught Harold's eye, and it was as though he had seen the treachery in my thoughts; why I was trying so hard to avoid being alone with Caleb. To provoke him, I said, "Why don't you come with us?" even though I suspected he was the kind of bookish person who hated beaches, swimming, sunshine, and the outdoors.

"No thanks," he said. "You'll have more fun without me."

"Oh," said Caleb, smiling. "Do you think so?"

Within the hour, we had set off for what Caleb promised was the best beach on the island, though it was also quite far away. Outside Elena's villa we turned left and followed the cobbled street up the hill until it petered out and became a dirt track that ran along a cliff top. Caleb led us inland and we followed a trail of goat droppings through a wilderness of prickly pears and what looked like rosemary bushes grown enormous and out of control. Away from the village the screech of cicadas was deafening and the heat was unbroken by trees or shade of any kind. I was close to melting when Caleb climbed to the top of a small, scrubby outcrop and pointed. "There," he said. "Told you it was worth the trek."

Below him, scrub gave way to a silver flash of sea and a crescent of yellow sand with a wreck of a taverna at one end. The descent was steep, an obstacle course of crumbling rock and aggressive, spiky plants, but we scrambled down in one piece to stand at the edge of a divinely blue stretch of water.

"Race you to the pancakes," said Caleb, pulling off his T-shirt and pointing to a ridge of flat rocks in the middle of the bay.

He was a scrappy swimmer and I beat him easily, climbing out of the water while he was still only halfway. Up close, the rocks were red and pitted, not flat at all, and burned my backside when I laid down on them. When Caleb finally climbed out of the water and plonked down next to me, I pretended not to notice him. For a few minutes he played along and we lay there soaking up the sun, our skin slowly crusting with salt. I made the mistake of looking down at my blue-white skin, and noticed a small crop of hairs sprouting in a place where there ought not to be any. My swimsuit was old and threadbare, and I suddenly felt self-conscious, exposed. Turning, I saw Caleb had been staring at the same place. He looked away, and I quickly rolled onto my stomach, but not before our eyes met and a guilty look passed between us.

"Race you back," I said, standing up and diving into the cold shower of the ocean.

Back on the beach, Caleb suggested we hire a paddleboat from the taverna, which had no roof or walls but still functioned as a kind of kiosk. Lying on a mat on the floor was the old codger who owned it, a man whose leather face cracked open to reveal a single gold tooth as we approached. We didn't have enough drachmas on us to match his fee, but Caleb persuaded him to lend us a paddleboat for a couple of hours by claiming Ari was the old man's cousin. He gave us his rustiest bucket, an orange relic from the seventies that leaked oil and lost traction when you pedaled too hard. Undeterred, we chopped out past the pancake rocks, where the water was deep and green and so clear that you could see wrinkled sand on the ocean floor.

For a spell we simply drifted, tired after all that fierce pedaling, and let the boat swing round to reveal whatever part of the view it fancied. Even though the vegetation there was different, being out on the water reminded me of home—and I realized that by home I meant New Zealand. The next thought I had was that I couldn't imagine ever living in London again. Caleb had closed his eyes, and his not looking at me made me want to confess to him all the strange things that had been happening at the villa. "You remember how I told you about the presence?" I began.

"Uh-huh."

"Well, it did follow me here."

Caleb opened his eyes a second. "You saw the ghost?"

"Not exactly, it's more like I'm the ghost and I keep revisiting the past, our old garden, because there's something I have to do there. There's this bunker—and I think someone's trapped down there." I told him what I'd seen and heard—even imitating the yelp of the child.

When Caleb yawned, it struck me that he hadn't been listening, he'd been zoning out like you do when someone bores you to death with their detailed recollection of a dream. "Anyway," I said. "It's probably nothing."

"Hmmm," said Caleb, sleepily.

We had started out drifting in the middle of the bay but slowly and almost imperceptibly the ocean currents were pulling us toward a jagged cliff face.

"Caleb," I said, tapping him on the arm. "We're drifting toward the rocks."

He sat up. "Bummer."

"Should we turn back?"

"No, I want to show you something—it's near here." He scanned the cliff face up ahead then urged me to pedal toward the opposite edge of the crescent-shaped bay.

"Where are we going?" I said.

"You'll see."

Around the headland we pedaled into a small cove, banked by sheer cliffs that plunged into deep water. The cove was completely shaded, and my skin chilled as we moved out of the sun. "Are you sure this is it?"

"Positive."

Caleb steered straight for a rock face that jutted out into the cove, swerving to the right just meters before hitting it. Behind its bulk, a body of water swelled and smacked against a second rock face that arched over the entrance to a cave. I'd suspected as much, but it wasn't until the yawning black mouth of it was in front of me that my feet slammed into the pedals and refused to rotate them. "We can't go in there," I said.

"Relax," he said. "It's just a cave. I've been in hundreds of times with Dad."

But already, a hammering had started in my stomach and was moving to my ears and throat. "Please, can we just go back?"

Caleb must have sensed my panic because he squeezed my hand, but he didn't turn the boat around. "You really don't want to miss this," he said. "Come on. Don't be a pussy."

People who adore caves never understand the terror they inspire in those who do not, and as the boat moved forward into a space that made me think of a waterlogged tomb, Caleb said, "See? I told you it was amazing!"

Obediently, I looked around, trying to find the beauty he could, but everything in front of me was awful. The cave was roughly the size of a small church, with a high grotto on one side that peaked in a cluster of sharp brown stalactites. Their yellow reflections—drowning-men's fingers—clawed at the surface. Elsewhere, the water was black and impenetrable and flowed into side caves even more horrible than this one. The ceiling was hidden in shadow, and water bled from the walls.

"Is this place ever submerged?" I said.

"I don't know," said Caleb. "But sometimes the entrance is blocked."

"By what?"

"Water." He saw my expression and laughed. "Don't worry, it's low tide."

The paddleboat rocked and a splash sounded next to it. Caleb's seat, when I turned to it, was empty. A meter away, he surfaced and waved. "Ahoy!" he shouted, then duck-dived, his feet kicking briefly above the water before it zipped shut behind him. An orange streak passed under the boat, then disappeared.

Alone in the cave, I fixated on the spot where I thought Caleb would come up, but the boat was drifting, and the water tricked me. The hideous silence was broken by the thunk of fiberglass hitting rock, and the boat jammed up against a wet cave wall, close enough to it that I could make out wormholes in the limestone. I tried to steer the boat away, to turn the pedals, but it had snagged on something, and I couldn't get it to budge. I tried to rock the boat back and forth to free it, and was so charged with adrenaline that I barely noticed when a large plastic halo broke off in my hand.

"Suki! What the hell are you doing?" Caleb clutched the side of the craft and hauled himself in.

"The boat's stuck," I said. "We can't get out."

Caleb had to use his full weight to restrain me, to calm me down, and even then I was shaking. "You pulled the steering wheel off," he said, picking up the plastic ring. "What happened?"

I pushed him off, angry that he'd brought us in here; that he didn't understand. "I told you I didn't like caves."

He looked at me as if I was a crazy person but finally must have gotten that I was afraid. "It's okay, we'll go," he said. "Just sit down."

I sat down. It turned out that the boat wasn't really stuck—in my frenzy I had tried to pedal in reverse, a maneuver the rusty old vessel couldn't handle. Steering was tricky without the wheel, but the rudder was intact and Caleb managed to guide us out of the cave and into daylight. But it wasn't until we were well away from the cove and I felt sun on my skin that I relaxed.

"You really freaked out in there, huh?" he said, his skinny arm still around me.

I managed a smile, but felt wretched. "I tried to warn you."

"Anyway, check these out," he said, reaching into the pocket of his swimming trunks and taking out three or four small metal cylinders. "Pretty cool, huh?" He handed them to me.

"What are they?"

"Empty shells from World War Two. There're thousands of them down there. Dad says it must have been used as an ammunition dump."

I examined the casings. To a boy they were treasure but the only thing they reminded me of was the air-raid shelter, that other waterlogged tomb.

"You can keep them if you want," Caleb said.

"Thanks." I put the shells in my bag.

After the rescue and the gift, Caleb had a new heroic confidence about him, but I felt diminished. The beach wasn't far away, but my legs pedaled feebly, and it took us forever to get there. As we drew nearer to shore, I saw that other people had arrived on the beach, most clustered in a group at one end.

"It's Yanni," said Caleb, steering in their direction and waving. "I hope he brought lunch. I'm starving. His mum makes the most amazing baklava."

A few meters from shore, a lanky youth with caramel skin waded out to meet the paddleboat and Caleb introduced us.

"Caleb has talk so much about you," said Yanni, his absurdly white teeth fixed in an exuberant and slightly mocking grin.

"Pleased to meet you," I said, feeling uneasy about what Caleb might have told him.

More waifs waded out to greet us, some of them children, others slightly older with chin fluff or budding poached-egg breasts. Two skinny girls with nut-brown skin put their arms around Caleb and tickled his ribs, and he batted them off in a relaxed, brotherly way. All in all, I was introduced to a dozen teens but barely noticed their names, and with every handshake, I felt more and more out of place among these lithe, tan saplings. Led by Yanni, the group drifted back to where they had set up a camp of raffia beach mats, and Caleb cleared a space for me to sit next to him. But I stayed standing. My skin was bright red, burned to a crisp because I hadn't applied sunscreen. The skinny girls were staring at me, at my ratty swimsuit, at my sunburn, and whispering to each other in nimble Greek.

"I have to go," I said to Caleb. "I promised to get back and help with Peggy."

"No you didn't," he said. "They'll be fine without you. Elena's like supernurse. She can change sheets one-handed—and Mum loves it when there's too much to do."

For a moment, his eyes were just a bit pleading, but I ignored them and gathered up my towel and knapsack, anxious to leave. "I'll see you back at the villa," I said. "Thanks for showing me the cave."

"You don't mean that," said Caleb. "You hated it." He didn't get up to follow me, and I marched up the goat track at a ferocious pace, relieved to get away. At the top of the hill I drank the last of my bottled water and steeled myself for the long trek back.

By the time I reached Elena's I was dehydrated and starving, but couldn't face returning to the hospice just yet. Instead, I walked toward the village, fixated on a mouth-watering souvlaki. In the piazza, I discovered where all the men spent their days: under the canopy of a knotty fig tree, a dozen of them sat sipping ouzo, hard at work over backgammon boards. Some even gave me the glad eye as I walked past, and I felt vaguely flattered but mostly insulted by the way Mediterranean men could have one foot in the grave and still think they had it.

I found Ari at his brother's taverna, sitting out front with a glass of pale yellow liquid in his hand. His cheeks were flushed, but not, I thought, from exertion. "Sit down a while," he said. "Would you like a bite to eat?"

"Yes, please. I'm ravenous." I inhaled the first souvlaki, and when another was brought out I devoured that too. After two liters of water, my thirst was almost quenched, but I declined Ari's offer of an ouzo for the road. "I better get back," I said. "There's so much to do." It hadn't been a dig at Ari, but he took it that way.

"I tried to help," he said. "But I got sick of them telling me I was doing everything wrong, so I just left them to it."

Back at the villa, sickbed chores were in full swing, and I was soon swept up in a flurry of sheet folding and bed moving. Ari was right—Pippa did have a particular way of doing things, but I didn't mind conforming to her standards as I had none of my own. In my absence, Peggy had rallied briefly, and demanded to be moved outside again. They'd been waiting for an extra pair of hands with which to accomplish the task. So with Harold and I on one side, Pippa and Elena on the other, we shunted the trolley bed—with Peggy in it—across the pebbled courtyard, its wheels snagging constantly and its cargo threatening to tip over or jump out. Once she was in place, with Pippa's help I fashioned an awning out of an old quilt and two broom handles, but the quilt was too heavy and the tent sank in the middle. A sheet worked better, but still left Peggy partly exposed to the sun, and Pippa and I spent a good half hour applying industrial-strength sunscreen to her desiccated skin. By then Peggy had lapsed into a state resembling a coma—or so it appeared.

"She'd kill us if she knew what we were putting on her skin," said Pippa, not bothering to lower her voice. "In her day it was baby oil or nothing."

"I can hear you," said Peggy, her eyes still shut.

"Good," said Pippa. "Do you want your sunglasses?"

Peggy half-opened one eye to the bright sun. "No, I want to see Madeline."

Her request was ignored. "Mummy, we've put you in the sun so you can work on your tan—remember how keen you were to get one?"

"What have you done with her?" Peggy gave her daughter a black stare, then looked away. When she saw me, her eyes widened and she seemed to do a double take. She tried to reach for my hand. "Suki, you must know where Madeline is? I know she talks to you too."

"The statue's in London," I said, backing away. "We had to leave it behind."

A look of pure madness crossed Peggy's face. "Why are you all lying to me?" She tried to drag me onto the bed, but Pippa intervened, pulling Peggy's hands off. While she was doing so, Peggy turned on Pippa, grabbing a handful of her hair.

"Ouch!" said Pippa, trying to shake loose from her mother, who was snarling like a cornered cat. "I know she's here," she said. "I've talked to her. She comes to me at night and sits by my bed."

Caught at an odd angle, Pippa flailed. "Mummy, stop it. Let go!" But still Peggy held on, surprisingly strong for someone so frail. I tried to prise Peggy off, but her hand was clamped as though rigor mortis had set in. And then, just as suddenly as she'd woken up, the old lady collapsed, and her hand, holding a few strands of her daughter's hair, fell to the sheet.

Pippa clutched her scalp and retreated slowly from the bed. Her face was white, as though she might faint. "I can't handle any more of this," she said.

Just then, Harold and Elena appeared in the courtyard to see what all the fuss was about, and I gestured to them to withdraw. I put an arm around Pippa's shoulders, and felt how shaken she was. "Why don't you take off for a bit?" I said. "Go for a swim or a walk. The rest of us can hold the fort for a few hours." I didn't like the idea of being left alone with Peggy, but Pippa seemed on the verge of a meltdown.

She agreed to stay away until at least teatime, and Harold and Elena and I arranged to take one-hour bedside shifts. The main task was to make sure Peggy stayed hydrated by dripping water onto her lips from a sponge. Late in the afternoon, I took over from Harold, who went to the village in search of an English newspaper. He told me Peggy had slept most of the time he was with her, and I sat by her bed with a book, hoping she'd continue to do the same. Elena was somewhere in the villa, praying or cleaning or chopping vegetables. At half past four, Peggy's eyelids flickered and she woke up. She scanned the courtyard, disoriented, and I took her cold, frail hand and gently squeezed it.

"It's okay, Peggy, I'm here. You're safe."

Her eyes locked on mine. "Suki, I'm so glad it's you. Where's Pippa?"

"She's gone for a walk, but she'll be back soon."

"I hope she's gone for longer than that," Peggy said. "Quickly. Bring me my fur coat. And my photographs." When I wavered, she snapped, "And don't make a meal of it."

The suitcase we'd brought from London was in Pippa and Ari's room, and had been unpacked and hastily restuffed, so that items were bursting out of its sides. Carrying the fur coat back to Peggy, I read on its label: GENUINE MINK; BY APPOINTMENT TO HER MAJESTY THE QUEEN, and felt how heavy it was—more than the two photograph albums put together.

Peggy was waiting expectantly for my return, but when I offered to help her put on the mink, she said, "I don't want to wear it, I want you to unpick it."

Following her instructions, I fetched a pair of scissors, and began to unstitch the satin lining of the coat, starting near the hem.

"Not there, farther up," ordered Peggy, grabbing the scissors and stabbing them near an inside pocket. "There, look."

Where she had indicated, the lining bulged and, hands trembling, I began to unpick the nearest seam. Propped next to me on her elbow, Peggy wheezed heavily, from either excitement or exertion, it was hard to tell which. Under the lining, I found an envelope glued to the pelt.

"Rip it off," urged Peggy. "But don't look inside."

I tried to do as she instructed, but the old, yellowing envelope tore and a wad of pound notes cascaded to the floor.

"Well, don't just sit there, pick them up!" Peggy said.

I got to my knees and scooped up the bills. They were all fifty- and hundred-pound notes, and I realized I had thousands of quid in my hands. The envelope was in pieces, but I did my best to patch it together, and Peggy pulled me close and wheezed in my ear, "There's a pocket in the back of the photo album, behind the last photo." She paused to gasp for air. "Don't let Pippa see. She'll try and take it."

She collapsed back onto the bed, eyes not quite closed, and for a whole minute I thought she was dead, that the sight of so much money had killed her. But it hadn't; holding my hand in front of her mouth, I felt shallow, rasping breaths.

When Elena appeared for her shift, I tried to explain that Peggy had been upset, and perhaps ought to be moved back to her room, but Elena misunderstood, and instead gave Peggy a medicinal nip of ouzo—"No tell Peepa," she made me promise—as well as an extra dose of morphine. Watching the tiny pump do its work, I thought of my mother, how she too had been hooked up to one of those near the very end.

In Elena's room, behind the curtain of my sleeping platform, I discovered that one of the photograph albums had a pocket exactly like the one Peggy had described. The pocket wasn't empty—other bits of paper had been stuffed in there too—but I crammed in the cash and ignored them. I had to return the album quickly to the suitcase before anyone noticed it was missing. I'd have to tell someone about the money too, but I wasn't sure whom, or when would be the right moment. I knew I should tell Pippa about the money, but I also thought it might be better to wait until the others weren't around.

When Pippa returned that night, I was exhausted and had a new respect for the stress she was under. Not only did Peggy require constant attention but she had also turned against the one person who really cared for her, and that could only have hurt Pippa deeply. She would be braced for grief, conscious at every step of the loss she was about to suffer. At least when my mum was dying I'd been oblivious to what I was about to go through, and directly afterward, too immature to feel anything but numb. But had that really been any better? Instead of grieving and getting over it, I had run away to the other side of the world, gotten into bad relationships, taken drugs—really pushed myself to the edge—then wondered what was wrong with me. It should have been obvious what was wrong with me. It couldn't be more obvious now.

With everyone on a round-the-clock vigil by Peggy's bedside, we ate and slept in irregular patterns, and household routines disappeared. Shortly after Pippa got home from her walk, I went to bed while it was still light and fell into a feverish sleep. Later on, I woke to the sound of voices chattering, plates clunking, but felt too tired to get up and eat. The crypt was particularly hot and airless that night and I stripped down to just my knickers and covered myself with a sheet. The events of the day were a blur and sleep came on strong, blitzing all thoughts and replacing them with crooked nightmares of fishing for bullets in a flooding cave.

I was in such a deep sleep that later on, when a hand tapped me gently on the shoulder and a voice whispered softly in my ear, I thought I was dreaming. I couldn't make out any of the whispered words, but the delicate breath they were carried on sent a secret voltage to the base of my spine. From there, the current spread to my arms and legs then fizzed to the ends of my fingers and toes. I had never experienced a dream quite like this, and then I realized it wasn't one.

"Why did you run away from the beach?" said the whisperer.

I opened my eyes halfway, enough to confirm his outline, kneeling by the bed. I was lost without my glasses but didn't reach for them; absurdly, I didn't want him to see me in spectacles. "You can't be here," I said. "You have to go."

He took off his T-shirt and put a finger to my lips. "Shhh." He smelled of the sea, of sunscreen, and I knew he hadn't showered since he'd been in the ocean. He lay down next to me on the mattress and, very carefully, as though either one of us might detonate, he rested one hand lightly on my shoulder. Next to my ear, he exhaled, a tiny puff of air that was a fuse to my nerve endings. His body next to mine was molten, too pliant, and on the other side of the sheet, I floundered.

"I'm serious," I said. "Your parents will kill me."

"No one saw me coming in here," he said. "They're too busy with Peggy."

He shifted his weight, slid a hand under the sheet and down past my shoulder blade. When he reached the rise of my breast and an attendant nipple, he timidly went around it. For a moment his mouth hovered in front of mine, awaiting permission, and in that second or two of sweet, urgent breath, everything was written, and everything came undone.

"Please," I said, on a sharp inhale. "Please don't." But his mouth inched forward, and my hand sought the downy cleft on the back of his neck, and finally his lips settled on mine. He tasted of summer fruit, nectarines and cherries, all the joyous, uncomplicated times in life that I had forgotten about, and rolling toward him on the stiff, horsehair mattress, I was a girl of sixteen again, having my first kiss—finally—with the boy of my dreams.

It was the presence of a firm, insistent nub that, moments later, brought me back to earth. Caleb's breathing had quickened, and I pulled back to listen while he nuzzled my neck. I knew that sound, what it meant. My knickers were still on, and so were his boxers, but the sheet was no longer between us, and on the crest of my hip bone, where the skin is taut and sensitive, a dot of moisture landed. Instinctively, I shrank from it, twisted away, just as an animal, guttural sound escaped from Caleb's throat.

He sprang back, as shocked as I was, and cringed next to me on the mattress. At the same time, blinded by darkness but senses burning, I registered a slow, trickling stickiness close to my hip, and covered it with the sheet.

In the silent, airless crypt our shame was mercilessly amplified, and for something like a full minute, neither of us moved or spoke.

There were so many things I could have said to patch his crushed ego and make it all better for him, but the magnitude of my own folly had hit me like a wrecking ball, and I needed reassuring as much as he did. "It doesn't matter," I managed. "You should go."

For once obedient, Caleb put on his T-shirt and pulled it down to cover his boxer shorts. Under his breath, he said, "You're not going to write about this in your diary, are you?"

"Of course not," I said, thinking that would be the last thing I'd do. "Just go back to bed."

So caught up was I in the mood of reckless humiliation that a few moments passed before I realized the implications of his plea. "What diary?" I said, already dimly aware of an approaching apocalypse.

"I don't know," he said. "I'm just going to go."

I couldn't see his face. It was too dark. But I already knew the answer to my question. It was written in my own handwriting in all those notebooks and journals that I had left behind in London under the bed. They went back years, to the very beginning, when I'd had my real first kiss in Ladbroke Gardens under a cloud of marijuana smoke. Caleb was worried he'd end up in them, another specimen in my collection. "You read my journals, didn't you?"

He said nothing.

"So that's a yes?"

A sigh of defeat signaled Caleb's confession.

"How could you?" But of course he had. Who wouldn't? Diaries were written to be read. If not now, then in a hundred years' time. If you really wanted to keep something secret, you kept your mouth shut and your pen capped. "They were private," I said, my final attempt to make Caleb feel bad.

"Private?" he said, scoffing. "You mean like the stuff in Dad's shed?"

"That's not the same—and you know it."

"Dad's shed was locked," Caleb said. "I'd call that private, wouldn't you?"

I didn't respond. Like any hypocrite, I wasn't about to admit that I was one.

Caleb was right, though. On the moral low ground, we were about even. But a sheet was stuck to my leg, and before another word was said, I needed to clean myself up without anyone seeing.

CHAPTER TWENTY-ONE

Skyros, 2003

WHEN GRILLED, CALEB ADMITTED he'd accidentally unearthed the first installment of my journals while I was out shopping for groceries one afternoon, and had gone back to read the next by torchlight while I slept on the bathroom floor. To make sure I stayed put while he read, he'd tried to make me more comfortable by propping up my head with a towel and covering me with a quilt. Then, once he discovered the diaries had "sexy bits," and episodes involving booze and drugs, he confessed he'd gotten addicted to reading them and had even risked going into my room one night while I was in the shower.

"I remember that night," I said. "Only I thought it was Harold in my room."

"That was me," he said. "But I didn't look at you in the shower."

"Are you sure?"

"Yes," he said, and a second later: "No."

We had moved from Elena's crypt to the courtyard by then, and were huddled under the fig tree, whispering like fugitives.

Caleb showed zero remorse about the snooping, and I found that I couldn't really blame him for it. (After all, had I shown any?) All he wanted to know was if everything he'd read in the diaries was true, particularly the stuff about his mother "shagging" some guy in a bathroom.

I said I wasn't sure what had happened that night, that he'd have to ask her.

He screwed up his face. "No thanks."

I noticed that all the tension had gone from our conversation, just as I noticed that a dusting of fine black hair had appeared, seemingly overnight, on Caleb's top lip. Had I really been even a little bit in love with this downy adolescent, this presumptuous boy who had bowled into my room to seduce me without even taking a shower? Alone on the sleeping platform after he'd gone to bed, I felt like a prizewinning idiot, with only myself to blame. How daft of me to think Harold had been the shower spy when it was Caleb who'd lurked and gone AWOL and generally behaved appallingly from the start. Or had he? What if he had followed my journals like a manual for delinquency? Certainly it was their contents that had given him the confidence to appear in my room late at night in his boxer shorts, the knowledge he needed to play me—that, and perhaps, *Lolita*.

I would not write about Caleb in my journal, but I saw already how he fit into the sorry narrative they outlined. He was only the latest in a long line of futile attractions—and yet he was also the zenith. With Caleb, I had finally set my sights on a beau so inappropriate that the folly of the whole scheme had been made obvious, even to me.

I thought of Arthur the therapist, who had tried through kindness to get close enough to cure me. At the time, I'd supposed it was his methods that had failed, that I was too smart to get sucked in by transference, but in actual fact, transference had worked so well on me that the second he invoked it I had run for my life.

Arthur would have known that was a risk. It was why he had taken his time, hoping that would make a difference. It would all be written down in his notes: "This girl has been neglected and then abandoned by her father. Withheld affection is what she has come to think of as love. Discomfort will arise from any other kind, and she will bolt."

If only he had been meaner, I might have stuck around.

While I had been cogitating, the crypt had turned from black to gray without my noticing. I started to doze, but only a short while later Pippa pulled back the curtain of my sleeping platform and tapped me on the shoulder. I started awake and, seeing her face, my first thought was that she'd found out about the tryst with Caleb and had come to give me a roasting. But what she said was, "The doctor thinks there isn't long, and I thought you'd want to be there with us."

I followed Pippa into Peggy's room, thinking that I ought to have taken a proper shower, and not just sluiced myself down. I was too grubby—both literally and spiritually—to sit by anyone's deathbed. My only consolation—and I felt like a crook even admitting it to myself—was that Caleb would be far too ashamed to mention the incident to anyone, especially his mother.

I was the last to arrive in the sickroom. Harold, Ari, Elena, and Caleb were already there, seated in a horseshoe around the bed where Peggy lay unconscious. Caleb wouldn't look at me, and all I saw when I looked at him was a skinny little boy with bags under his eyes. I couldn't even remember what it was about him that had so bewitched me. I caught Harold's eye, and realized how badly I'd behaved toward him, when he'd been right about me all along.

But it was time to put all that aside because Peggy was about to die. The air around us was weighed down with the anticipation of it, and everyone was watching her, not really breathing, unsure how we'd react when it finally happened.

Like all solemn occasions, however, it wasn't without bursts of comedy. Against family wishes, Elena had summoned the local priest, a man so vast he might have smuggled in half the village under his cassock. When he leaned over Peggy to administer the rosary, she woke up, saw the antique gold pendant around his neck, and lunged for it. "That's mine, you rotter!" she shrieked, refusing to let go. "I know you—you're the dirty thief from downstairs."

Pippa explained to the priest—who was no doubt used to such nuttiness—that Peggy had mistaken him for her old neighbor Jimmy, who had in fact been a thief, but I noticed that from then on, to avoid a repeat performance, he discreetly maintained his distance.

Unfortunately for the gathered family, Peggy's outburst turned out to be the last coherent words she would utter. Soon after, she began to shout out random names and objects, like a baby does when it first learns to talk but without any of the delight a baby expresses, just fury and agitation. Slowly, horribly, even the names and objects deteriorated until they were simply grunts and moans.

"The brain shuts down first, but patients can remain very vocal during that process," explained the village doctor, who had done his medical training in Hull and spoke with a queer northern accent. He tried to reassure us that Peggy wasn't suffering at all, even though it sounded that way. In fact, he said, she wouldn't be aware of anything. I wanted to ask how such a thing had ever been proved, but sat still and said nothing.

Instead, I watched from the end of the bed and thought of my mother, of the only other death I'd seen. Except that I hadn't seen her die. For hours and hours, I'd held her hand in the ICU, had watched the machines and pumps do their work, had prayed, and talked, and even eaten, but then, in the end, when she had taken her last breath, I had not been paying attention.

Not long after the doctor's reassurances, Peggy's grunts and moans declined to the most distressing noise I had ever heard: a high, sharp intake of breath, followed by a long, low, drawn-out cry of agony on each exhale. Despite what the doctor had said, I pictured Peggy being dragged into hell one fingernail at a time. After we had endured it for close to half an hour, the doctor purposefully opened up his medical bag. "I am going to make her more comfortable," he said, quietly. He held up a series of glass vials to the light to better read their labels. He selected two, and showed them to Pippa. I didn't hear what he said to her, but whatever it was, she nodded emphatically, and put her hand over her mouth and started crying. The doctor took out two syringes from his bag and filled them from the vials, flicking each needle to get rid of air bubbles. Holding one syringe in his teeth and the other in his hand, he reached under the sheet of Peggy's bed and rolled her over slightly, discreetly injecting the vials into what was left of her backside. The indignity went unnoticed by Peggy, and the doctor gently repositioned her before smoothing down the sheet.

Almost instantly, her groans became softer, less anguished, as if someone had turned down the volume. No more than five minutes later she skipped an inhalation, and her mouth froze open in an expression of surprise—her pupils fixed upward, staring at a view she didn't much seem to like.

Pippa climbed onto the bed and cradled her mother, weeping. Ari moved to his wife's side and stroked her arm, tight mouthed but blinking. Harold looked at the doctor, who gave him a benign smile and said, "Yes," very quietly, as though someone in the room was asleep and he didn't want to wake them. Timidly, Harold went to the bed and leaned over Peggy's rib cage. His back shuddered, but he made no sound, and when Pippa looked up and saw him standing across the bed from her, quaking, she leaned over to pat his shoulder. Her touch released a series of violent spasms, and he flailed for his sister's hand and pulled it to his face. Mumbling to themselves but not to each other, they voiced pet names and regrets, while the priest and doctor discreetly left the room.

After a short interval, Elena slipped between the siblings and popped up next to Peggy's head, where her busy hands closed the old woman's eyes and mouth. Peggy looked more serene after that, like people in death are supposed to look, and I tried to un-remember a little of the horror she had gone through to get there.

On the other side of the bed, I noticed Caleb sitting on his hands, staring at his feet, his face pinched in a scowl. To get his attention, I had to say his name twice, and when he finally looked up, I nodded toward Pippa. He didn't understand at first, but then he rushed forward and wrapped his arms around her and burst into childish tears. Seconds later, a surge of such strong emotion hit me that I had to steady myself against the bed rail. Some long-buried canister of unshed tears had burst, and out they all came. Tears for my mother, pure grief, and hot, angry tears for my father, who had been such a jerk. For Caleb, tears of shame and regret. I cried for the bottle-top girl who'd found a hand in the cupboard that nobody else believed in, and for the loser that she had turned into. I cried because I hated her, hated myself, but did not know how to change. A few tears were even for Peggy, who would never host charades in a Kabuki gown again.

For about an hour, I let it all hang out, and so did everyone else. Then I blew my nose once, twice, three times for good measure, and went to the kitchen to make a pot of tea, the first of dozens that I would brew, pour, and sip with others in the ensuing days. While I was waiting for the stovetop kettle to boil, it struck me that I hadn't missed the moment of my mother's death because I was unfeeling or unobservant, but because there probably hadn't been one. She hadn't fought it like Peggy; one minute she had been breathing very quietly with her eyes shut and then a few minutes later not breathing at all. It had been a gradual fading out and nothing to feel ashamed of for missing, yet that was still the emotion I associated with her death—along with remorse that I had lied about losing her locket.

So much of what I remembered about my mother was like that, obscured by my own preoccupations. I thought of her constantly, but the image I had was only a sketch, its lines drawn from the self-centered perspective of my eighteen-year-old self. I wished I could have seen her, just once, as an adult, to take in everything about her I had missed.

At lunchtime the family assembled at the large outdoor dining table and failed to make a dent in the dozen moussakas dropped off by relatives and neighbors. Around the table, we were all cried out and had arrived at a plateau of hyperaware silence. Our skins were thinner, our hearing more receptive, and each time anyone so much as sighed, a ripple of emotions passed among us. The small wire-spectacled man who had joined us to discuss funeral arrangements was treated like an interloper. He passed around a folder of coffin styles and prices, and each of us flicked through it before passing it on to the next person, until it had been round the circle three or four times without anyone taking in a thing. The man chatted on, a fresh pot of tea was made, and it wasn't until he suggested their top-selling model—basic pine with a matte varnish—that anyone seemed to realize a decision was expected. "Basic pine?" exclaimed Harold, actually standing up from his chair. "Mummy would never consent to that!"

He had spoken so forcefully that Pippa looked quite shocked. "What do you suggest?" she said.

Harold turned to the bespectacled man. "Do you have anything vintage—an antique perhaps?"

"A secondhand coffin?" The undertaker shook his head. "Only new," and Harold cringed at the battiness of his request.

Once Harold had picked one out (brass handles, mahogany stain) the man with the wire spectacles informed us, perhaps not as delicately as he might have, that his embalmer would be round to start work "right away." In this heat, he said, they had to move fast or nature did it for them. He wasn't exaggerating: the embalmer appeared so quickly he must have been waiting outside. His arrival triggered a secret signal to the village that a funeral was imminent, and within the hour, an army of elderly women in shawls descended on the villa and transformed it from muted hospice to hive of burial activity.

While the village women scuttled back and forth with wire brushes and pots of boiling water under a canopy of incense, the family was stranded at the dining table, almost afraid to leave the circle. Only Ari had about him an air of impatience, and nearing twilight, the source of it was revealed. His brother Soteris came to the door of the villa, and after offering his condolences, he and Ari had huddled near the fig tree discussing something in hushed voices. Once Soteris had left, Ari returned to the table with a small piece of paper and stood looking nervously at Pippa. "A few days ago," he began, "Peggy asked me to carry out her final request."

"She asked *you*?" Pippa exclaimed.

"Yes," said Ari. "And she asked me to keep it a secret"—he looked guiltily at his wife—"from you."

Pippa's expression was neutral—neither surprised nor upset—and Ari hurriedly continued. "She wanted everyone in the village to have a shot of Johnny Walker at her wake, and, well, the stuff doesn't exactly grow on trees around here."

"So you ordered some ahead of time?" said Pippa.

"Yes." Ari started to fold up the piece of paper, but Pippa snatched it from his hand and read it.

"Three cases?" she said, incredulous. "And you're going to pay for that how?"

"I thought . . ." he began, then looked hopefully at Harold. "Any ideas?"

"Sorry, old chum, those brass handles don't grow on trees either."

"Wait," I said, remembering the stash of pound notes. "I think Peggy left something to pay for it." I fetched the photograph album that had been moonlighting as a bank, and explained that the money had been hidden in Peggy's fur coat. With all of them watching intently, I was nervous opening the album and my hands jittered on its yellowing, vellum pages. Done in haste, my attempt at stuffing had been poor, and the notes came out creased and in bunches. Harold held out his hands to form a collecting bowl, and Ari took the notes from him and acted as bank teller. The album was wide, and I had to reach far into the corners of the pocket to pull out the stragglers. As well as the money, a clutch of folded scrap paper—the papers I hadn't looked at before—fell out.

"Two thousand, seven hundred and fifty pounds," announced Ari, counting the last pile of notes. "But just to make sure, I'm going to count it again."

Pippa was flabbergasted. "But she always needed to borrow money off us to pay for gas and electricity—and her phone was always getting cut off."

"Well, now you know why," said Harold. "She was hoarding it."

"Maybe she forgot it was there," said Caleb. "She was pretty mental at the end."

"I don't think so," Pippa said. "She was adamant about bringing her mink over, even though it's ninety degrees in the shade."

"No wonder that effing coat weighed a ton," said Harold, cracking a smile for the first time that day.

"She knew where the money was, all right," I confirmed. "And when I stayed at her flat, I caught her hiding jewelry in the curtains."

"Oh God," said Pippa. "She was still hiding stuff from Jimmy."

"But Jimmy's dead—right?" I said.

"We think so," said Pippa. "But no one really knows what happened to him. One day he just disappeared from his flat, leaving everything in it. The police came to ask us if we'd seen him, but no one had. He was a sitting tenant, like Peggy, so after a while, when he still hadn't reappeared, they presumed he was dead and the landlord sold the flat."

"And that's when they renovated and found out what he'd done?" I asked.

Pippa nodded. "Mummy said she felt like he had been spying on her. It was awful."

"But he didn't spy on her—did he?"

"We don't think so," said Ari. "But who knows what he got up to. A man like that was capable of anything." He gathered the pound notes into a wad and smacked it on the table. "Well, this should pay for the wake," he said, smiling.

"Not all of it, darling," said Pippa. "Peggy will have bills to pay."

She held out her hand, but Ari hesitated. "Do you always have to spoil my fun?"

Pippa smiled, and Harold touched her shoulder. "You don't need to this time," he said. "I'll find a way to help out with the bills. I believe it's probably my turn."

Pippa looked sharply at her brother, and I thought, for a second, she was going to refuse his offer. But she softened. "Thanks. That would really help."

The whole time we'd been talking, I had been sitting with the photograph album and a pile of scrap-paper notes in my lap. Now I picked one up and unfolded it. Scrawled on it in curly, old-fashioned script, was a short sentence: "To Caleb, I leave my birdcage." I unfolded another, written in the same handwriting. "To Harold," it said, "I leave my photographs."

"I think Peggy has left a sort of will," I said. "Look." I handed Harold and Caleb their bequests.

"Lame," said Caleb, after reading his. "Those stuffed birds are utterly rank."

"It's the thought that counts," said Pippa.

"No it isn't," said Caleb. "She could have left me some coin."

Everyone was curious to see what was written on the remaining pieces of paper, so I unfolded them and handed them to the various beneficiaries. One or two were for Harold and Ari, plus another for Caleb, before one finally came up for Pippa. "One dress for Pippa—the rest to the Victoria and Albert museum," it read.

Pippa laughed when she saw it. "So begrudging, to the end."

"At least you can see the funny side," said Harold.

"I have to," said Pippa. "Otherwise I'd slash my wrists."

One piece of paper was left, and I unfolded it, then read and reread the message, for I could not believe my eyes. "I want Suki to have Madeline," it said, and then: "She is to be treasured, not left on the curb."

I showed the note to Pippa, who smiled. "I told you she remembered your name. And how thoughtful of her to leave you that ghastly old thing."

"Ghastly is right," I said. "I can't think of anything I'd less like to own."

By evening, the black-shawled women had left the villa, but other than to take toilet and tea breaks, none of the family except Caleb had moved from the table. A few hours earlier, he'd stood up and announced he was going to hang out at Yanni's house where, he said, at least people would be acting "normal." It was a warm night, the air thick with chirruping cicadas and Saturday-night festivities—unnatural, boisterous sounds, so discordant with our mood. We had all forgotten about the embalmer, about his work, so it was a shock when he emerged in the courtyard to inform us that Peggy, in her coffin, had been laid out on a trestle table and was ready to receive visitors.

It seemed so like her to have kept us waiting until she was ready to make her entrance, and I forgot, for a second, that he was talking about a corpse. We filed in to see her, to stare at her garishly made-up face, a face that looked more alive in death than it had in months. But no one commented on her appearance—it would have been too obvious, too tasteless—and Pippa, Harold, and Ari went to stand wordlessly at her side. Another wave of sorrow engulfed the room, but I felt immune from it this time, and left the family alone to grieve for their loss.

CHAPTER TWENTY-TWO

Skyros, 2003

I HAD A WALK IN MIND, and set off down a steep cobbled street toward the village, but a little way along I was taken aback by the sight of so many people not stricken with grief and turned back toward the villa. I went to bed, wanting only to pass out, but I was overtired and my body trilled with nerves that made it impossible to sleep. My mind was a shambles, overrun with chaotic thoughts of Caleb and coffins and my mother, all of it incoherent. I tried to think of nothing—the insomniac's meditation—but I was too wired even for that. I had left the others still sitting round the table, but after an hour or two there was a brief flurry of noises—toilets flushing; faucets turning on and off; Elena shuffling past, switching off her halos—followed by the deep hush of collective slumber.

When I was sure they had all gone to sleep, I climbed down from my bed and crossed over to the courtyard door. I'd not heard scraping metal or any other noise, but as I put my hand on the door to push it open I was still apprehensive and held my breath a little, just in case. But on the other side of the door were only the ordinary features of Elena's courtyard—the olive tree, low white wall, and a dark expanse of sky. No garden, nor anything even to suggest a recent death.

That the courtyard should be so oblivious seemed a little disrespectful, and I crossed to Peggy's room to remind myself that she had really passed away. Since I'd last been in there, the family had lit candles, a whole flotilla of them, and the room smelled strongly of hot, melting wax. Under their golden flames, Peggy's skin was at last glowing with her longed-for tan, and I smiled for her benefit. Her body looked heavier than it had, but also deserted, and I remembered how my mother's corpse had looked the same way, unoccupied by the person I loved.

For good measure, I added another candle to the blaze and bent to kiss Peggy's forehead, bidding her farewell. Beneath my lips, her skin felt cold but firm—blood turned marble—and I was still thinking about how unexpectedly dense it was when out of the corner of my eye I saw something move. It was very fast, a shadow passing quickly from one side of the room to the other, and when I looked behind me to see what it was, Peggy's door clicked shut, as though whatever it was had slipped outside.

I remembered what Peggy had said near the end about how Madeline would visit her at night and sit by her bed. How she would keep vigil. I had thought at the time that it was only the ravings of a dying woman, but now I couldn't help but wonder: had the spirit of Madeline come to pay her final respects? It seemed to make an absurd sort of sense that if I could return to Ladbroke Gardens from Greece, Madeline might be able to travel the other way, that perhaps she had been doing so all along. A chill went through me and I was seized with an urge to bolt from the room. In a fraction of a second, I reached the door, swung it open, and strode out into the courtyard—then abruptly came to a halt. Spread out in front of me was not Elena's courtyard but the garden, my old garden, only viewed from a different angle than on previous nights.

Behind me, the door closed with a satisfied thud, and I froze, too stunned even to breathe.

I stood in the center of the patio looking straight out toward the white picket fence and the narrow gate to the communal lawn. I had not come out of the service door this time, but had walked out through the French doors—straight out from our old flat. When I turned around, I could see into my parents' old bedroom, and farther, all the way through to the living room beyond, where dim lights and laughter flared. The sight of the impromptu party in full swing was too much for me, and I hurried toward the service entrance to make my way out.

But the door there was shut—literally painted into its frame, unopened since the paint had been applied. As my fingers scrabbled at its edges, desperate to find an opening, I heard a man's footsteps land on the stone patio and turned around, my own feet betraying me with a shuffling noise. The man—my father—looked over in my direction just as I ducked behind the barbecue and waited, chest sucked in, paralyzed, for him to walk over and find me. But he didn't, and after a time I peered over the brick ramparts and searched for him in the garden. He was weaving in the direction of the air-raid shelter, tripping on uneven flagstones and flowerpots and I could tell he was drunk. The hatch was open, and he bent loosely over the heavy iron trapdoor and tried to lift it. When it didn't budge, he wedged something long and thick underneath it—a branch perhaps—and the familiar scrape of metal on concrete sounded out across the yard.

The hatch moved a few inches before the branch snapped and my father tossed it aside and gave up. He turned around and stomped across the patio, this time kicking aside whatever got in his way.

I knew what had to happen next, had been over it in my head a thousand times. I had ten minutes, perhaps fifteen—the length of time it would take for my father to round up Jean Luc and Henri.

The open hatch was about ten meters away, and I crossed that distance in no time at all. I got down on my knees, peered into the hole, and braced myself against the side. A waft of cold air reached my face, followed by a faint whine, and I got to my feet and shook off the soil that had already stuck to my hands. Balancing my weight on one leg, I slowly lowered the other foot onto the top step and pressed down on it to make sure the surface was as solid as it looked. Though the stairs appeared to be made of concrete, I half-thought they might be an illusion that would give way and swallow my foot, then the rest of me. But the step held my weight, and I placed both feet on it and stared squarely into the dark cavity in front of me. I thought of all the candles burning so brightly in Peggy's room, how useful they would have been for what lay ahead.

The staircase was narrower than I remembered, and when I passed beneath the opposite side of the hatch I had to duck my head. Once I had gone under the hatch, it became harder to see, and I remembered how the time I had been down there as a child, it had at least been daylight outside. This time, only a pale wash of moonlight filtered down, and after a few more steps even that was gone—when I waved my hand in front of my face, I sensed the air displace but could not see my fingers. Without visual bearings I was forced to use the wall to steady myself, even though I cringed each time my fingers touched the cold, wet surface. With every step, I fought the urge to turn back, but when some moist thing writhed under my palm, and I cried out, my short yelp was answered by a soft whimper from farther down in the bunker. Someone was definitely down there—a child who needed my help.

The stairs seemed to go on forever, though I'd been too frightened to count them, and when I finally reached the bottom my leg jarred as it tried to continue down another step. I was standing in a puddle an inch or two deep; ice-cold water sluiced the soft skin between my toes.

The child, or whoever it was, was sobbing again, a wretched whine that would curdle milk. It sounded like a girl, and I thought she must be somewhere in front of me. I stepped in what I thought was her direction then stopped. If I went any farther, I wasn't sure how I would find my way back to the foot of the stairs. I could only hope that once I was really in the pit of the chamber, the stairs, dipped in that faint wash of moonlight, would appear fractionally less dark than their surroundings.

I took another step forward, and another, until I hit a hard lump that gave way under my foot and made a sickening squelching sound. I hoped it was nothing more than a beetle or a snail, but remembered the grisly textures that had been in the bottom of the bunker when my hand had closed around the shoe. My breathing quickened to a shallow rasp, and I moved forward another ten or so steps before stopping abruptly. I could see no boundaries, had no idea of the bunker's dimensions, and I felt suddenly disoriented, as though I were standing on a tiny fragment of rock in some deep undersea cavern. No sounds issued from the chamber, and I wondered if the child had been nothing more than a decoy to lure me down here. But who would play such a joke? Was some malevolent force really out to get me, or was this all my own creation—an elaborate manifestation of the list?

I'd read somewhere once that if you died in a dream you died in real life too, and I wondered if that was what was happening to me now. All the visions, hallucinations, whatever they were, of a decaying body in a watery hole had been leading to this: my own grave. I had been the one buried here, the one who did not get out alive.

In perfect despair, I dropped to my hands and knees and felt myself give in to the self-destructive thoughts I had tried for so long to resist. Released from its bindings, the list unfurled with violent force. I was stuck inside a dream that wasn't a dream, but there was no exit and no way to wake up. For several minutes I crouched there in the muck, lacking the courage even to turn around and crawl for the stairs. But then something kicked in, not self-preservation exactly, but the threat of a terror more prolonged than any other I had known. I did not want to become the diabolical soup of hair and teeth, to rot in a place where no one would find me.

I meant only to turn around, to search for a haze of light, but in so doing, my hand swept forward and hit human skin so warm it burned my fingers. My hand closed around a slender ankle, perhaps a wrist, and traveled up to find a swatch of fabric, a cotton dress, sopping wet. Enfolded in the dress was a girl, motionless. She was all arms and legs, a spidery tangle of limbs, but I managed to feel my way toward her head. Her hair was wet, with blood or water I could not tell. Nor did I stop to check if she was breathing—her warmth was enough. Moving fast, I linked my arms behind her slim waist and pulled her to me in a loose bear hug. She was heavier than I expected—roughly half my size—but the fact that I had found her, and that she was alive, boosted my strength. I was no longer alone in this dungeon and, feeling my spirits soar, I hauled us both to our feet.

As I'd hoped, the darkness was less concentrated at the other end of the bunker. With the girl hoisted under one arm and bolstered by the other, I made my way toward the grayish haze. Halfway across the flooded chamber, one of my flip-flops got hooked on something under the water and came off, but I wasn't about to waste time trying to find it. Instead I limped on with one bare foot, trying not to slip in the soft, buttery mulch.

At the foot of the stairs, I leaned on the wall to rest for a few moments. In my arms, the girl stirred, and coughed once or twice. Even though she felt hot to the touch, she was also shivering, and I guessed she had some kind of fever. Pulling her closer to my body, I began the ascent, each step slow and torturous. The girl's head lolled at an impossible angle, hiding her face from me, and I worried that her skull might scrape against the narrow stairway, or worse, that I would drop her.

But I didn't drop her, at least not until we had climbed out of the bunker and I had stumbled a few feet across the grass. My arms literally gave way then, and she slid down the length of my body and landed in a pile at my feet. The jolt must have roused her, because she started to cough again—a little more violently this time—and I crouched next to her and rubbed her back. She was turned away from me, and long strings of wet hair covered her face, but I finally had enough of my wits about me to notice what she was wearing: a simple dress, made from a cotton printed with strawberries. The dress was soaked and stained, but I recognized it immediately. It had been my favorite, a dress made for me by my mother. I had been wearing it the day after the party.

I stopped rubbing her back, and sat down heavily on the grass, watching her. She lifted her head and I caught her profile—her nose had a small bump from wearing spectacles, and her full lips turned down in a sulk. A thin line of blood trickled from one corner of her mouth, but what took away my breath was her big mole eyes, the way she was straining to see me without her glasses on; the way she gave up trying and looked away, frustrated. My whole life, I had been doing that, been blind when I most needed to see.

There was no mistaking who the girl was, but what was this other Suki doing out here? I recalled being rescued from the bunker by my father—in which case she should have been safely tucked up in bed, like I had been. So why wasn't she? What strange glitch had occurred that the two us could coexist?

For a second or two she squinted at the garden before fixing her eyes on the French doors, the brightest, and only, source of light. Too dazed to move, I looked in the same direction, until the doorway swarmed with the silhouettes of a trio of men who were walking toward us, coming out into the garden.

Though I did not understand why this other Suki was here, I did not think it would be a disaster if the men stumbled across her in the garden—whereas if they stumbled across me it would be catastrophic.

The nearest cover was a small holly bush to the right of the patio—in the opposite direction from the service door—and I dived for it, hoping the leaves would be dense enough, and the men drunk enough, that the plant would hide me. It did, but only just, and I noticed, once I was stuck behind it, that I was shivering, I supposed in shock.

None of the strange and irrational events leading up to this one had prepared me for the strangeness and irrationality of meeting myself as a girl. And I couldn't work out what I had just done, or how it was even possible. How had she been left in the bunker, while I remembered being carried out by my father? Where were her glasses and why did blood trail from her mouth, while I had made it to the surface with my spectacles and teeth intact?

From behind the holly bush, I had a clear view of the men, and I watched intently as they made their first, failed attempt to lift the hatch then stopped to regroup. I wondered why they hadn't noticed Suki sitting on the grass, but I did not have a clear view of her myself, and thought perhaps they had missed her because they were drunk.

The sequence of the men's actions was familiar to me by now, but on other nights I had not been close enough to hear what they were saying. From my new vantage point, I could hear each word as though it were being piped directly into my ear.

They were talking about sex, and Henri was miming a recent encounter. "The rail for the bath was at just the right height," he said and smacked his lips. "*C'était parfait,*" he said. "*Parfait.*"

Jean Luc held two hands in front of his chest and squeezed a pair of imaginary breasts. "And what about these?"

"*Parfait aussi,*" said Henri.

"*Merde,*" said Jean Luc, laughing. "I chased the wrong chicken."

"Yes," agreed my father. "Lulu's what around here we call a cock tease."

"But not Pippa," said Henri, almost singing. "She is wonderful!"

Jean Luc turned to my father. "And she likes an audience, *n'est-ce pas*?"

A low, dirty laugh went round the men and Ludo put a finger to his lips. "Shhhhh, you'll get me in trouble," he said.

"With which one?" said Jean Luc, and the three of them laughed some more.

They had not so much as bent over the hatch yet, but stopped talking and laughing for a moment to concentrate on their task. So it had been Henri and Pippa having sex in the bathroom, and my father had been a spectator—which he didn't want either his wife or his mistress to find out about. I felt a familiar flare of anger toward him. Not just for cheating on my mother with Rowan or for watching the babysitter have sex, but for having no conscience about any of it.

When their work was done—with much huffing and puffing and swearing in both English and French—the men left the garden, just as they had on previous occasions, with Jean Luc staying behind to water the potted geraniums. I'd been right about the zipper—halfway up it got stuck, and he struggled for some time to close it.

Once he had gone, I came out from behind the holly bush and stopped dead in my tracks. The patch of grass where I'd left the young Suki was empty, though in the spot where she'd been sitting there was a slight indentation. No wonder the men hadn't seen her. But where was she? I looked around the garden, then again at the patch of grass. Something was there, partly hidden, and when I got a little closer I recognized the locket, on its chain. The locket part was blackened and gritty, as though it had been submerged in silt, and I wiped it clean with my T-shirt and settled it, tenderly, around my neck.

I thought Suki must have gone inside—though I wasn't sure how she could have done so without anyone seeing her. My childhood bedroom overlooked the patio, and I tiptoed to the window and peered in. Bars in front of the glass made it hard to see, but enough light filtered through from the hall that it was just possible to make out the bed and a figure sleeping in it: Suki.

Was this the same Suki I had rescued from the bunker? I realized there was no way of knowing, but I saw that there might be a way to return the locket—to right the mistake I had made so long ago.

The French doors were open, but at the threshold I hesitated, wondering what would happen if I stepped through them.

I had gotten as far as putting my foot in the door, experimentally, when I heard movement inside the flat. Someone was heading straight for me, then at the last minute they veered off to the right, toward Suki's room. In the light of the hall, I recognized Hillary, my mother, and froze, not knowing what to do.

She went into Suki's room for a minute or two then came out carrying a bucket—and I still hadn't moved. I knew I should leave but my feet had decided, independently of me, to stay put. I must have gasped then or made some other noise for she turned in my direction and appeared to be staring straight at me. She looked so young, so vital, that every cell in my body yearned to go to her.

My mother approached me with an expression of open curiosity, but as she got nearer she looked troubled—and then plain frightened. I noticed she was looking in my direction but not straight at me, not meeting my gaze, and I wondered what it was she was seeing. Perhaps I was in shadow—or maybe I resembled a ghost. A few steps in front of me she halted, eyes wide, and put her hand to her throat. When I mirrored her actions, my hand collided with the locket. Was that what transfixed her?

"Mum, it's me," I said, and she tilted her head so that for one brief second I thought she had heard me and was going to respond. But instead whatever had caused her to tilt her head also galvanized her into action, and she reached out and shut the French doors, then pulled the curtains across in front of them.

She was gone, but not the ache, and I remembered what she'd told me just before she died, about seeing each other again in the garden. This had been it. Only her motivation had not been to reproach me for taking the locket but to gift me a moment of hope. She had wanted me to know, in some small way, that her dying wasn't the end of us—that we would share another moment of connection, even if for her, that moment had been and gone.

I was so relieved I wanted to cry—but not yet. I was still trapped in the garden, and before anything else, I had to get out.

I returned to the service door hoping it had somehow opened during the time I had been in the bunker, but it was still stubbornly painted shut. The French doors, the way I'd arrived, were locked, so I went to the edge of the patio and peered into the communal garden, or what I could see of it: the large stretch of lawn bordered by towering oak trees. I tried to make out what was beyond those trees, but no matter how much I strained, the buildings that should have been there remained murky and in shadow—the edge of a world I did not have the courage to explore.

Heavy rain started, surprising me, for I hadn't been so aware this time of moisture in the air. Almost instantly I was soaked through, my glasses so streaked with water that I found it hard to see. Getting wet didn't bother me, but I minded that I had nowhere to run, and that the garden, with me in it, was about to dissolve. Even through my streaked lenses, I could see the edges of the garden were losing definition, rinsing away. So I did what anyone would do when faced with no other option: I crouched on the ground and covered my head with my hands, and prayed for it all to be over.

CHAPTER TWENTY-THREE

Skyros, 2003

AND SOONER THAN I HAD THOUGHT POSSIBLE, it was. The rain stopped, abruptly, and I opened my eyes and looked down at a surface that was covered with pebbles. Dry pebbles inlaid in concrete. I was back in Elena's courtyard, crouching next to the wall. Someone was patting my shoulder, talking to me in a soft voice: "Suki, are you okay?"

It was Pippa.

"She's gone to a better place," she was saying. "They both have."

To uncurl myself took some effort—my muscles had been clenched clamshell tight, and now they felt weighed down with lead. My clothes weren't soaked through this time, but they were damp, as though I'd been sweating.

"I thought this might happen," said Pippa. "That Peggy dying would bring back all the memories from when Hillary passed away." She pointed to my neck. "Your mother's locket. I had no idea you still had it." She smiled. "It looks well loved."

I touched the locket, scarcely able to believe it was still around my neck. The temporary psychosis of sleep deprivation could explain many things, but not this, a solid, tangible object. My voice, when I spoke, was strangely waterlogged. "Yes," I said. "It is." I did not know what else to say. I tried to stand up, but immediately had to steady myself against the wall. One of my flip-flops was missing, left behind in the bunker. "I'm sorry, I haven't slept for days."

"I know how you feel," said Pippa. "I've been sitting with Peggy for hours and I actually thought we were having a conversation. She was telling me not to wear anything that draws attention to my waist, because I didn't really have one. And I was telling her that if she'd actually eaten food once or twice during her lifetime she might not be so dead."

I laughed, although I wasn't sure if it was the appropriate response. I was only sure that I needed to lie down. "Do you mind," I said, "do you mind if I—?" I pointed in the direction of Elena's room, but couldn't think what the word was for a place where one slept.

"Don't even think about getting up for breakfast," said Pippa. "We'll start tomorrow with lunch."

For twelve hours straight, I slept better than I had in years, and woke sometime around sundown, just a few hours before Peggy's funeral.

In the shower, trying to work out what exactly had occurred the night before in the bunker, I realized a curious thing. Alongside my original memory of the day after the party was a new version in which I had a few of my baby teeth knocked out on the steps of the bunker and was rescued many hours later by a woman who looked like me. The strangest thing about this new memory was that it broke off in the garden, right after Suki was rescued—around the same time I last sighted her. After that point, the little Suki, and her consciousness, seemed to vanish like smoke.

Thinking it all over, I started to feel a little like Narcissus, staring endlessly into the lake at his own reflection. Except that in the end it hadn't been all about me. My mother was there, and so was her locket. Where was the locket? I had shrugged it off the night before and hadn't seen it since.

I found it on the sleeping platform, partially tucked under the mattress. It was a little grubby, and the catch was still broken where I'd sliced it off, but it was otherwise intact and I was suddenly desperate to open it. On Elena's dresser, I found a nail file, and much more carefully this time, I wedged it between the two halves of the locket and slowly nudged them apart. When the gap was wide enough, I prised it the rest of the way open with my thumb.

The inside of the locket was caked in silt, but in the heat it had almost dried and when I tapped it against the hard pebbled floor, the bulk of it fell out. Under the silt, I expected to see pictures of my mum and dad, looking young and in love, perhaps when they first met. But what I saw instead was a tiny photo of a toddler and another one of a child—both of them me. The first one was taken before I needed glasses, when I was under two, and in the second I would have been about five.

I did not have any formal black clothes with me in Skyros, but put on a charcoal gray dress that was plain and also modest. Just as we were leaving the villa, Pippa handed me an emerald feather boa and a heavy diamante necklace. She herself had on a garish array of beads and brocade. "These belonged to Peggy," she explained. "She loathed it when people wore black to funerals, and I'm terrified she's going to complain."

"I felt like that about the food at my mother's wake," I said, putting on the necklace over the locket and resting the boa across my shoulders. "All those tea cakes and sausage rolls. She hated that stodgy, old-fashioned stuff."

The coffin was placed on a simple wooden cart harnessed to two donkeys and we followed behind it, dressed in our finery, carrying beeswax candles that flickered as we walked. The service was held in the island's largest and most airless Greek Orthodox church, which seemed inappropriate until I saw how heavily it was festooned on the inside with swaths of lapis and gold. Afterward, at a taverna that opened out onto the village square, we toasted Peggy's life with Johnny Walker, neat, and ouzo for the locals who preferred it. Worn out from sleepless nights and sorrow, inebriation came quickly to those who sought it, and even Pippa broke months of sobriety with a tipple or two. Ari was in his element, and was ready to smash plates once the tributes were through, despite being reminded by the old folks that it was a custom at Greek weddings, not funerals. "Well, *malakas* to that," he said by way of vindication. "Since when was the old biddy Greek?"

Harold drank too, but he became withdrawn, and wandered off into the night on his own. Quite understandably, Caleb had been avoiding me since the sticky sheet incident, and had disappeared with his friends right after the service.

In the crowded taverna, Pippa sat wedged between two old widows dressed in black, who leaned forward and talked to her in English or across her in Greek, depending on the topic. I had been cornered by a couple of Ari's young nieces who wanted to practice their English, and at their request, found myself teaching them swear words and slang. I'd switched from whiskey to ouzo by then, and everyone in the room was beginning to seem jovial and kind. Ari and his backgammon cronies formed a singing circle around a couple of lads with balalaikas, and the decibel level rose inexorably. To a tremendous cheer, towers of white plates arrived in a crate, and I noticed that Pippa had disappeared. A few minutes later I found her in the kitchen, rinsing glasses and scraping dishes—the beads, brocade, and boa discarded to one side.

"I've always hated balalaikas," she said, looking up when she saw me. "They make my teeth vibrate."

"I hadn't realized Peggy was so popular."

Pippa smiled. "Imagine what it's like when a local dies."

I had a sudden urge to rescue her, just as, I now realized, she had rescued me, and pointed to the back door. "Why don't we get some fresh air?"

She looked relieved that someone had given her permission to leave. "What a bloody good idea."

The alley behind the restaurant reeked of rotten fish heads and deep-fryer fat and we had to walk a fair distance to reach this mythical fresh air I had spoken of. Then, we just kept on walking, right through the square and down a long cobbled street toward the port. On a low, white plaster wall with a jaw-dropping view, Pippa sat down and closed her eyes, letting the breeze wash over her face. "God, the end was horrible," she said, to the sky. "I can't get that awful moaning noise out of my head."

"Death is awful even when it's quiet. I guess we should hang on to what the doctor said, that she wasn't actually in pain."

"I don't believe that for a second," Pippa said. "She was in agony." She opened her eyes and I saw they had tears in them. "All day, I've been trying to replace it with a good memory of her, but I just don't have any. She's been cross with me for the last forty years."

"What about before that?"

"I'm forty-one," she said drily.

"Maybe she loved you more than she let on," I said, thinking of my own mother. "I think that's why Hillary didn't tell me she was dying. It was too awful. She couldn't face doing it."

"You might be right," said Pippa. "But I don't think Peggy was like other mums—especially not like yours. Hillary was worse than I am with Caleb. I remember her telling me this crazy story once about how she loved you so much that she actually thought she'd killed you. It was that day you all went down in the bunker. She said one minute you were standing next to her on the step, when she had this awful premonition that you were going to fall down the stairs and hit your head—and the next thing she knew, you had fallen. Almost as if she had pushed you."

The hair on my head stood on end. "She told you that?"

"Something like that—it was a long time ago."

I felt a residue of tingling on the back of my neck, almost like an aftershock. "Don't you think that's sort of creepy?"

Pippa shrugged. "I thought it was at the time, but now that I'm a mother myself I don't. I'm always having visions of the horrible things that could happen to Caleb . . . and if something did, I might blame myself for it."

I understood what Pippa meant, but it wasn't the track my thoughts had taken. I had been wondering if my mother *had* killed me—or at least a piece of me—that day in the bunker. That's what it had felt like all these years, that hunger, that emptiness, like some vital part of me was missing. But did that also mean it had now been restored?

Pippa stood up from the wall, seeming lighter than when she'd sat down. "Let's go swimming. I haven't put my feet in the water since we got here."

The main beach was reached by a narrow, cobbled path that snaked down the hillside to the water, then veered up again toward an ancient acropolis on the hill. Despite a steady flow of tourists and donkeys, the path had never been widened, and we had to walk down it in single file.

When we got down to the beach, we were not the only ones there. At the far end, some kids had lit a bonfire, and from their ghetto blaster the tinny sounds of Euro house-music spilled out across the bay. Pippa took off her shoes and walked straight to the water's edge. I thought she was going to paddle in the shallows and leave it at that, but in one stealthy movement, she discarded her shirt and pants, bra and knickers, and waded in. "Come on, you! It's magic," she said, and dove underwater, surfacing a few meters out.

I glanced up the beach toward the revelers and, reasoning that if I couldn't see them, they couldn't see me, stripped off to my underwear and ran in after Pippa. She was right; the water was dreamy—warm and refreshing at the same time—and after a few minutes under, I felt revitalized, clearheaded, albeit still a little tipsy. I watched Pippa thrash out toward the middle of the bay—swimming the last six months out of her system—and floated on my back with my eyes closed. Held by the water, my body relaxed, each bone letting go of the muscle that surrounded it. The tinny Eurobeats had been replaced by an even cheesier tune that I recognized, a club hit from the nineties. For a minute or so, I flashed back to that time, and to the emotion I had associated with the record, a kind of chafing isolation that had always gnawed away at me in social situations. Then, just as quickly, the emotion passed and I settled back into the present, realizing, with some relief as I did so, that I no longer felt like that all the time.

"Christ, I needed that!" said Pippa, striding out of the water in her birthday suit and getting dressed on the sand.

I paddled back to the shore to join her. "Me too. You were right about the water. It was divine."

"Cooped up in that villa," she said, "I've been thinking the most awful things about everyone—especially Mummy—but it's only because I couldn't breathe."

My dress was damp from doing the work of a towel, but it was a warm night, and the sensation wasn't unpleasant. Halfway up the beach I realized I needed to pee. I told Pippa and she led us toward a building site, some tourist apartments that were going up in the lee of the cliffs.

"No one will see you in there." She glanced up the beach. "But I'll keep watch if you like."

Among the slabs of concrete masonry and twisted iron cables was a perfectly concealed space, and I squatted there, trying not to pee on my feet–or the emerald boa.

"Are you done yet?" called Pippa from the lookout spot. "I think someone's coming."

I remembered the teen revelers and tried to hurry but had only just put my dress back in place when Pippa came round the corner, covering her mouth to suppress laughter.

"What is it?" I whispered.

She pulled me behind a concrete block wall and, still stifling giggles, pointed to the cliffs behind the building site. Squinting into the shadows, I heard sucking noises, and quiet sighs, and made out a nebulous pair of figures. They were kissing and frantically groping, trying to find a level spot in the dunes where they could lie down. For a second, they were swathed in moonlight and I saw Caleb, shirtless, with his hand between a pair of long, nut-brown legs.

"I *knew* it," Pippa said, unable to contain her delight. "I knew he'd eventually run off with one of Yanni's sisters. I just didn't know which one."

"You're *pleased* about this?"

"I'm relieved," she said. "He's been in so much trouble lately, hanging out with the most awful gang of brutes—drinking, smoking, stealing, lord knows what else—and I just knew he'd lose interest in them once he found a girlfriend."

"She might not be his girlfriend," I said, realizing, and then cringing at, what a horny teen Caleb had been all along. "It might only be a casual fling."

"Do you think so?" said Pippa, very interested. "I don't think Athena would put up with that."

"Not like me," I wanted to say, but I had already said too much. I could never tell Pippa, or anyone else, what had happened. I'd not had a secret before that had to be taken to the grave, and I saw how, over the years, it would lead to many casual, well-intentioned lies. I would lie to protect Caleb and myself and I would also lie to avoid hurting Pippa.

Knowing that, ahead of time, made me feel crummy, and for a second or two, I saw that I was not the decent person I'd always imagined myself to be. I was flawed, just like everyone else. Just like my father. I did not think I could ever forgive him for abandoning my mother and me, but I could sort of understand why, once he had abandoned us, he could never look back. Starting afresh, not repeating the same mistakes, was sometimes the only way to make amends for what you'd done.

We had walked up the steep hill from the beach to the town, but Pippa was reluctant to return immediately to the wake. Instead she suggested we stop at a pint-size taverna in a narrow, cobbled alley for coffee and a slice of baklava. My arm did not need much twisting, and we were soon settled at an outside table, alongside a pair of toothless backgammon fiends. "By the way," she said, suddenly looking up, spoon in hand. "I've a bone to pick with you."

Her tone was light, almost mischievous, but my conscience was heavy, and I braced for an accusation.

"Last night, Caleb asked me a strange question," she began. "He wanted to know if I'd ever 'shagged' some bloke in the bath. He said it was at a costume party, back in the eighties, at your parents' flat." She paused. "For someone who wasn't even born yet, he seemed to know a lot about it."

It was a chance to come clean—about one thing at least—and I took it. "That was my fault. I told him about something I saw that night."

Pippa was no less amused, but she had started to blush. "What on earth were you doing? Looking through the bloody keyhole?"

I coughed through my embarrassment, pretending a piece of baklava had lodged in my throat.

Pippa studied me for a moment, and then took a sharp inhale of breath. "Oh dear God," she said. "You didn't think, all this time, that I was bonking your father, did you?"

"No," I said, horrified that she had guessed the truth. "Absolutely not!"

"Good, because I never would have crossed that line." She laughed, high and tinkling, and for a moment, her green eyes flashed eighteen again. "Though I crossed all the others," she added.

With relief, I laughed too, and then we fell into an easy silence, broken only by the occasional clinking of ouzo glasses and a frenzied rattling of dice. It was the first time in a long, long while that my mind had been comfortably blank.

"You know, if you wanted to, you could stay here until the end of the summer," Pippa said. "There's plenty of space at Elena's—so long as you don't mind sleeping in the crypt—and you might even get work at Soteris's taverna."

Her mention of the coming months caught me off guard, for the present had been so consuming that I hadn't given any thought to what I'd do next. The idea of going back to London, to an endless, fruitless job hunt was abhorrent, but so was the thought of returning so soon to New Zealand—even though I'd worked out that it was my hang-ups, not the country, that had pushed me to the edge.

In the absence of a long-term plan, spending what was left of the summer on a Greek island with a family that wasn't my family, but who'd nonetheless made room for me, was about the most idyllic situation I could think of. I was sure that by the end of it, I would have an idea of what to do. "Thank you," I said at last. "That's a very kind offer."

When our baklava had been reduced to a few sticky crumbs, we ambled toward the taverna, where Peggy's wake had quadrupled in size and was spilling out in waves across the cobblestoned piazza. Around the impromptu band, a group of men and women had gathered in a circle, and were clapping wildly in time to the music. Some distance from the mayhem, Pippa hesitated, and I thought perhaps she didn't want to get any closer, that the balalaikas were wigging her out, but then the crowds parted a little, and she ran forward eagerly to get a closer look at what everyone was going so crazy over. In front of the band, a traditional Greek dance was under way: a line of women at the back and in front of them a line of men with their arms around each other. The music they were dancing to was repetitive and getting faster, building up a head of steam. At the center of the male line were Harold and Ari, kicking up their heels in manic imitation of the locals they were arm in arm with, their pink, shiny faces creased with unbridled joy. With something like a whoop of delight, Pippa dashed forward to link arms with her husband and brother, and before I could talk myself out of it, I followed her into the fray.

# Acknowledgments

MY FANTASTIC AGENT, Lisa Grubka, committed to this book when it was a long way from finished, and her dedication and enthusiasm continue to impress me. At Morrow, my editor, Katherine Nintzel, nimbly located the last piece in the puzzle but kindly let me think I'd found it myself. (So that's what the very best editors do!) Her patience, acuity, and wit made the final phase of writing this book a most pleasurable collaboration. My sincere gratitude goes out to everyone else at Foundry and Morrow who have helped launch this book, but in particular to Stephanie Abou, Hannah Brown Gordon, Caspian Dennis, Mary Sasso, and Katie Steinberg.

Without the (extremely premature) encouragement of Curtis Sittenfeld, this novel would never have got off the ground, and without the tireless cheerleading of the Sittenfelds—Michelle Arathimos, Sarah Bainbridge, Janis Freegard, Jared Gulian,

Anna Jackson, Amanda Samuel, Kate Simpkins, and especially Sarah Laing—it would never have made it to a first draft. (Who knew there would be ten or fifteen more?)

For creative contributions and support of all kinds, I'd like to thank Rob Appierdo, Wallace Chapman, Anita Coulter, Jen Craddock, Marianne Elliott, Jess Feast, Rachael King, Emily Simpson, Jane Ussher, and Juliette Veber. A special warm fuzzy thank you to Kirstin Marcon for the manifesto. (Can you believe we did it?!)

I'm so lucky to have great and loving parents, David and Azedear, who have been steadfast supporters of my unpredictable career. My beloved brother, Nick, I sincerely hope you read this and decide to do better (as I know you can). Chris and Lesley Saville, thank you for giving us a home, and so much more. Charlie, Zoe, Adrienne, and Alex, thanks for all the babysitting. And Gillian, whose battle is all through this book, rest in peace.

Matthew, my lion-hearted husband, thank you for believing in me all the way; I know it hasn't been easy. Hector, special boy, thank you for being so awesome.

Last but not least, a big thank you to all my generous "sponsors" (most of whom are loyal family and friends). Long after the funds ran out, your allegiance kept me going (translation: after four years, I had to bloody finish it or you'd all come after me): Rob Appierdo and Jess Feast, Shandelle Battersby, Namila Benson, Helena Brooks, Jaquie Brown, Heather and Greg Bryant, Olivia Bryant, Clare Burgess, Kathryn Carmody, Paul Casserly, Wallace Chapman, Desiree Cheer, Nick Churchouse, Jacki Condra, the Coulters (Anita, John, Klara, Xavier, and Francesca), Jen Craddock and Will Smart, Liz DiFiore and Kevin Donovan, Lucy and Zelda Edwards, Raga D'silva, Patrick Fife, Janis Freegard, Tanya Fretz, Joanne Ganley, Hayley Garrett, Gemma Gracewood, Caroline Grose,

Jared Gulian, Robyn Harper, Jason Hebron and Louise May, Cass Hessom-Williams, Nathan Hickey, Mei Hill, Matthew J. Horrocks, Anna Jackson and Simon Edmonds, Mel James, Matthias Jordan and Charlotte Ryan, Natasha Judd, Jonathan King and Rebecca Priestley, Rachael King and Peter Rutherford, Richard King, Rebecca Laffar-Smith, Bevin Linkhorn, Fiona MacKenzie, Peter Malcouronne, Kirstin Marcon and Paul Swadel, Aimee McCammon, Nic McCloy, Nathan and Miriam Meister, Carly Neemia, Suzy O'Brien, Dale and Geoff Olsen, Françoise Padellec, Rebekah Palmer and Bernard Steeds, Sibilla Paparatti, Mary Parker, Susan Pearce, Vicky Pope, Mark and Marion Prebble, Laura Preston, Vanessa Rhodes, Rose from Oxford, Marcia Russell, Peter Salmon, Lesley and Chris Saville, Lisa Schulz, Kate Simpkins, Emily Simpson and Steve Braunias, Mailene Tubman, Juliette Veber, Victoria University English Class 243: Contemporary Fiction (2007), Paul Ward, Neville and Jan Zander, the Zander-Joneses (Mel, Karen, Caitlin, and Oliver), and Margaret Zube. The following people must be singled out for their ridiculous generosity: Marianne Elliott, Eric Holowacz and Mo Hickey, David Stubbs, Mum and Dad. (I'm really sorry if I've left anyone out.)

Insights,
Interviews
& More . . .

About the author

About the book

Read on

About the author

Homeland Insecurity
(an essay)

by Bianca Zander

I WAS BORN IN LONDON and grew up there, but it took me a long time—perhaps thirty years—to figure out I wasn't really English.

The signs were there from day one; I just didn't know how to read them. At my upright prep school in Kensington, this sense of being different was muddied with the usual British anxieties about class. The kids I went to school with—Arabella, Henrietta, Leanda—had country "hises" and great-uncles who were titled; we had renovations that were never finished. (My father managed building sites but seldom managed ours.) A shy seven-year-old girl called Nell once came over to play at our flat, took one look around, screwed up her nose, and said, in all seriousness, "What would happen if the queen came to tea?"

Jane Ussher

"The queen?"

"Yes," said Nell, "She would be appalled."

Nell was appalled—and Nell lived in a world where, conceivably, the queen might pop 'round for afternoon tea.

Around the same time, I started to notice that my parents spoke with funny accents—accents that were a notch above cockney, but only just. My father did strange, un-English things, like wear shorts around the house in the middle of winter, and when even the sniff of a rugby match came on the TV, he yelled so much he lost his voice. (He still does this, at age sixty-seven.) My mother, on her part, was too cool, too Bohemian. She picked me up from school wearing tight blue jeans and carelessly got pregnant with her second and last child when I was, gasp, eleven.

Actual proof that we were foreign came later, at my private, all-girls secondary school. My class was going on a day trip to Calais to eat cheese, but at the last minute, just as we were about to board the coach, I was hauled aside and told I couldn't go. The night before, the visa laws had changed unexpectedly, and only those with British or EU passports were being let into France. Mine wasn't either of those.

At thirteen, the worst thing imaginable happened: My parents announced we were moving to New Zealand, a country where all the dads wore shorts in the winter. My father was from there; my mother was Australian. It was the mid '80s, Chernobyl had just blown, and my mother wanted to be as far away as possible from the threat of acid rain. I was so embarrassed about emigrating to an island on the other side of the world that I didn't tell a single classmate I was going until a few days before we left.

We had been there not quite two years when I begged to return to England. That we did so surprised me, ▸

“My father did strange, un-English things, like wear shorts around the house in the middle of winter.”

Homeland Insecurity ***(continued)***

and it wasn't until years later that I realized I couldn't have been the only one in the Zander camp unready to be a New Zealander. My father was so unready for repatriation that he had been commuting back and forth between London and Auckland every other month, in those days a trip of thirty-two hours or more each way.

Arriving back in London at the age of fifteen, I was appalled to discover that I no longer fit in at the school I had dreamed of returning to. (This, after two years in New Zealand of pretending, for the sake of survival, not to be British.) I had changed, become something else: the perpetual outsider, a writer in training—the member of a club that no one wants to belong to at that age.

A few years later, when my mother and I took a train to Cambridge University, where I was to be interviewed for a place, I gazed around at the absurdly beautiful grounds of Emmanuel College and felt almost seismically, if a little longingly, out of place. I was suddenly aware in a visceral way that nothing in my heritage had prepared me for this. It didn't make sense. I had gone to a fancy academic school, my grades were good enough to get me an interview, and yet, walking into the dean's office to be grilled, what I felt was a profound lack of entitlement.

I didn't get in. I went to art school for a few months, dropped out, then went to New Zealand for a holiday, and ended up staying a decade.

Almost ten years after that, I'm still here.

In between those two decades Down Under, just like Suki, I went back to London at the age of twenty-eight to see if I had made the right decision. I had left in such an unplanned fashion, so impulsively, that I didn't ever feel as though I had chosen to live in New Zealand but had simply washed up here, a beached pilot whale. In the meantime, I had picked up the disease that afflicts almost every New Zealander: a crippling insecurity that living on a tiny island in the Pacific makes us less sophisticated, less interesting, less intelligent than people in other parts of the world. The only cure for this provincialism is to escape.

What happened to me on that trip back to London is a bit like what happened to Suki, only without all the time travel, grisly discoveries, and underage sex. In other words: nothing like it at all, except in spirit. I did feel locked out of my childhood, that I no longer belonged in the place that had once been my home. It wasn't a happy experience, but it was at least decisive.

After six months, I returned to New Zealand, where I had perched for ten years without ever feeling settled, and claimed it as my home. I got married (to a misplaced South African writer) and had a son (with a Greek name, Hector), who will no doubt grow up wondering why he doesn't quite feel like a New Zealander. I stopped thinking I would have been smarter, better educated, a better writer, had I stayed in England and started to feel lucky that I had lived in a place that had allowed me to gain so much experience in so many different areas. The patchwork career is a uniquely New Zealand thing, and in my twenties I had tried my hand at journalism, screenwriting, radio producing, documentary-making, and even DJing, all fields that, in England, are too competitive to be able to dabble in.

I felt luckier still that I had grown up in a place as stimulating as London but that I wasn't still trying to live there, where the living isn't easy. I started to enjoy all things that had made me different, insecure about my place in the world—faux-English and a half-baked New Zealander—and then I started to write about them.

Getting to Know *The Girl Below*

Journalist Emily Simpson interviews her friend, Bianca Zander, about the book.

Suki grows up in London and spends periods of her life in New Zealand and Greece—as did you. Clearly there are some autobiographical elements, but are there aspects of Suki's character that you definitely don't share?

When people ask if my novel is about me, I say that it's geographically autobiographical, in that Suki and I both grew up in London, then returned there at the same age (twenty-eight), after living in New Zealand for ten years. However, what happens to Suki in London is, by anyone's standards, fairly fantastical, and nothing like that ever happened to me.

Where it gets tricky though is that the psychological arc underpinning the book is one that I share with Suki—I definitely had some of the same epiphanies that she does. In that sense, it's a deeply personal book, and intentionally so.

In fact, one of the hardest things to do in the later stages of writing the book was to remain true to my twenty-eight-year-old self. The writing process took five years, and in that time I got married, became a mother, and did a lot of growing up, but I couldn't retrospectively go and give Suki more wisdom than she could be expected to have at that age. As a character, she

"The psychological arc underpinning the book is one that I share with Suki."

seems self-absorbed to me now, quite screwed up, but when I started writing the book, I couldn't see that stuff about her—I was too much like that myself.

Having convinced everyone that the events of the novel are not autobiographical, I'm now going to turn that on its head. One of the weirdest and most fantastical incidents in the book—the hand in the cupboard at the start of chapter two—is lifted straight out of my childhood. I too had a playful hand in the cupboard that came out and untied the bows on my dresses, and this memory, however bizarre, is very vivid, very fixed.

Significantly, it was this hand in the cupboard that kicked off the whole novel. I started writing *The Girl Below* in 2007, in a summer writing class at Victoria University, Wellington, taught by American writer Curtis Sittenfeld. (It was in this class that my writing group, The Sittenfelds, was born.) Sittenfeld assigned us a writing exercise and a scene about the hand in the cupboard is what I came up with—and everyone went, "Wow!" Prior to that, I had written screenplays and attempted a few short stories, but nothing, ever, with a magical realism bent. I had tried something new, and suddenly everyone was responding to it. From that moment on, I sort of became fearless in terms of what I could dream up, what I could imagine. Whether or not the hand was "real," I have a lot to thank it for.

You've written a ghostly novel. Was this hard to manage as a writer, without it ▸

“One of the weirdest and most fantastical incidents in the book—the hand in the cupboard—is lifted straight out of my childhood.”

dissolving into B-grade horror or comedy? What was your touchstone for this—other fiction or experiences of your own?

I read some great advice, while I was writing *The Girl Below*, that was about getting readers to believe in magical or fantasy elements that crop up in otherwise believable worlds—as opposed to writing in the fantasy genre, where the entire world is make-believe. The advice was basically that the more far-fetched the scene, then the plainer and less adorned your writing should be. (This advice applied in reverse, too, in that a mundane scene about plumbing could be made less so with metaphor and so on.) I had already been doing this to a certain extent—my natural writing style is quite unadorned, typical ex-journalist—but after reading that advice, I kept things very matter-of-fact.

Another thing that came in handy is that I have what you might call an architecture fetish. As a kid, I liked to draw plans of boats and buildings, and imagine myself in the spaces I had created. My writing is full of that, almost like a tic, but I think it does have the handy side effect of tethering the reader within a concrete physical space while something fantastical is going on.

I actually don't read a lot of contemporary magical realism—especially the whimsical chocolate-shop sort—but the books I most loved

> "I wanted to re-create that slightly woozy feeling of entering an imaginary world."

as a child were of that ilk. Books like *The Wizard of Oz*, *Alice in Wonderland*, and *The Phoenix and the Carpet* (E. Nesbit) were huge for me, and I wanted to re-create that slightly woozy feeling of entering an imaginary world.

Probably the last great magical novel I read, as a teenager, was Margaret Mahy's *The Changeover.* Then throughout my twenties I read mostly realist novels.

All that changed when I discovered Japanese writer Haruki Murakami. In his novels anything is possible, but the crazy stuff happens alongside episodes of listening to jazz records and eating bowls of ramen noodles. He takes his characters on these mind-bending metaphysical journeys, but they are always rooted in a recognizable reality—and the language is so plain it's almost casual. If I hadn't read Murakami, I don't think I would have realized how far out you can take your adult reader without losing them. His books are extremely compelling, even when they don't make sense.

“If I hadn't read Murakami, I don't think I would have realized how far out you can take your adult reader without losing them.”

Just getting back to "the hand in the cupboard," you've said people responded to it and that it opened doors for you as a writer, but which doors were they? Why do you mix that magical element in with what is otherwise quite autobiographical realism?

What appeals to me about magic realism, as opposed to straight realism, is that ▸

you can use the uncanny to explain psychological truths that are difficult to approach head-on or to write about in a literal way.

Before I discovered Murakami, I went through a Jung phase, reading about his theories of the subconscious and dream symbolism. (Note that I read *about* his theories; Jung's actual writing is unreadable.) Then I read an amazing book about the meaning of myth and fairy tale that is disguised as a self-help book and whose title is so off-putting that most serious writers wouldn't go near it: *Women Who Run with the Wolves*, by Clarissa Pinkola Estés, is weapons-grade Secret Women's Business, but it's also the book that, for me, unlocked the secret language of storytelling. (I may be opening myself up for ridicule here . . .)

Estés's book explains why myths and fairy tales (and ergo, magic realism) can be so powerful, and why they don't always make sense—so much brutality, no neat or happy endings. The reason is that fairy tales explain psychological truths—the murky stuff of the subconscious—and such dark matter is not always understood by, or very appealing to, the conscious mind.

So part of what I was trying to do with *The Girl Below* was to tell a story on two levels: to harness the subterranean power of myth and fairy tale but without alienating the modern reader who doesn't go in for that kind of thing.

As I explain all of this, I'm very

“You can use the uncanny to explain psychological truths that are difficult to approach head-on.”

conscious that I might not have succeeded in achieving what I set out to do, which is also the answer to why so many novelists write the same book twenty times over. They're just trying to nail that one thing they want to say.

Going back to Murakami, his books are often quite perplexing because they contain metaphysical riddles, but he generally doesn't solve them. Their dream logic cannot necessarily be decoded, even by a skilled interpreter—or Jungian shrink. Now, I was aiming to create a psychological metaphor, not a riddle, but that enigmatic quality is a huge part of Murakami's appeal, and I was very mindful, particularly in the later stages of writing, that I didn't want to give the reader all of the answers. The books I most enjoy are the ones where the reader has to do a bit of work.

Having started out as a journalist, you've said it took seven years to properly shed that mind-set in order to write fiction. What is it about that background that hampers creative writing?

It has to do with finding an authentic voice. I was a feature writer, not a news reporter, but a lot of what you do in journalism in general is strike a pose. You have a certain number of pages to fill about a topic, and often you adopt a persona or a standpoint because that makes it easier to write and more interesting to read. You manufacture ▸

“A lot of what you do in journalism in general is strike a pose.”

an opinion that sounds authentic but often isn't, not really. You're always one step removed.

I didn't discover this inauthenticity, this pose, until I tried to write fiction. Everything I wrote at first was false. I would try so hard to be clever, but always the feedback I got was that my stories lacked heart. I was completely miffed, of course, because the feedback I'd always had about my journalism was that it was a little too "creative." I was always teetering on the edge of actually making things up for the sake of a more entertaining read. I took this criticism very personally too. If my writing lacked heart, perhaps I lacked it as well. Then gradually, it dawned on me that I had to stop being clever, stop posing, and expose something of my inner workings on the page. Fiction is the opposite of journalism in that instead of trying to make facts sound interesting, you're making stuff up that has to come across as real. In fiction, you have to write honestly about all the emotions that make you human—rage, humiliation, sadness, shame—and you can't write about them as though other people experience those things but you don't. This is risky stuff, and in the beginning you feel very exposed. But then, when you get it right, people don't say, "You're a weirdo." They say, "There is a sense of a soul underneath the words." So, yeah, you have to put a piece of your soul into it or it comes across as phony.

“Fiction is the opposite of journalism in that instead of trying to make facts sound interesting, you're making stuff up that has to come across as real.”

The process I have just described took about seven years, which is why, I think, it's wrongheaded to think you can take a year off your journalism job and spit out a novel.

You also have screenwriting experience. How does that influence you as a novelist?

It makes me enter a scene late and leave early! This is one of the fundamentals of screenwriting. You never, ever start a scene with someone opening a door and saying hello to the person outside. If you do start with a door, there has to be a surprise waiting on the other side—it isn't who was expected, or the expected person is wearing a gorilla suit. Small talk, introductions, are superfluous. You cut all that out and you start straight in with the nitty-gritty. What needs to happen in this scene to move the story forward?

It also influences the way I write dialogue. Rarely do people say what they mean, or even what they are really thinking, in a conversation. The interesting stuff goes on underneath, in subtext. Every time your characters speak, they have an agenda, and you're trying to tease that out. That's why two characters discussing their political viewpoints sounds so dreadful, so false, but it happens all the time in novels—never in films or in real life. There are some points in the novel where my characters speak exposition—they ▸

“It's wrongheaded to think you can take a year off your journalism job and spit out a novel.”

reveal something that happened in the past for the sake of driving the plot forward—and let's just say, I wish I knew how to avoid that.

By far the biggest tool you learn from screenwriting is how to build drama and tension in a scene. But it can also backfire when scenes become too dramatic at the expense of subtlety or meaning. Your readers have wet their pants with fear when you were trying to make them feel heartbroken—that kind of thing.

Would* The Girl Below *make a good movie and would Bianca Zander be the only person who could write the script?

It would make an excellent movie (of course I would say that), but I would like absolutely nothing to do with writing the script. Ideally, I would hand it over to some amazingly talented filmmaker and they would go for gold. To make something work as a movie, you need to take liberties with the story, and I would be happy to give someone the license to do that. The trickiest thing to pull off would be the timespan. The novel covers a period of about twenty years, whereas film, as a medium, lends itself better to stories that take place over a single weekend or a year at the most. The time travel aspect might also present challenges . . .

“To make something work as a movie, you need to take liberties with the story, and I would be happy to give someone the license to do that.”

Over the course of writing this book you've been childless, then pregnant,

then a mother. How did those three writing experiences differ from one another?

The childless writer has endless amounts of time to sit around dreaming and writing, but that time has no shape so you often waste it; procrastination becomes a problem. Pregnancy sharpened my focus. The birth became my second-draft deadline because I was terrified I might never write again. I sent the manuscript off to various editors the night before my son was born. They all rejected it. I did write again; I had to. Writing as a mother teaches you that it's possible to write two thousand words in four hours because you might not get another four hours free for a week. What you really miss is reading and thinking time, and I do worry that my work, from now on, will suffer from inadequate consideration.

"The birth became my second-draft deadline because I was terrified I might never write again."

Ten books that inspired me while I wrote *The Girl Below*

1. *The House of Mirth* by Edith Wharton
2. *Wonder Boys* by Michael Chabon
3. *Kafka on the Shore* by Haruki Murakami
4. *The Great Gatsby* by F. Scott Fitzgerald
5. *The Ice Storm* by Rick Moody
6. *Atonement* by Ian McEwan
7. *Lolita* by Vladimir Nabokov
8. *Prep* by Curtis Sittenfeld
9. *The Little Stranger* by Sarah Waters
10. *Norwegian Wood* by Haruki Murakami